big NATE

PRAY FOR A FIRE DRILL

by LINCOLN PEIRCE

Andrews McMeel
Publishing®

a division of Andrews McMeel Universal

big NATE

PRAY FOR A FIRE DRILL

More

big NATE

adventures from

LINCOLN PEIRCE

Big Nate From the Top

Big Nate Out Loud

Big Nate and Friends

Big Nate Makes the Grade

Big Nate All Work and No Play

Big Nate: Game On!

Big Nate: I Can't Take It!

Big Nate: Great Minds Think Alike

Big Nate: The Crowd Goes Wild!

Big Nate's Greatest Hits

Big Nate: Say Good-Bye to Dork City

Big Nate: Welcome to My World

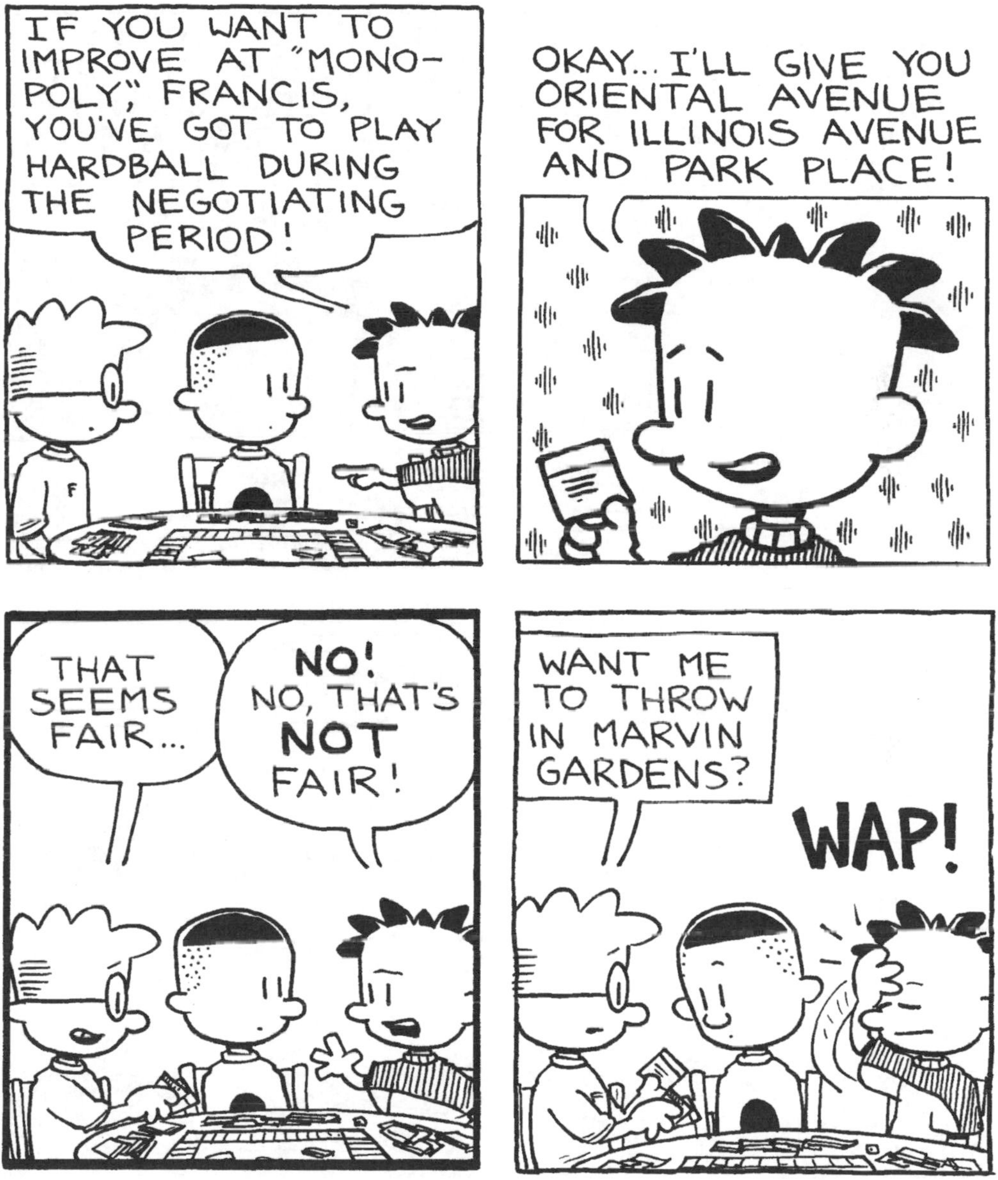
IF YOU WANT TO IMPROVE AT "MONOPOLY," FRANCIS, YOU'VE GOT TO PLAY HARDBALL DURING THE NEGOTIATING PERIOD!
OKAY... I'LL GIVE YOU ORIENTAL AVENUE FOR ILLINOIS AVENUE AND PARK PLACE!
THAT SEEMS FAIR...
NO! NO, THAT'S NOT FAIR!
WANT ME TO THROW IN MARVIN GARDENS?
WAP!

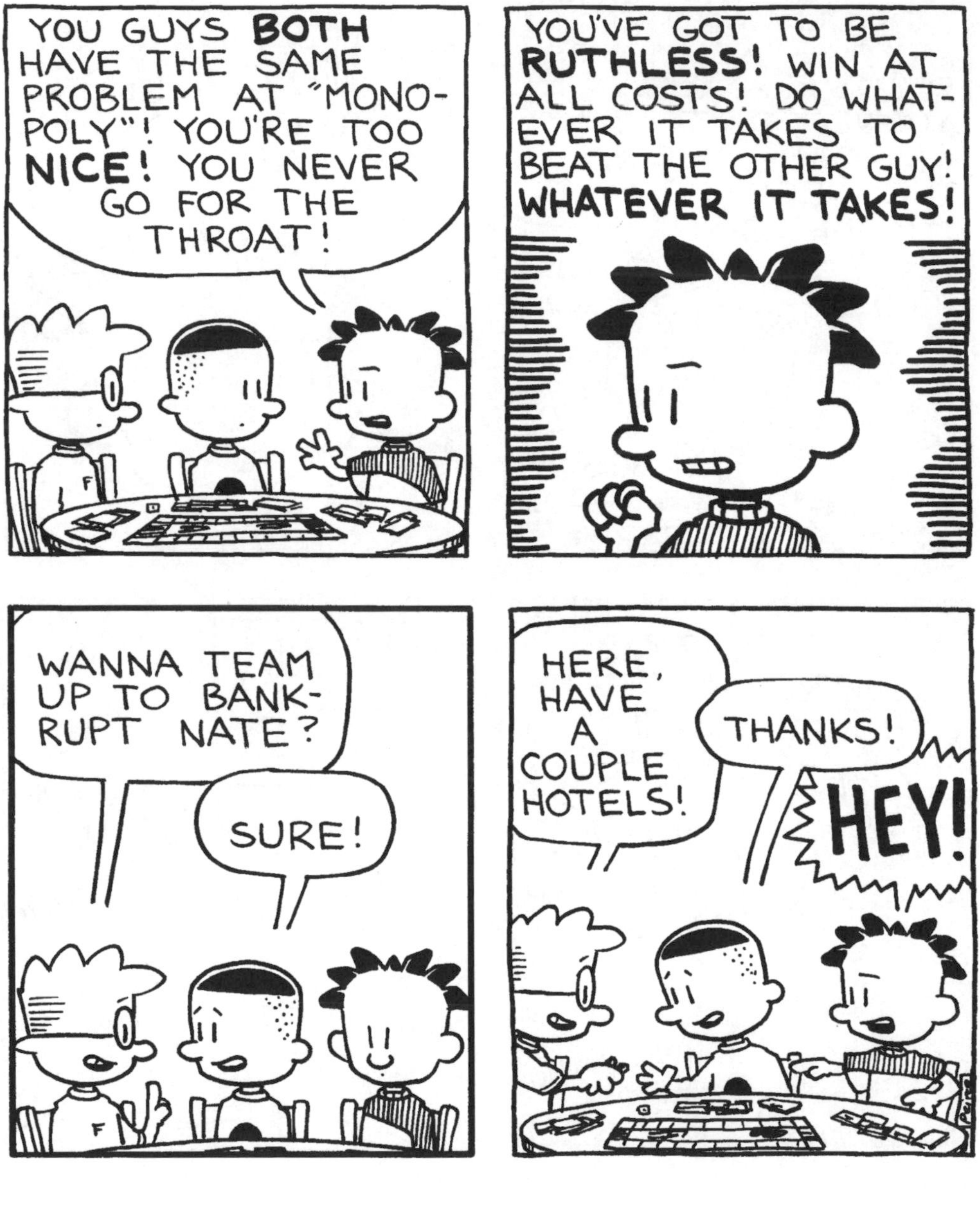
YOU GUYS **BOTH** HAVE THE SAME PROBLEM AT "MONO-POLY"! YOU'RE TOO **NICE**! YOU NEVER GO FOR THE THROAT!
YOU'VE GOT TO BE **RUTHLESS**! WIN AT ALL COSTS! DO WHAT-EVER IT TAKES TO BEAT THE OTHER GUY! **WHATEVER IT TAKES!**
WANNA TEAM UP TO BANK-RUPT NATE?
SURE!
HERE, HAVE A COUPLE HOTELS!
THANKS!
HEY!

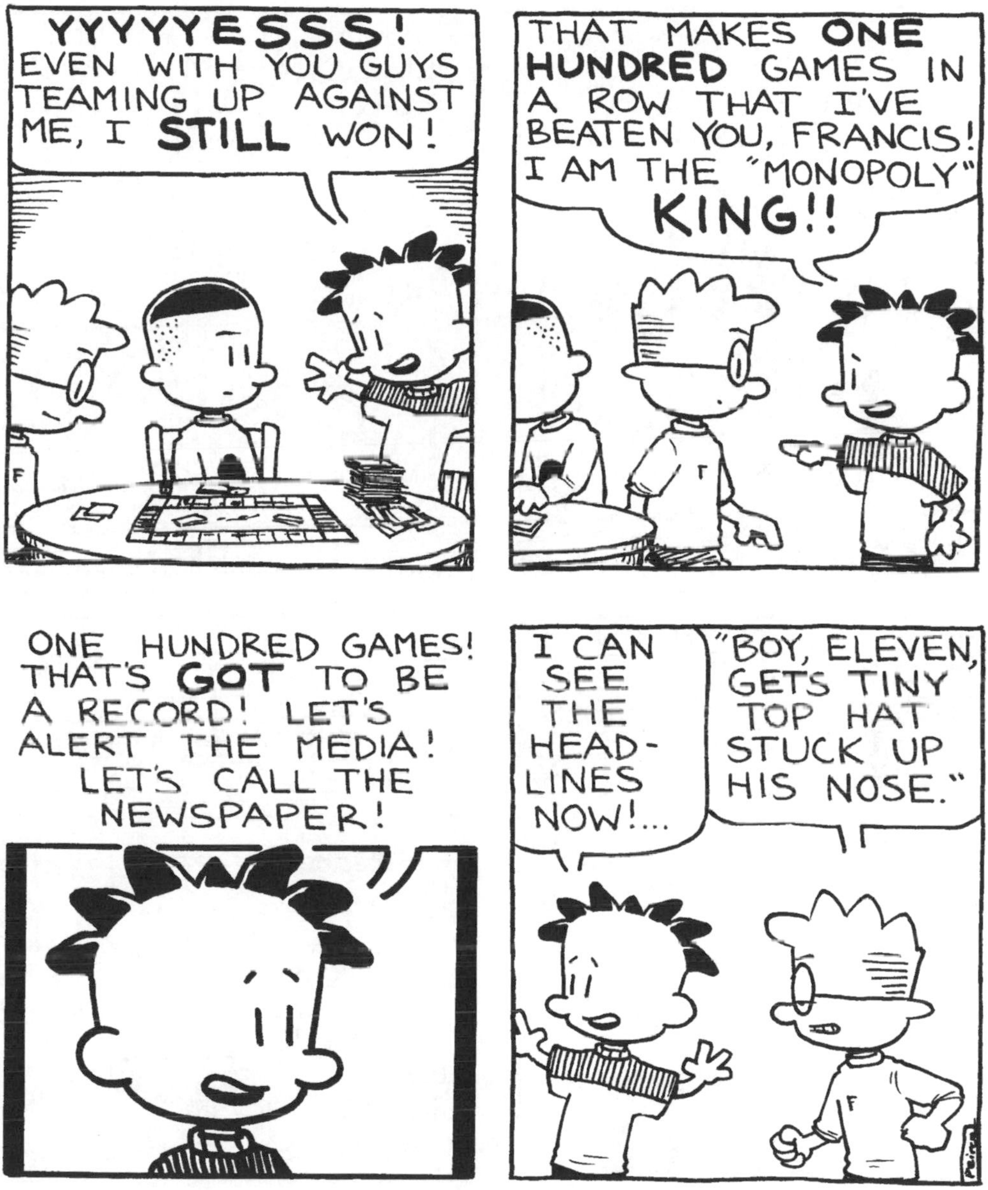
YYYYYESSSS! EVEN WITH YOU GUYS TEAMING UP AGAINST ME, I **STILL** WON!
THAT MAKES **ONE HUNDRED** GAMES IN A ROW THAT I'VE BEATEN YOU, FRANCIS! I AM THE "MONOPOLY" **KING!!**
ONE HUNDRED GAMES! THAT'S **GOT** TO BE A RECORD! LET'S ALERT THE MEDIA! LET'S CALL THE NEWSPAPER!
I CAN SEE THE HEAD-LINES NOW!...
"BOY, ELEVEN, GETS TINY TOP HAT STUCK UP HIS NOSE."
F
T
F
PEIRCE

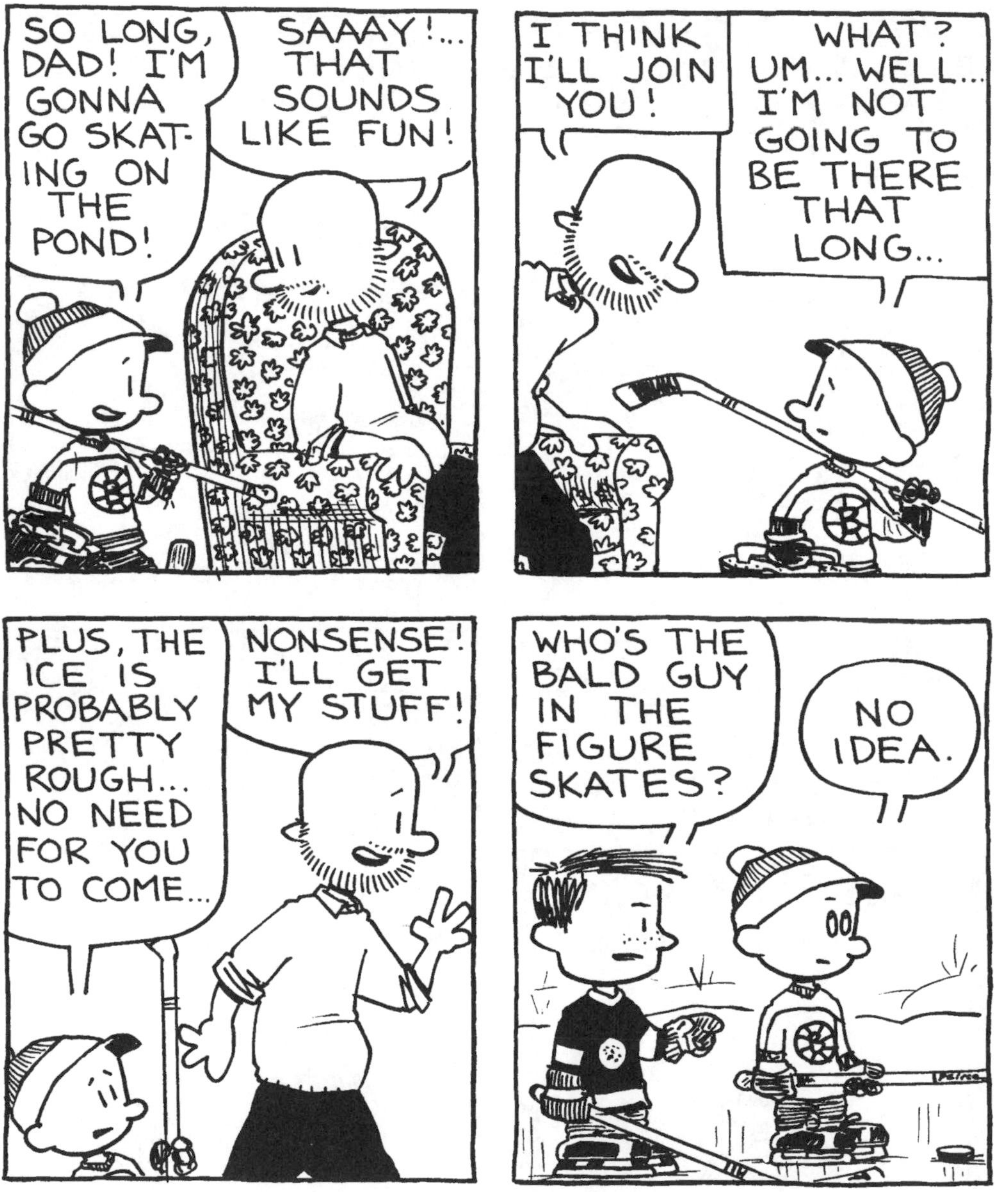
SO LONG, DAD! I'M GONNA GO SKAT-ING ON THE POND!
SAAAY!... THAT SOUNDS LIKE FUN!
I THINK I'LL JOIN YOU!
WHAT? UM... WELL... I'M NOT GOING TO BE THERE THAT LONG...
PLUS, THE ICE IS PROBABLY PRETTY ROUGH... NO NEED FOR YOU TO COME...
NONSENSE! I'LL GET MY STUFF!
WHO'S THE BALD GUY IN THE FIGURE SKATES?
NO IDEA.

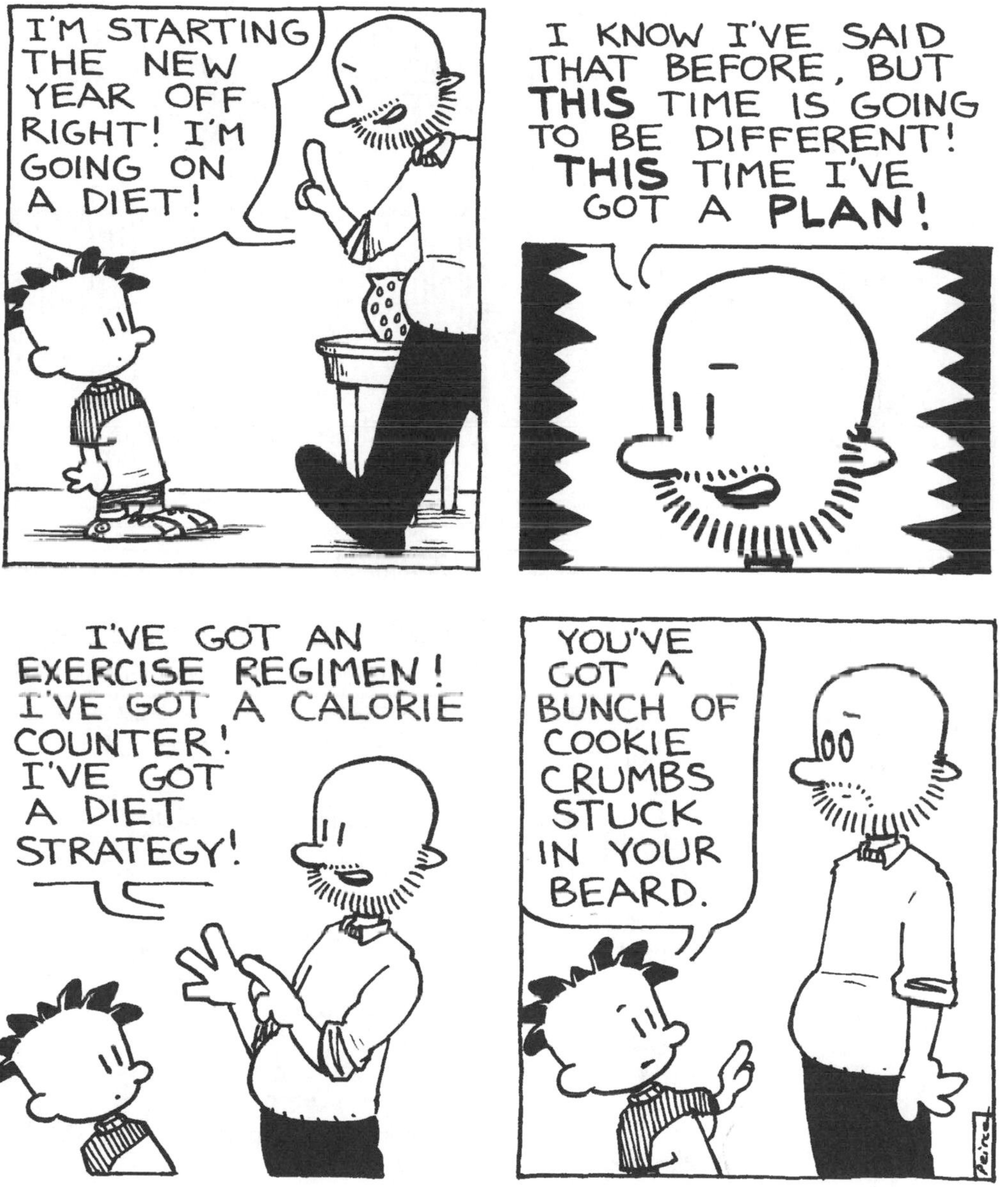
I'M STARTING THE NEW YEAR OFF RIGHT! I'M GOING ON A DIET!
I KNOW I'VE SAID THAT BEFORE, BUT **THIS** TIME IS GOING TO BE DIFFERENT! **THIS** TIME I'VE GOT A **PLAN**!
I'VE GOT AN EXERCISE REGIMEN! I'VE GOT A CALORIE COUNTER! I'VE GOT A DIET STRATEGY!
YOU'VE GOT A BUNCH OF COOKIE CRUMBS STUCK IN YOUR BEARD.
PEIRCE

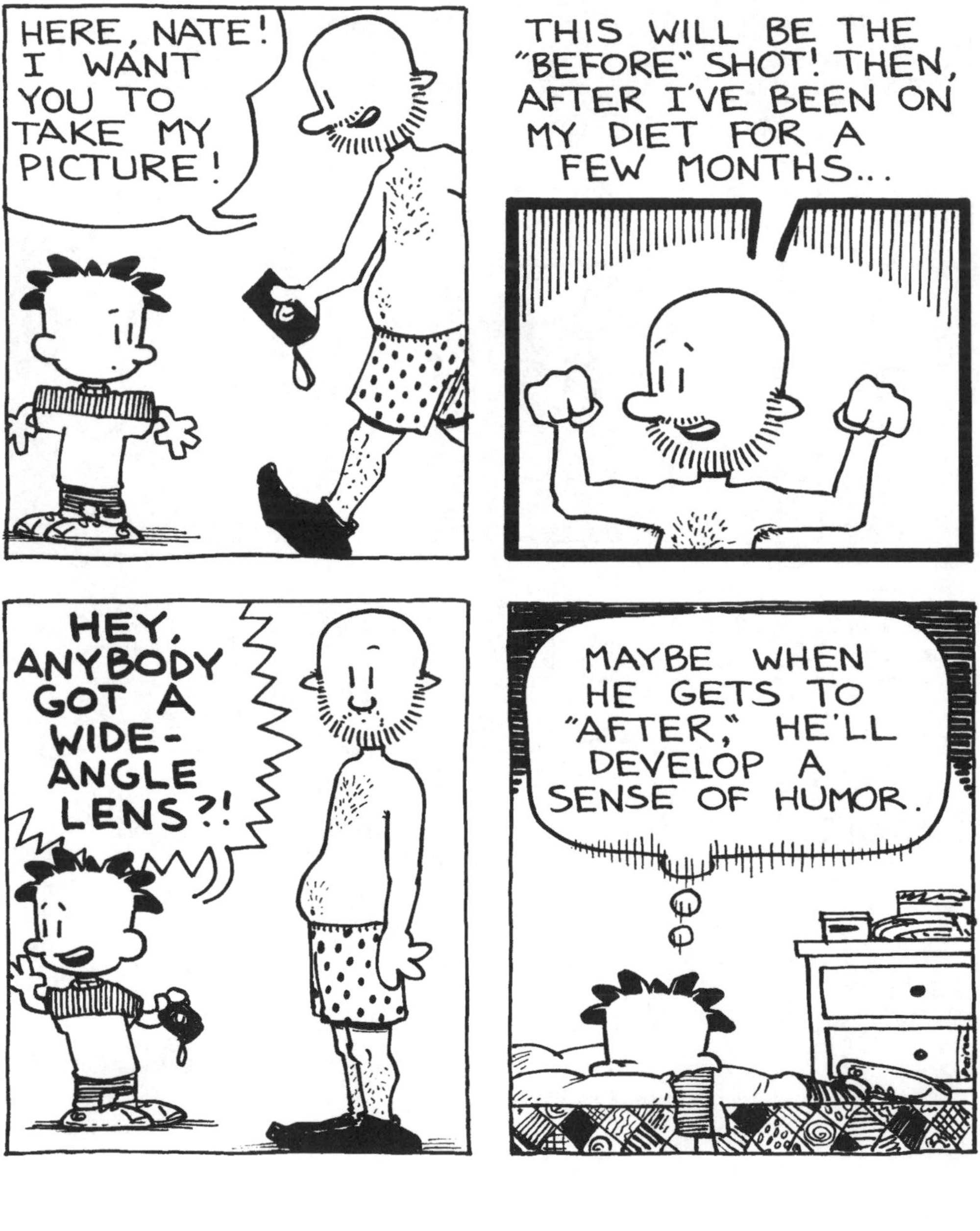
HERE, NATE! I WANT YOU TO TAKE MY PICTURE!
THIS WILL BE THE "BEFORE" SHOT! THEN, AFTER I'VE BEEN ON MY DIET FOR A FEW MONTHS...
HEY, ANYBODY GOT A WIDE-ANGLE LENS?!
MAYBE WHEN HE GETS TO "AFTER," HE'LL DEVELOP A SENSE OF HUMOR.

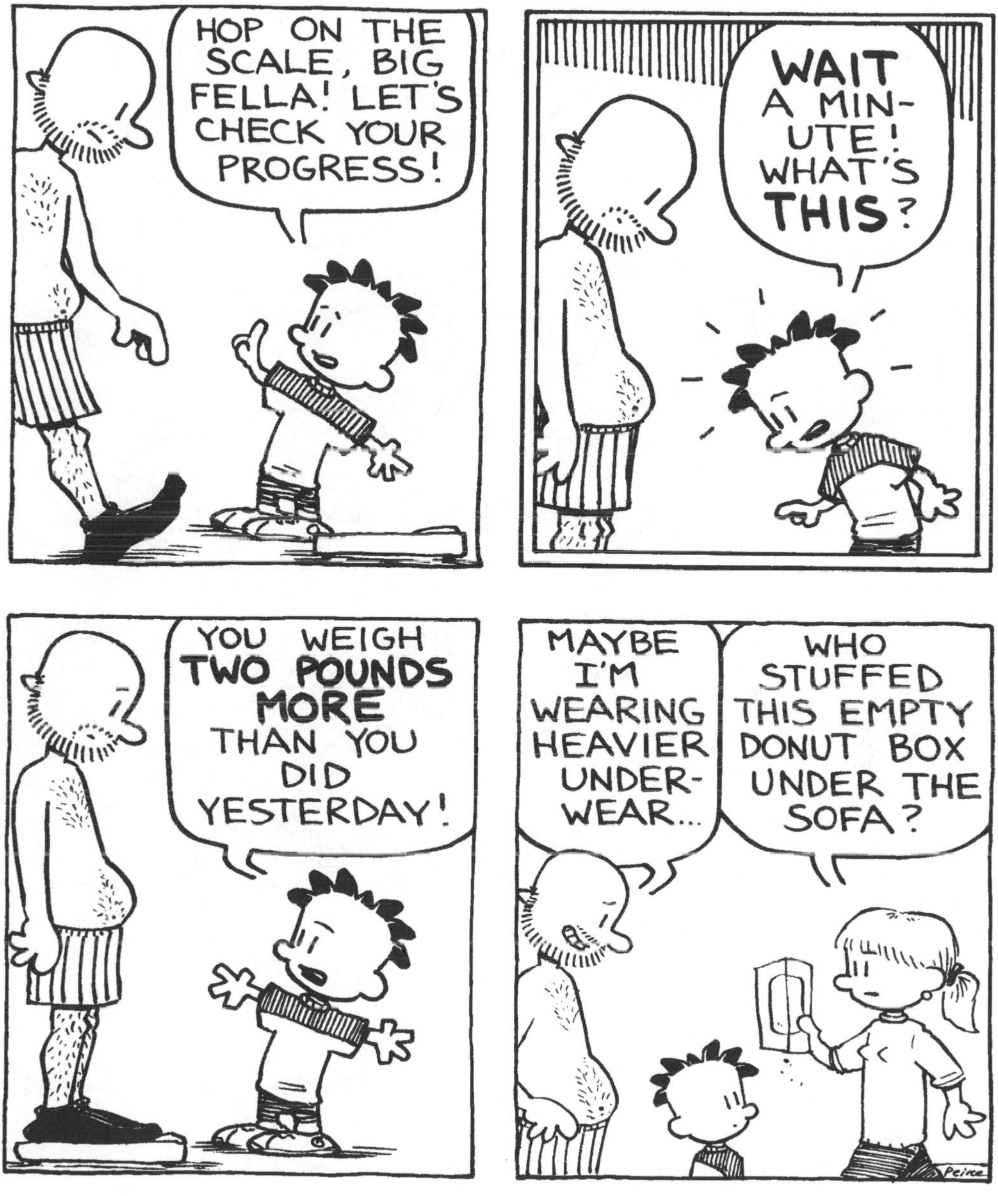
HOP ON THE SCALE, BIG FELLA! LET'S CHECK YOUR PROGRESS!
WAIT A MIN-UTE! WHAT'S THIS?
YOU WEIGH TWO POUNDS MORE THAN YOU DID YESTERDAY!
MAYBE I'M WEARING HEAVIER UNDER-WEAR...
WHO STUFFED THIS EMPTY DONUT BOX UNDER THE SOFA?
Peirce

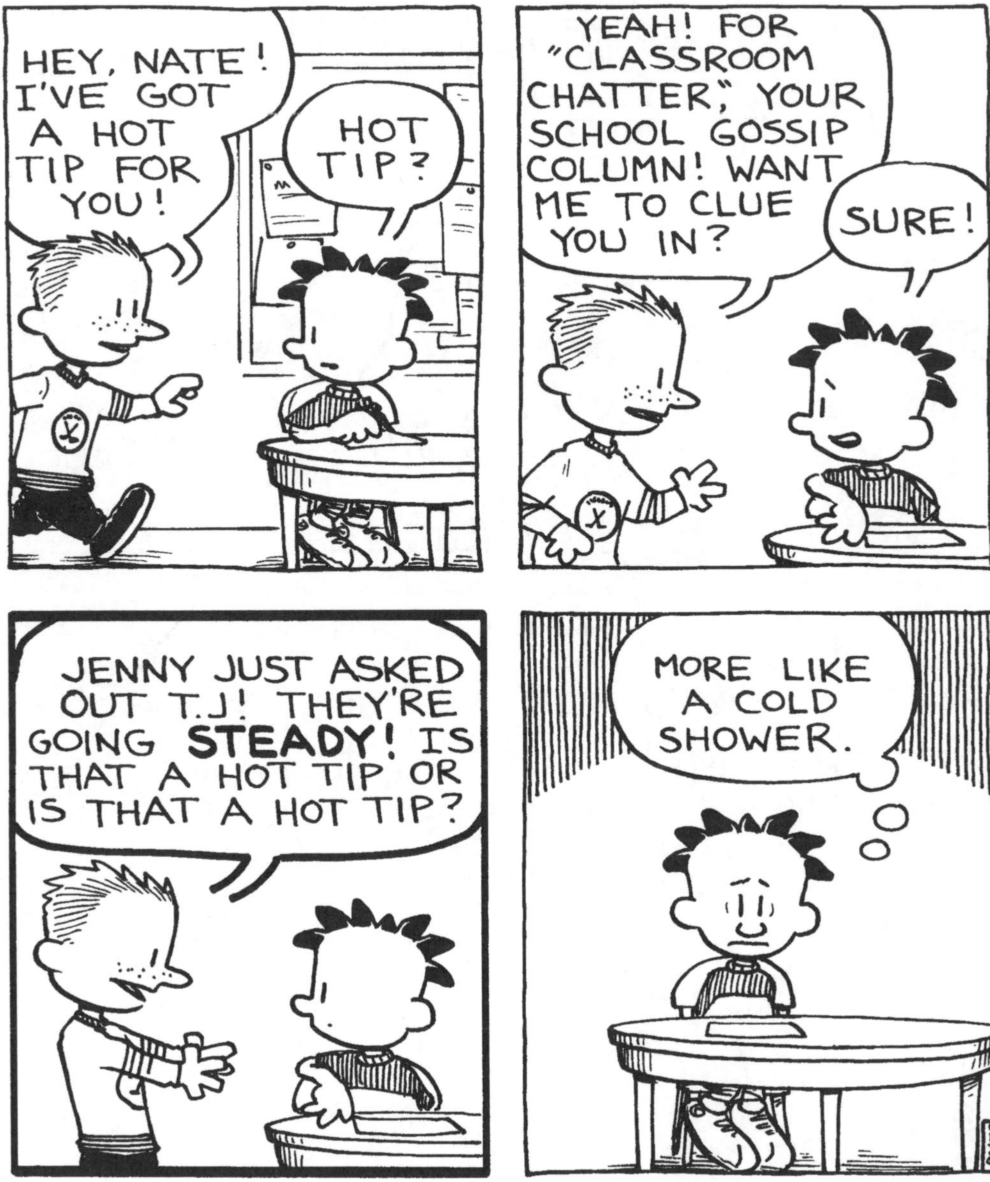
HEY, NATE! I'VE GOT A HOT TIP FOR YOU!
HOT TIP?
YEAH! FOR "CLASSROOM CHATTER," YOUR SCHOOL GOSSIP COLUMN! WANT ME TO CLUE YOU IN?
SURE!
JENNY JUST ASKED OUT T.J! THEY'RE GOING **STEADY!** IS THAT A HOT TIP OR IS THAT A HOT TIP?
MORE LIKE A COLD SHOWER.

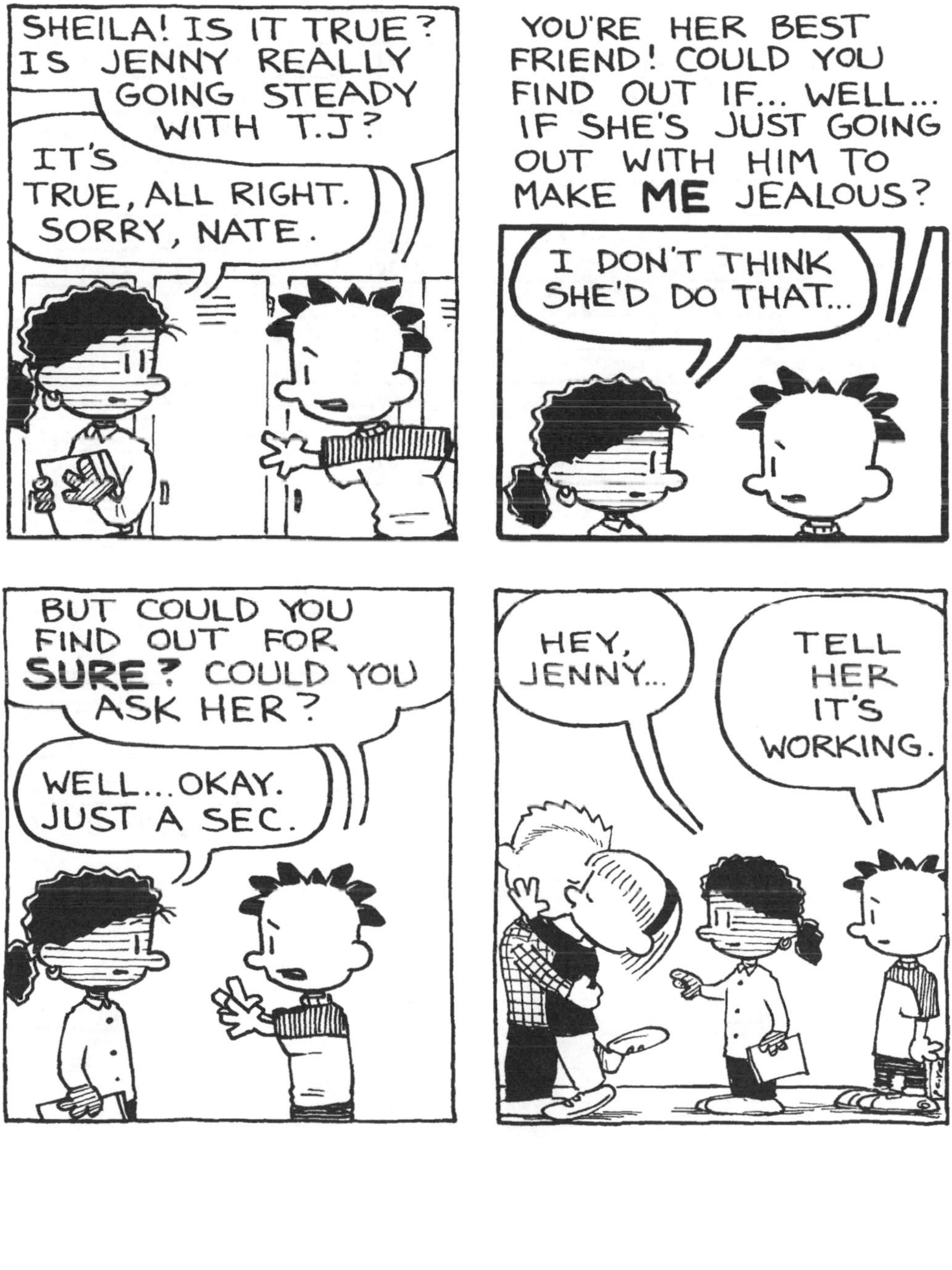
SHEILA! IS IT TRUE? IS JENNY REALLY GOING STEADY WITH T.J?
IT'S TRUE, ALL RIGHT. SORRY, NATE.
YOU'RE HER BEST FRIEND! COULD YOU FIND OUT IF... WELL... IF SHE'S JUST GOING OUT WITH HIM TO MAKE **ME** JEALOUS?
I DON'T THINK SHE'D DO THAT...
BUT COULD YOU FIND OUT FOR **SURE?** COULD YOU ASK HER?
WELL...OKAY. JUST A SEC.
HEY, JENNY...
TELL HER IT'S WORKING.

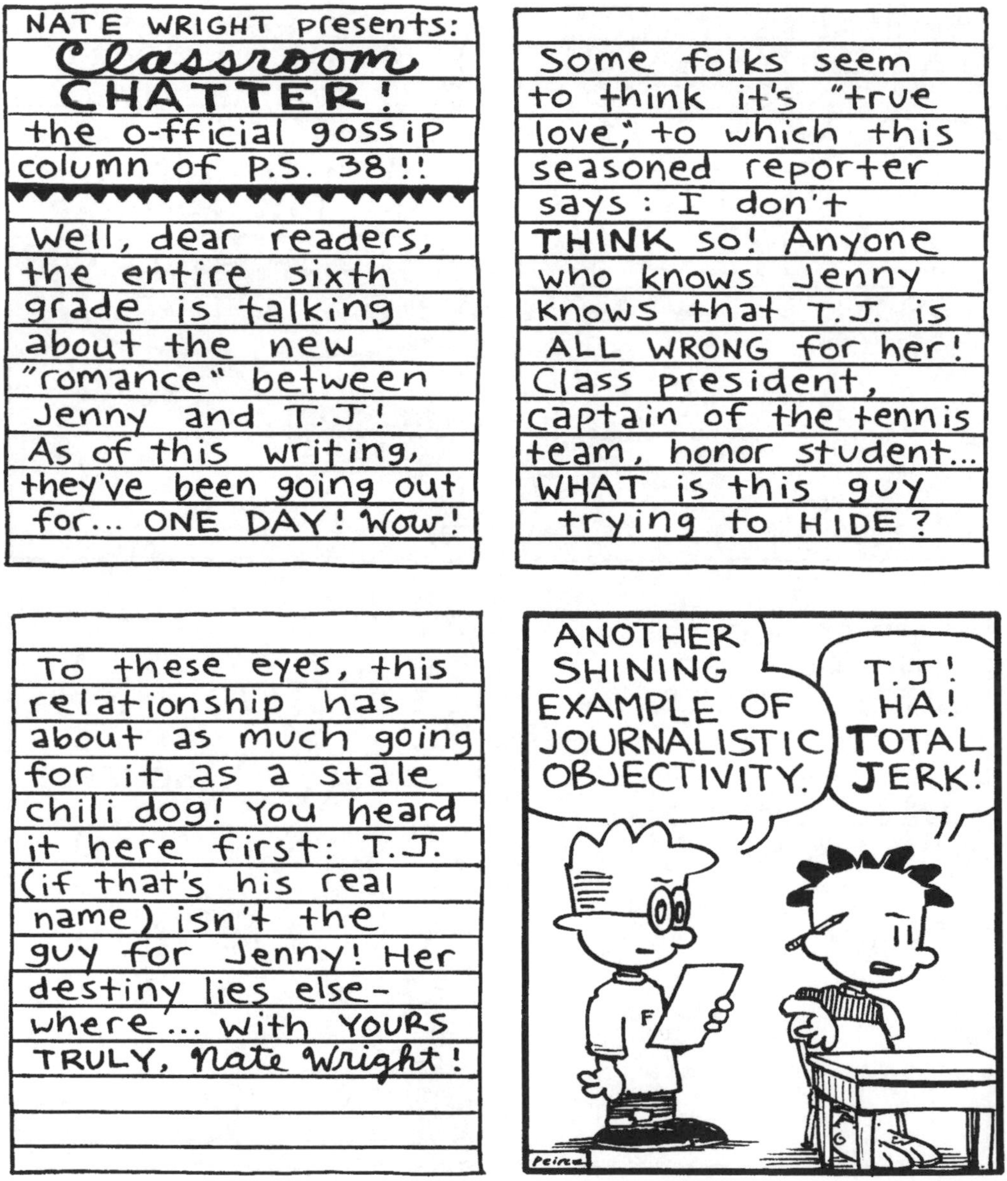

NATE WRIGHT presents:

Classroom CHATTER!

the o-fficial gossip column of P.S. 38 !!

Well, dear readers, the entire sixth grade is talking about the new "romance" between Jenny and T.J! As of this writing, they've been going out for... ONE DAY! Wow!

Some folks seem to think it's "true love," to which this seasoned reporter says: I don't THINK so! Anyone who knows Jenny knows that T.J. is ALL WRONG for her! Class president, captain of the tennis team, honor student... WHAT is this guy trying to HIDE?

To these eyes, this relationship has about as much going for it as a stale chili dog! You heard it here first: T.J. (if that's his real name) isn't the guy for Jenny! Her destiny lies else-where... with YOURS TRULY, Nate Wright!

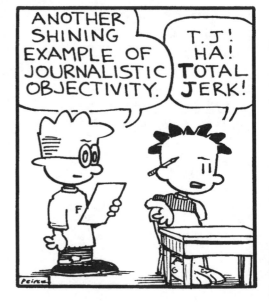

ANOTHER SHINING EXAMPLE OF JOURNALISTIC OBJECTIVITY.

T.J! HA! TOTAL JERK!

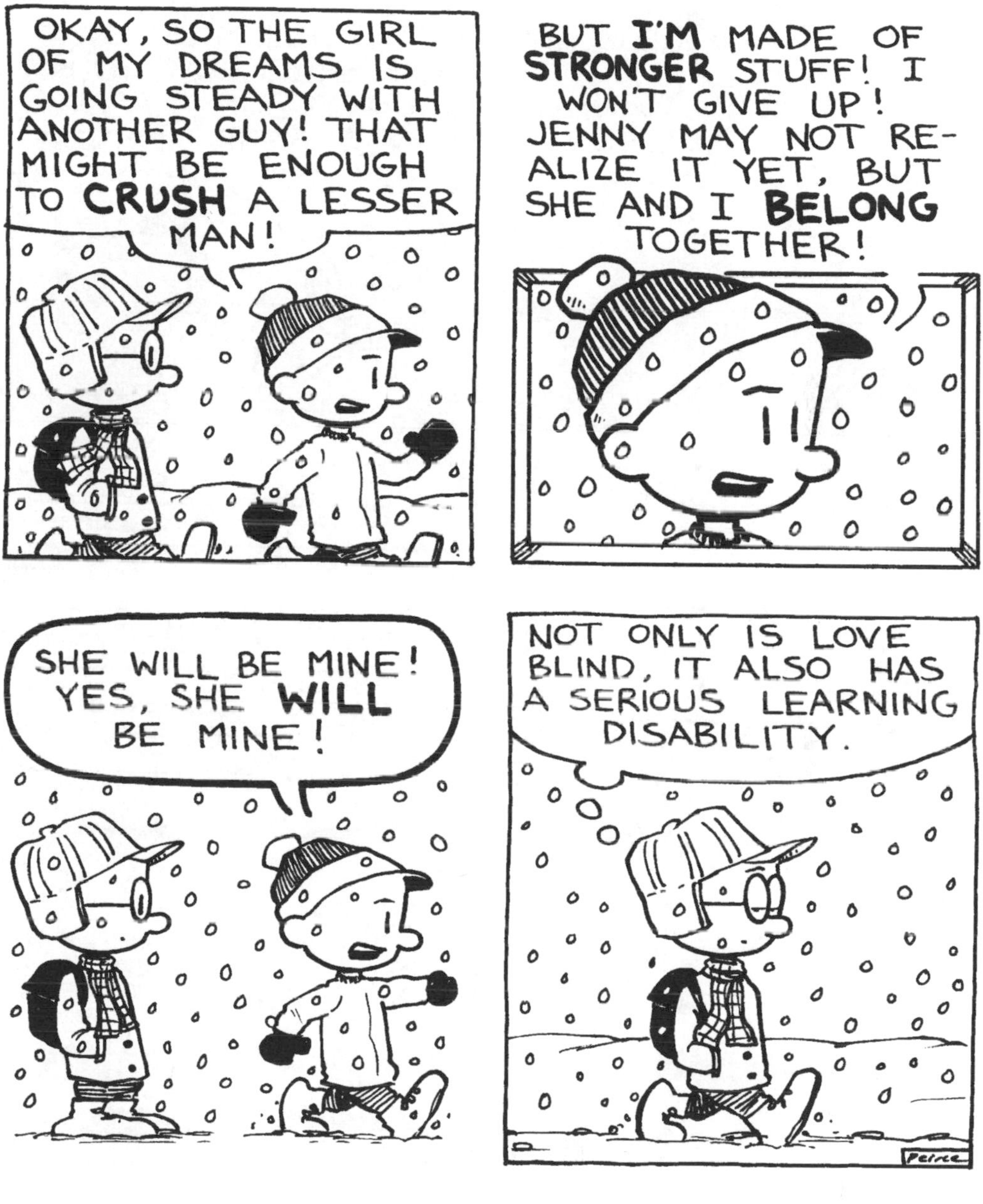
OKAY, SO THE GIRL OF MY DREAMS IS GOING STEADY WITH ANOTHER GUY! THAT MIGHT BE ENOUGH TO **CRUSH** A LESSER MAN!
BUT **I'M** MADE OF **STRONGER** STUFF! I WON'T GIVE UP! JENNY MAY NOT REALIZE IT YET, BUT SHE AND I **BELONG** TOGETHER!
SHE WILL BE MINE! YES, SHE **WILL** BE MINE!
NOT ONLY IS LOVE BLIND, IT ALSO HAS A SERIOUS LEARNING DISABILITY.
Peirce

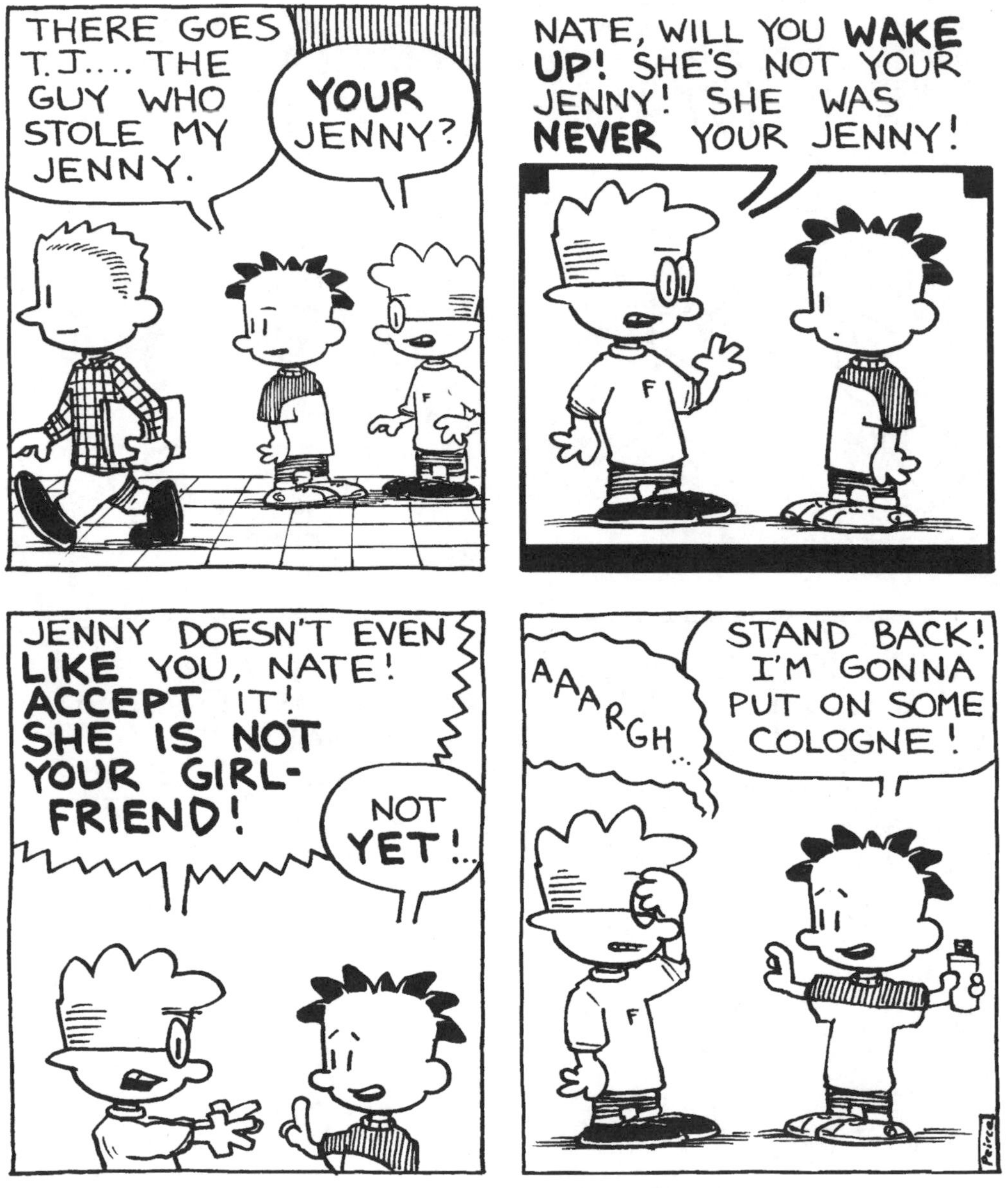
THERE GOES T.J.... THE GUY WHO STOLE MY JENNY.
YOUR JENNY?
NATE, WILL YOU WAKE UP! SHE'S NOT YOUR JENNY! SHE WAS NEVER YOUR JENNY!
JENNY DOESN'T EVEN LIKE YOU, NATE! ACCEPT IT! SHE IS NOT YOUR GIRL-FRIEND!
NOT YET!..
AAARGH...
STAND BACK! I'M GONNA PUT ON SOME COLOGNE!
Peirce

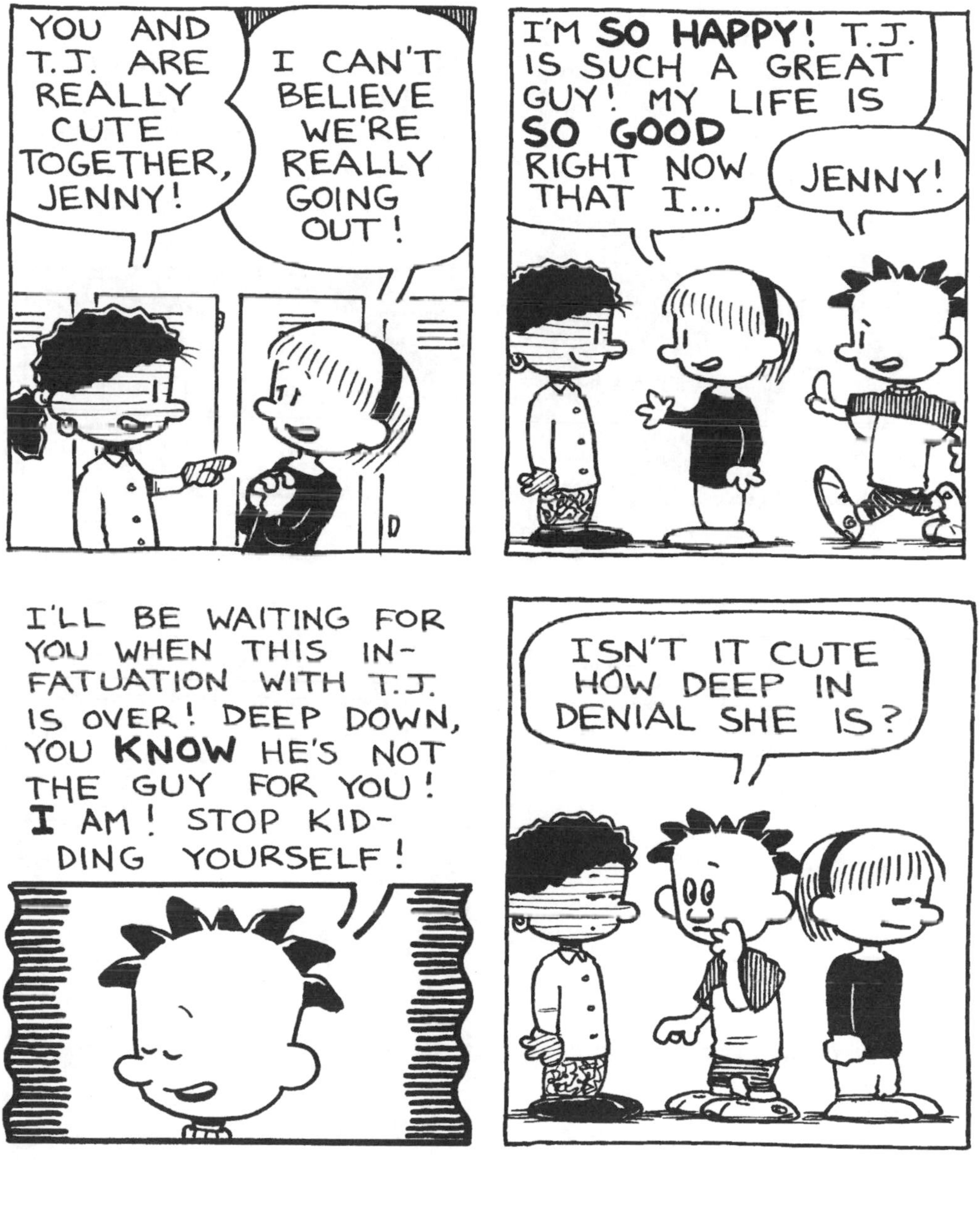
YOU AND T.J. ARE REALLY CUTE TOGETHER, JENNY!
I CAN'T BELIEVE WE'RE REALLY GOING OUT!
I'M SO HAPPY! T.J. IS SUCH A GREAT GUY! MY LIFE IS SO GOOD RIGHT NOW THAT I...
JENNY!
I'LL BE WAITING FOR YOU WHEN THIS IN-FATUATION WITH T.J. IS OVER! DEEP DOWN, YOU KNOW HE'S NOT THE GUY FOR YOU! I AM! STOP KID-DING YOURSELF!
ISN'T IT CUTE HOW DEEP IN DENIAL SHE IS?

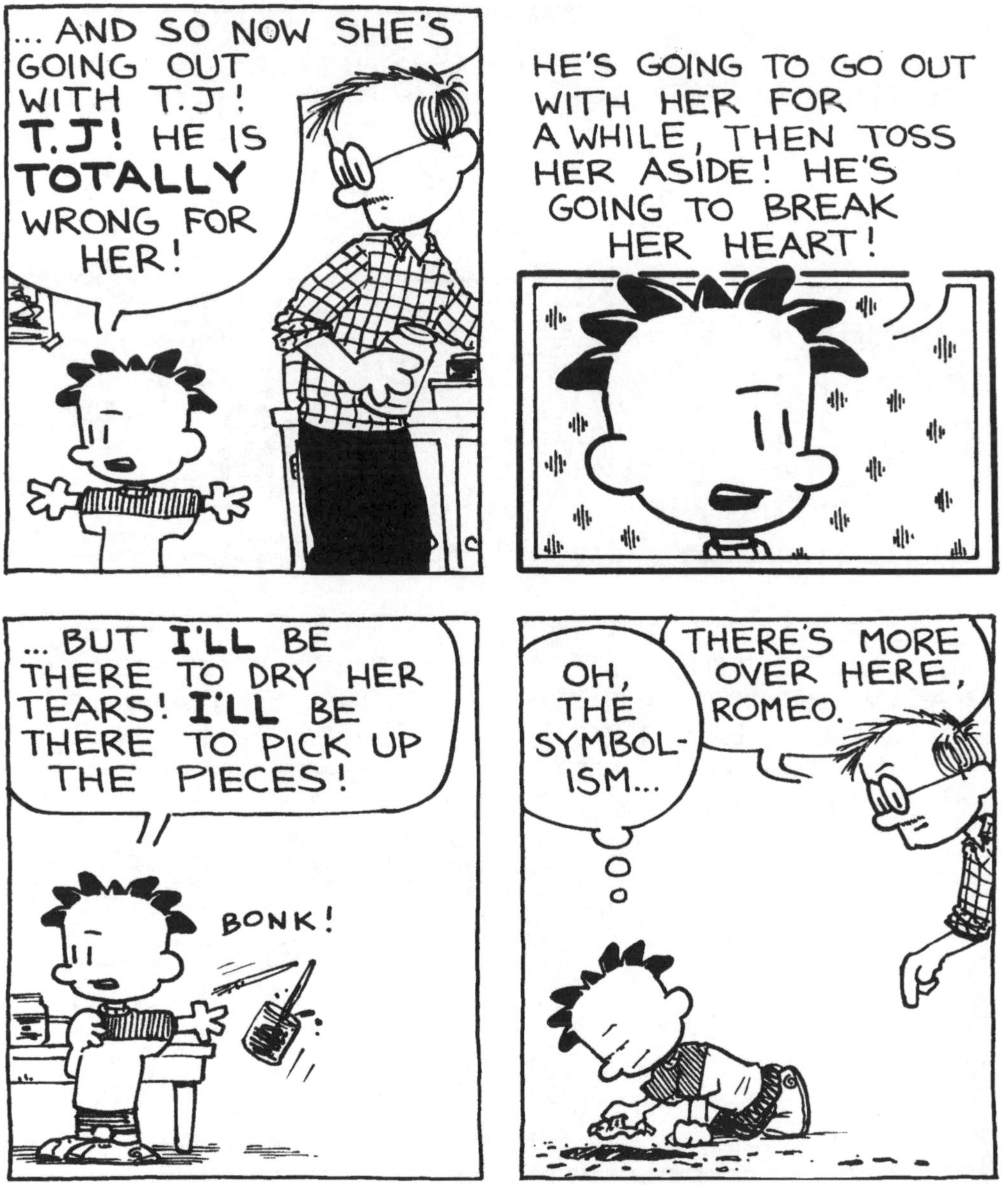

... AND SO NOW SHE'S GOING OUT WITH T.J! **T.J!** HE IS **TOTALLY** WRONG FOR HER!
HE'S GOING TO GO OUT WITH HER FOR A WHILE, THEN TOSS HER ASIDE! HE'S GOING TO BREAK HER HEART!
... BUT **I'LL** BE THERE TO DRY HER TEARS! **I'LL** BE THERE TO PICK UP THE PIECES!
BONK!
THERE'S MORE OVER HERE, ROMEO.
OH, THE SYMBOL-ISM...

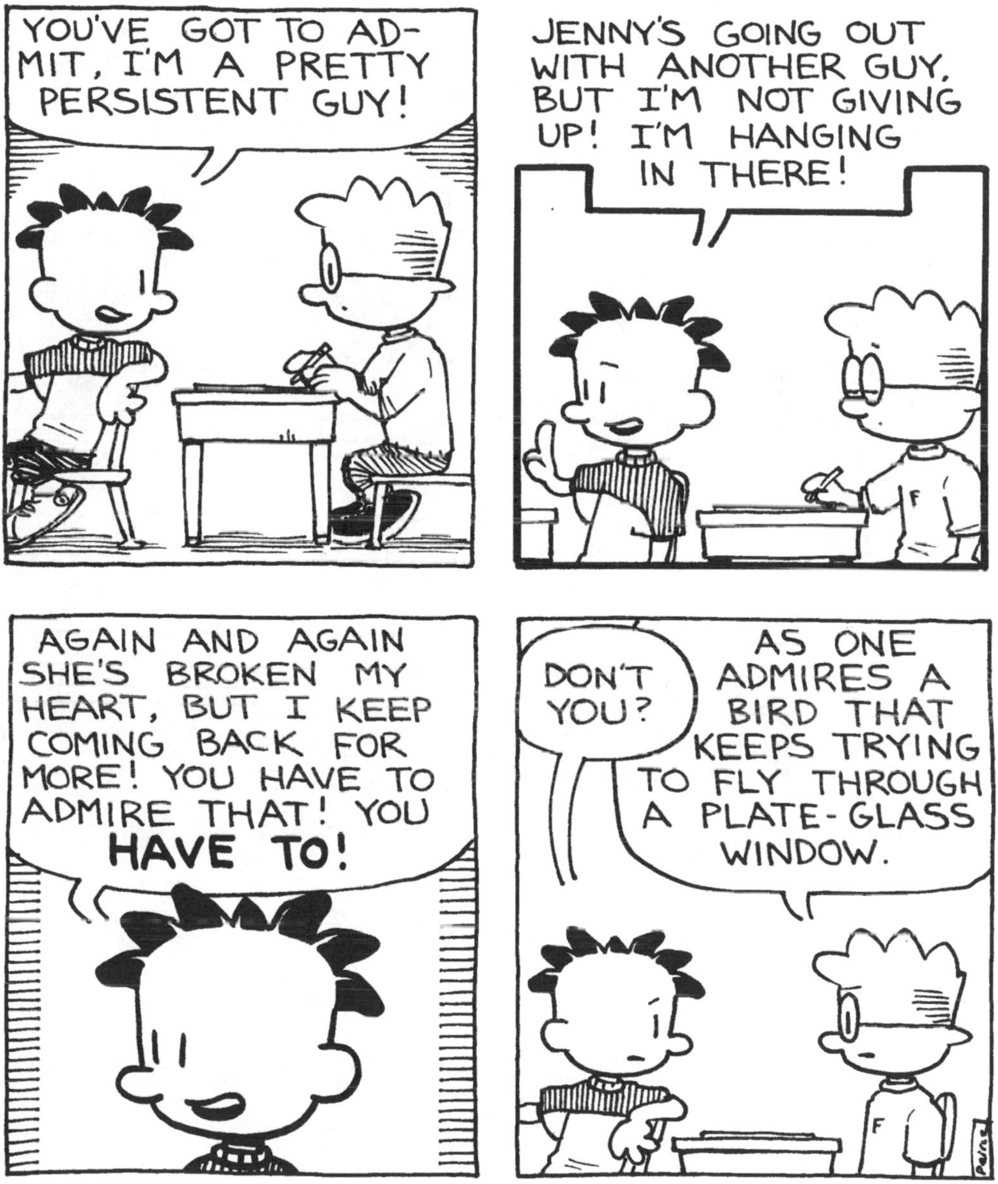
YOU'VE GOT TO ADMIT, I'M A PRETTY PERSISTENT GUY!
JENNY'S GOING OUT WITH ANOTHER GUY, BUT I'M NOT GIVING UP! I'M HANGING IN THERE!
AGAIN AND AGAIN SHE'S BROKEN MY HEART, BUT I KEEP COMING BACK FOR MORE! YOU HAVE TO ADMIRE THAT! YOU **HAVE TO**!
DON'T YOU?
AS ONE ADMIRES A BIRD THAT KEEPS TRYING TO FLY THROUGH A PLATE-GLASS WINDOW.
PEIRCE

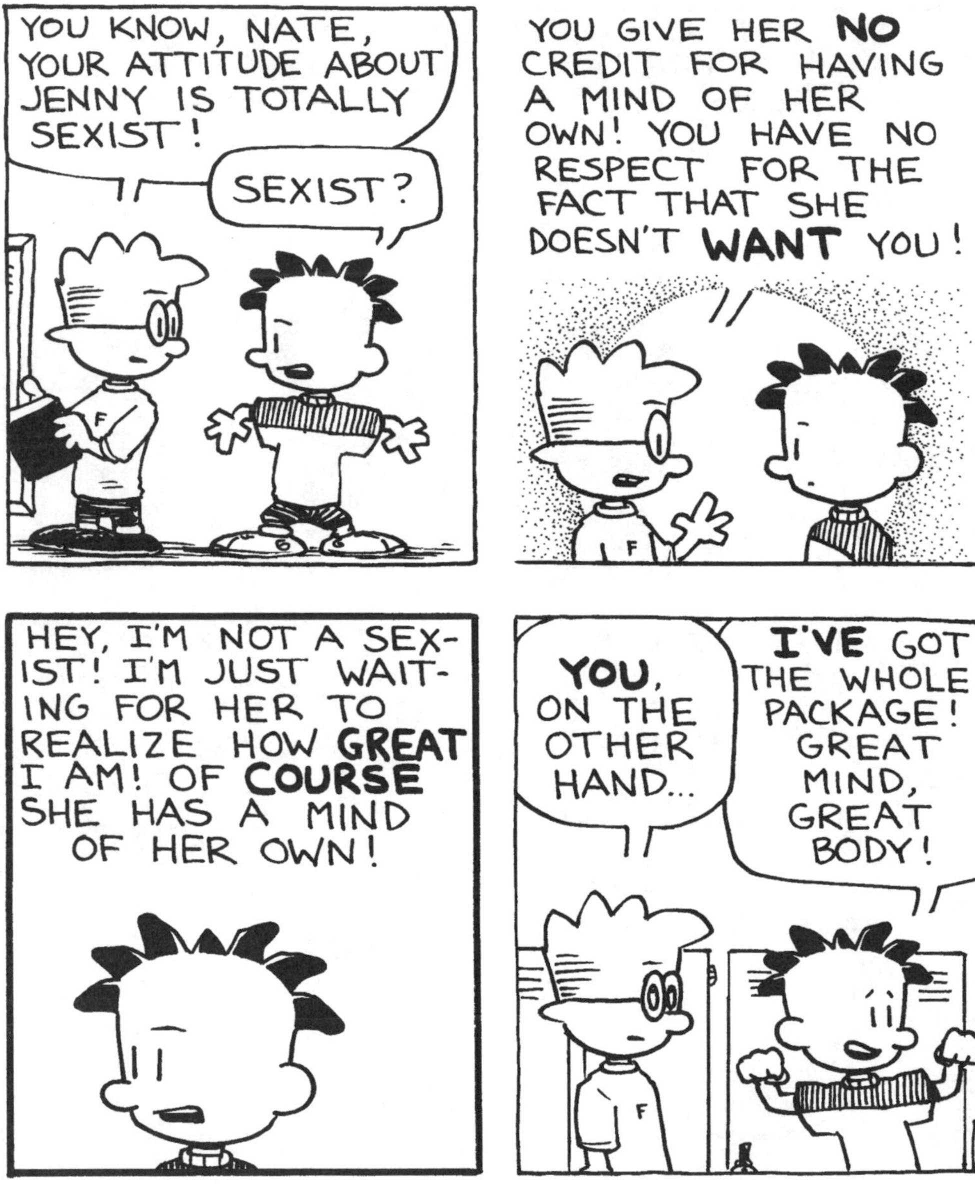
YOU KNOW, NATE, YOUR ATTITUDE ABOUT JENNY IS TOTALLY SEXIST!
SEXIST?
YOU GIVE HER NO CREDIT FOR HAVING A MIND OF HER OWN! YOU HAVE NO RESPECT FOR THE FACT THAT SHE DOESN'T WANT YOU!
HEY, I'M NOT A SEXIST! I'M JUST WAITING FOR HER TO REALIZE HOW GREAT I AM! OF COURSE SHE HAS A MIND OF HER OWN!
YOU, ON THE OTHER HAND...
I'VE GOT THE WHOLE PACKAGE! GREAT MIND, GREAT BODY!

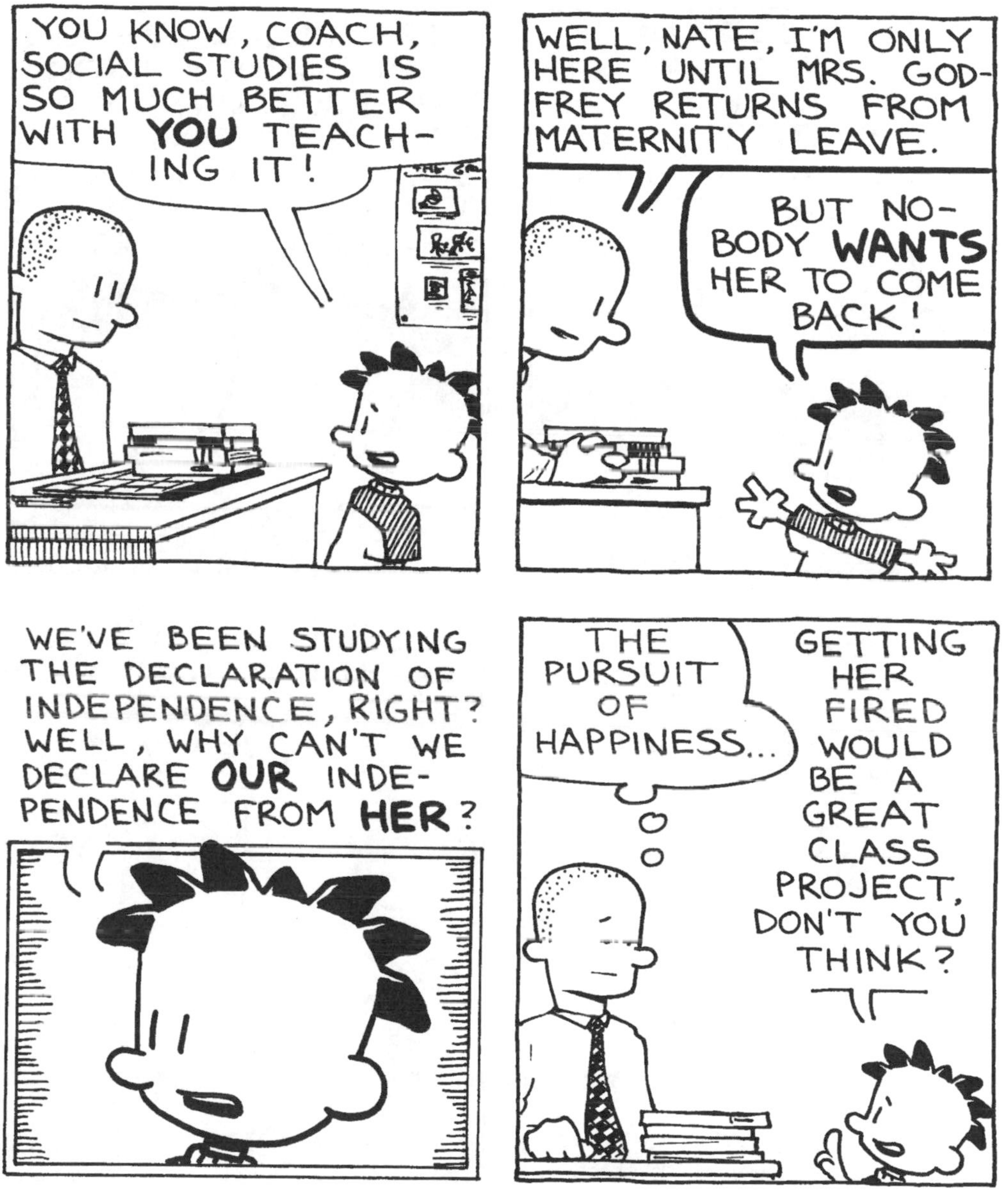
YOU KNOW, COACH, SOCIAL STUDIES IS SO MUCH BETTER WITH YOU TEACHING IT!
WELL, NATE, I'M ONLY HERE UNTIL MRS. GODFREY RETURNS FROM MATERNITY LEAVE.
BUT NOBODY WANTS HER TO COME BACK!
WE'VE BEEN STUDYING THE DECLARATION OF INDEPENDENCE, RIGHT? WELL, WHY CAN'T WE DECLARE OUR INDEPENDENCE FROM HER?
THE PURSUIT OF HAPPINESS...
GETTING HER FIRED WOULD BE A GREAT CLASS PROJECT, DON'T YOU THINK?

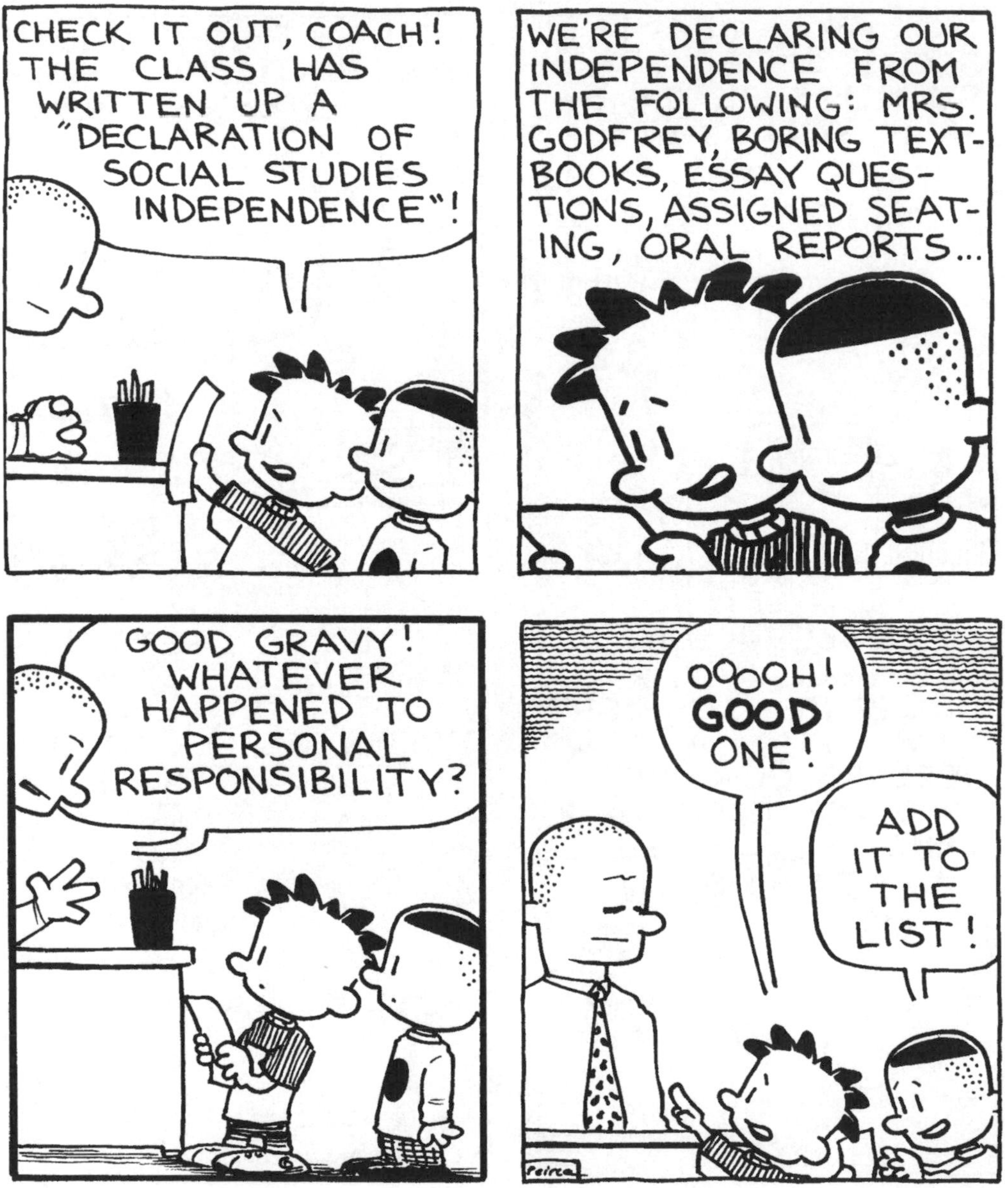
CHECK IT OUT, COACH! THE CLASS HAS WRITTEN UP A "DECLARATION OF SOCIAL STUDIES INDEPENDENCE"!
WE'RE DECLARING OUR INDEPENDENCE FROM THE FOLLOWING: MRS. GODFREY, BORING TEXT-BOOKS, ESSAY QUES-TIONS, ASSIGNED SEAT-ING, ORAL REPORTS...
GOOD GRAVY! WHATEVER HAPPENED TO PERSONAL RESPONSIBILITY?
OOOOH! GOOD ONE!
ADD IT TO THE LIST!
Peirce

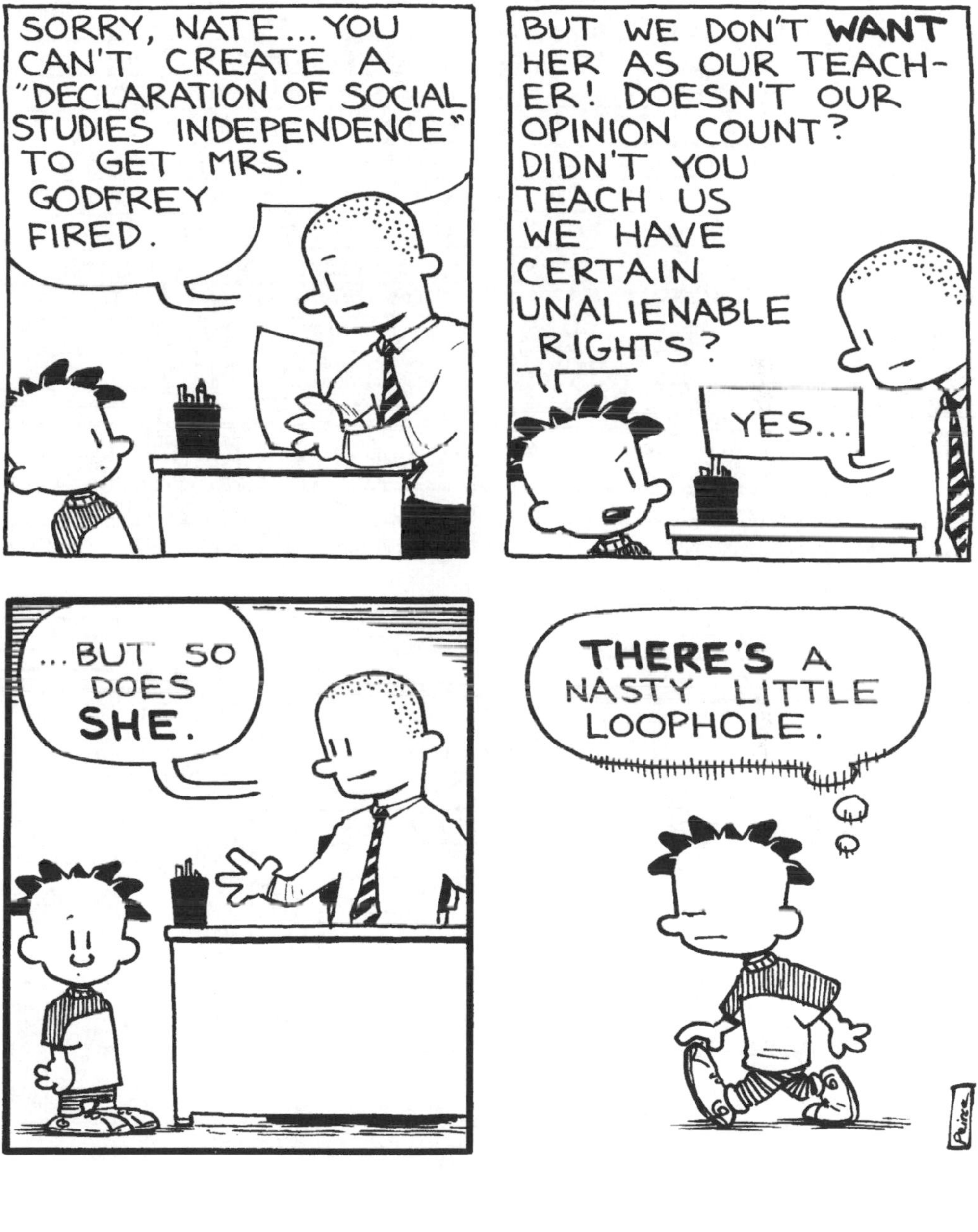
SORRY, NATE... YOU CAN'T CREATE A "DECLARATION OF SOCIAL STUDIES INDEPENDENCE" TO GET MRS. GODFREY FIRED.
BUT WE DON'T WANT HER AS OUR TEACH-ER! DOESN'T OUR OPINION COUNT? DIDN'T YOU TEACH US WE HAVE CERTAIN UNALIENABLE RIGHTS?
YES...
...BUT SO DOES SHE.
THERE'S A NASTY LITTLE LOOPHOLE.

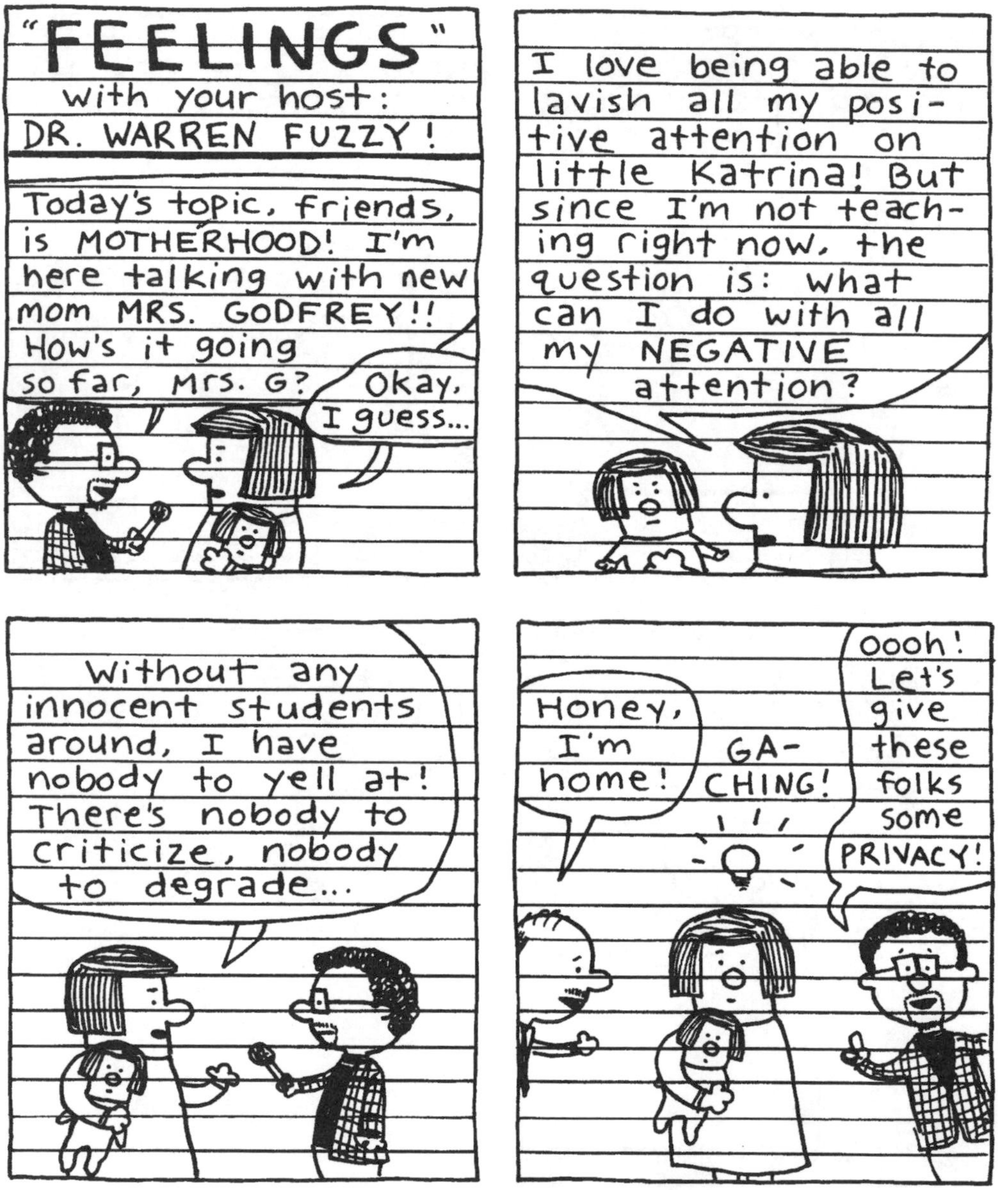
"FEELINGS"
with your host: DR. WARREN FUZZY!
Today's topic, friends, is MOTHERHOOD! I'm here talking with new mom MRS. GODFREY!! How's it going so far, Mrs. G?
Okay, I guess...
I love being able to lavish all my positive attention on little Katrina! But since I'm not teaching right now, the question is: what can I do with all my NEGATIVE attention?
Without any innocent students around, I have nobody to yell at! There's nobody to criticize, nobody to degrade...
Honey, I'm home!
GA-CHING!
Oooh! Let's give these folks some PRIVACY!

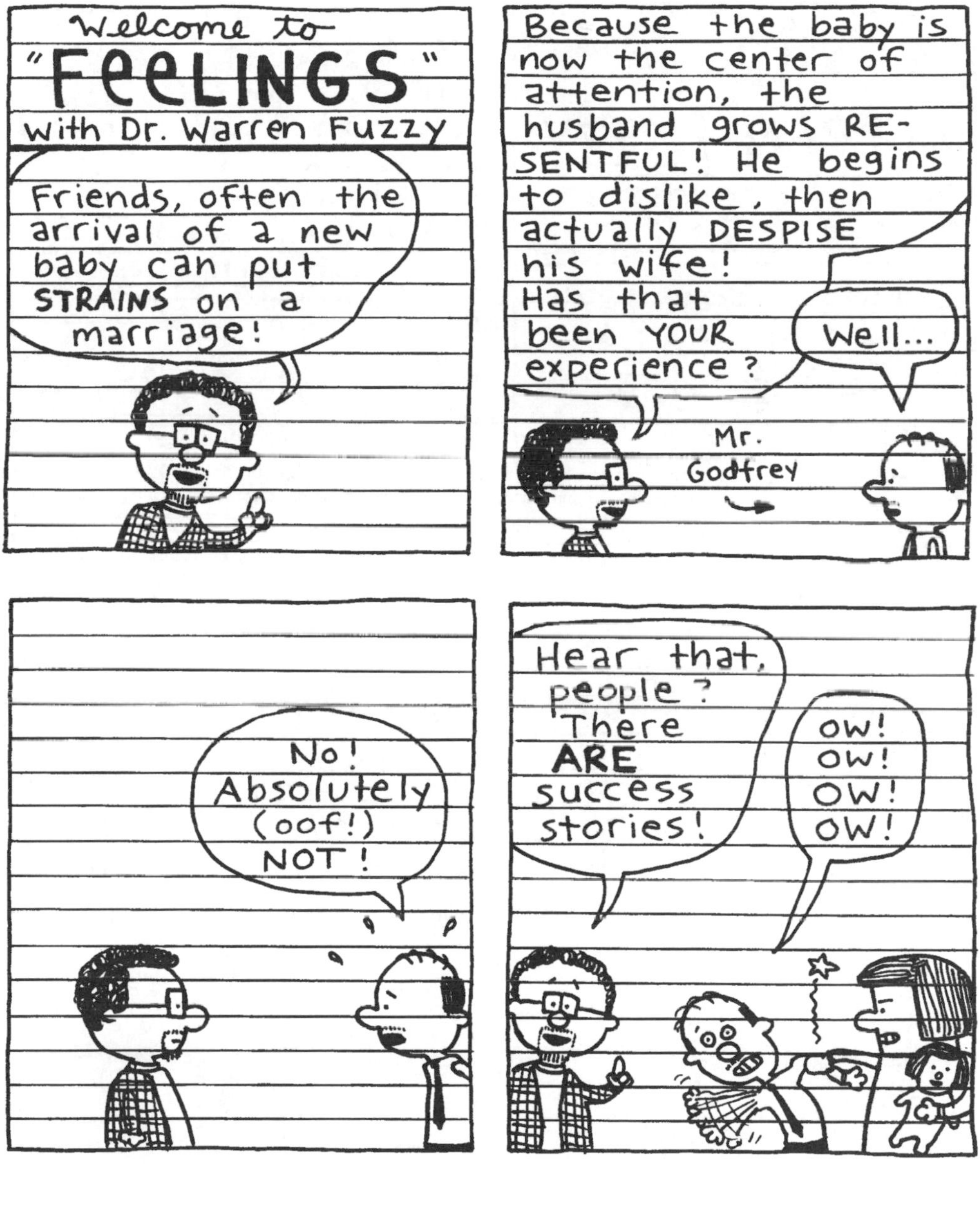
Welcome to
"FeeLINGS"
with Dr. Warren Fuzzy
Friends, often the arrival of a new baby can put STRAINS on a marriage!
Because the baby is now the center of attention, the husband grows RE-SENTFUL! He begins to dislike, then actually DESPISE his wife! Has that been YOUR experience?
Well...
Mr. Godfrey
No! Absolutely (oof!) NOT!
Hear that, people? There ARE success stories!
OW! OW! OW! OW!

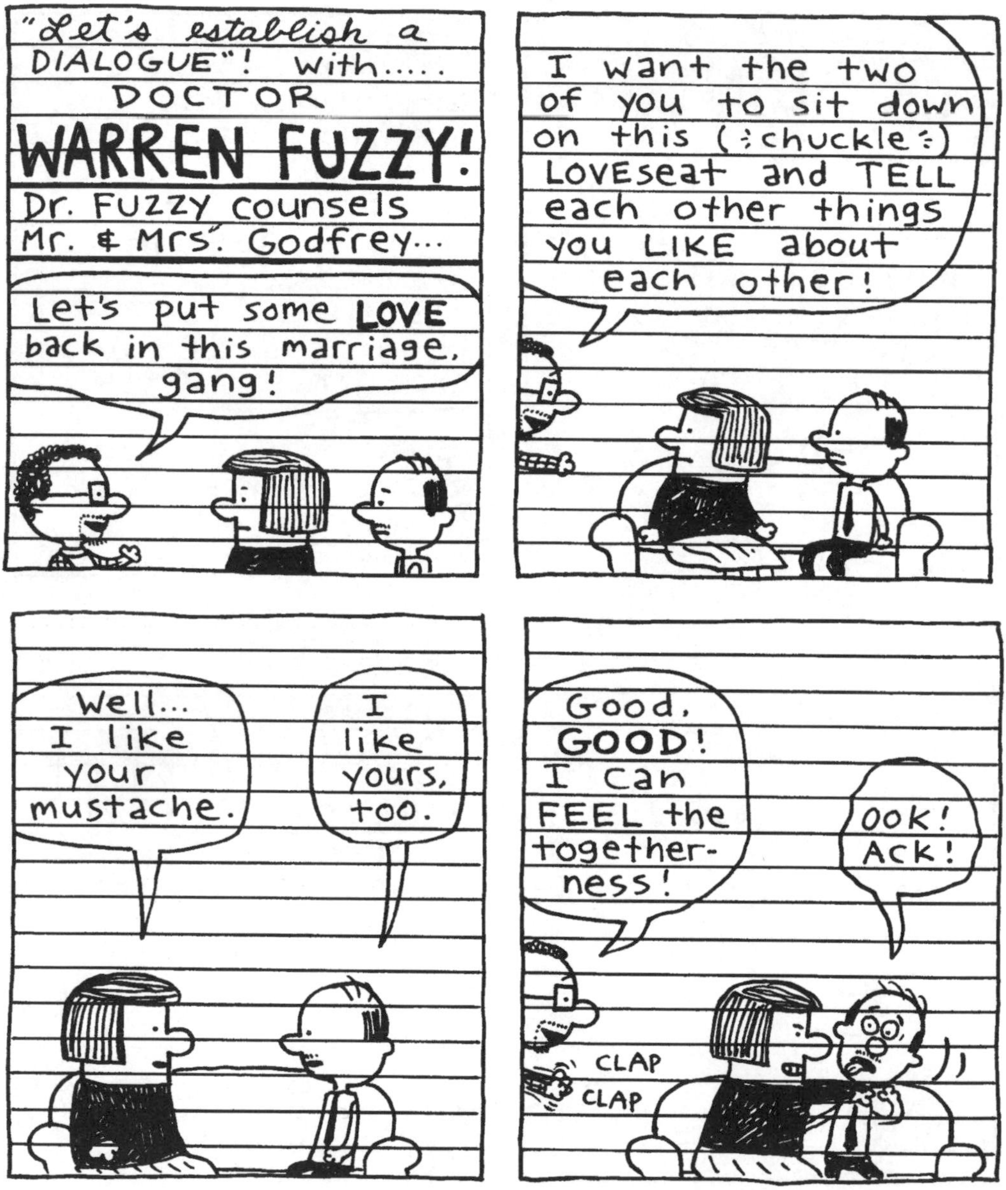

"Let's establish a DIALOGUE"! with..... DOCTOR
WARREN FUZZY!
Dr. FUZZY counsels Mr. & Mrs. Godfrey...
Let's put some LOVE back in this marriage, gang!
I want the two of you to sit down on this (chuckle) LOVESeat and TELL each other things you LIKE about each other!
Well... I like your mustache.
I like yours, too.
Good, GOOD! I can FEEL the together-ness!
OOK! Ack!
CLAP
CLAP

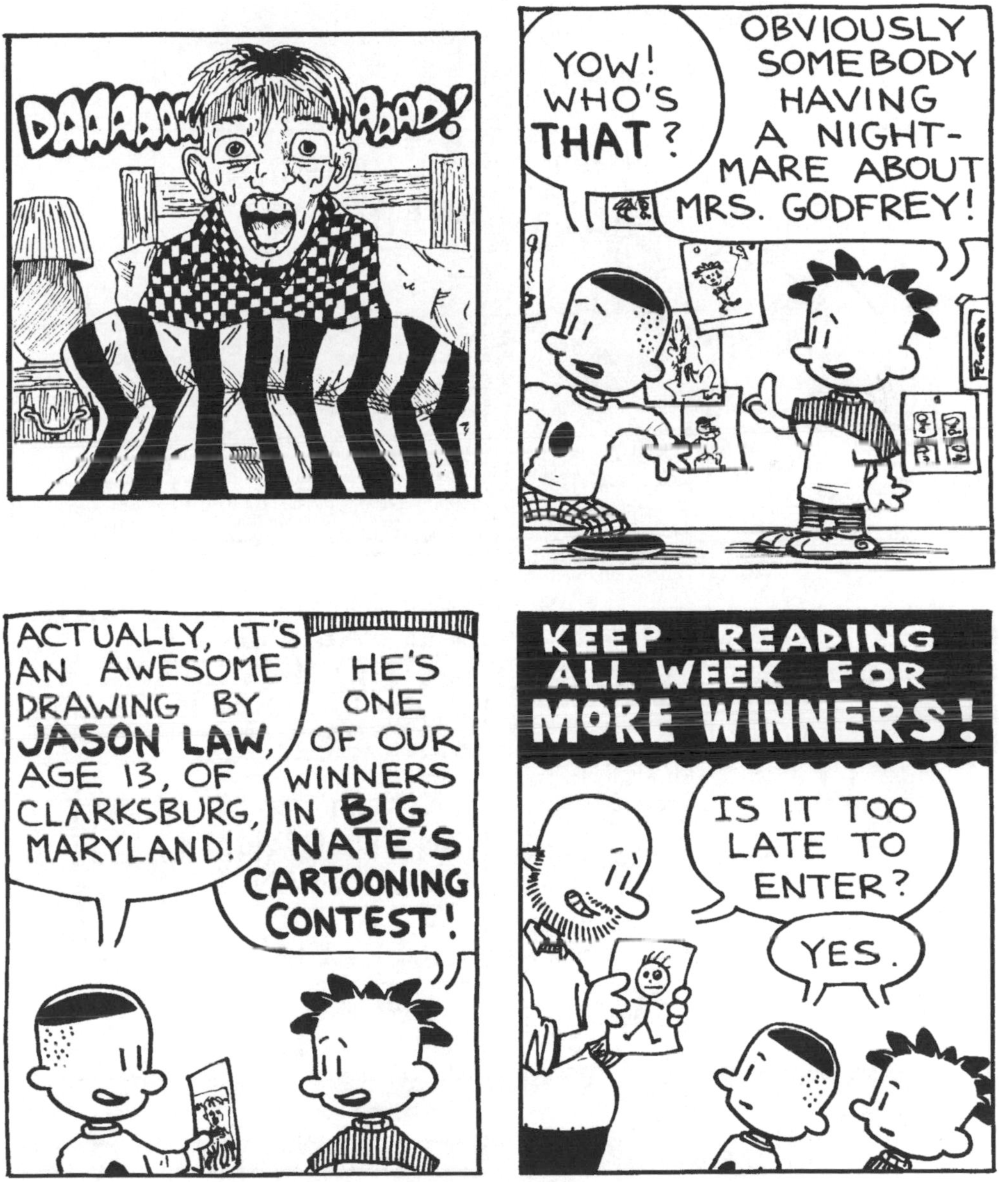
DAAAAA... AAAD!
YOW! WHO'S THAT?
OBVIOUSLY SOMEBODY HAVING A NIGHT-MARE ABOUT MRS. GODFREY!
ACTUALLY, IT'S AN AWESOME DRAWING BY JASON LAW, AGE 13, OF CLARKSBURG, MARYLAND!
HE'S ONE OF OUR WINNERS IN BIG NATE'S CARTOONING CONTEST!
KEEP READING ALL WEEK FOR MORE WINNERS!
IS IT TOO LATE TO ENTER?
YES.

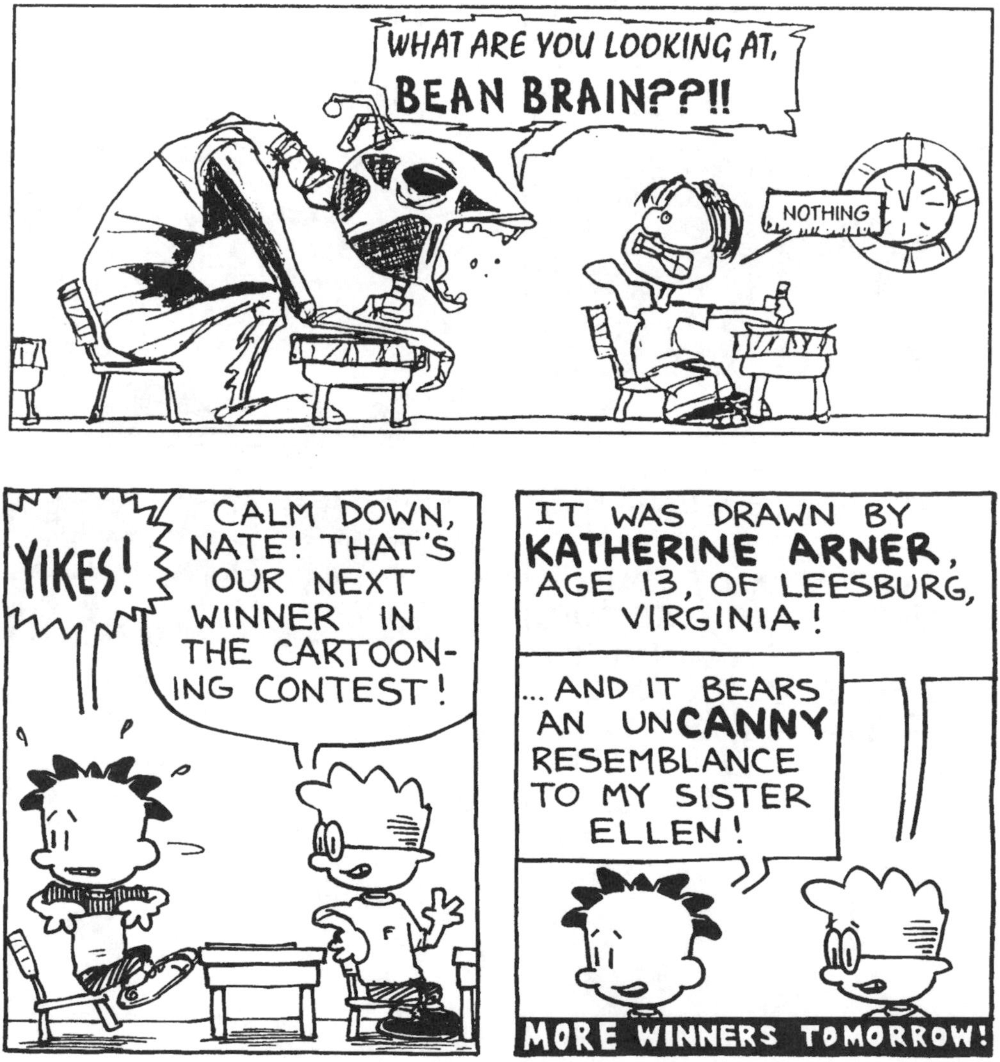
WHAT ARE YOU LOOKING AT, BEAN BRAIN??!!
NOTHING
YIKES!
CALM DOWN, NATE! THAT'S OUR NEXT WINNER IN THE CARTOONING CONTEST!
IT WAS DRAWN BY KATHERINE ARNER, AGE 13, OF LEESBURG, VIRGINIA!
...AND IT BEARS AN UNCANNY RESEMBLANCE TO MY SISTER ELLEN!
MORE WINNERS TOMORROW!

TODAY, CLASS, I'M GOING TO SHOW YOU HOW TO MAKE A VOLCANO!
WOW!
NEAT!
GEE, NATE, WHAT WOULD YOU DO IF YOU COULD MAKE A VOLCANO?
EASTER-BARNES
BOOM!
ELEMENTARY SCHOOL
SCHOOL
TODAY'S CONTEST WINNERS: ROB BARNES AND DAVID EASTER, TWO THIRTY-SOMETHINGS FROM THE STATE OF MISSOURI!
WHO SAYS OLD PEOPLE HAVE NO SENSE OF HUMOR?
MORE!

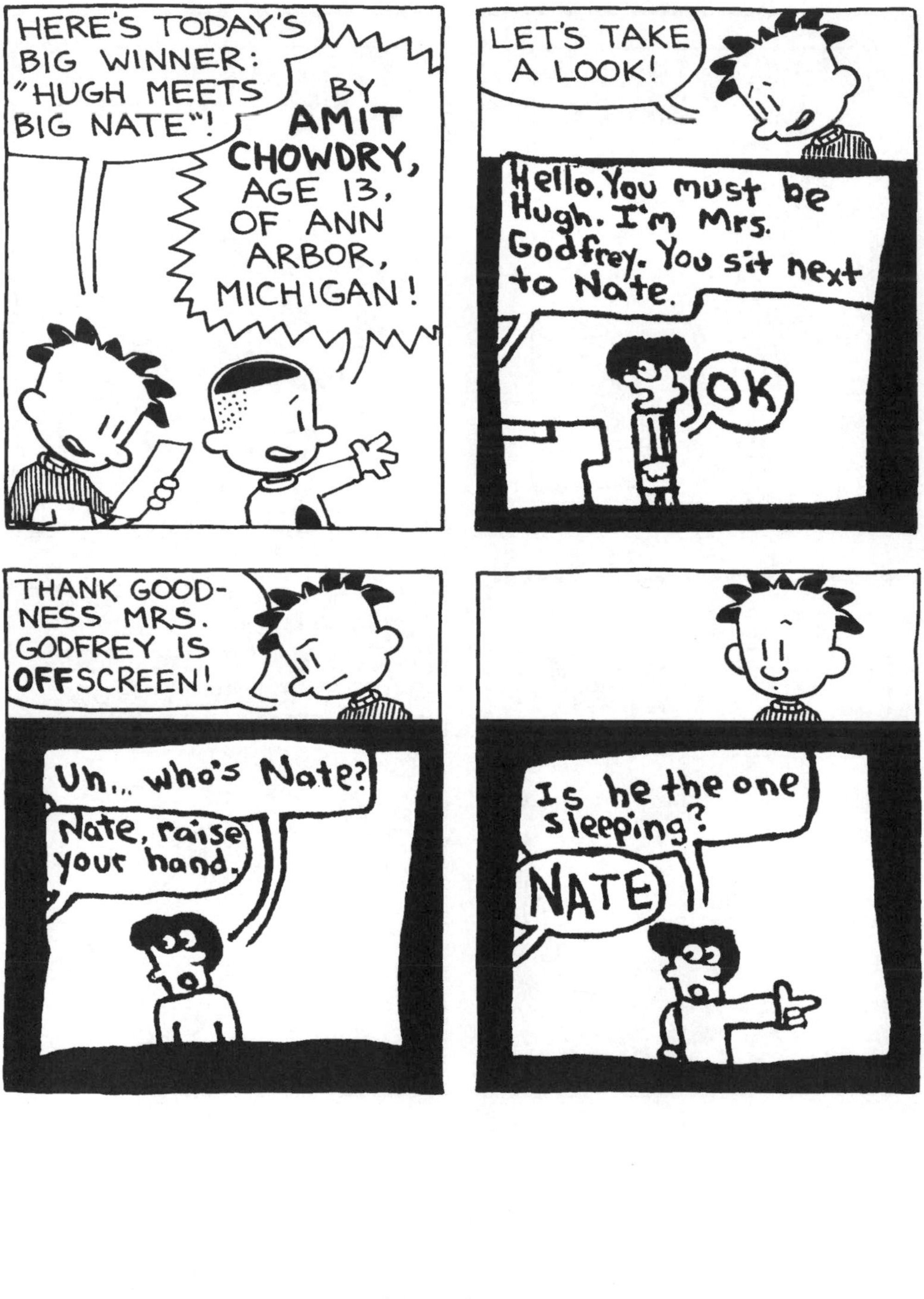
HERE'S TODAY'S BIG WINNER: "HUGH MEETS BIG NATE"!
BY **AMIT CHOWDRY,** AGE 13, OF ANN ARBOR, MICHIGAN!
LET'S TAKE A LOOK!
Hello. You must be Hugh. I'm Mrs. Godfrey. You sit next to Nate.
OK
THANK GOODNESS MRS. GODFREY IS **OFF**SCREEN!
Uh... who's Nate?
Nate, raise your hand.
Is he the one sleeping?
NATE

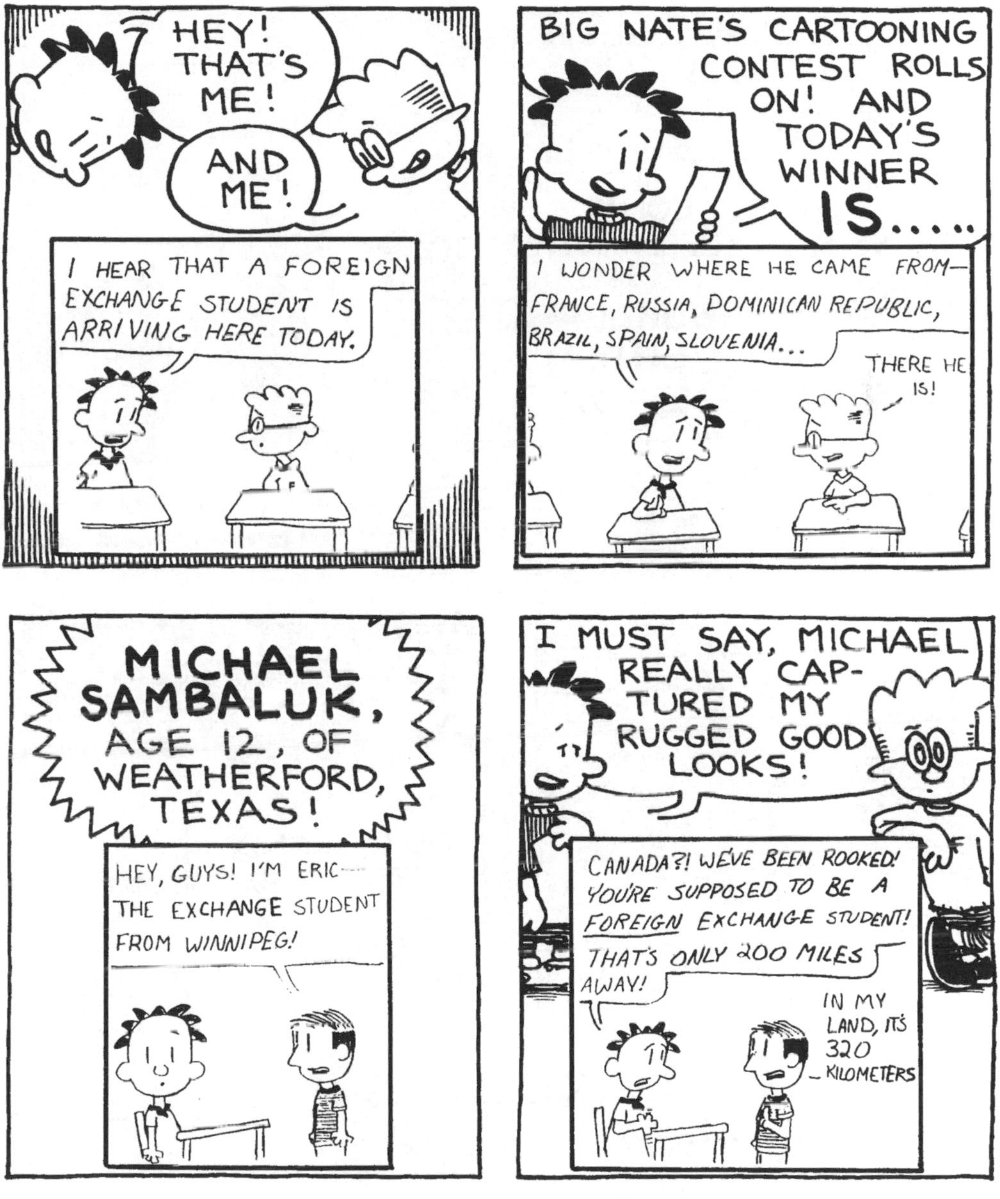
HEY! THAT'S ME!
AND ME!
I HEAR THAT A FOREIGN EXCHANGE STUDENT IS ARRIVING HERE TODAY.
BIG NATE'S CARTOONING CONTEST ROLLS ON! AND TODAY'S WINNER IS.....
I WONDER WHERE HE CAME FROM— FRANCE, RUSSIA, DOMINICAN REPUBLIC, BRAZIL, SPAIN, SLOVENIA...
THERE HE IS!
MICHAEL SAMBALUK, AGE 12, OF WEATHERFORD, TEXAS!
HEY, GUYS! I'M ERIC— THE EXCHANGE STUDENT FROM WINNIPEG!
I MUST SAY, MICHAEL REALLY CAPTURED MY RUGGED GOOD LOOKS!
CANADA?! WE'VE BEEN ROOKED! YOU'RE SUPPOSED TO BE A FOREIGN EXCHANGE STUDENT!
THAT'S ONLY 200 MILES AWAY!
IN MY LAND, IT'S 320 KILOMETERS

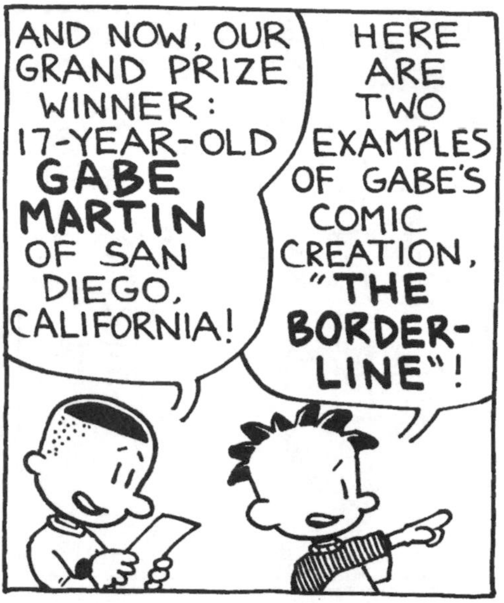
AND NOW, OUR GRAND PRIZE WINNER: 17-YEAR-OLD GABE MARTIN OF SAN DIEGO, CALIFORNIA!
HERE ARE TWO EXAMPLES OF GABE'S COMIC CREATION, "THE BORDER-LINE"!

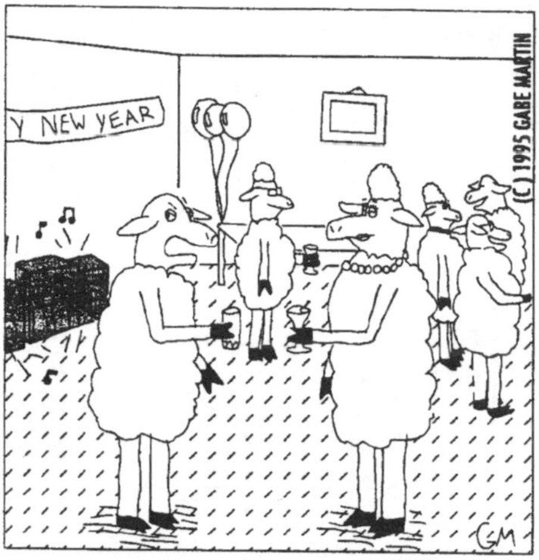
Y NEW YEAR
(C) 1995 GABE MARTIN
GM

" Oh for crying out loud! Not 'Barbara Ann' again! "

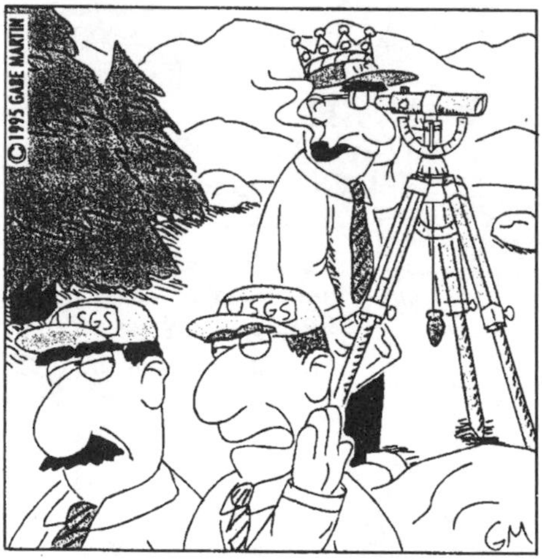
©1995 GABE MARTIN
USGS
USGS
GM

"There goes Lenny again–he thinks he's king of all he surveys."

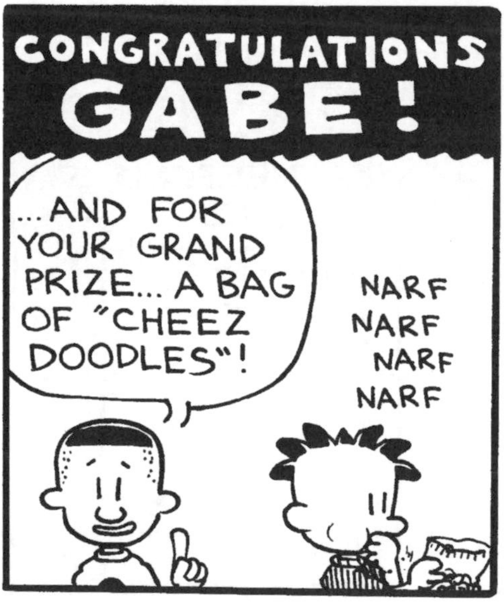
CONGRATULATIONS GABE!
...AND FOR YOUR GRAND PRIZE... A BAG OF "CHEEZ DOODLES"!
NARF NARF NARF NARF

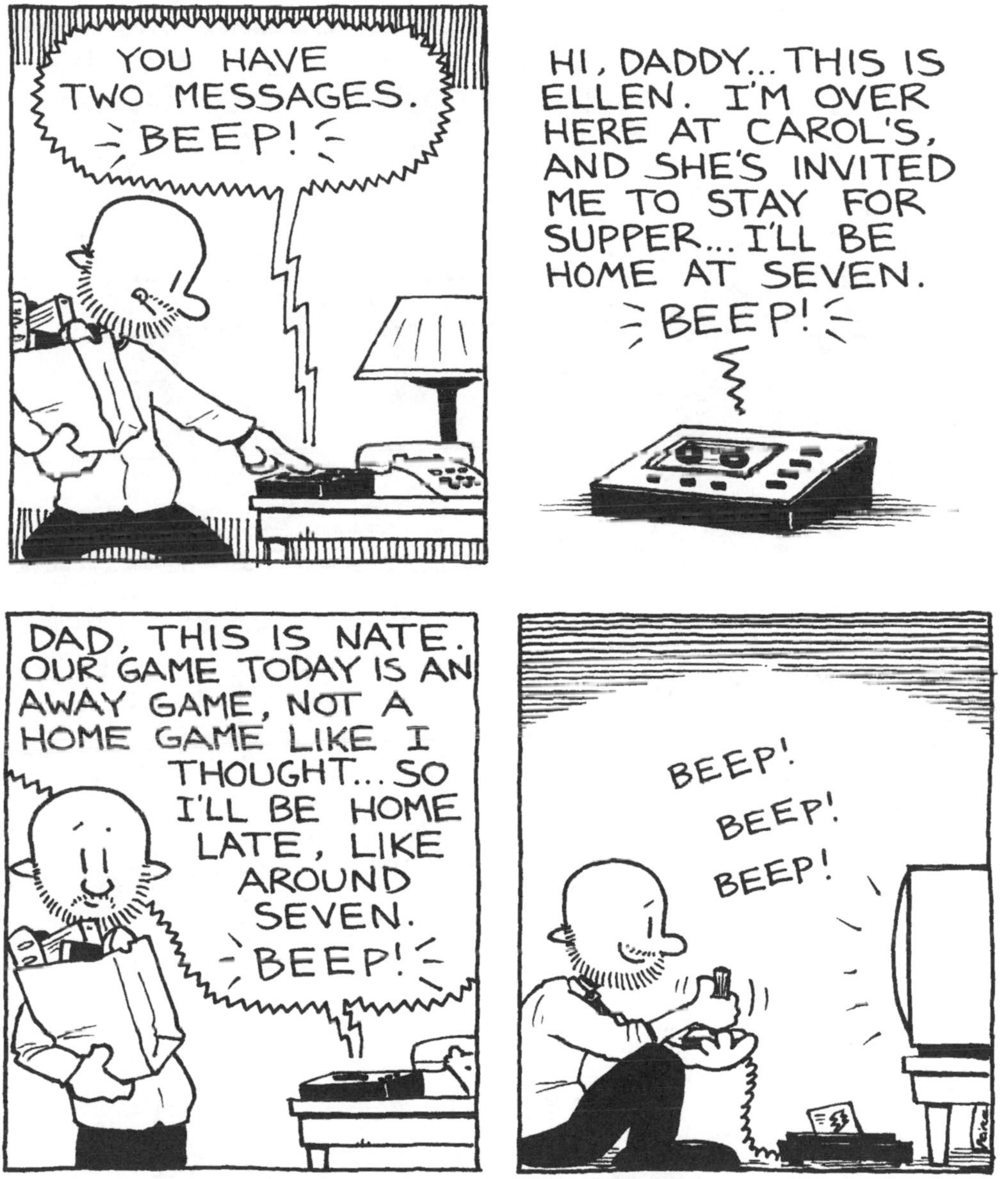
YOU HAVE TWO MESSAGES. BEEP!
HI, DADDY... THIS IS ELLEN. I'M OVER HERE AT CAROL'S, AND SHE'S INVITED ME TO STAY FOR SUPPER... I'LL BE HOME AT SEVEN.
BEEP!
DAD, THIS IS NATE. OUR GAME TODAY IS AN AWAY GAME, NOT A HOME GAME LIKE I THOUGHT... SO I'LL BE HOME LATE, LIKE AROUND SEVEN. BEEP!
BEEP!
BEEP!
BEEP!

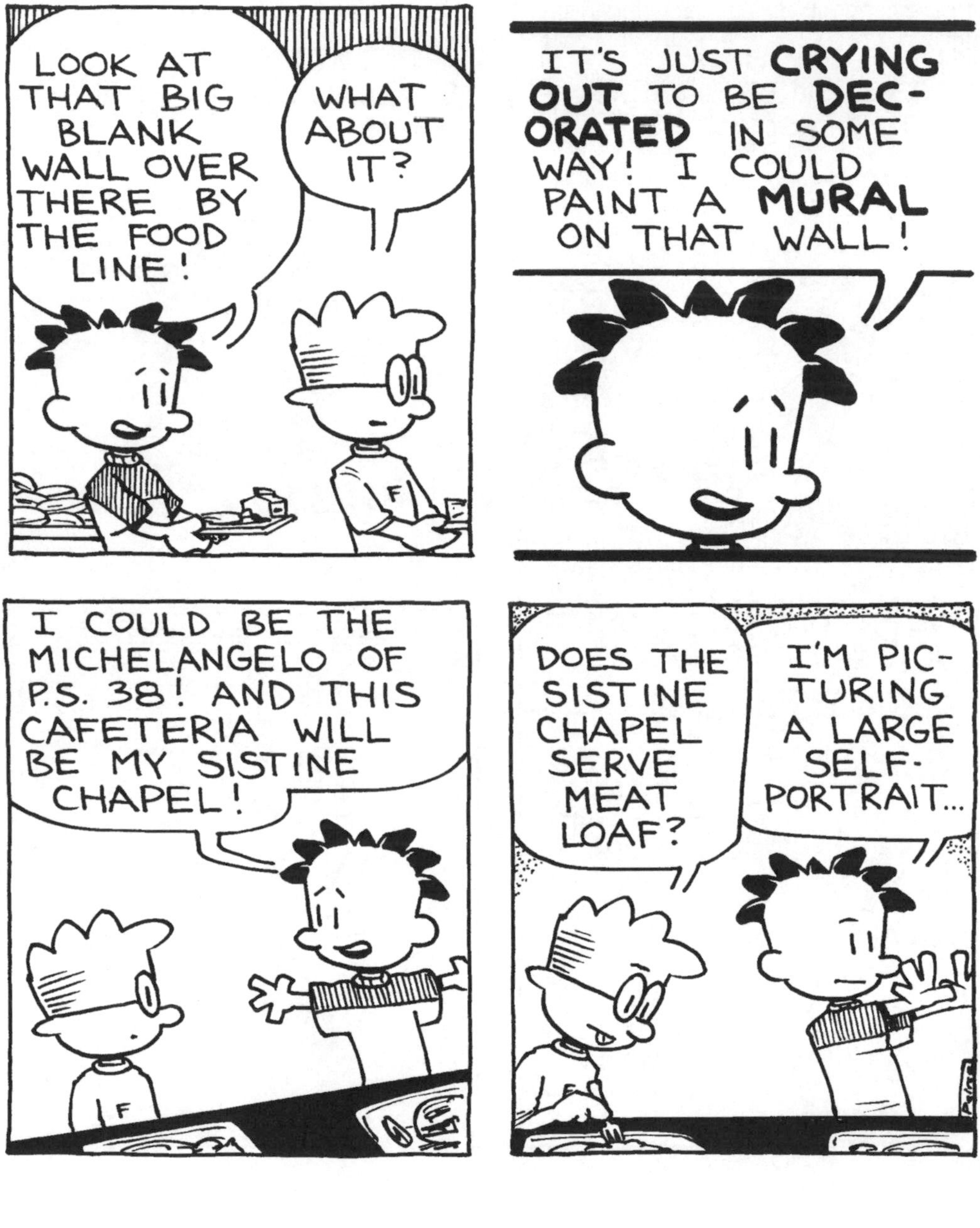
LOOK AT THAT BIG BLANK WALL OVER THERE BY THE FOOD LINE!
WHAT ABOUT IT?
IT'S JUST **CRYING OUT** TO BE **DECORATED** IN SOME WAY! I COULD PAINT A **MURAL** ON THAT WALL!
I COULD BE THE MICHELANGELO OF P.S. 38! AND THIS CAFETERIA WILL BE MY SISTINE CHAPEL!
DOES THE SISTINE CHAPEL SERVE MEAT LOAF?
I'M PICTURING A LARGE SELF-PORTRAIT...

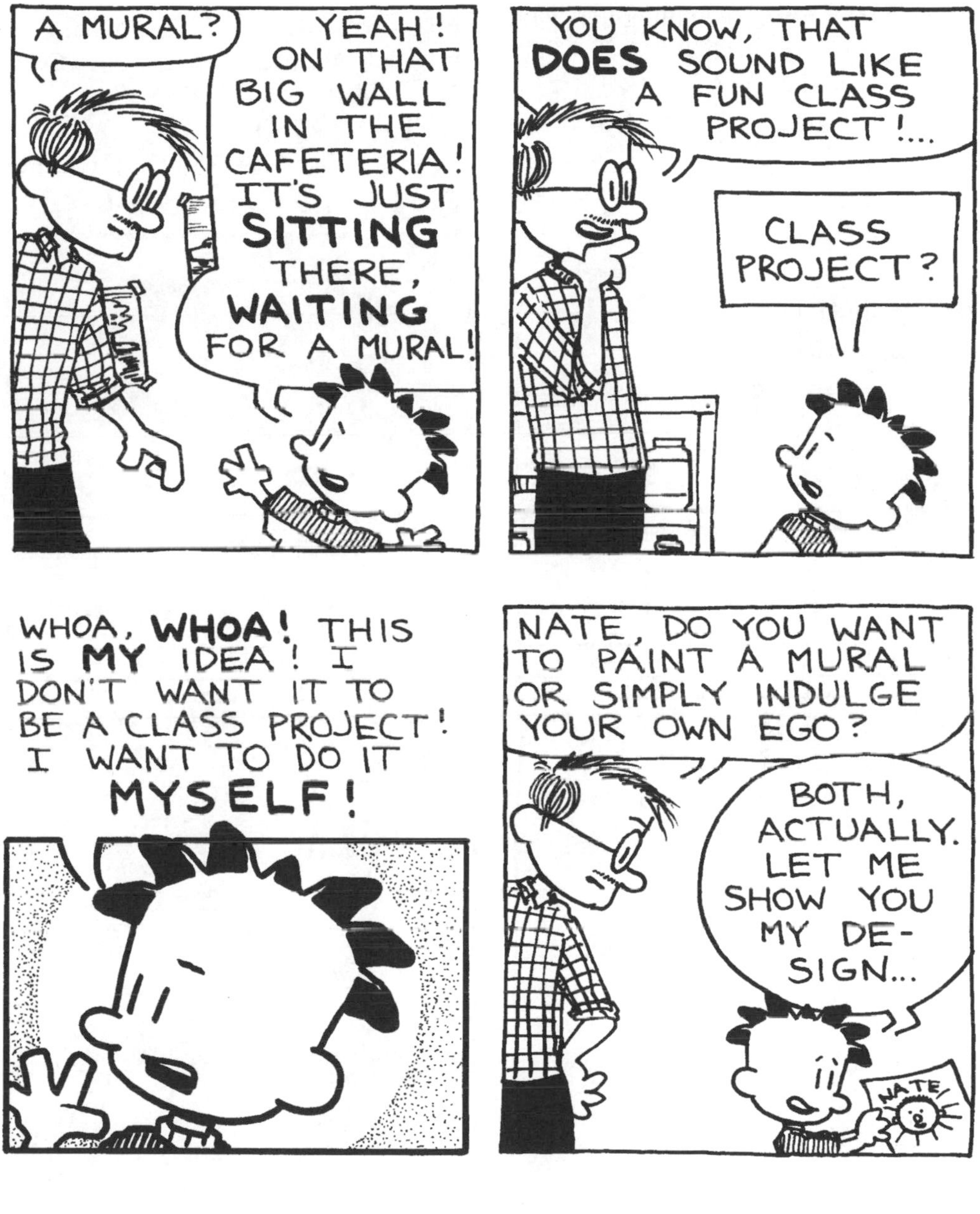
A MURAL?
YEAH! ON THAT BIG WALL IN THE CAFETERIA! IT'S JUST SITTING THERE, WAITING FOR A MURAL!
YOU KNOW, THAT DOES SOUND LIKE A FUN CLASS PROJECT!...
CLASS PROJECT?
WHOA, WHOA! THIS IS MY IDEA! I DON'T WANT IT TO BE A CLASS PROJECT! I WANT TO DO IT MYSELF!
NATE, DO YOU WANT TO PAINT A MURAL OR SIMPLY INDULGE YOUR OWN EGO?
BOTH, ACTUALLY. LET ME SHOW YOU MY DE-SIGN...
NATE

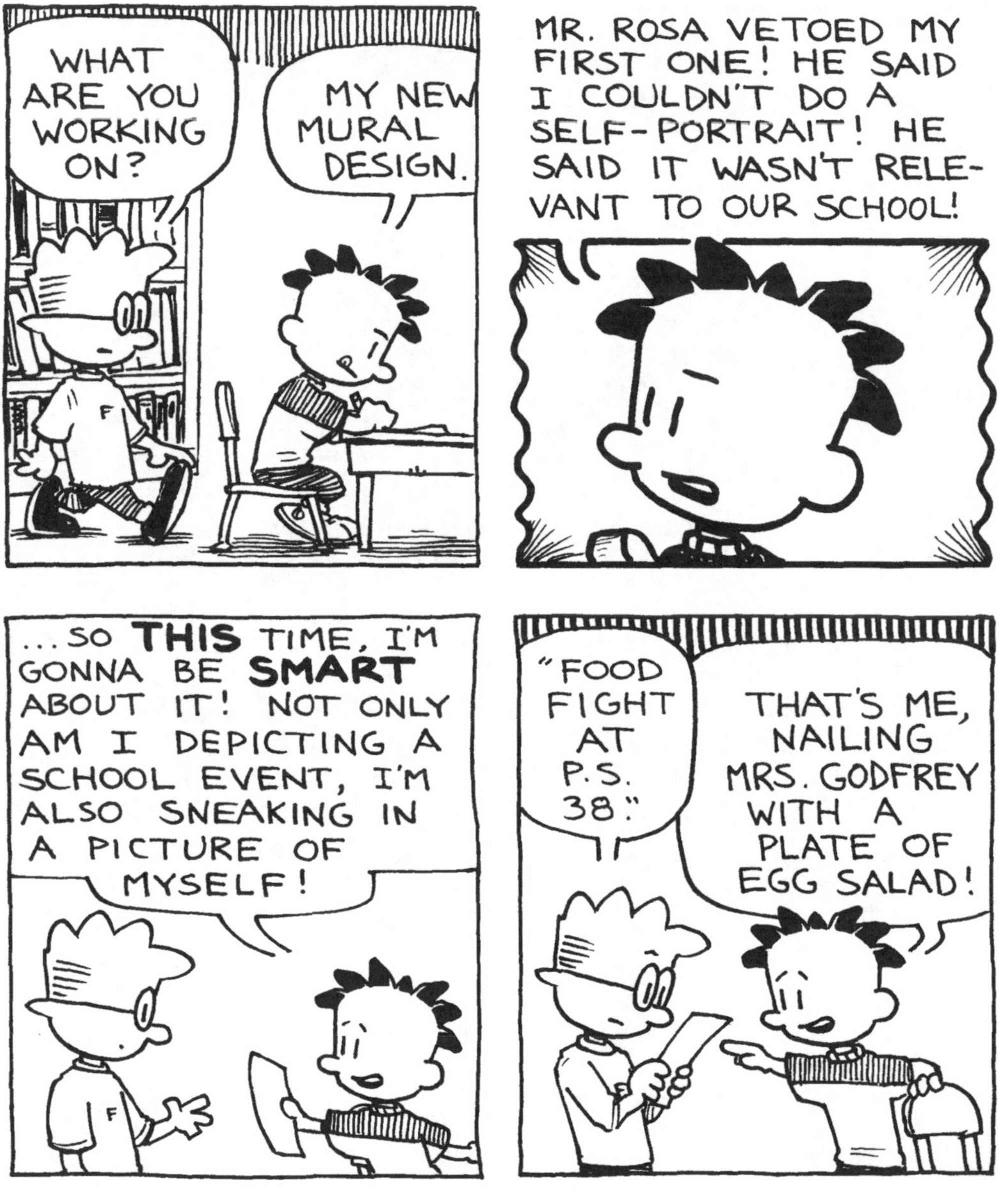
WHAT ARE YOU WORKING ON?
MY NEW MURAL DESIGN.
MR. ROSA VETOED MY FIRST ONE! HE SAID I COULDN'T DO A SELF-PORTRAIT! HE SAID IT WASN'T RELEVANT TO OUR SCHOOL!
...SO **THIS** TIME, I'M GONNA BE **SMART** ABOUT IT! NOT ONLY AM I DEPICTING A SCHOOL EVENT, I'M ALSO SNEAKING IN A PICTURE OF MYSELF!
"FOOD FIGHT AT P.S. 38."
THAT'S ME, NAILING MRS. GODFREY WITH A PLATE OF EGG SALAD!

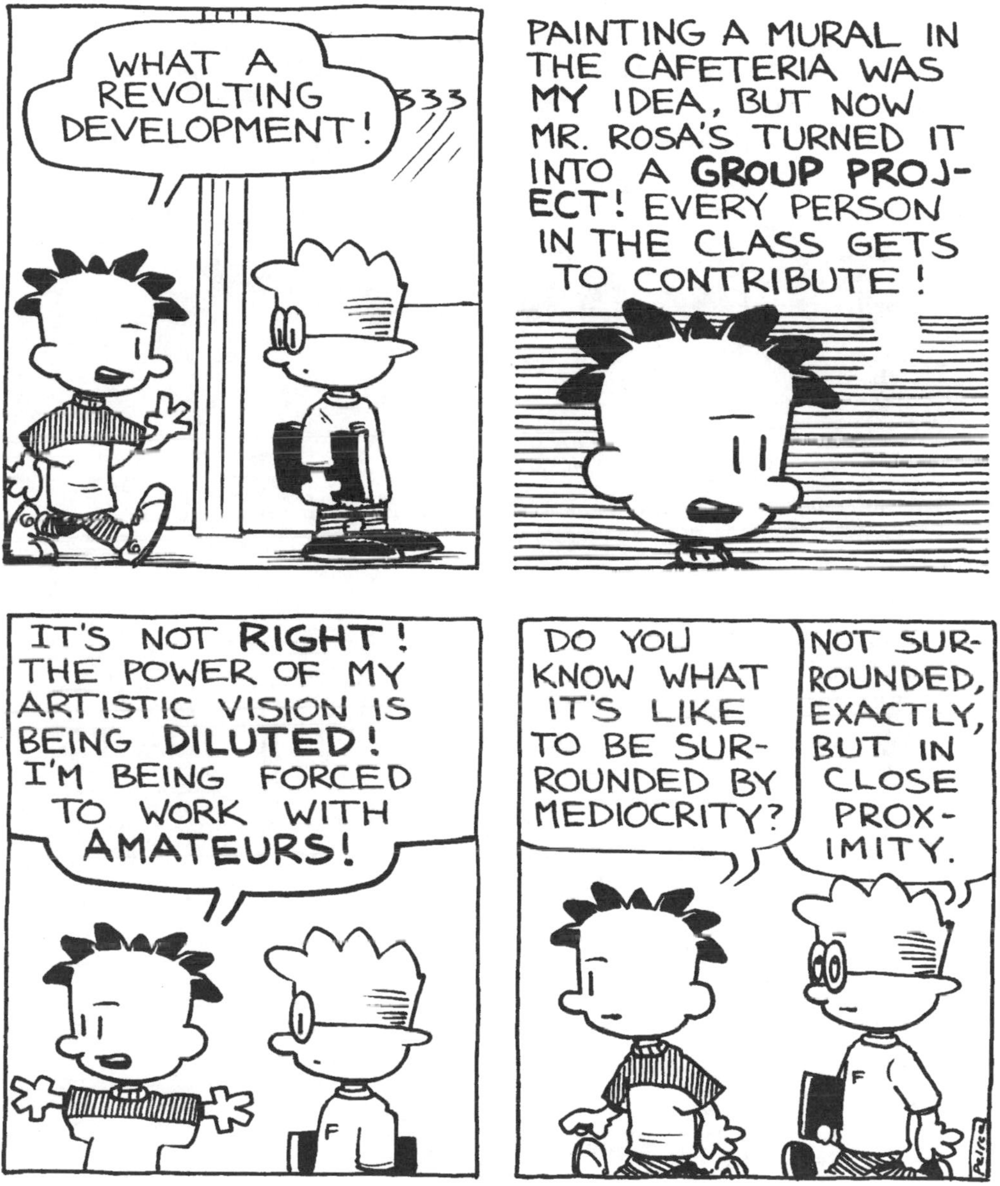
WHAT A REVOLTING DEVELOPMENT!
PAINTING A MURAL IN THE CAFETERIA WAS MY IDEA, BUT NOW MR. ROSA'S TURNED IT INTO A GROUP PROJECT! EVERY PERSON IN THE CLASS GETS TO CONTRIBUTE!
IT'S NOT RIGHT! THE POWER OF MY ARTISTIC VISION IS BEING DILUTED! I'M BEING FORCED TO WORK WITH AMATEURS!
DO YOU KNOW WHAT IT'S LIKE TO BE SURROUNDED BY MEDIOCRITY?
NOT SURROUNDED, EXACTLY, BUT IN CLOSE PROXIMITY.

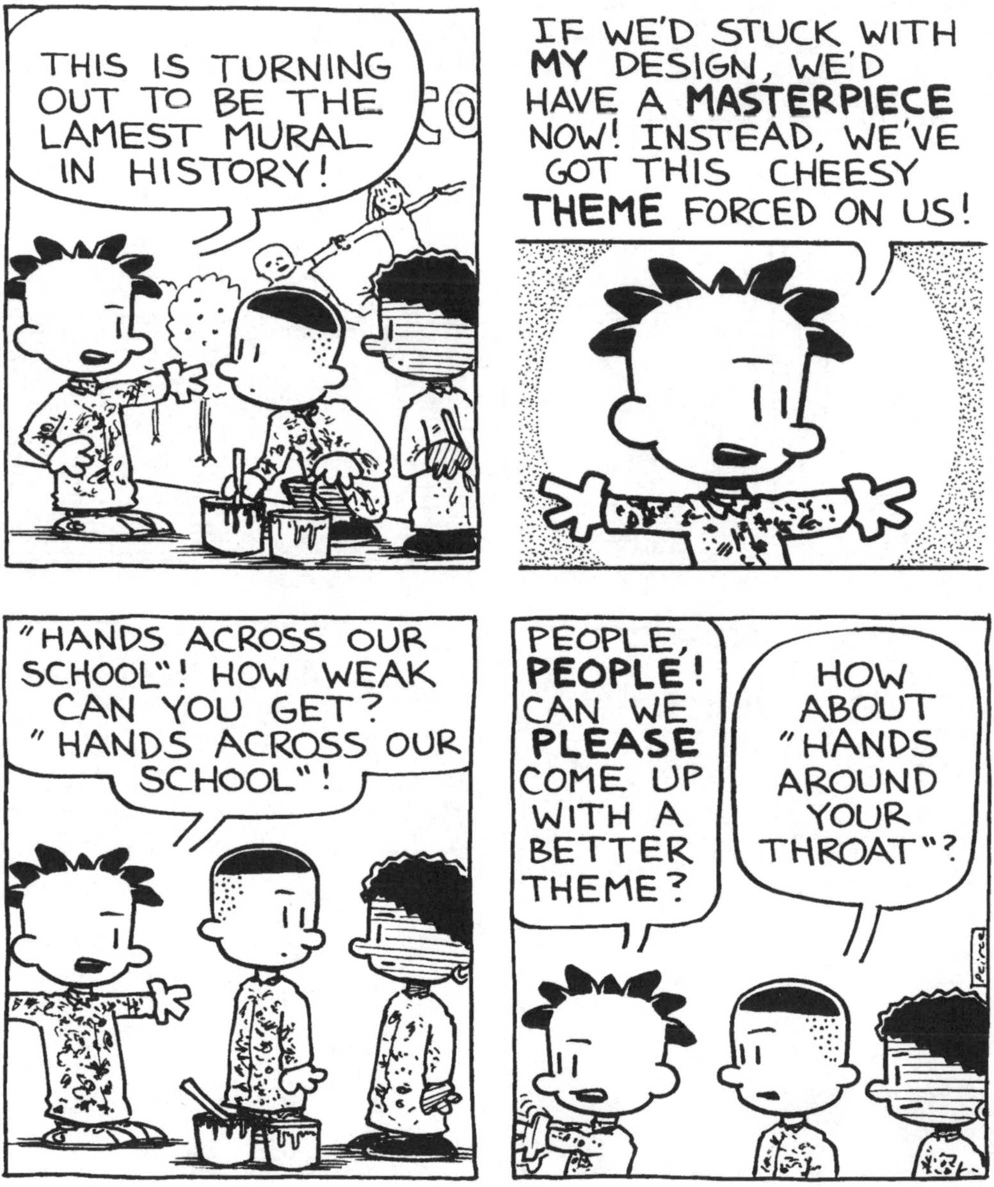
THIS IS TURNING OUT TO BE THE LAMEST MURAL IN HISTORY!
IF WE'D STUCK WITH **MY** DESIGN, WE'D HAVE A **MASTERPIECE** NOW! INSTEAD, WE'VE GOT THIS CHEESY **THEME** FORCED ON US!
"HANDS ACROSS OUR SCHOOL"! HOW WEAK CAN YOU GET? "HANDS ACROSS OUR SCHOOL"!
PEOPLE, **PEOPLE**! CAN WE **PLEASE** COME UP WITH A BETTER THEME?
HOW ABOUT "HANDS AROUND YOUR THROAT"?
PEIRCE

YOW! WHAT IS THIS MUSIC?
IT'S FROM THE SHOW "HAIR."
"HAIR"?
"HAIR."
LITTLE BIT OF WISHFUL THINKING THERE, EH, DAD?
PAT PAT!
THESE AGING HIPPIES JUST DON'T APPRECIATE IRONIC HUMOR...
PEIRCE

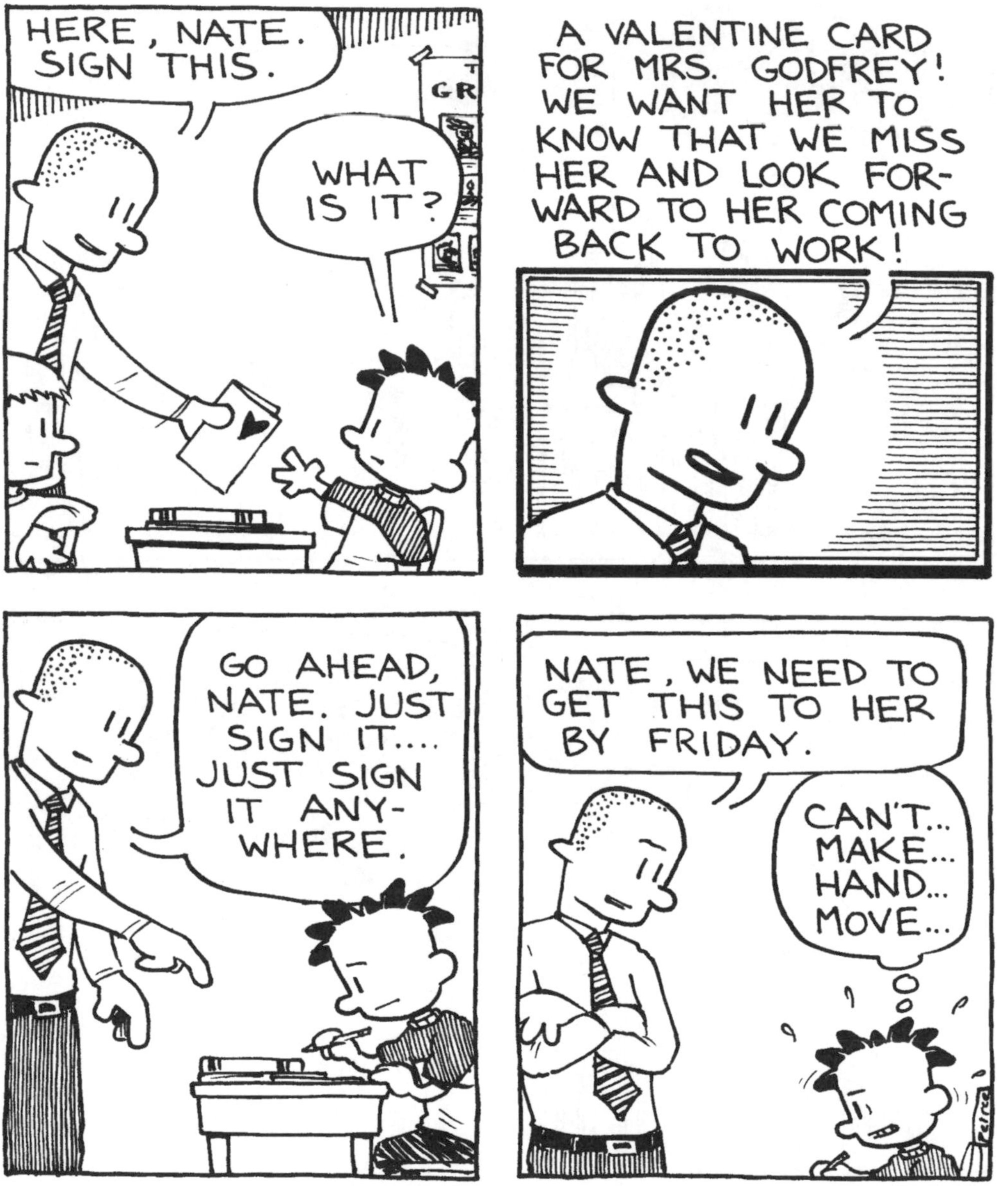
HERE, NATE. SIGN THIS.
WHAT IS IT?
A VALENTINE CARD FOR MRS. GODFREY! WE WANT HER TO KNOW THAT WE MISS HER AND LOOK FORWARD TO HER COMING BACK TO WORK!
GO AHEAD, NATE. JUST SIGN IT.... JUST SIGN IT ANYWHERE.
NATE, WE NEED TO GET THIS TO HER BY FRIDAY.
CAN'T... MAKE... HAND... MOVE...
PEIRCE

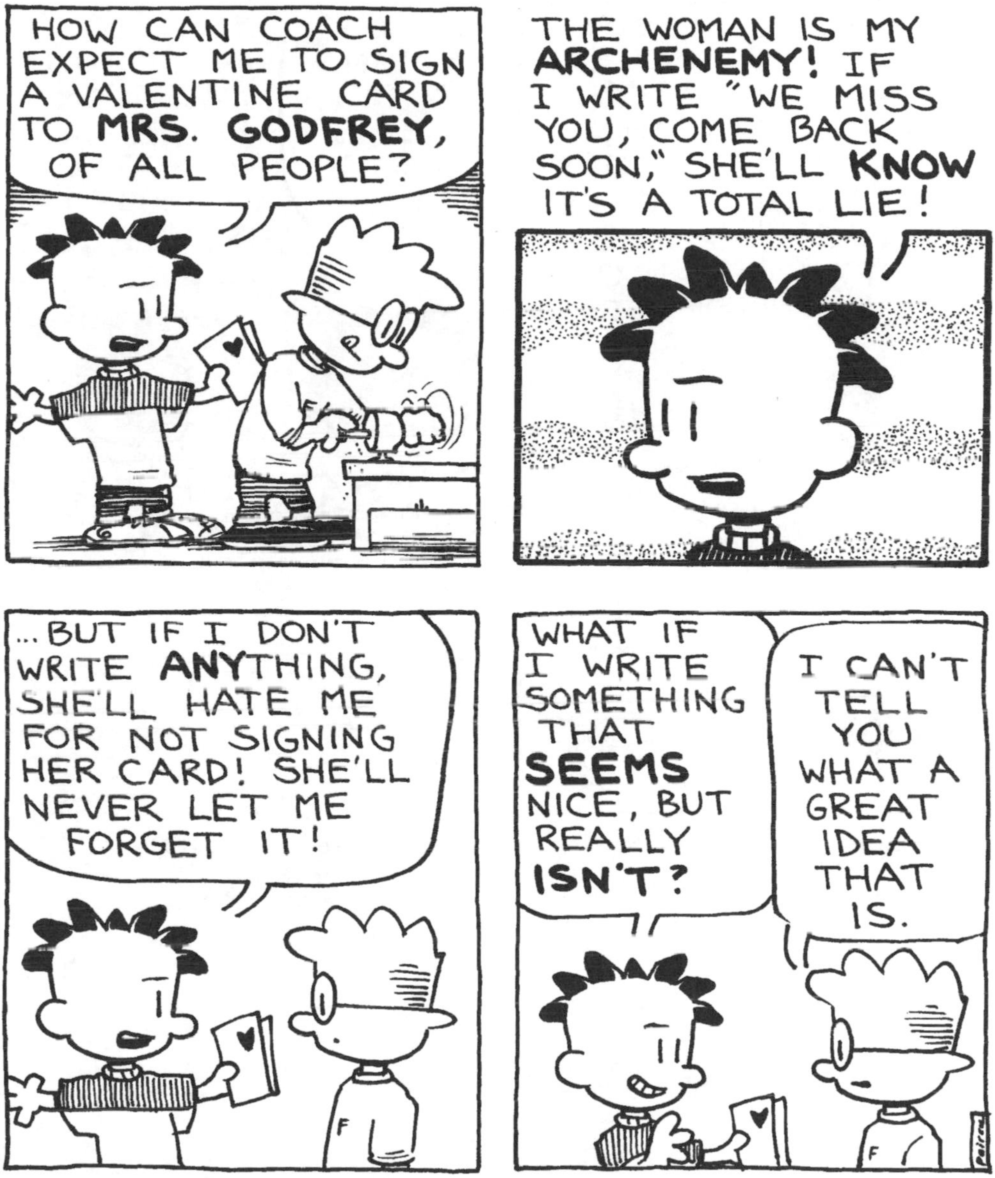
HOW CAN COACH EXPECT ME TO SIGN A VALENTINE CARD TO MRS. GODFREY, OF ALL PEOPLE?
THE WOMAN IS MY ARCHENEMY! IF I WRITE "WE MISS YOU, COME BACK SOON," SHE'LL KNOW IT'S A TOTAL LIE!
...BUT IF I DON'T WRITE ANYTHING, SHE'LL HATE ME FOR NOT SIGNING HER CARD! SHE'LL NEVER LET ME FORGET IT!
WHAT IF I WRITE SOMETHING THAT SEEMS NICE, BUT REALLY ISN'T?
I CAN'T TELL YOU WHAT A GREAT IDEA THAT IS.

I JUST DON'T KNOW WHAT TO WRITE ON THIS CARD TO MRS. GODFREY...
JUST WRITE **ANY-**THING! STOP MAKING SUCH A BIG DEAL OUT OF IT!
I'M NOT MAKING A BIG DEAL OUT OF IT!
YES, YOU ARE! YOU **ALWAYS** MAKE A BIG DEAL OUT OF **EVERYTHING**!
ME? I DO **NOT**! ASK ANYBODY! HECK, LET'S ASK THE WHOLE **CLASS**!
FOCUS GROUP, PEOPLE! DO I ALWAYS MAKE A BIG DEAL OUT OF EVERYTHING!?? LET'S SEE A SHOW OF HANDS!
CLAP
CLAP

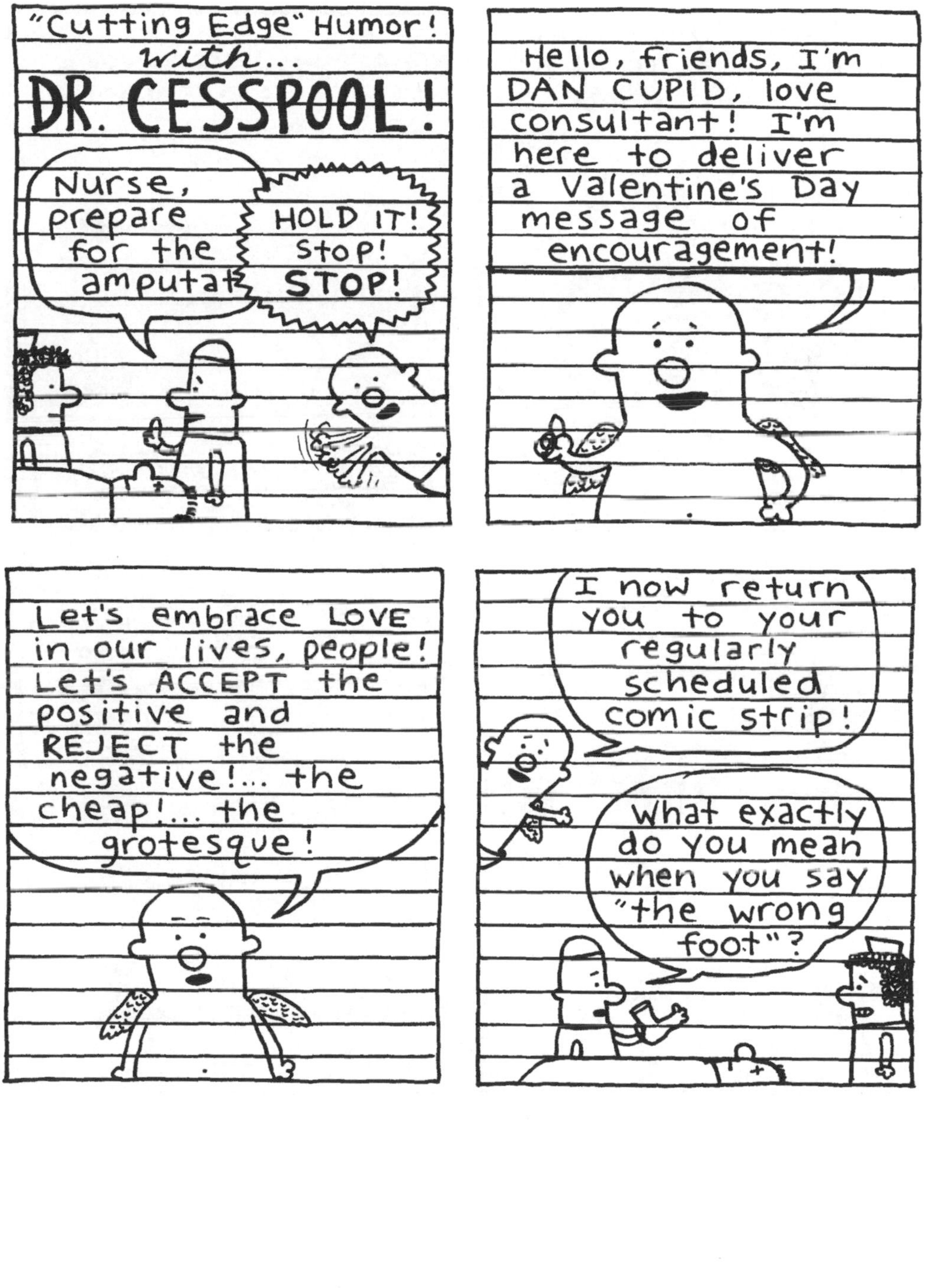
"Cutting Edge" Humor! with...
DR. CESSPOOL!
Nurse, prepare for the amputat
HOLD IT! Stop! STOP!
Hello, friends, I'm DAN CUPID, love consultant! I'm here to deliver a Valentine's Day message of encouragement!
Let's embrace LOVE in our lives, people! Let's ACCEPT the positive and REJECT the negative!... the cheap!... the grotesque!
I now return you to your regularly scheduled comic strip!
What exactly do you mean when you say "the wrong foot"?

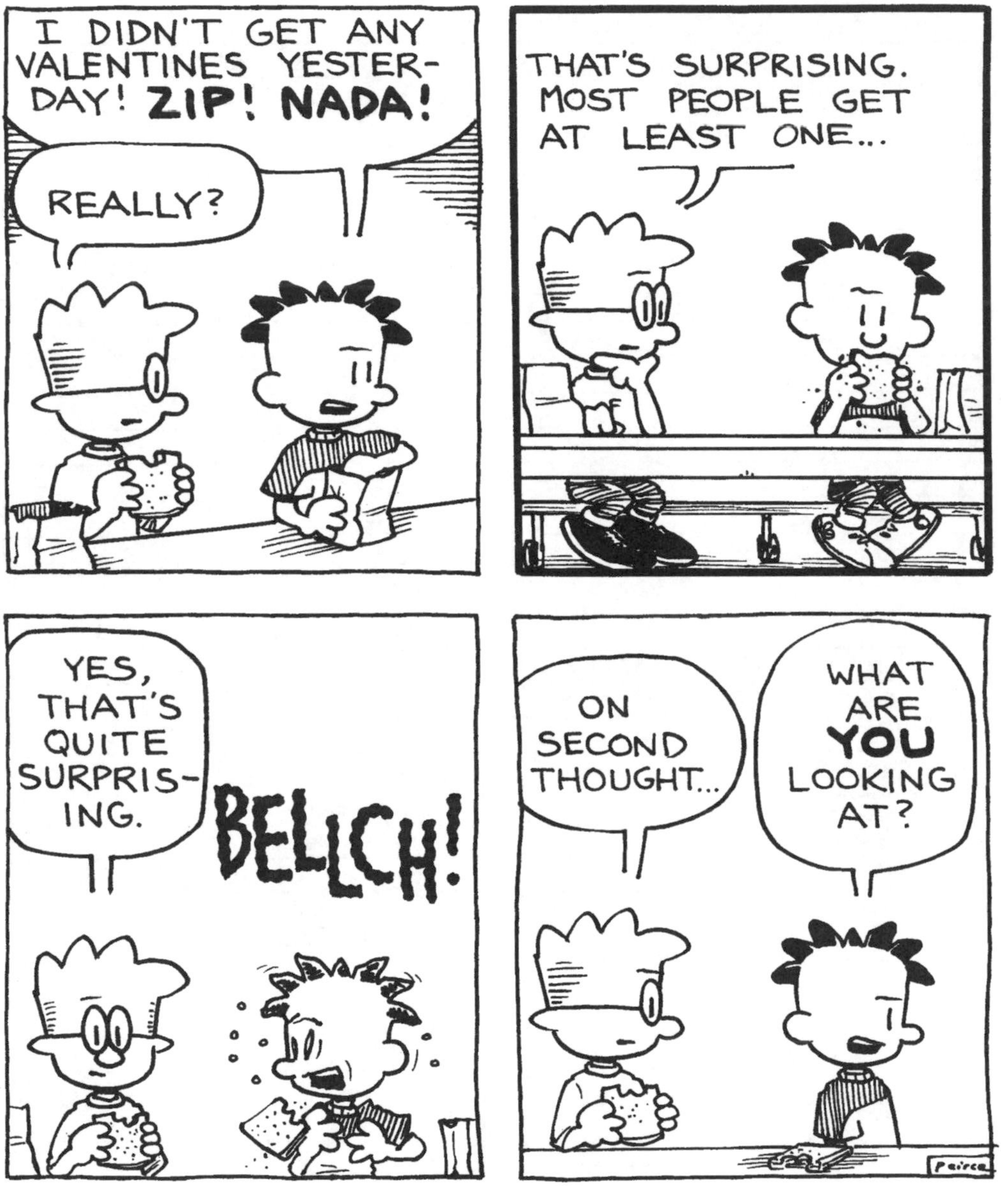
I DIDN'T GET ANY VALENTINES YESTERDAY! ZIP! NADA!
REALLY?
THAT'S SURPRISING. MOST PEOPLE GET AT LEAST ONE...
YES, THAT'S QUITE SURPRISING.
BELLCH!
ON SECOND THOUGHT...
WHAT ARE YOU LOOKING AT?
Peirce

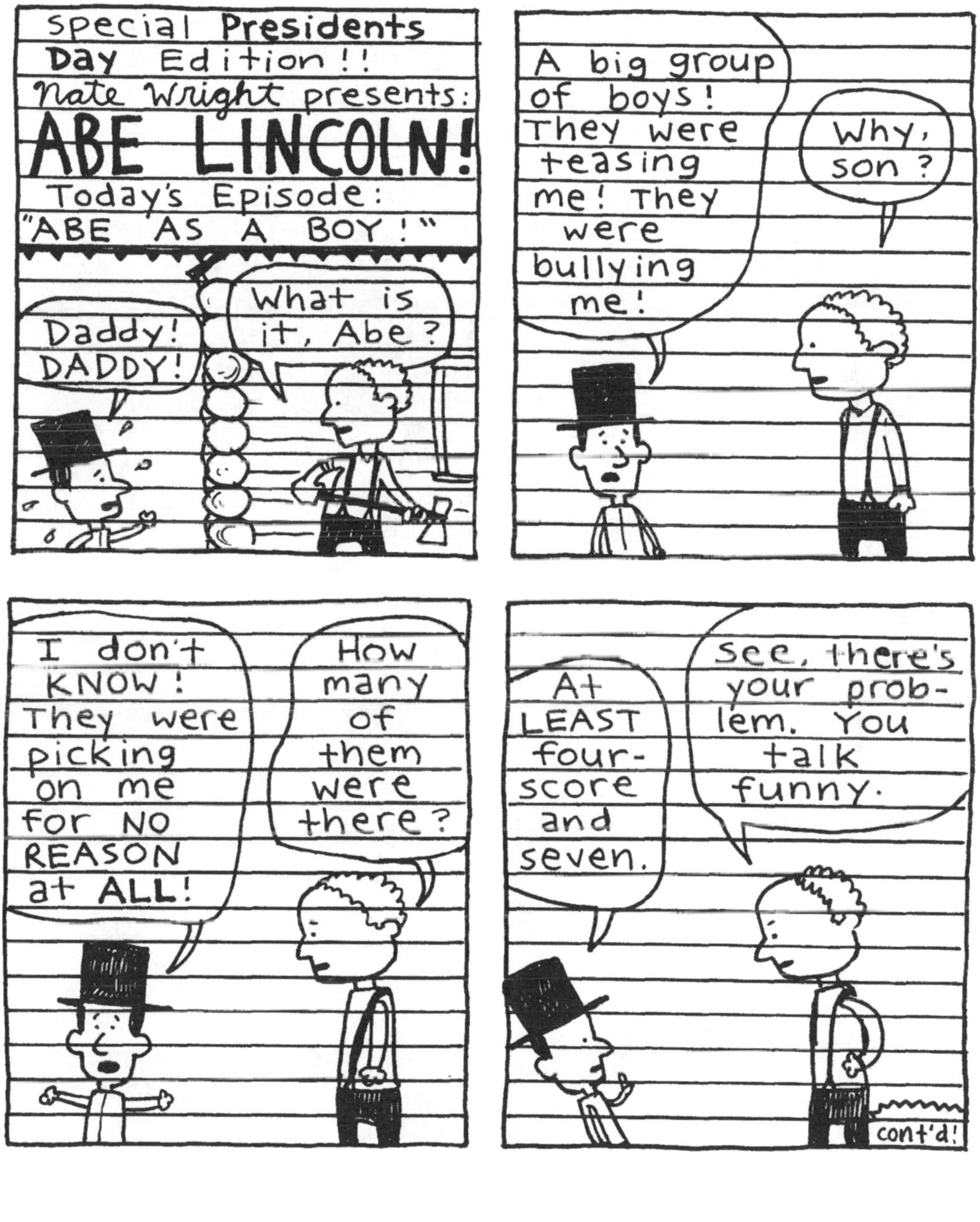
Special Presidents Day Edition!!
Nate Wright presents:
ABE LINCOLN!
Today's Episode: "ABE AS A BOY!"
Daddy! DADDY!
What is it, Abe?
A big group of boys! They were teasing me! They were bullying me!
Why, son?
I don't KNOW! They were picking on me for NO REASON at ALL!
How many of them were there?
At LEAST four-score and seven.
See, there's your problem. You talk funny.
cont'd!

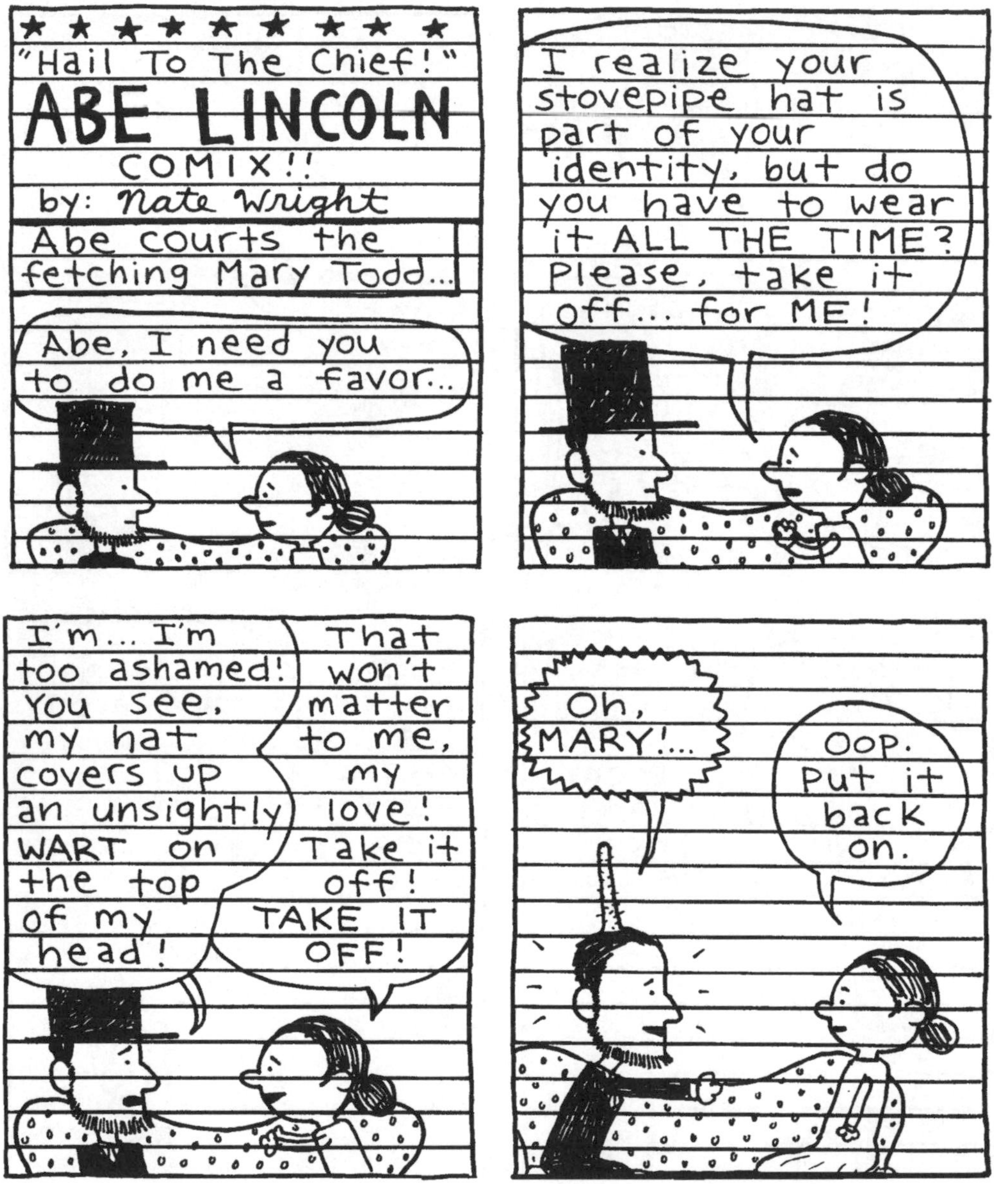
★ ★ ★ ★ ★ ★ ★ ★
"Hail To The Chief!"
ABE LINCOLN COMIX!!
by: Nate Wright
Abe courts the fetching Mary Todd...
Abe, I need you to do me a favor...
I realize your stovepipe hat is part of your identity, but do you have to wear it ALL THE TIME? Please, take it off... for ME!
I'm... I'm too ashamed! You see, my hat covers up an unsightly WART on the top of my head!
That won't matter to me, my love! Take it off! TAKE IT OFF!
Oh, MARY!...
Oop. Put it back on.

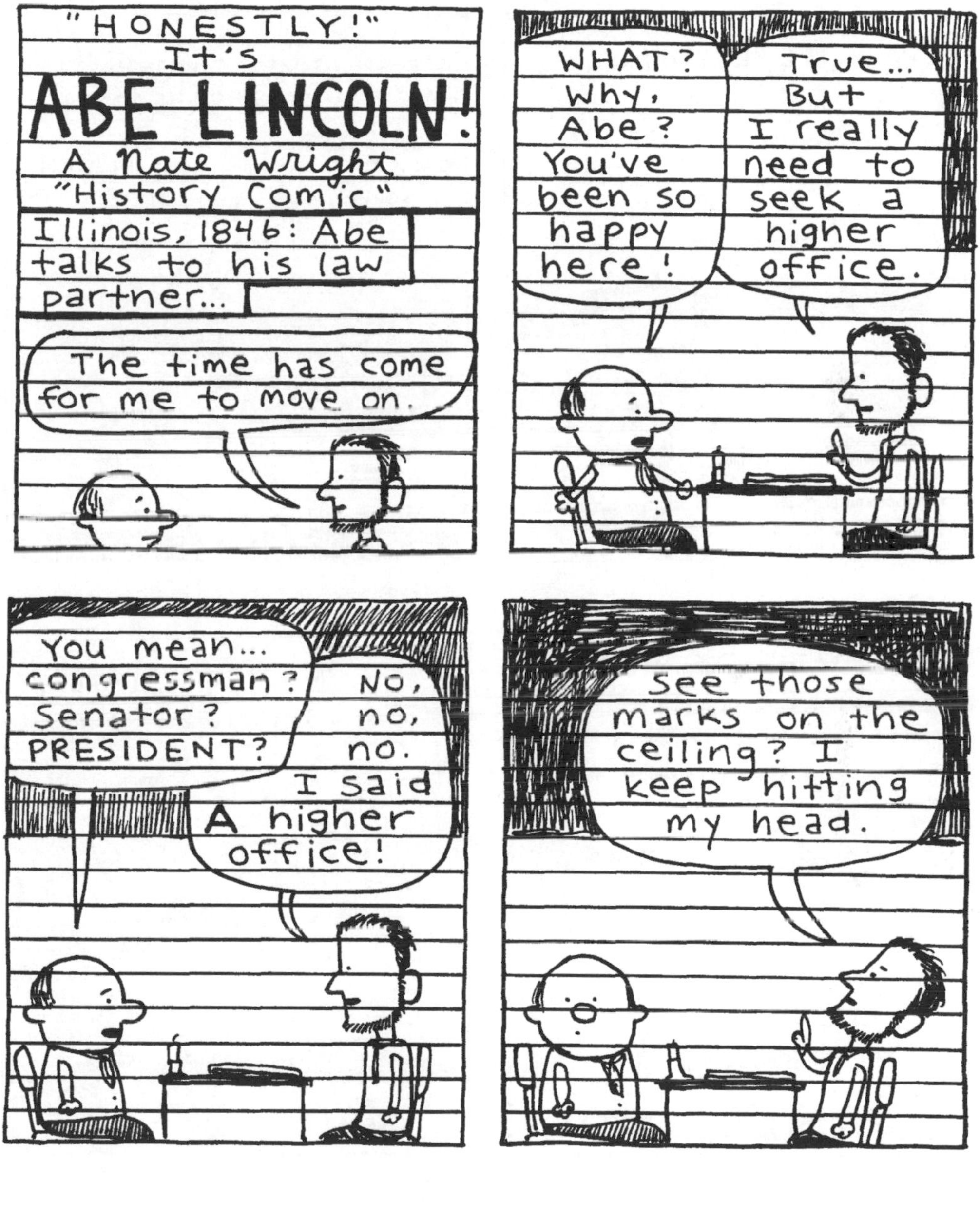
"HONESTLY!" It's ABE LINCOLN!
A Nate Wright "History Comic"
Illinois, 1846: Abe talks to his law partner...
The time has come for me to move on.
WHAT? Why, Abe? You've been so happy here!
True... But I really need to seek a higher office.
You mean... congressman? Senator? PRESIDENT?
No, no, no. I said A higher office!
See those marks on the ceiling? I keep hitting my head.

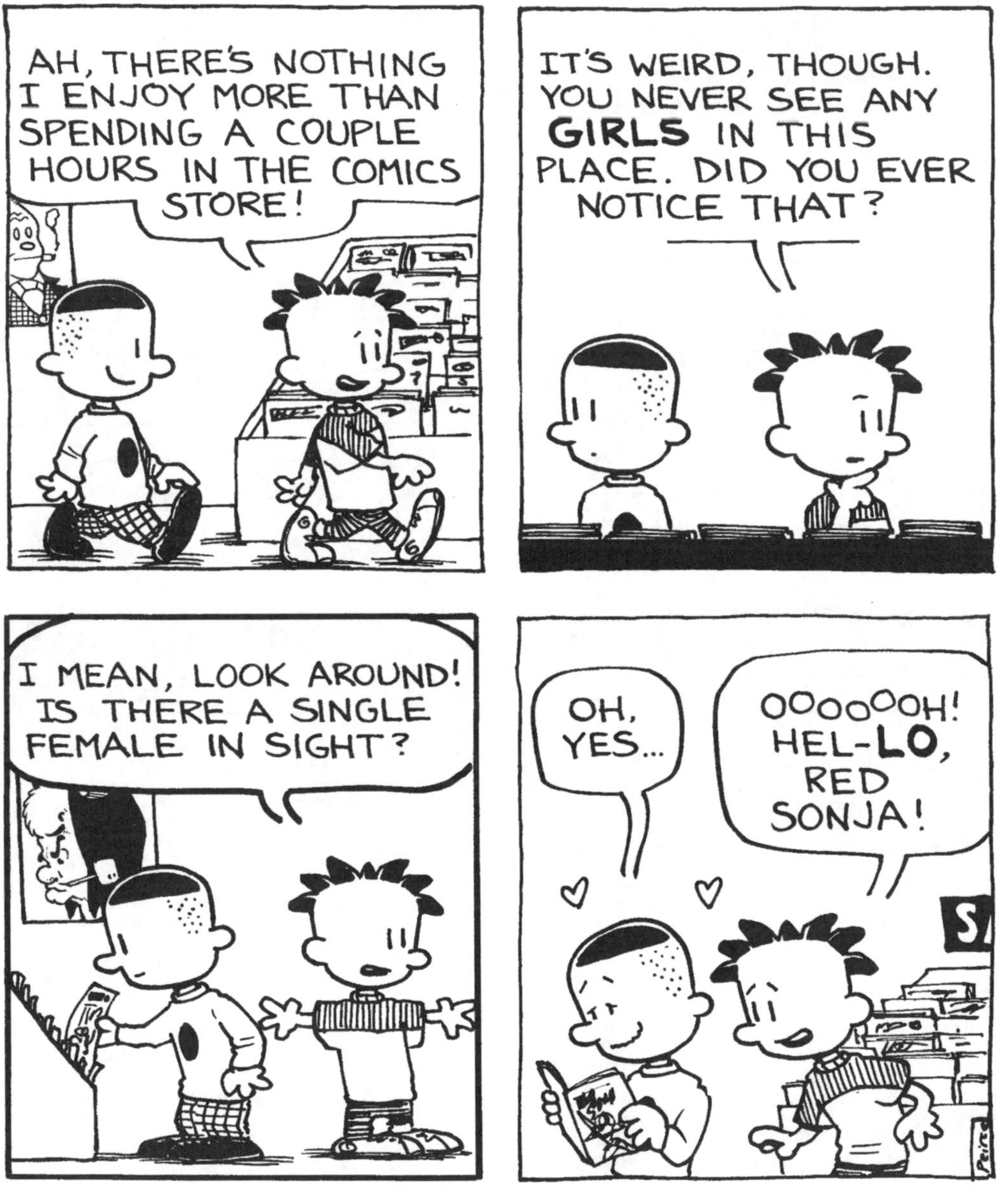

AH, THERE'S NOTHING I ENJOY MORE THAN SPENDING A COUPLE HOURS IN THE COMICS STORE!
IT'S WEIRD, THOUGH. YOU NEVER SEE ANY **GIRLS** IN THIS PLACE. DID YOU EVER NOTICE THAT?
I MEAN, LOOK AROUND! IS THERE A SINGLE FEMALE IN SIGHT?
OH, YES...
OOOOOOOH! HEL-**LO**, RED SONJA!

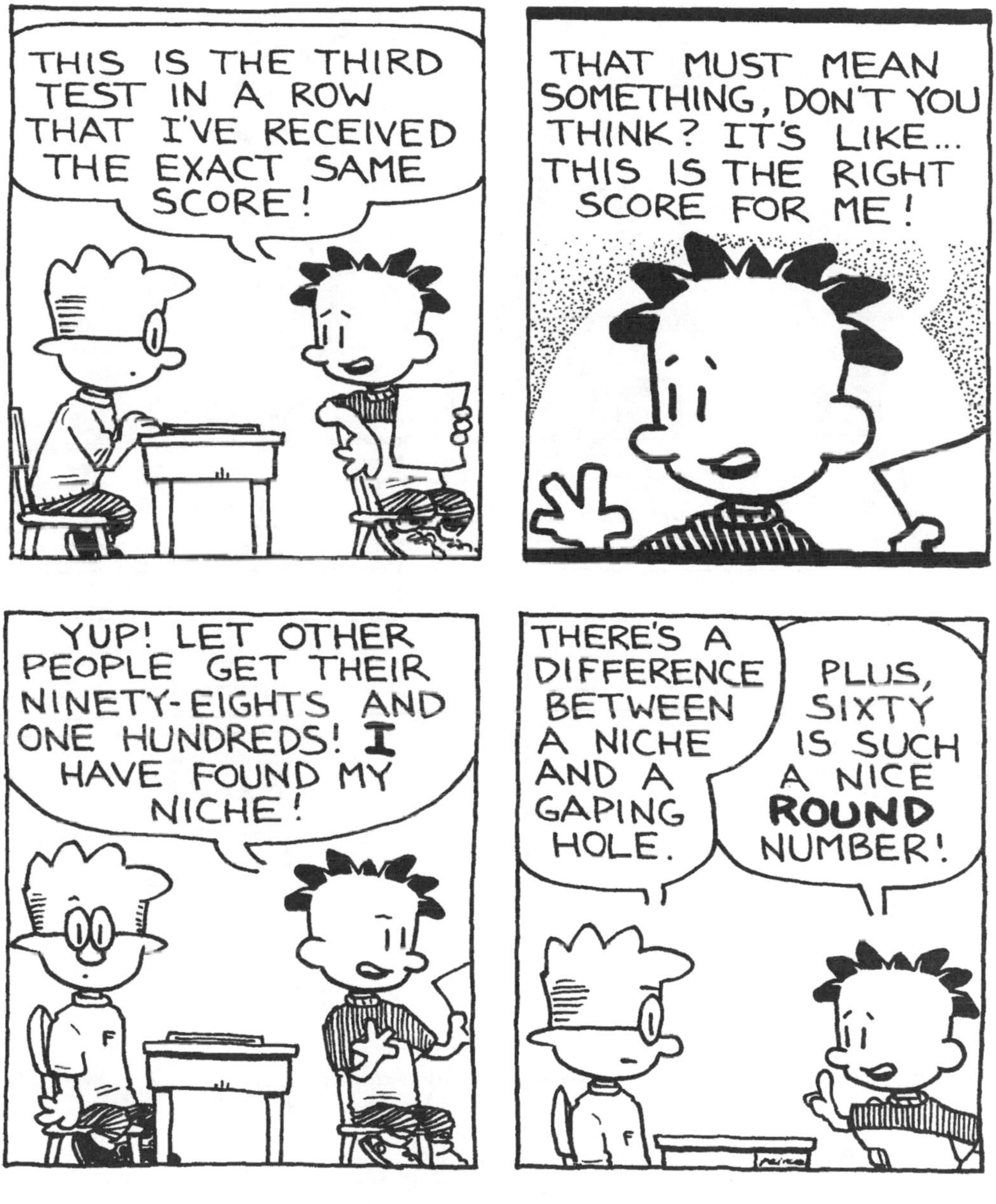

THIS IS THE THIRD TEST IN A ROW THAT I'VE RECEIVED THE EXACT SAME SCORE!
THAT MUST MEAN SOMETHING, DON'T YOU THINK? IT'S LIKE... THIS IS THE RIGHT SCORE FOR ME!
YUP! LET OTHER PEOPLE GET THEIR NINETY-EIGHTS AND ONE HUNDREDS! **I** HAVE FOUND MY NICHE!
THERE'S A DIFFERENCE BETWEEN A NICHE AND A GAPING HOLE.
PLUS, SIXTY IS SUCH A NICE **ROUND** NUMBER!

I'M HANDING BACK YOUR QUIZZES, FOLKS!

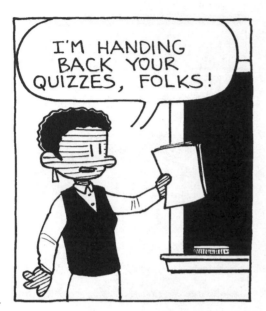

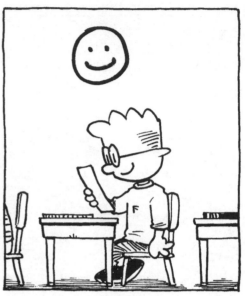

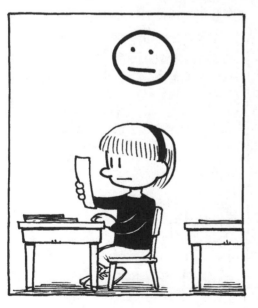

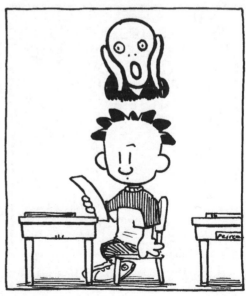

THE WEIRDEST THING HAPPENED YESTERDAY WHILE I WAS WATCHING TV! I BUMPED MY HEAD ON THE END TABLE, SEE...

I GOT KNOCKED UNCONSCIOUS! THEN, ALL OF A SUDDEN I WAS WALKING DOWN A TUNNEL! I SAW A BRIGHT WHITE LIGHT...

I THINK... I THINK I MIGHT HAVE HAD A **NEAR-DEATH EXPERIENCE!**

TO HAVE A NEAR-DEATH EXPERIENCE, DON'T YOU NEED TO HAVE A LIFE?

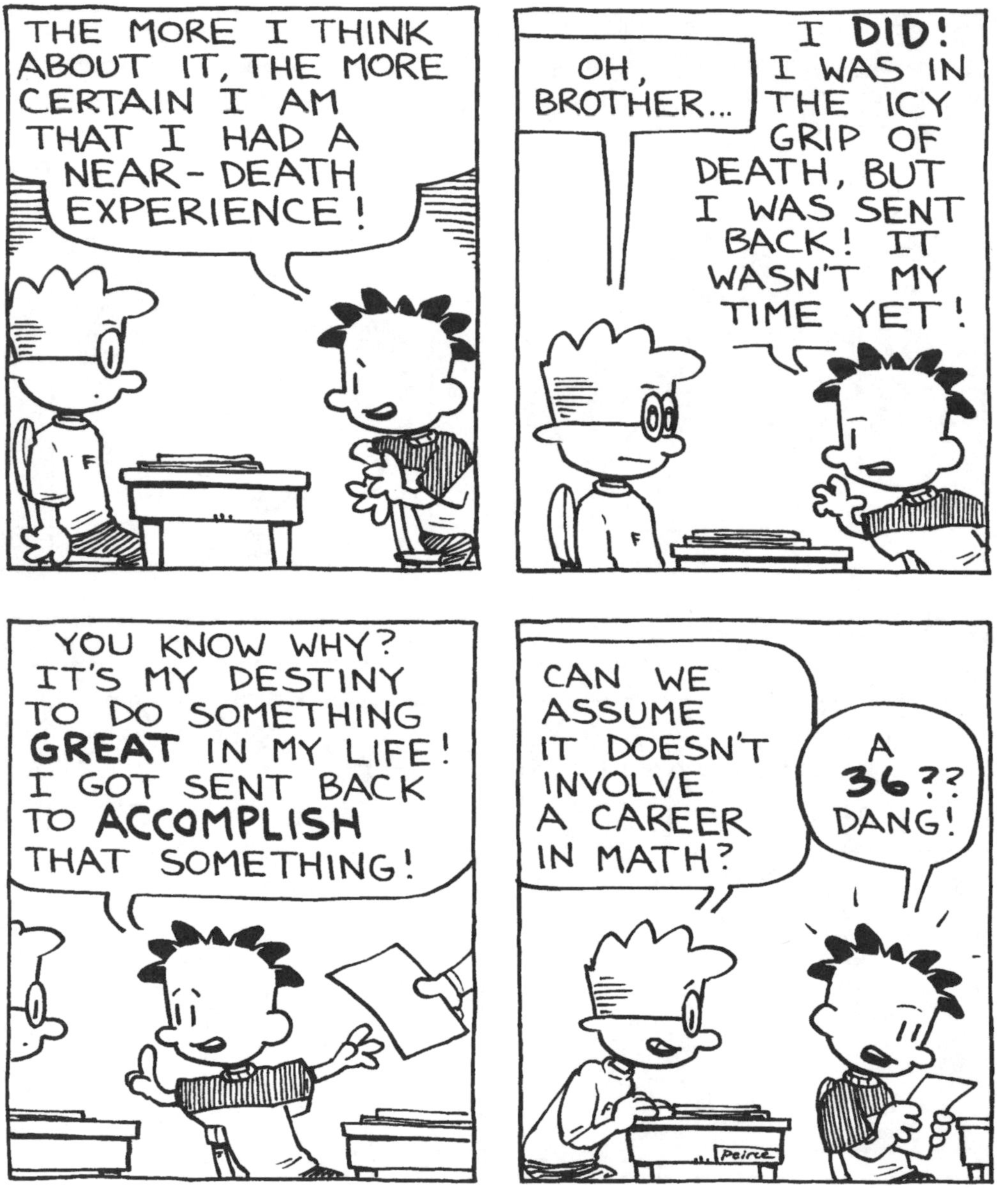
THE MORE I THINK ABOUT IT, THE MORE CERTAIN I AM THAT I HAD A NEAR-DEATH EXPERIENCE!
OH, BROTHER...
I **DID**! I WAS IN THE ICY GRIP OF DEATH, BUT I WAS SENT BACK! IT WASN'T MY TIME YET!
YOU KNOW WHY? IT'S MY DESTINY TO DO SOMETHING **GREAT** IN MY LIFE! I GOT SENT BACK TO **ACCOMPLISH** THAT SOMETHING!
CAN WE ASSUME IT DOESN'T INVOLVE A CAREER IN MATH?
A **36**?? DANG!
Peirce

...AND THEN I FLOATED OUT OF MY BODY! I WAS IN A TUNNEL, WALKING TOWARD A BRIGHT WHITE LIGHT!...

BUT THEN SOMETHING PULLED ME BACK! YES, I WAS YANKED BACK FROM THE ABYSS!

YAWNNN

I'M IMPRESSING THESE BABES WITH THE GRIPPING TALE OF MY NEAR-DEATH EXPERIENCE!

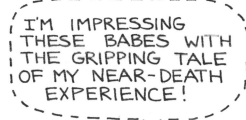

WHAT ABOUT YOUR **BRAIN-DEATH** EXPERIENCE?

HEY, WHERE'D THEY GO?

YOU'RE UNBELIEVABLE, YOU KNOW THAT?

WHATTA YA MEAN?

YOU'RE TELLING EVERYBODY YOU HAD A NEAR-DEATH EXPERIENCE! THAT YOU **LEFT** YOUR **BODY**! IT'S JUST UNBELIEVABLE!

HMM... I GUESS IT **IS** HARD TO BELIEVE...

I MEAN, WHY LEAVE A BODY LIKE **THIS** ONE? IT MAKES NO SENSE!

NO **WONDER** I'VE BEEN GETTING SO MANY FUNNY LOOKS!

ACCORDING TO THIS ARTICLE, FIRSTBORN CHILDREN ARE LESS CREATIVE THAN THEIR YOUNGER SIBLINGS!
THERE'S **MORE**, ELLEN! YOU FIRST-BORNS ARE LESS LIKELY TO TAKE RISKS! MORE CONSER-VATIVE! STODGIER! STIFFER!
BIGGER.
!
BUMMER.
Peirce

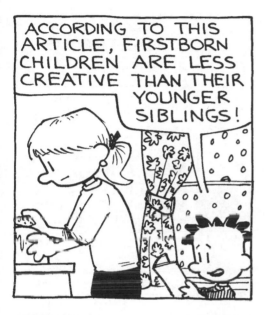

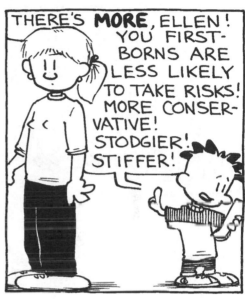

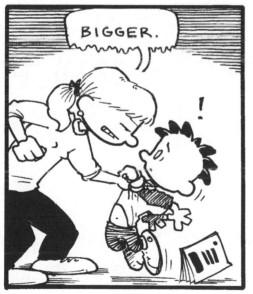

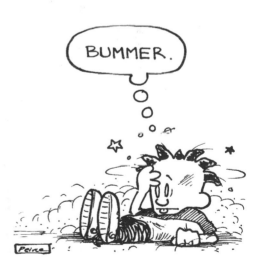

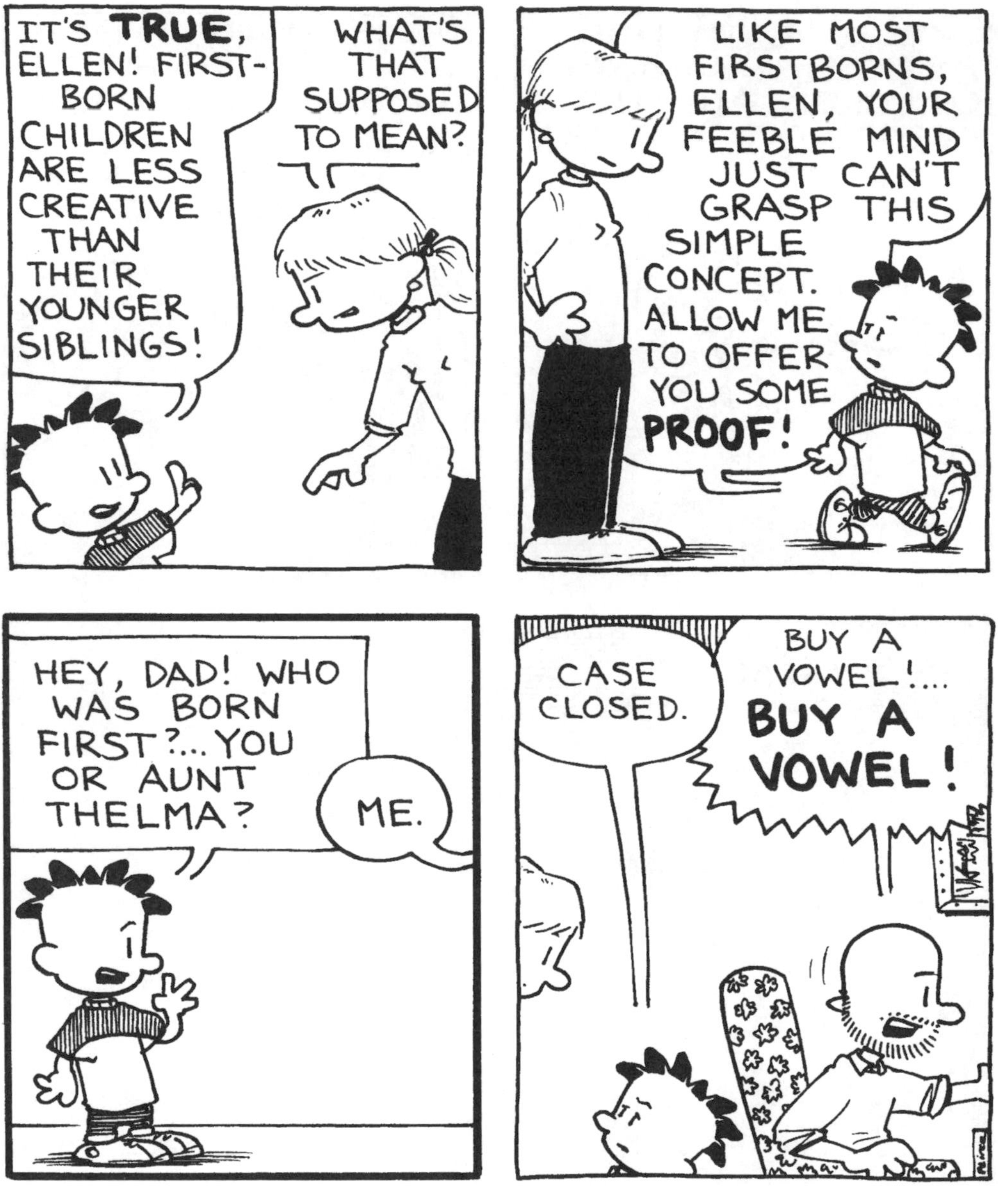
IT'S TRUE, ELLEN! FIRST-BORN CHILDREN ARE LESS CREATIVE THAN THEIR YOUNGER SIBLINGS!
WHAT'S THAT SUPPOSED TO MEAN?
LIKE MOST FIRSTBORNS, ELLEN, YOUR FEEBLE MIND JUST CAN'T GRASP THIS SIMPLE CONCEPT. ALLOW ME TO OFFER YOU SOME PROOF!
HEY, DAD! WHO WAS BORN FIRST?... YOU OR AUNT THELMA?
ME.
CASE CLOSED.
BUY A VOWEL!... BUY A VOWEL!

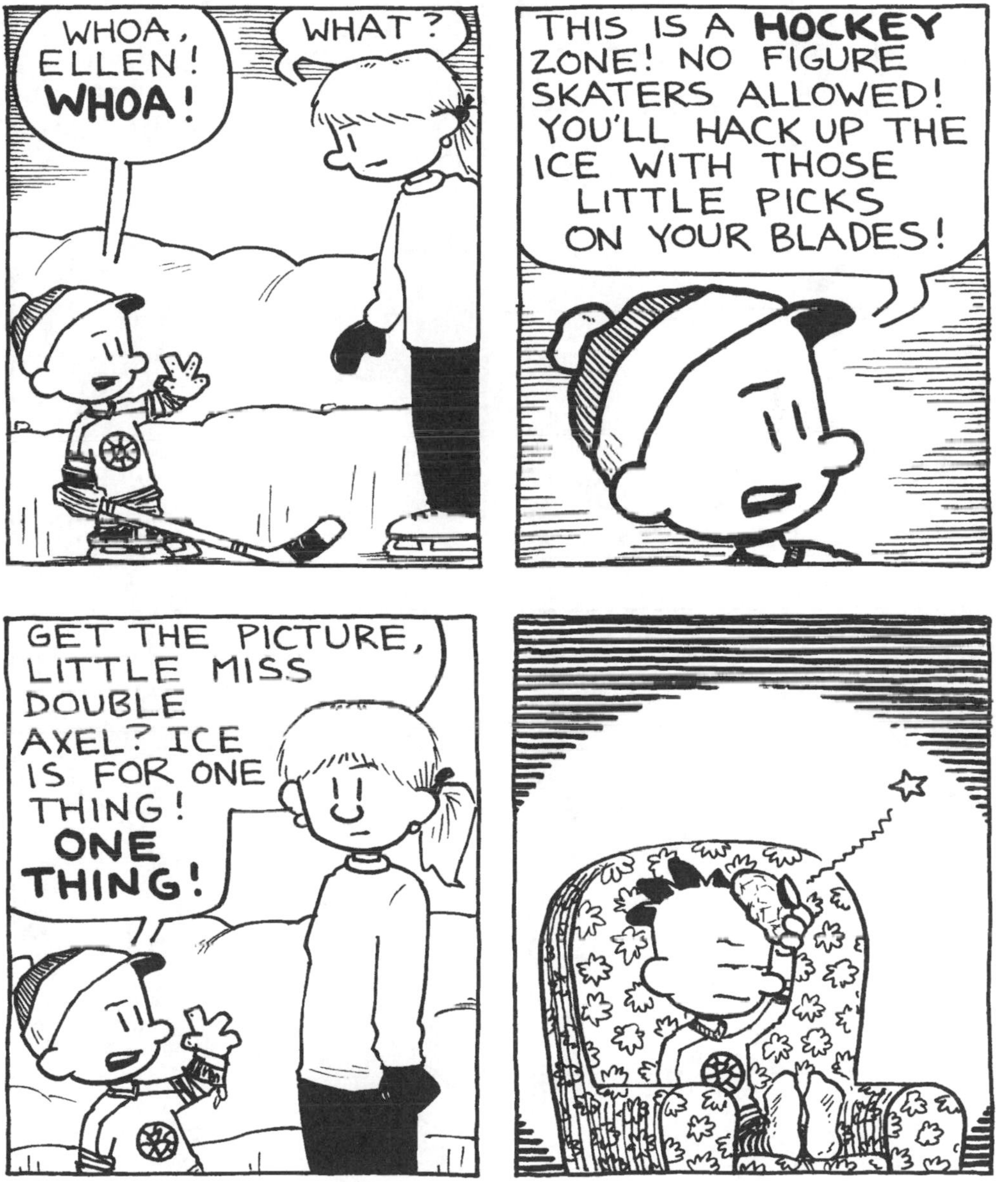
WHOA, ELLEN! WHOA!
WHAT?
THIS IS A HOCKEY ZONE! NO FIGURE SKATERS ALLOWED! YOU'LL HACK UP THE ICE WITH THOSE LITTLE PICKS ON YOUR BLADES!
GET THE PICTURE, LITTLE MISS DOUBLE AXEL? ICE IS FOR ONE THING! ONE THING!

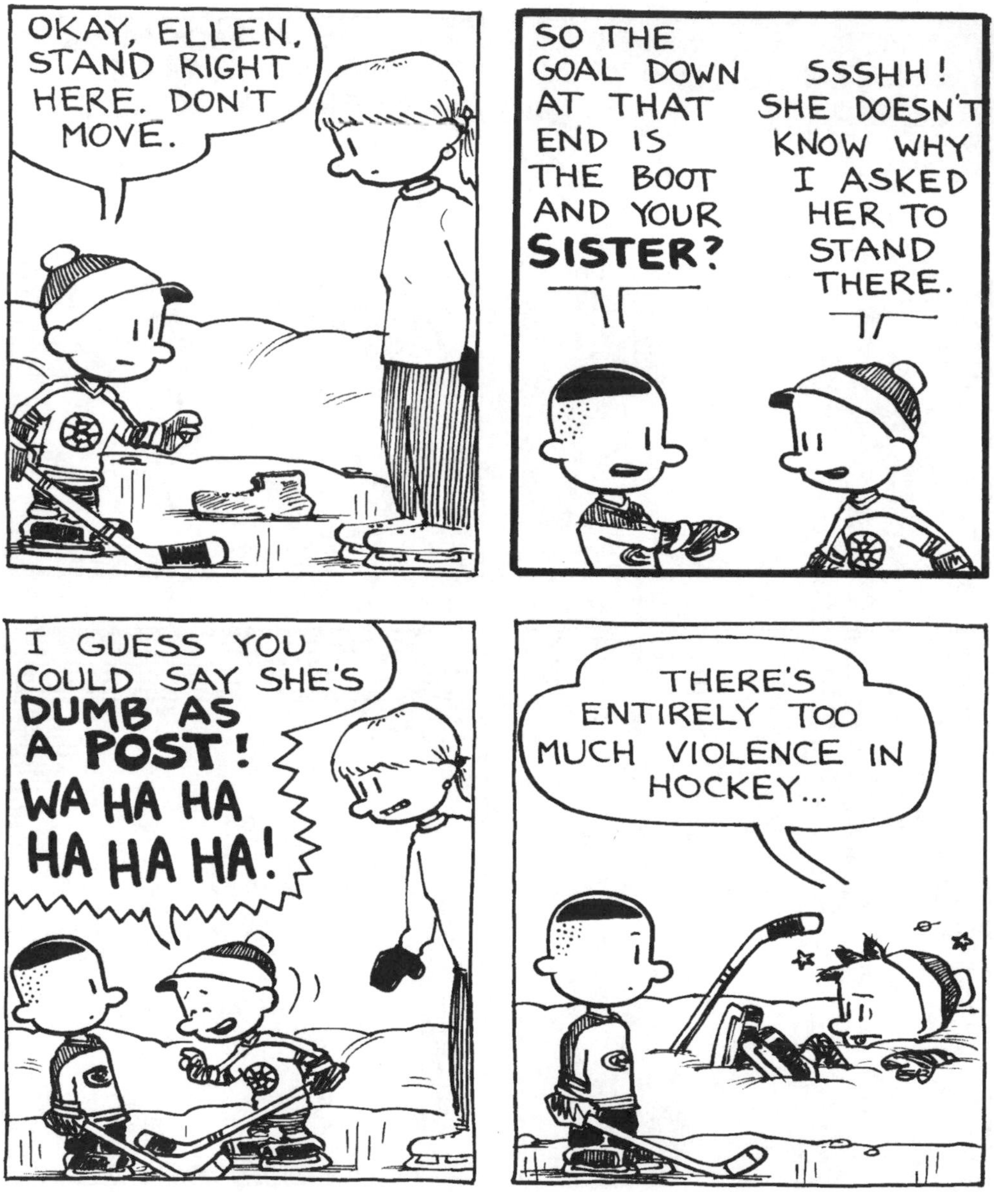
OKAY, ELLEN, STAND RIGHT HERE. DON'T MOVE.
SO THE GOAL DOWN AT THAT END IS THE BOOT AND YOUR **SISTER?**
SSSHH! SHE DOESN'T KNOW WHY I ASKED HER TO STAND THERE.
I GUESS YOU COULD SAY SHE'S **DUMB AS A POST! WA HA HA HA HA HA!**
THERE'S ENTIRELY TOO MUCH VIOLENCE IN HOCKEY...

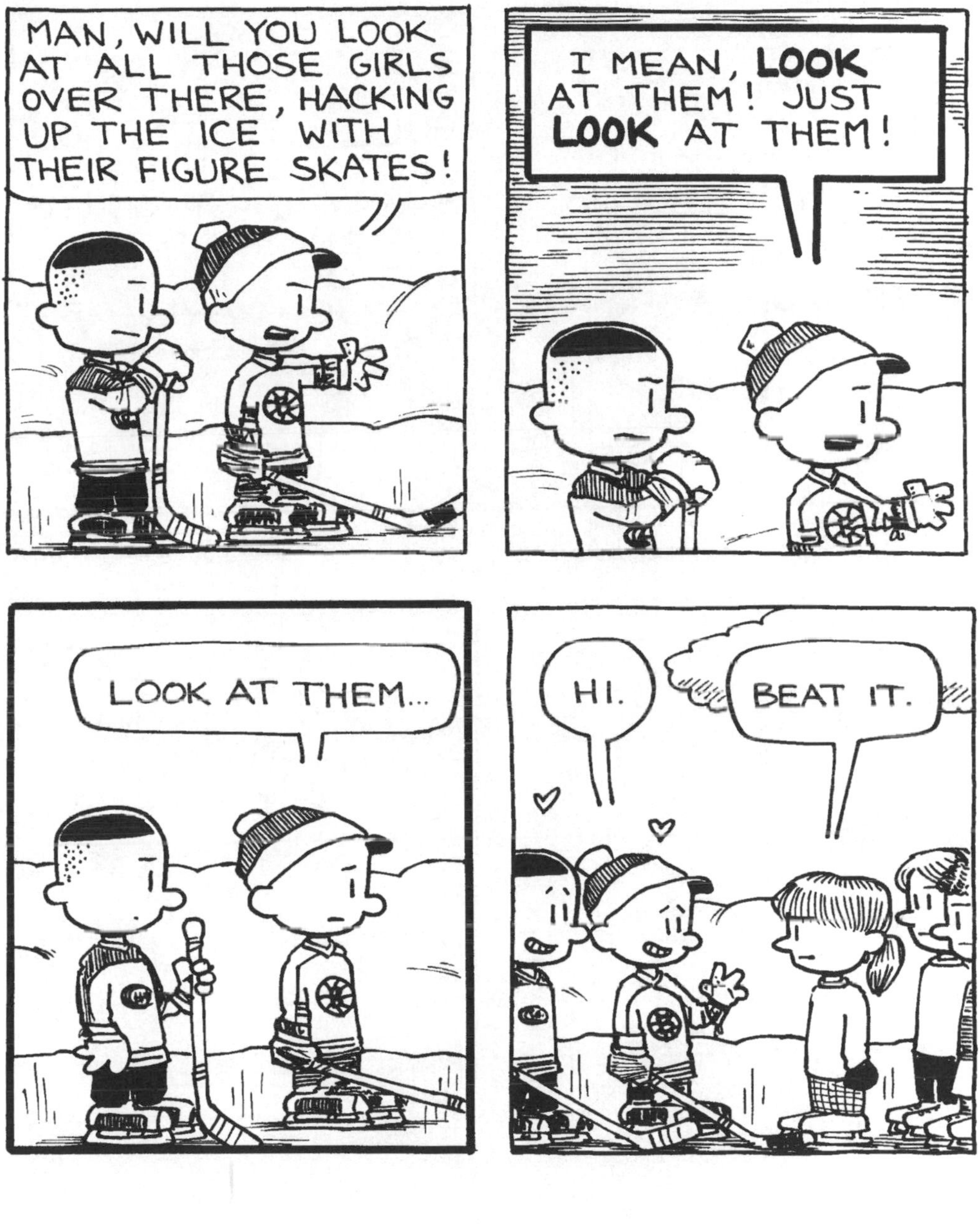
MAN, WILL YOU LOOK AT ALL THOSE GIRLS OVER THERE, HACKING UP THE ICE WITH THEIR FIGURE SKATES!
I MEAN, **LOOK** AT THEM! JUST **LOOK** AT THEM!
LOOK AT THEM...
HI.
BEAT IT.

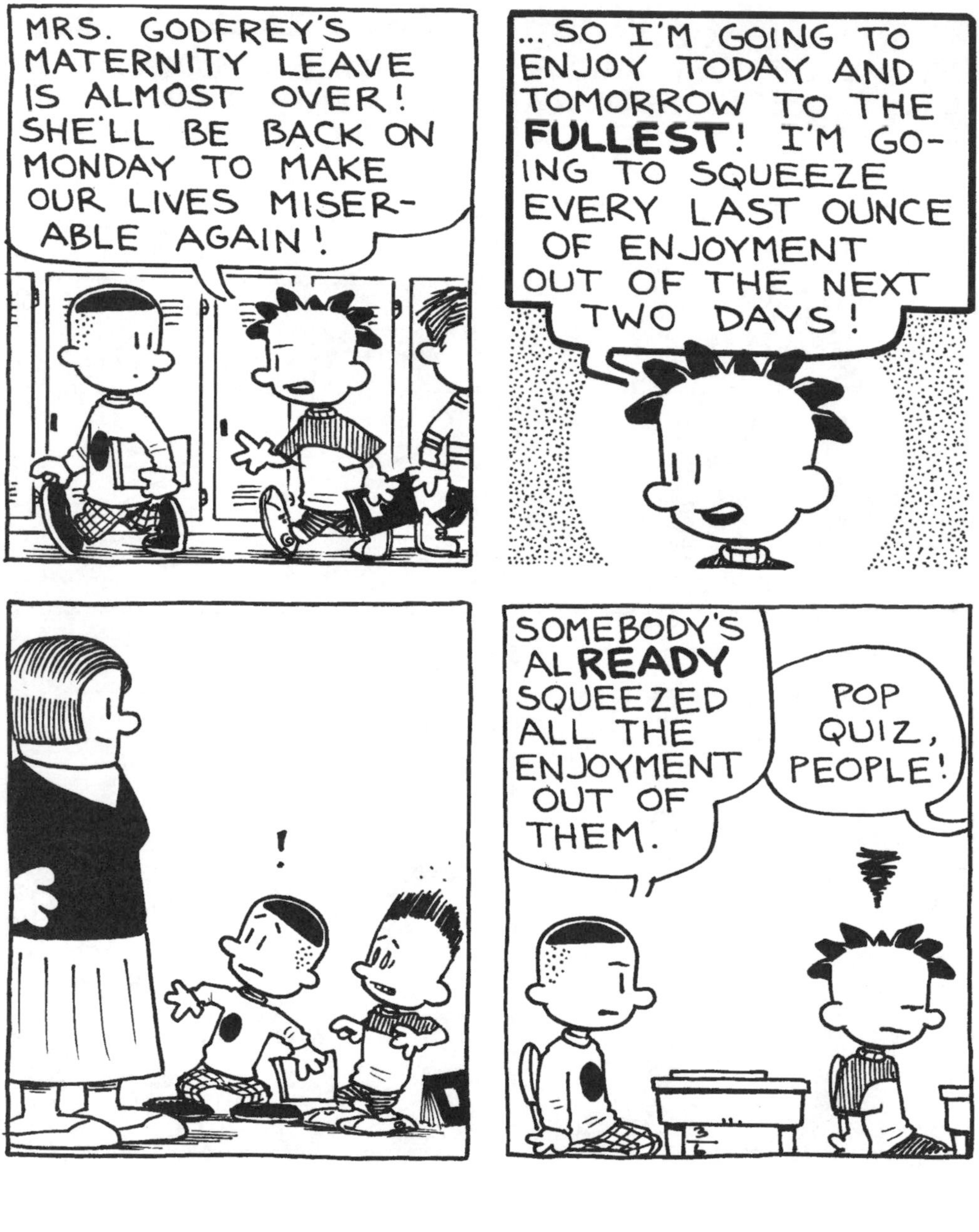
MRS. GODFREY'S MATERNITY LEAVE IS ALMOST OVER! SHE'LL BE BACK ON MONDAY TO MAKE OUR LIVES MISER-ABLE AGAIN!
...SO I'M GOING TO ENJOY TODAY AND TOMORROW TO THE FULLEST! I'M GO-ING TO SQUEEZE EVERY LAST OUNCE OF ENJOYMENT OUT OF THE NEXT TWO DAYS!
!
SOMEBODY'S ALREADY SQUEEZED ALL THE ENJOYMENT OUT OF THEM.
POP QUIZ, PEOPLE!

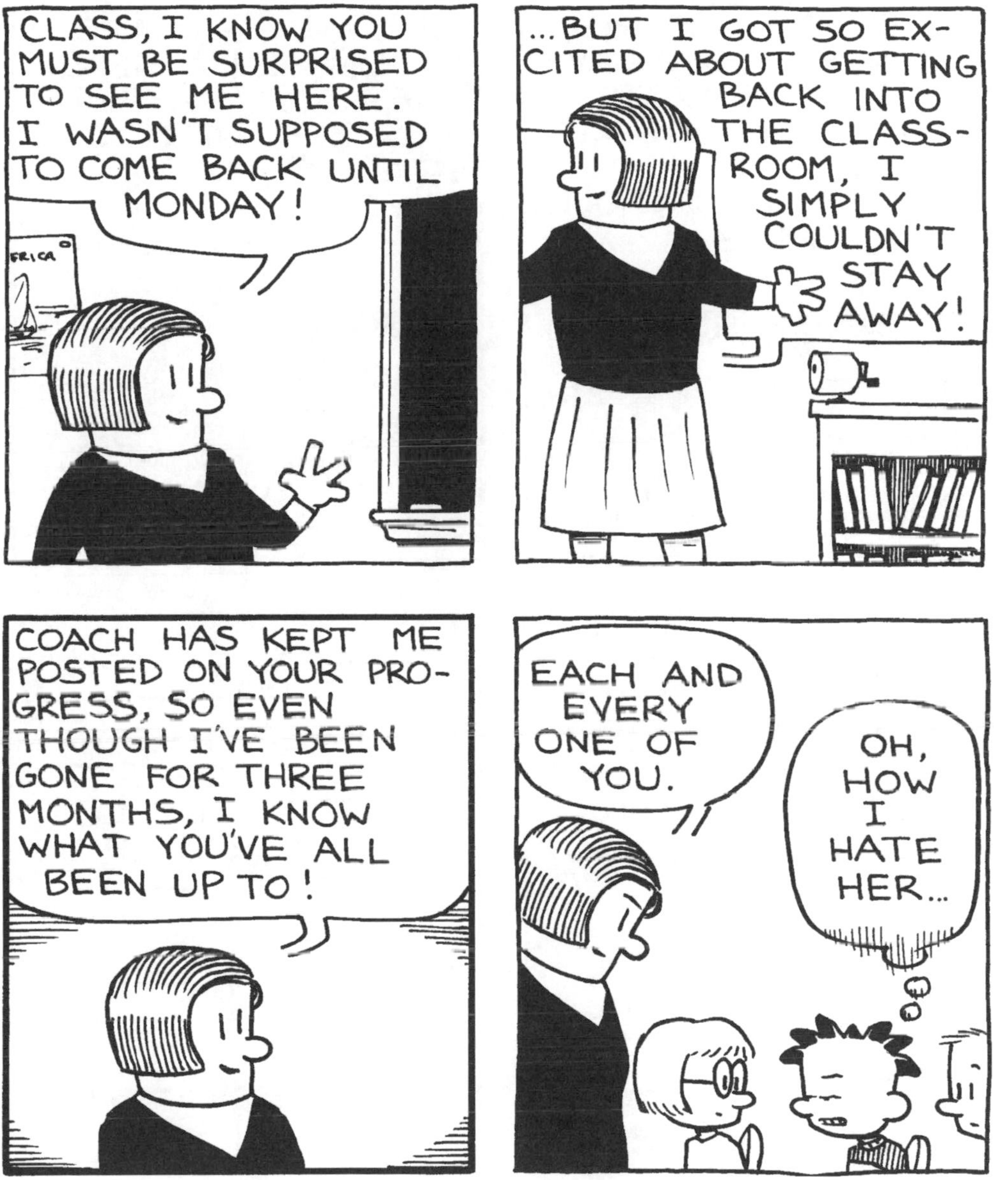
CLASS, I KNOW YOU MUST BE SURPRISED TO SEE ME HERE. I WASN'T SUPPOSED TO COME BACK UNTIL MONDAY!
...BUT I GOT SO EXCITED ABOUT GETTING BACK INTO THE CLASSROOM, I SIMPLY COULDN'T STAY AWAY!
COACH HAS KEPT ME POSTED ON YOUR PROGRESS, SO EVEN THOUGH I'VE BEEN GONE FOR THREE MONTHS, I KNOW WHAT YOU'VE ALL BEEN UP TO!
EACH AND EVERY ONE OF YOU.
OH, HOW I HATE HER...

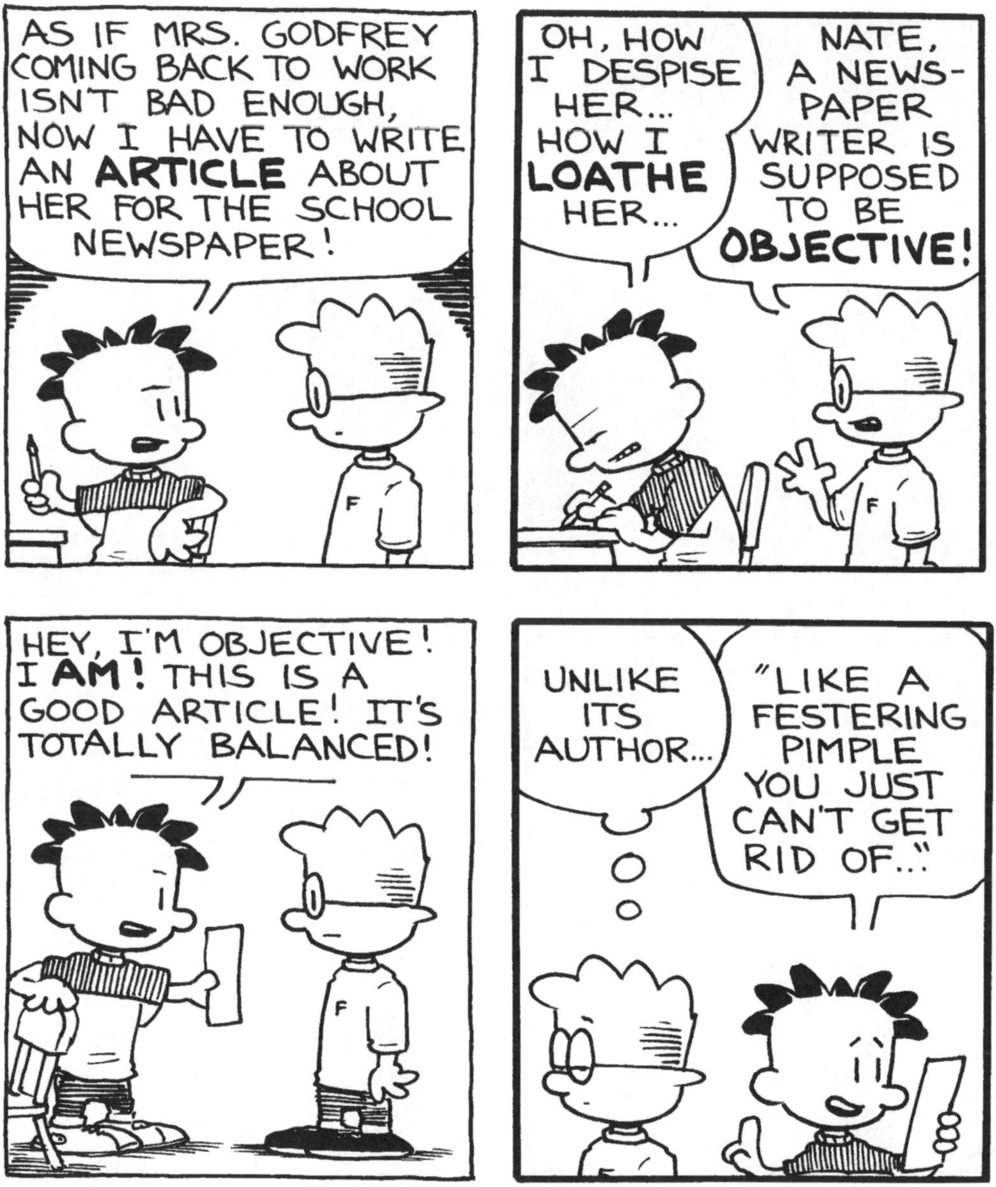
AS IF MRS. GODFREY COMING BACK TO WORK ISN'T BAD ENOUGH, NOW I HAVE TO WRITE AN **ARTICLE** ABOUT HER FOR THE SCHOOL NEWSPAPER!
OH, HOW I DESPISE HER... HOW I **LOATHE** HER...
NATE, A NEWSPAPER WRITER IS SUPPOSED TO BE **OBJECTIVE**!
HEY, I'M OBJECTIVE! I **AM**! THIS IS A GOOD ARTICLE! IT'S TOTALLY BALANCED!
UNLIKE ITS AUTHOR...
"LIKE A FESTERING PIMPLE YOU JUST CAN'T GET RID OF..."

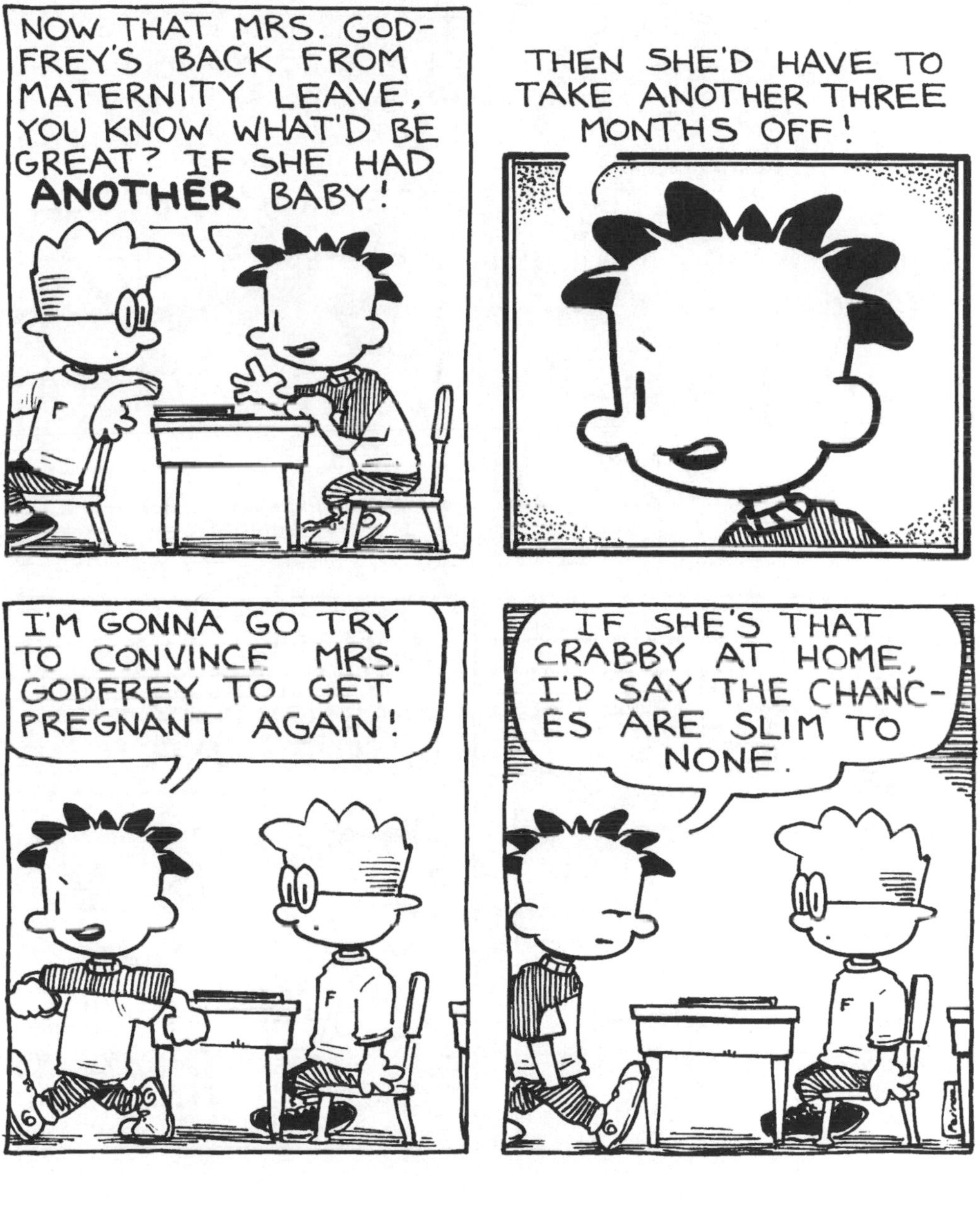
NOW THAT MRS. GODFREY'S BACK FROM MATERNITY LEAVE, YOU KNOW WHAT'D BE GREAT? IF SHE HAD **ANOTHER** BABY!
THEN SHE'D HAVE TO TAKE ANOTHER THREE MONTHS OFF!
I'M GONNA GO TRY TO CONVINCE MRS. GODFREY TO GET PREGNANT AGAIN!
IF SHE'S THAT CRABBY AT HOME, I'D SAY THE CHANCES ARE SLIM TO NONE.

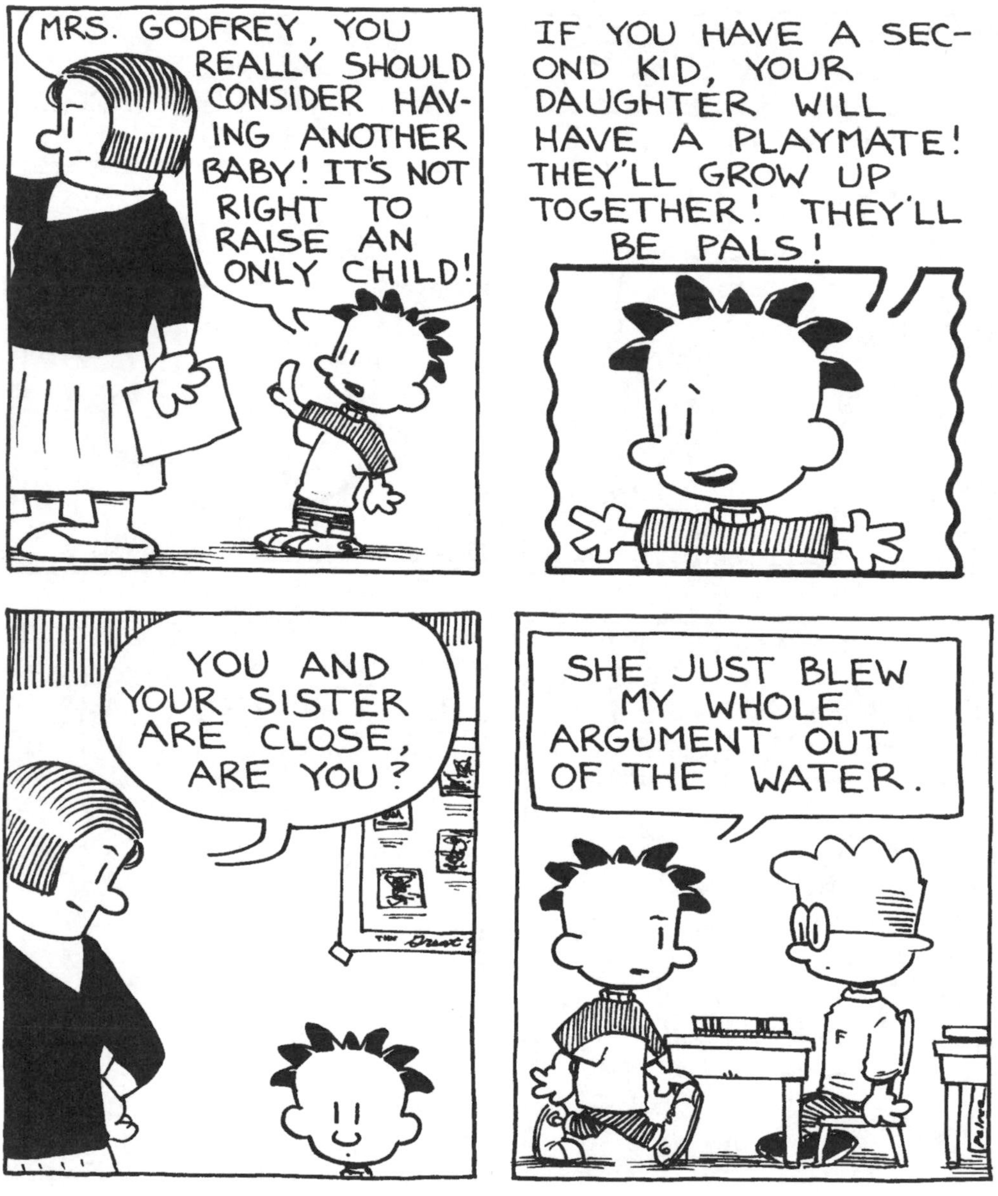

MRS. GODFREY, YOU REALLY SHOULD CONSIDER HAVING ANOTHER BABY! IT'S NOT RIGHT TO RAISE AN ONLY CHILD!
IF YOU HAVE A SECOND KID, YOUR DAUGHTER WILL HAVE A PLAYMATE! THEY'LL GROW UP TOGETHER! THEY'LL BE PALS!
YOU AND YOUR SISTER ARE CLOSE, ARE YOU?
SHE JUST BLEW MY WHOLE ARGUMENT OUT OF THE WATER.

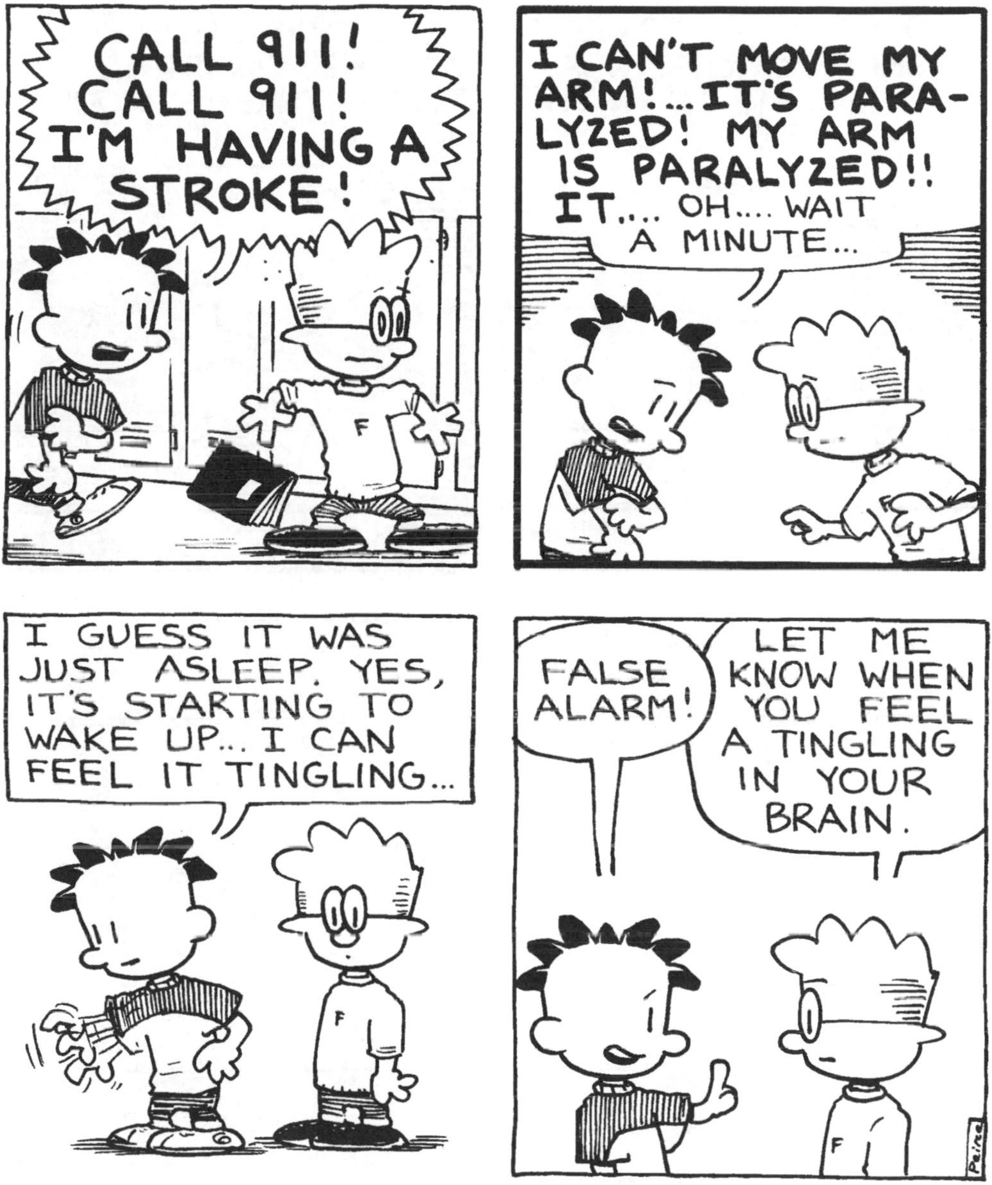
CALL 911! CALL 911! I'M HAVING A STROKE!
I CAN'T MOVE MY ARM!...IT'S PARALYZED! MY ARM IS PARALYZED!! IT.... OH.... WAIT A MINUTE...
I GUESS IT WAS JUST ASLEEP. YES, IT'S STARTING TO WAKE UP... I CAN FEEL IT TINGLING...
FALSE ALARM!
LET ME KNOW WHEN YOU FEEL A TINGLING IN YOUR BRAIN.
Peirce

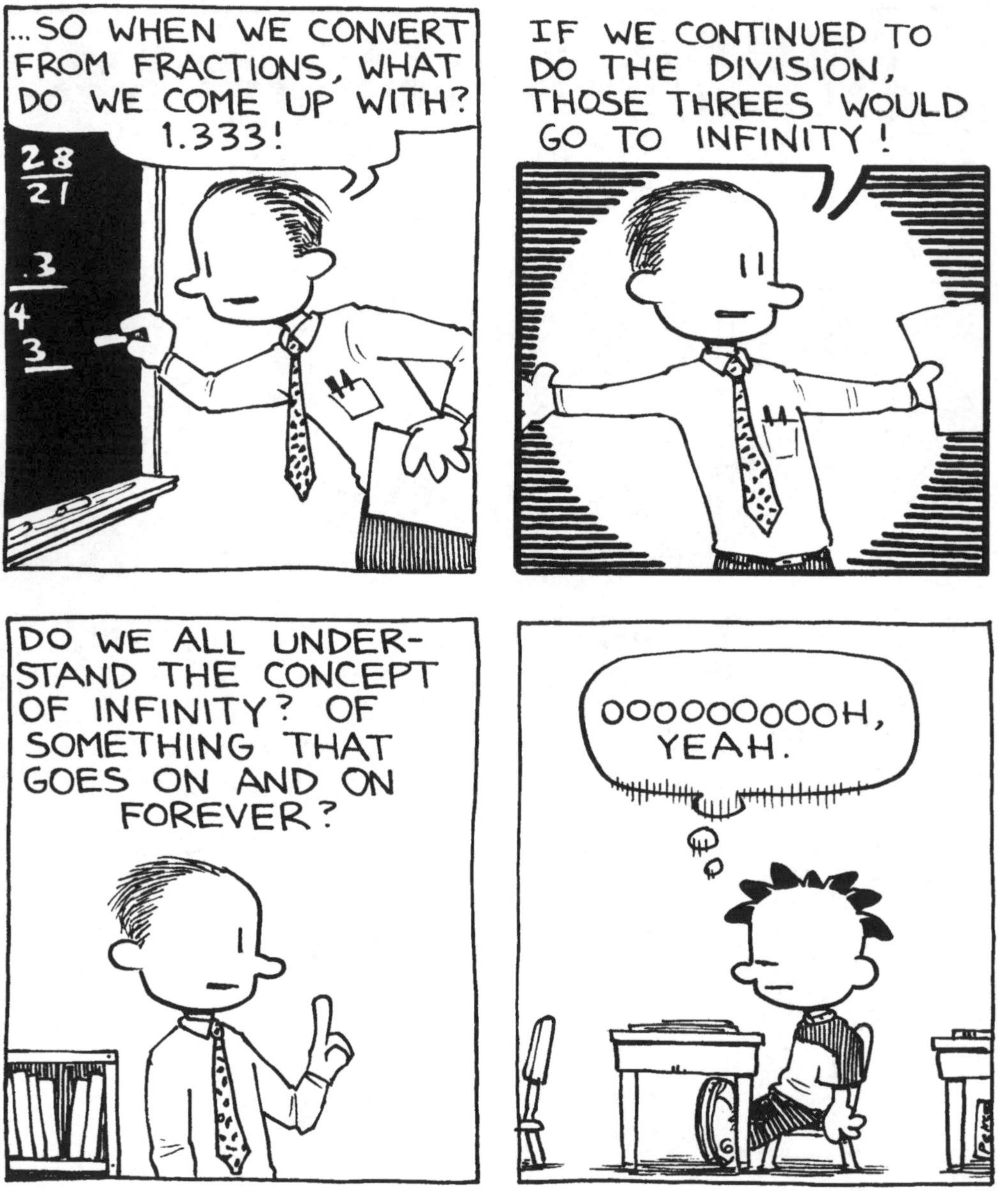
...SO WHEN WE CONVERT FROM FRACTIONS, WHAT DO WE COME UP WITH? 1.333!
28
21
.3
4
3
IF WE CONTINUED TO DO THE DIVISION, THOSE THREES WOULD GO TO INFINITY!
DO WE ALL UNDERSTAND THE CONCEPT OF INFINITY? OF SOMETHING THAT GOES ON AND ON FOREVER?
OOOOOOOOOOH, YEAH.
6
Peirce

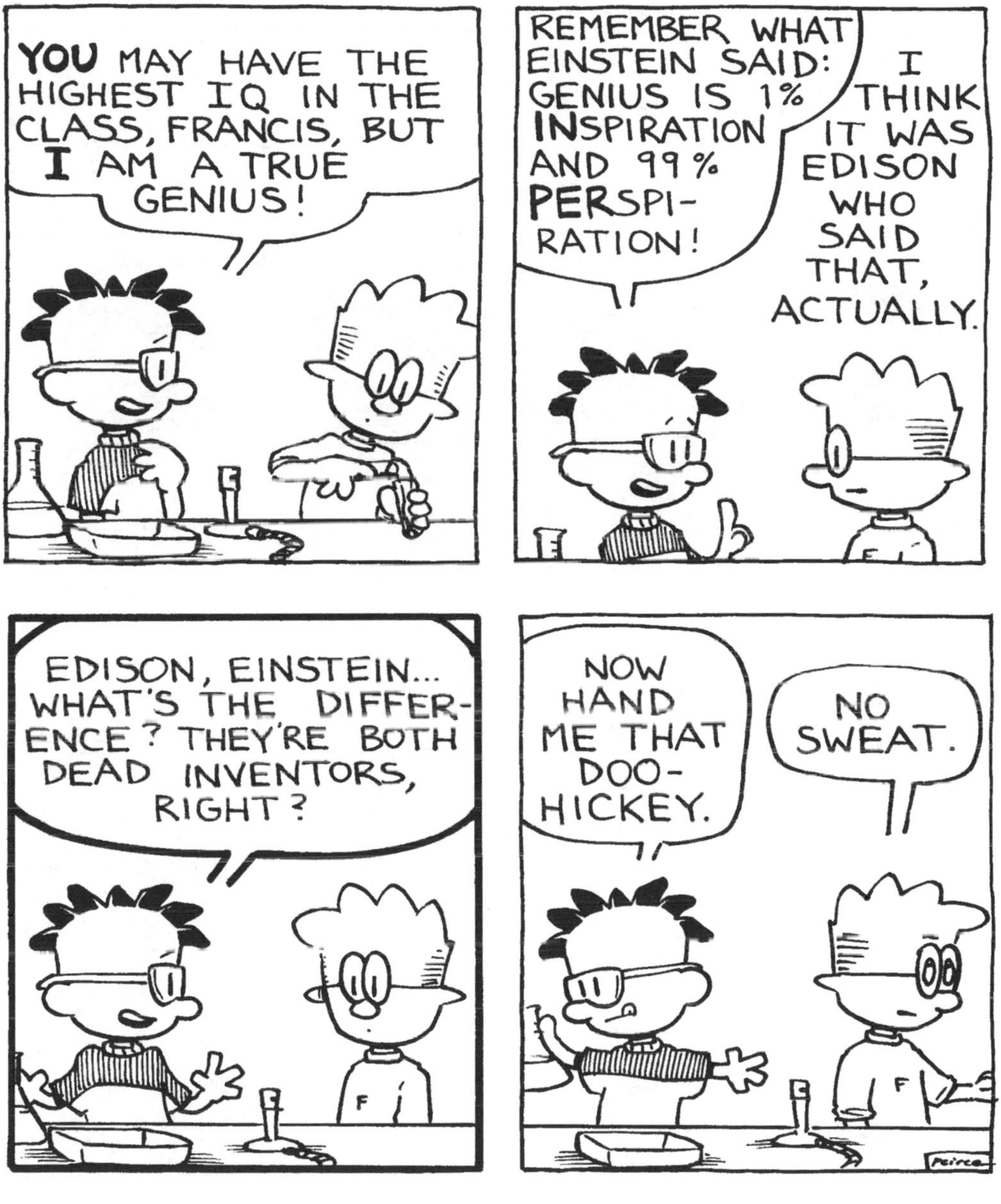
YOU MAY HAVE THE HIGHEST IQ IN THE CLASS, FRANCIS, BUT I AM A TRUE GENIUS!
REMEMBER WHAT EINSTEIN SAID: GENIUS IS 1% INSPIRATION AND 99% PERSPIRATION!
I THINK IT WAS EDISON WHO SAID THAT, ACTUALLY.
EDISON, EINSTEIN... WHAT'S THE DIFFERENCE? THEY'RE BOTH DEAD INVENTORS, RIGHT?
NOW HAND ME THAT DOO-HICKEY.
NO SWEAT.
Peirce

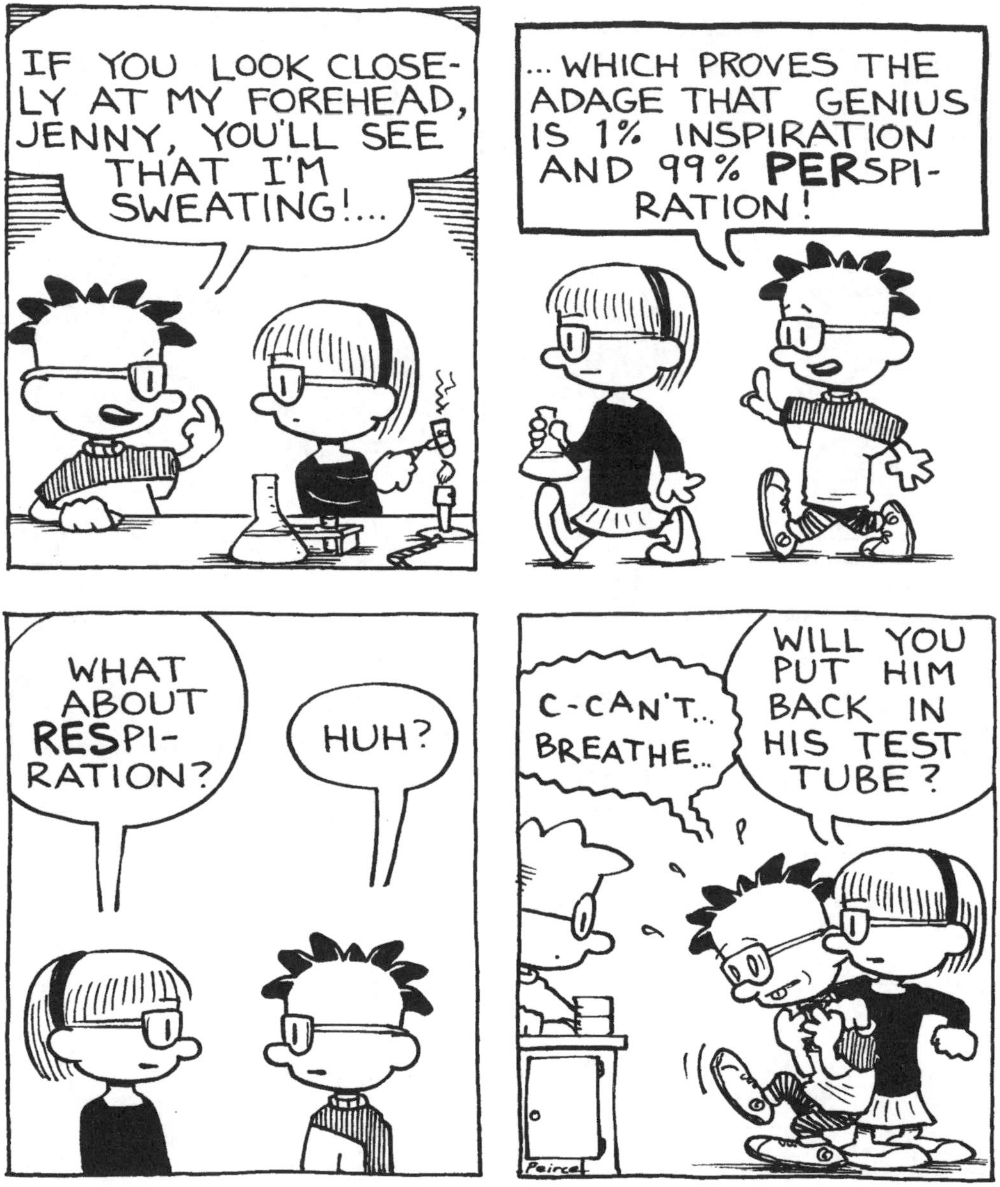
IF YOU LOOK CLOSELY AT MY FOREHEAD, JENNY, YOU'LL SEE THAT I'M SWEATING!...
...WHICH PROVES THE ADAGE THAT GENIUS IS 1% INSPIRATION AND 99% **PER**SPIRATION!
WHAT ABOUT **RES**PIRATION?
HUH?
C-CAN'T... BREATHE...
WILL YOU PUT HIM BACK IN HIS TEST TUBE?
Peirce

KISS ME I'M IRISH
KISS ME I'M IRISH
KISS ME I'M IRISH

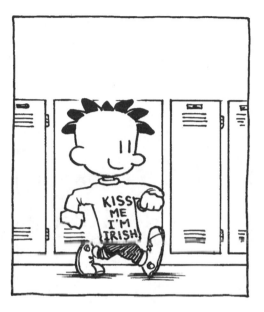

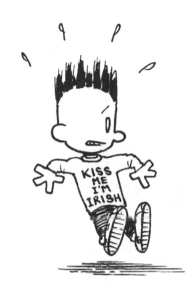

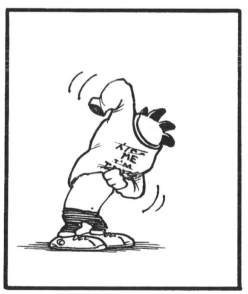

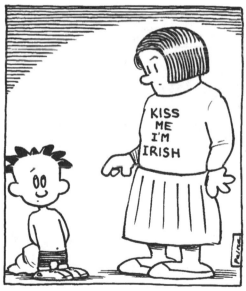

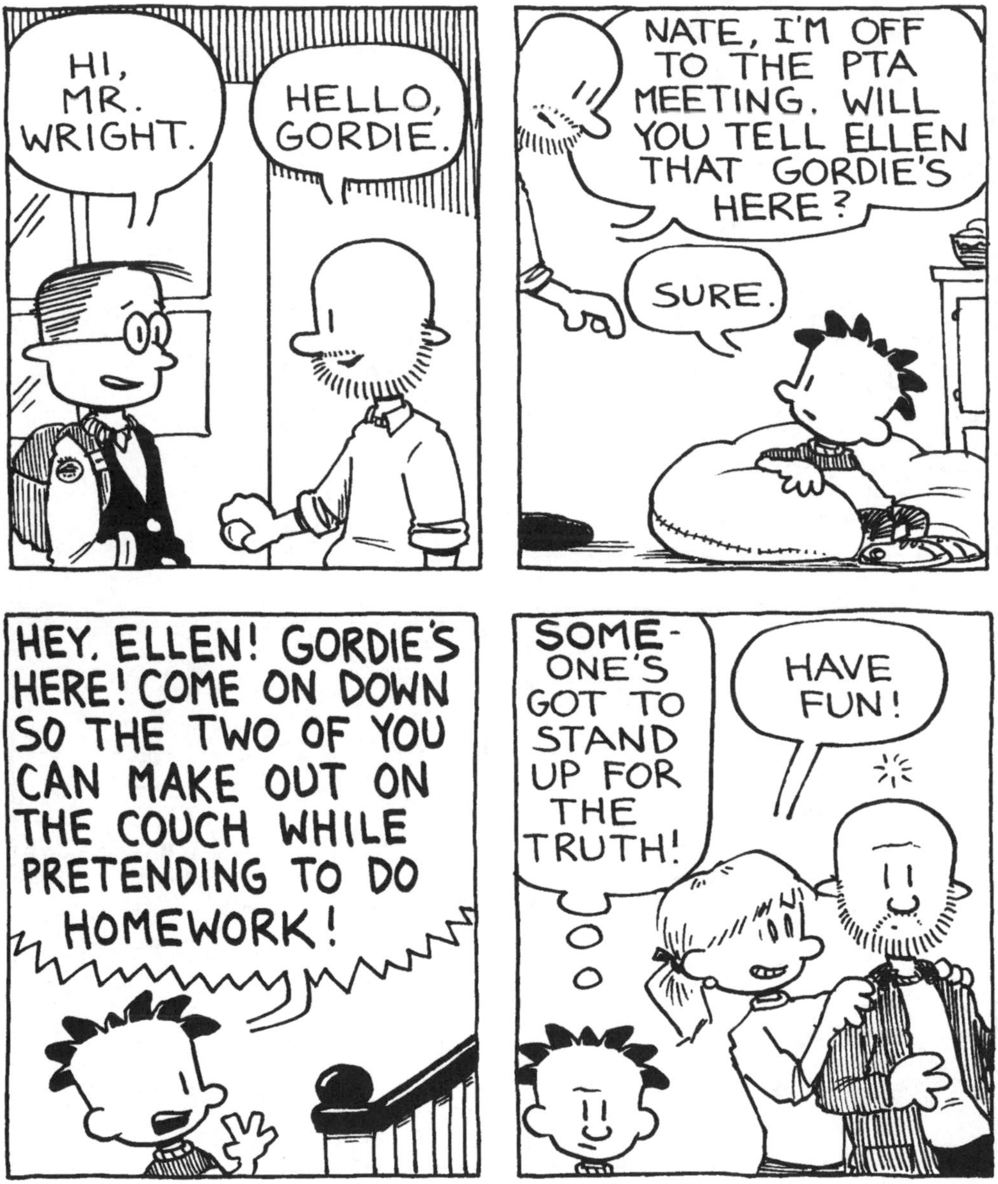
HI, MR. WRIGHT.
HELLO, GORDIE.
NATE, I'M OFF TO THE PTA MEETING. WILL YOU TELL ELLEN THAT GORDIE'S HERE?
SURE.
HEY, ELLEN! GORDIE'S HERE! COME ON DOWN SO THE TWO OF YOU CAN MAKE OUT ON THE COUCH WHILE PRETENDING TO DO HOMEWORK!
SOME-ONE'S GOT TO STAND UP FOR THE TRUTH!
HAVE FUN!

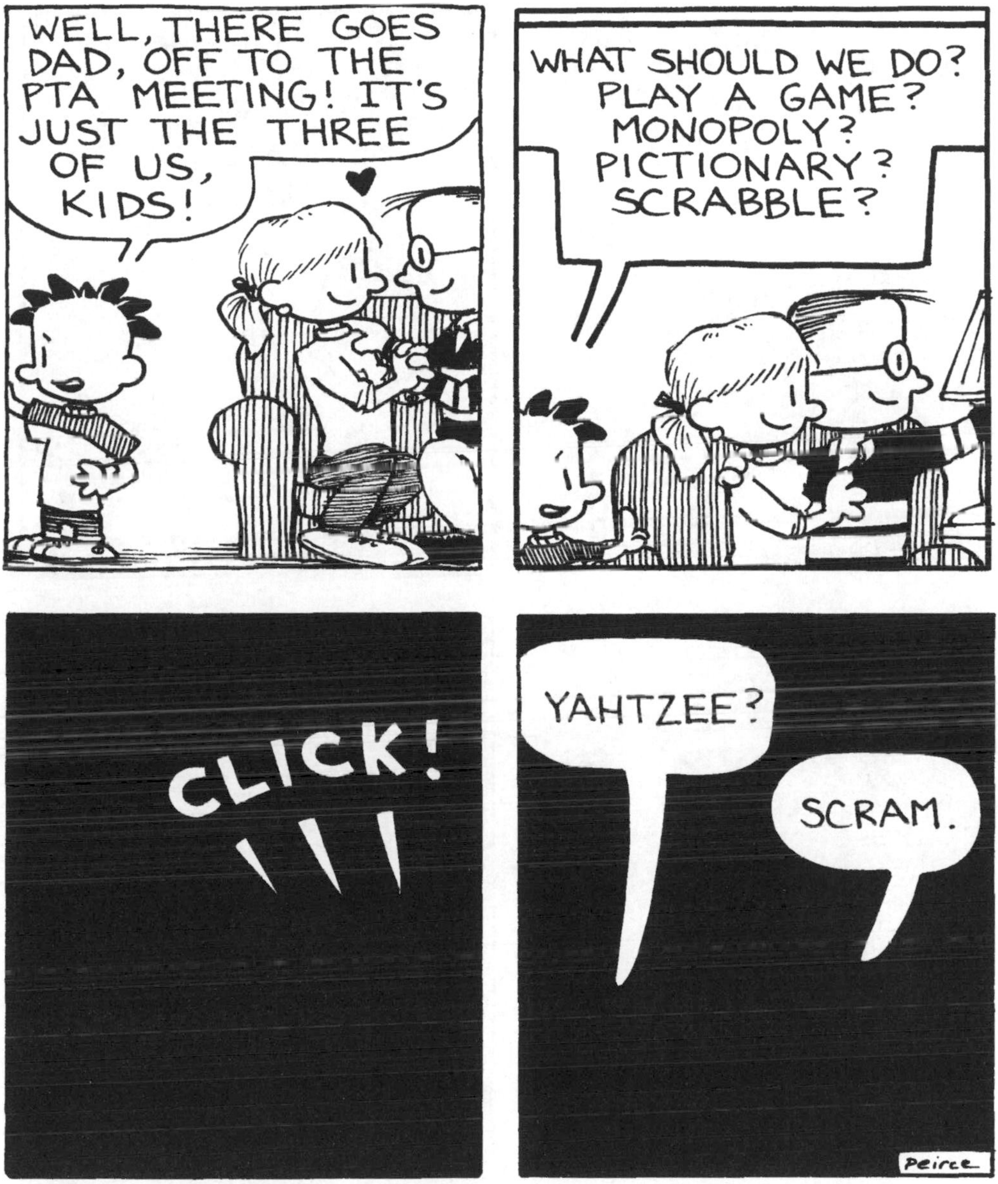
WELL, THERE GOES DAD, OFF TO THE PTA MEETING! IT'S JUST THE THREE OF US, KIDS!
WHAT SHOULD WE DO? PLAY A GAME? MONOPOLY? PICTIONARY? SCRABBLE?
CLICK!
YAHTZEE?
SCRAM.
Peirce

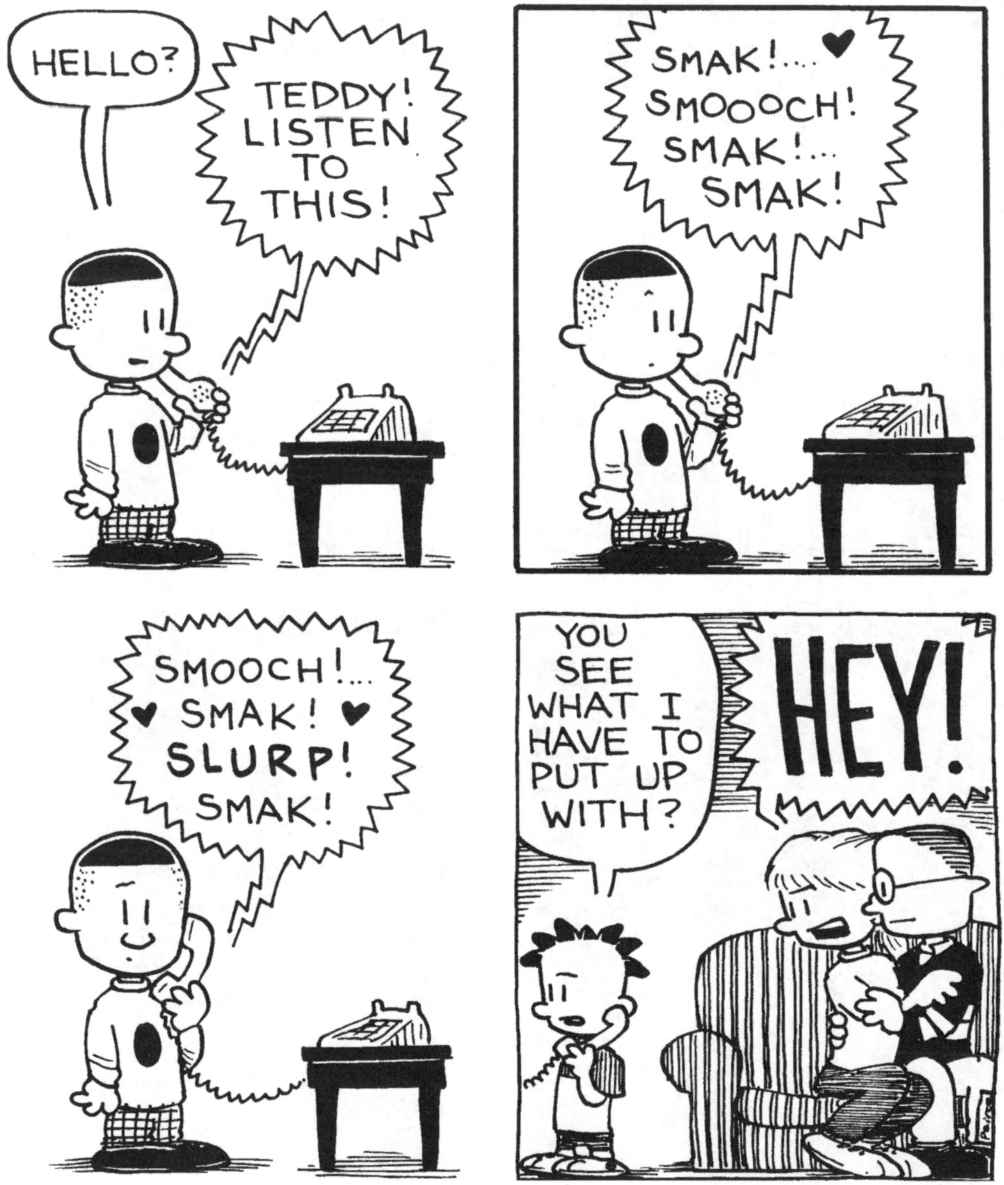
HELLO?
TEDDY! LISTEN TO THIS!
SMAK!... ♥ SMOOOCH! SMAK!... SMAK!
SMOOCH!... ♥ SMAK! ♥ SLURP! SMAK!
YOU SEE WHAT I HAVE TO PUT UP WITH?
HEY!

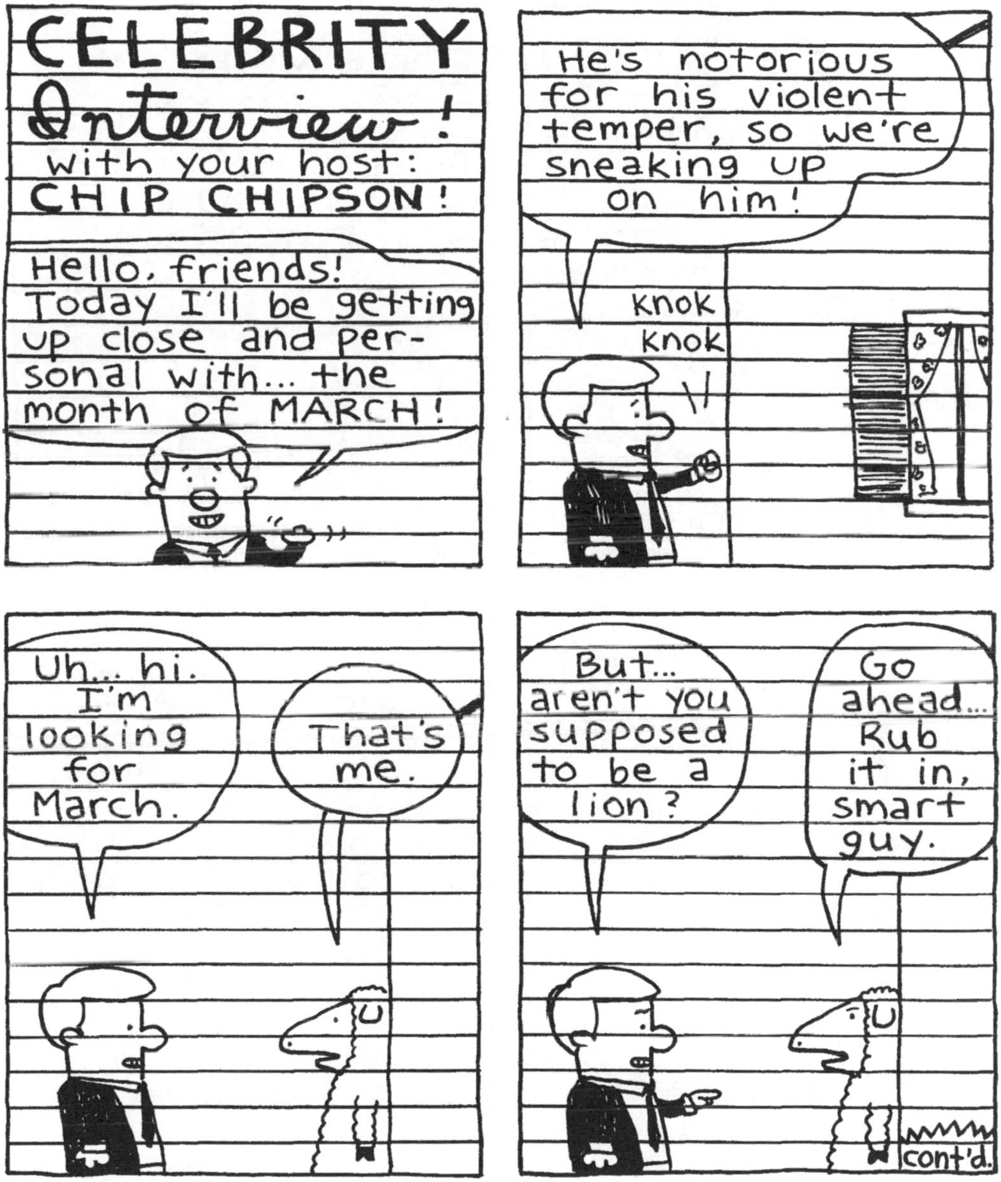
CELEBRITY Interview! with your host: CHIP CHIPSON!
Hello, friends! Today I'll be getting up close and personal with... the month of MARCH!
He's notorious for his violent temper, so we're sneaking up on him!
KNOK KNOK
Uh... hi. I'm looking for March.
That's me.
But... aren't you supposed to be a lion?
Go ahead... Rub it in, smart guy.
cont'd.

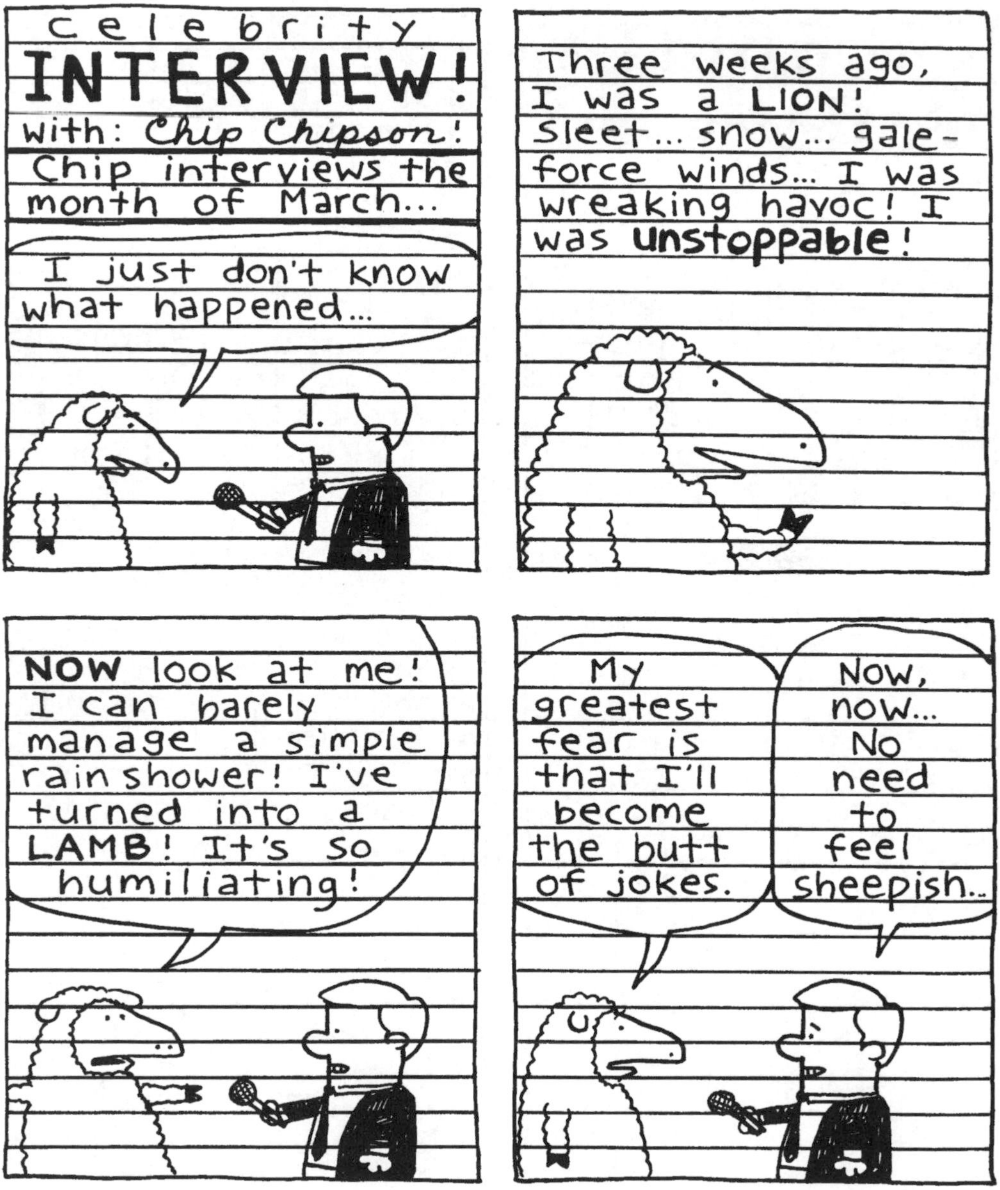
celebrity INTERVIEW!
with: Chip Chipson!
Chip interviews the month of March...
I just don't know what happened...
Three weeks ago, I was a LION! Sleet... snow... gale-force winds... I was wreaking havoc! I was unstoppable!
NOW look at me! I can barely manage a simple rain shower! I've turned into a LAMB! It's so humiliating!
My greatest fear is that I'll become the butt of jokes.
Now, now... No need to feel sheepish..

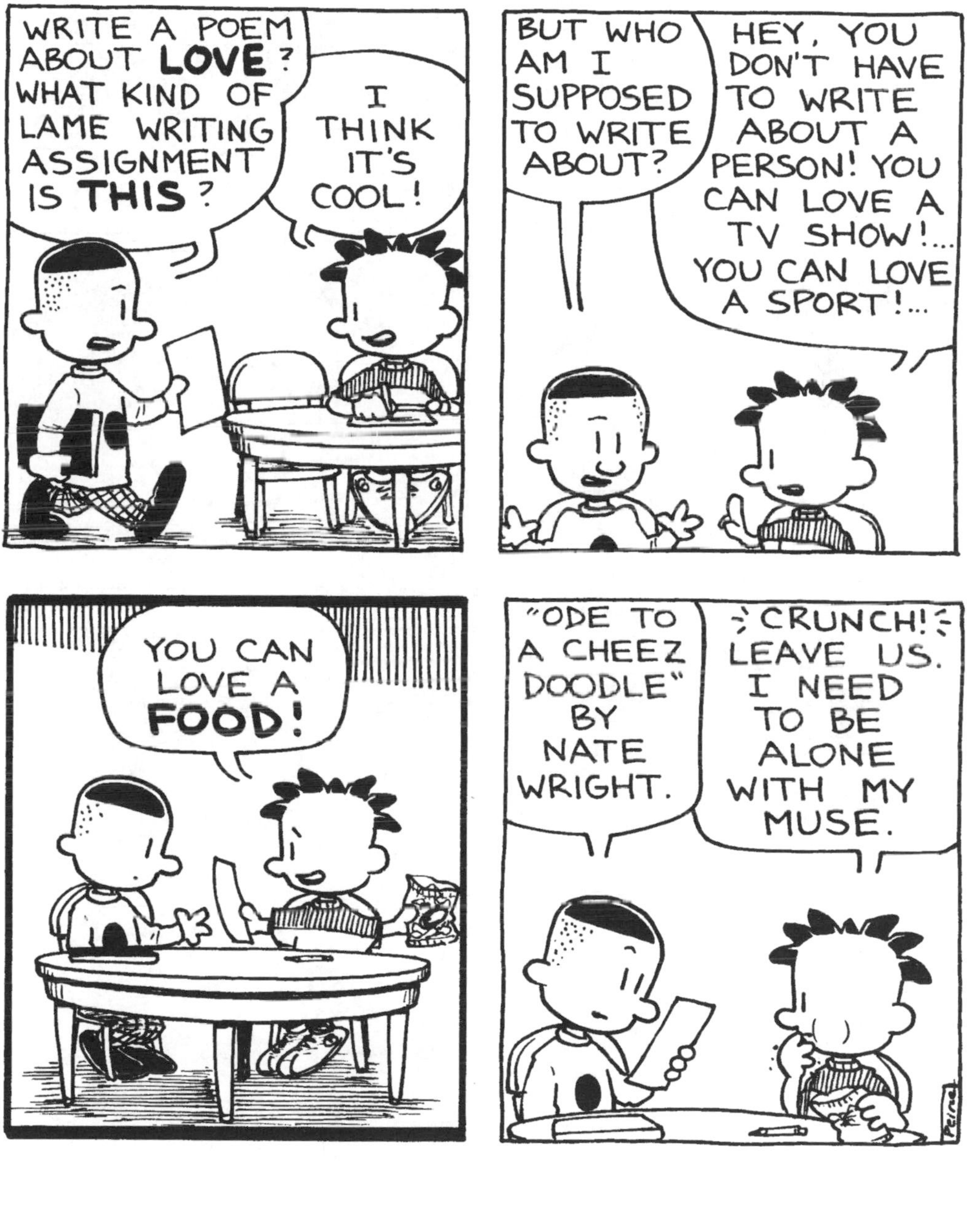
WRITE A POEM ABOUT **LOVE**? WHAT KIND OF LAME WRITING ASSIGNMENT IS **THIS**?
I THINK IT'S COOL!
BUT WHO AM I SUPPOSED TO WRITE ABOUT?
HEY, YOU DON'T HAVE TO WRITE ABOUT A PERSON! YOU CAN LOVE A TV SHOW!... YOU CAN LOVE A SPORT!...
YOU CAN LOVE A **FOOD**!
"ODE TO A CHEEZ DOODLE" BY NATE WRIGHT.
CRUNCH! LEAVE US. I NEED TO BE ALONE WITH MY MUSE.
Peirce

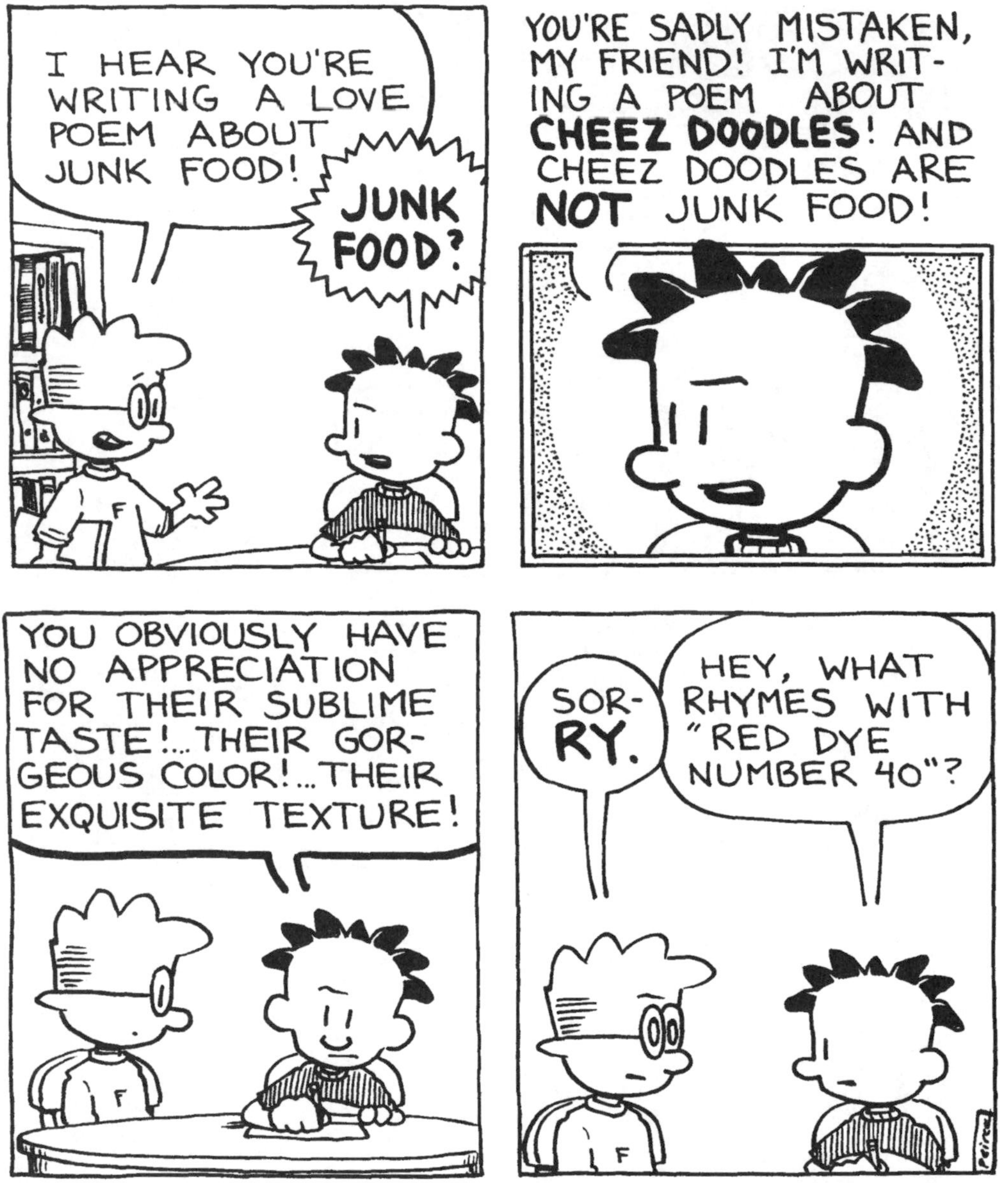
I HEAR YOU'RE WRITING A LOVE POEM ABOUT JUNK FOOD!
JUNK FOOD?
YOU'RE SADLY MISTAKEN, MY FRIEND! I'M WRITING A POEM ABOUT CHEEZ DOODLES! AND CHEEZ DOODLES ARE NOT JUNK FOOD!
YOU OBVIOUSLY HAVE NO APPRECIATION FOR THEIR SUBLIME TASTE!... THEIR GORGEOUS COLOR!... THEIR EXQUISITE TEXTURE!
SORRY.
HEY, WHAT RHYMES WITH "RED DYE NUMBER 40"?
Peirce

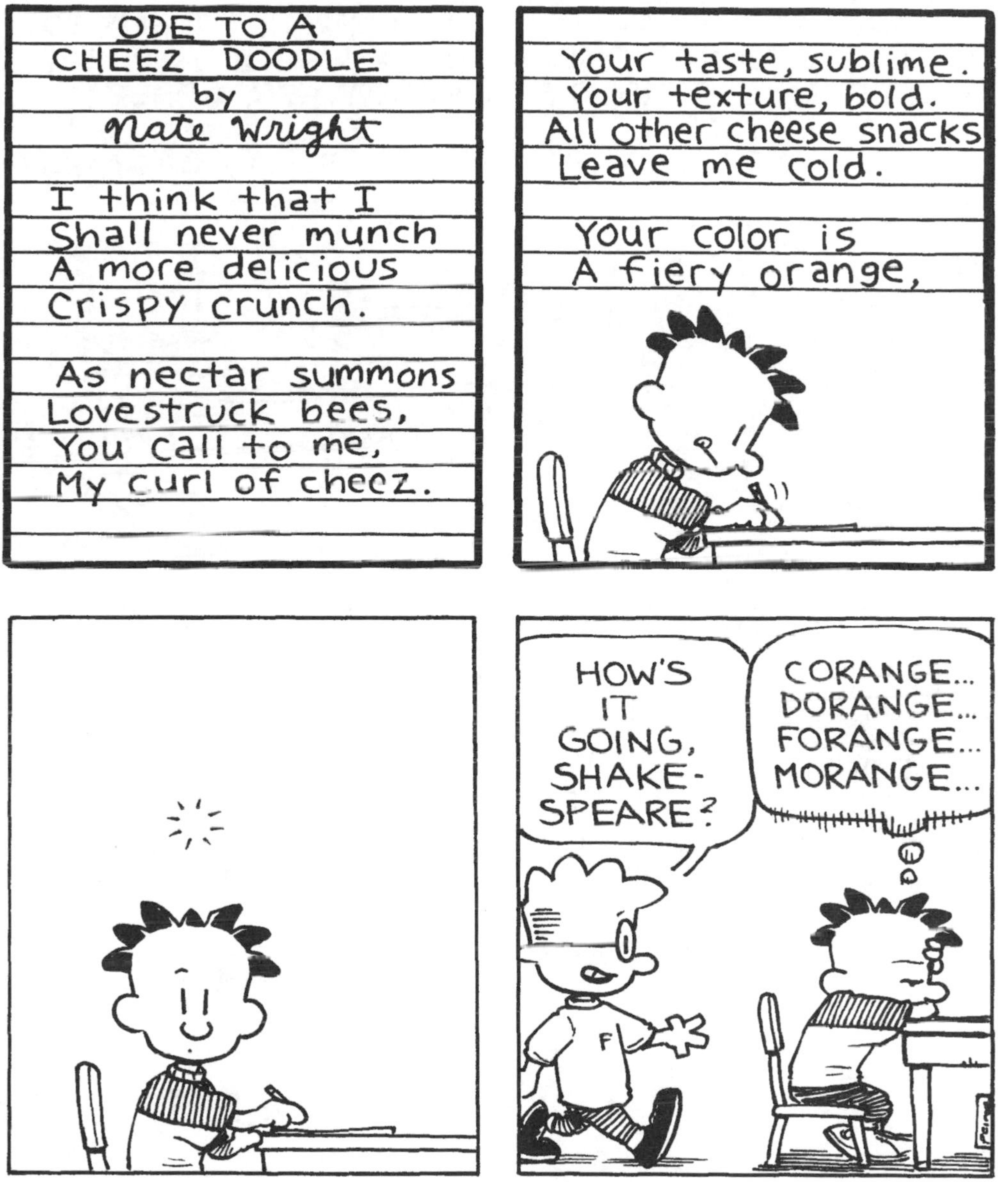
ODE TO A CHEEZ DOODLE
by
Nate Wright
I think that I
Shall never munch
A more delicious
Crispy crunch.
As nectar summons
Lovestruck bees,
You call to me,
My curl of cheez.
Your taste, sublime.
Your texture, bold.
All other cheese snacks
Leave me cold.
Your color is
A fiery orange,
HOW'S IT GOING, SHAKE-SPEARE?
CORANGE... DORANGE... FORANGE... MORANGE...

THANK YOU, GINA! WE'RE HEARING SOME WONDERFUL POEMS ON THE THEME OF LOVE, AREN'T WE, CLASS?

CLAP CLAP CLAP CLAP

WONDERFUL POEMS?? GINA WROTE A POEM ABOUT HER **GERBIL**! I MEAN, COME ON! THAT IS SO **SHALLOW**!

NATE, YOU'RE ABOUT TO GO UP THERE AND READ A POEM ABOUT **CHEEZ DOODLES**!

EXACTLY! CHEEZ DOODLES ARE **DEEP**!

THERE'S DEEP, AND THEN THERE'S UNFATHOMABLE.

NICE TRY, GINA. WE CAN'T ALL BE HEROES.

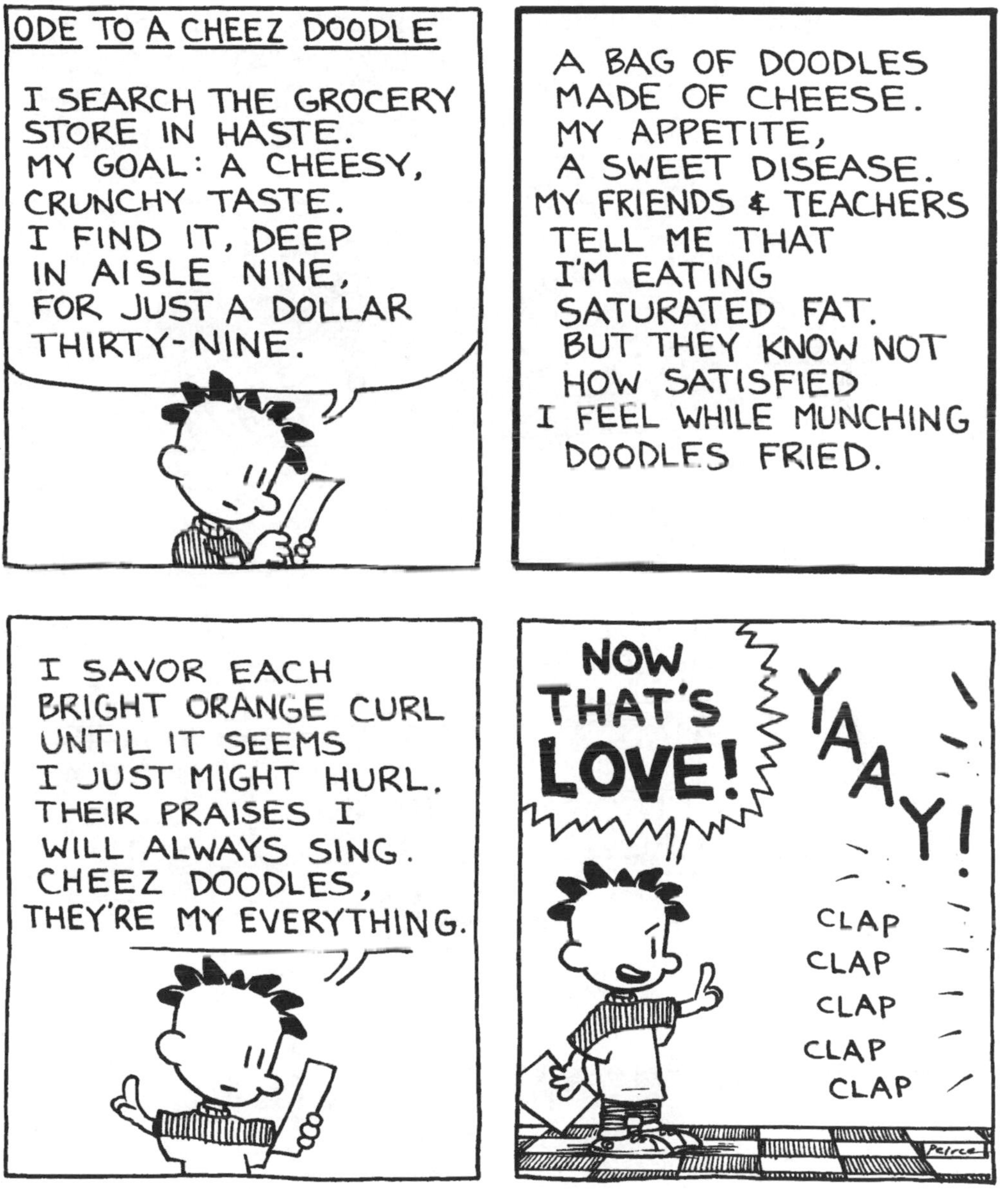
ODE TO A CHEEZ DOODLE
I SEARCH THE GROCERY STORE IN HASTE. MY GOAL: A CHEESY, CRUNCHY TASTE. I FIND IT, DEEP IN AISLE NINE, FOR JUST A DOLLAR THIRTY-NINE.
A BAG OF DOODLES MADE OF CHEESE. MY APPETITE, A SWEET DISEASE. MY FRIENDS & TEACHERS TELL ME THAT I'M EATING SATURATED FAT. BUT THEY KNOW NOT HOW SATISFIED I FEEL WHILE MUNCHING DOODLES FRIED.
I SAVOR EACH BRIGHT ORANGE CURL UNTIL IT SEEMS I JUST MIGHT HURL. THEIR PRAISES I WILL ALWAYS SING. CHEEZ DOODLES, THEY'RE MY EVERYTHING.
NOW THAT'S LOVE!
YAAAY!
CLAP
CLAP
CLAP
CLAP
CLAP
Peirce

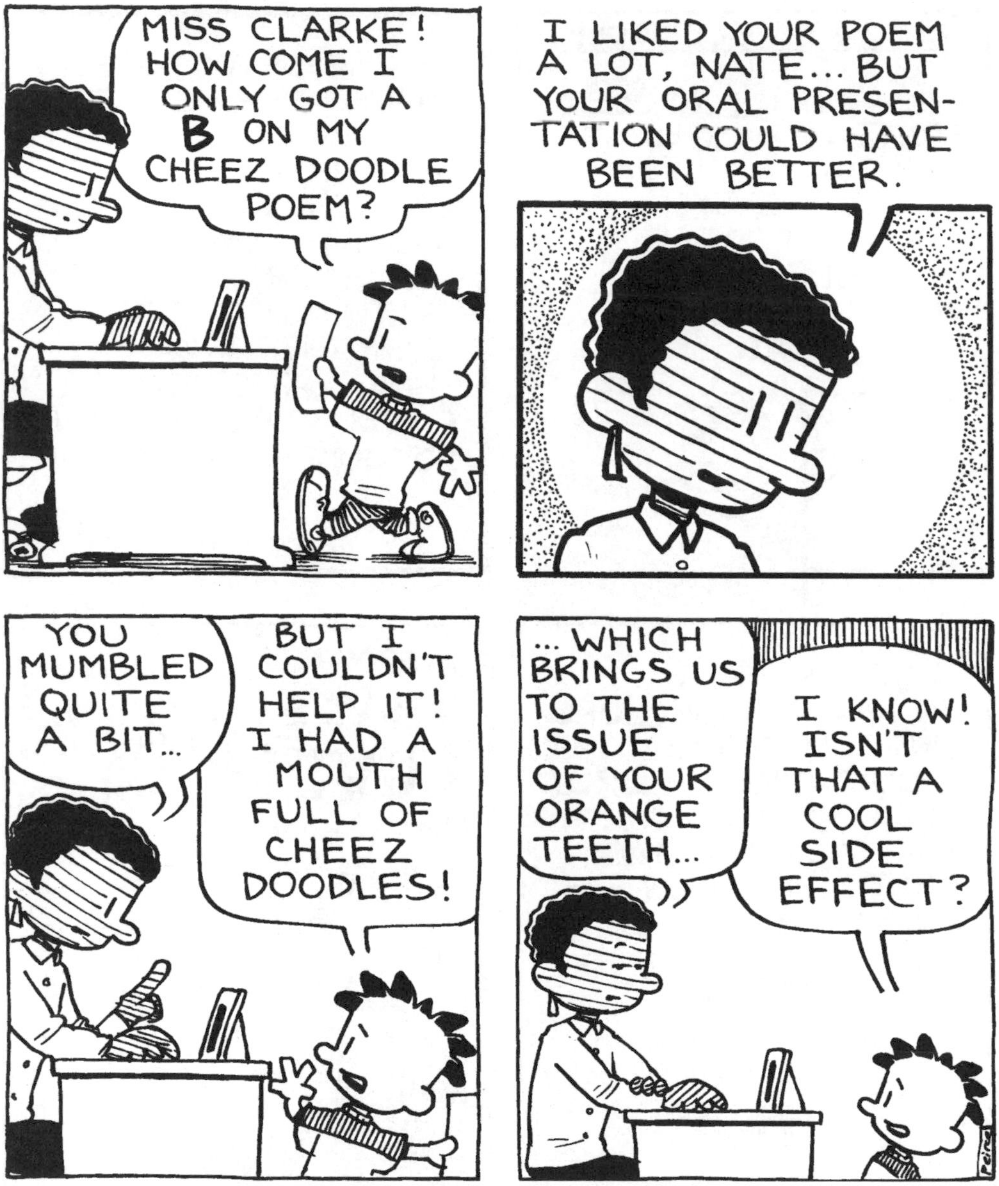
MISS CLARKE! HOW COME I ONLY GOT A B ON MY CHEEZ DOODLE POEM?
I LIKED YOUR POEM A LOT, NATE... BUT YOUR ORAL PRESENTATION COULD HAVE BEEN BETTER.
YOU MUMBLED QUITE A BIT...
BUT I COULDN'T HELP IT! I HAD A MOUTH FULL OF CHEEZ DOODLES!
...WHICH BRINGS US TO THE ISSUE OF YOUR ORANGE TEETH...
I KNOW! ISN'T THAT A COOL SIDE EFFECT?
Peirce

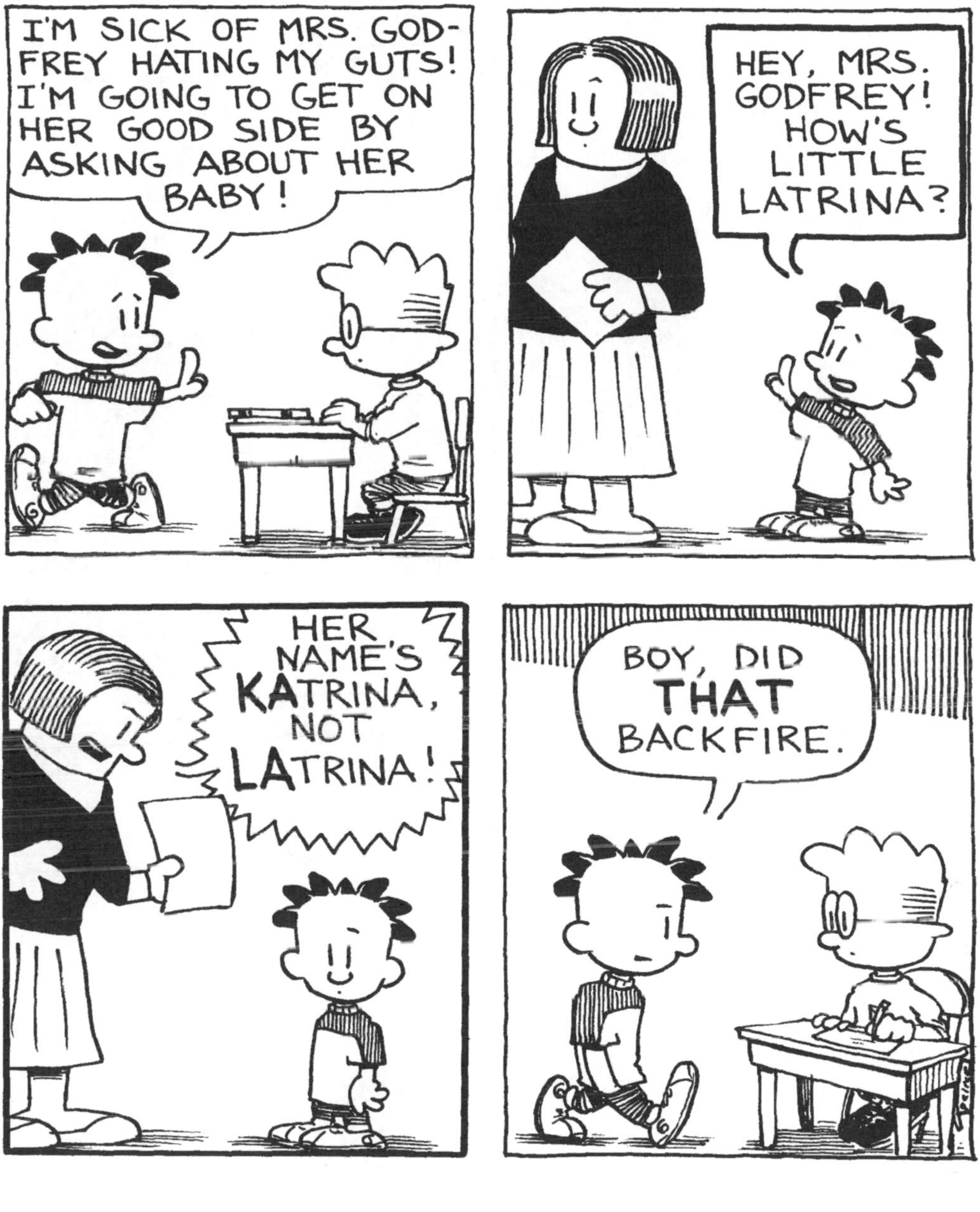
I'M SICK OF MRS. GOD-FREY HATING MY GUTS! I'M GOING TO GET ON HER GOOD SIDE BY ASKING ABOUT HER BABY!
HEY, MRS. GODFREY! HOW'S LITTLE LATRINA?
HER NAME'S KATRINA, NOT LATRINA!
BOY, DID THAT BACKFIRE.

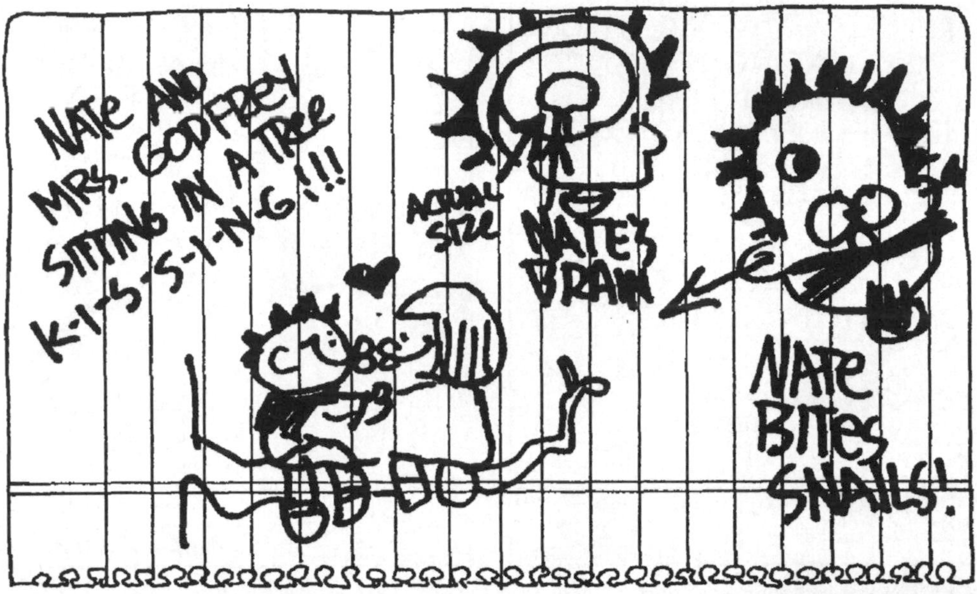

NATE AND MRS. GODFREY SITTING IN A TREE K-I-S-S-I-N-G!!!
ACTUAL SIZE
NATE'S BRAIN
NATE BITES SNAILS!

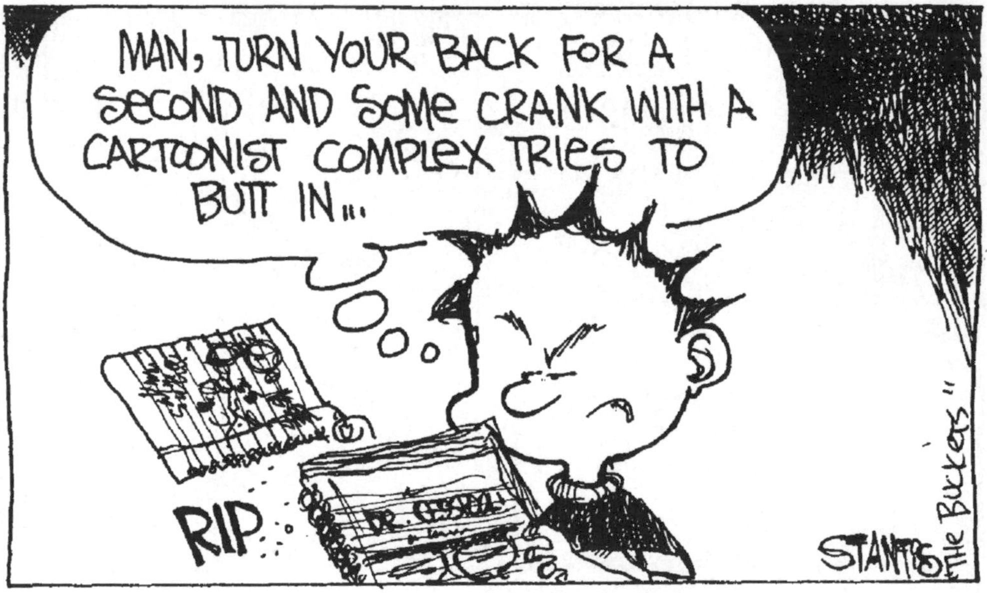

MAN, TURN YOUR BACK FOR A SECOND AND SOME CRANK WITH A CARTOONIST COMPLEX TRIES TO BUTT IN...
RIP
STAN'85
"THE BUCKETS"

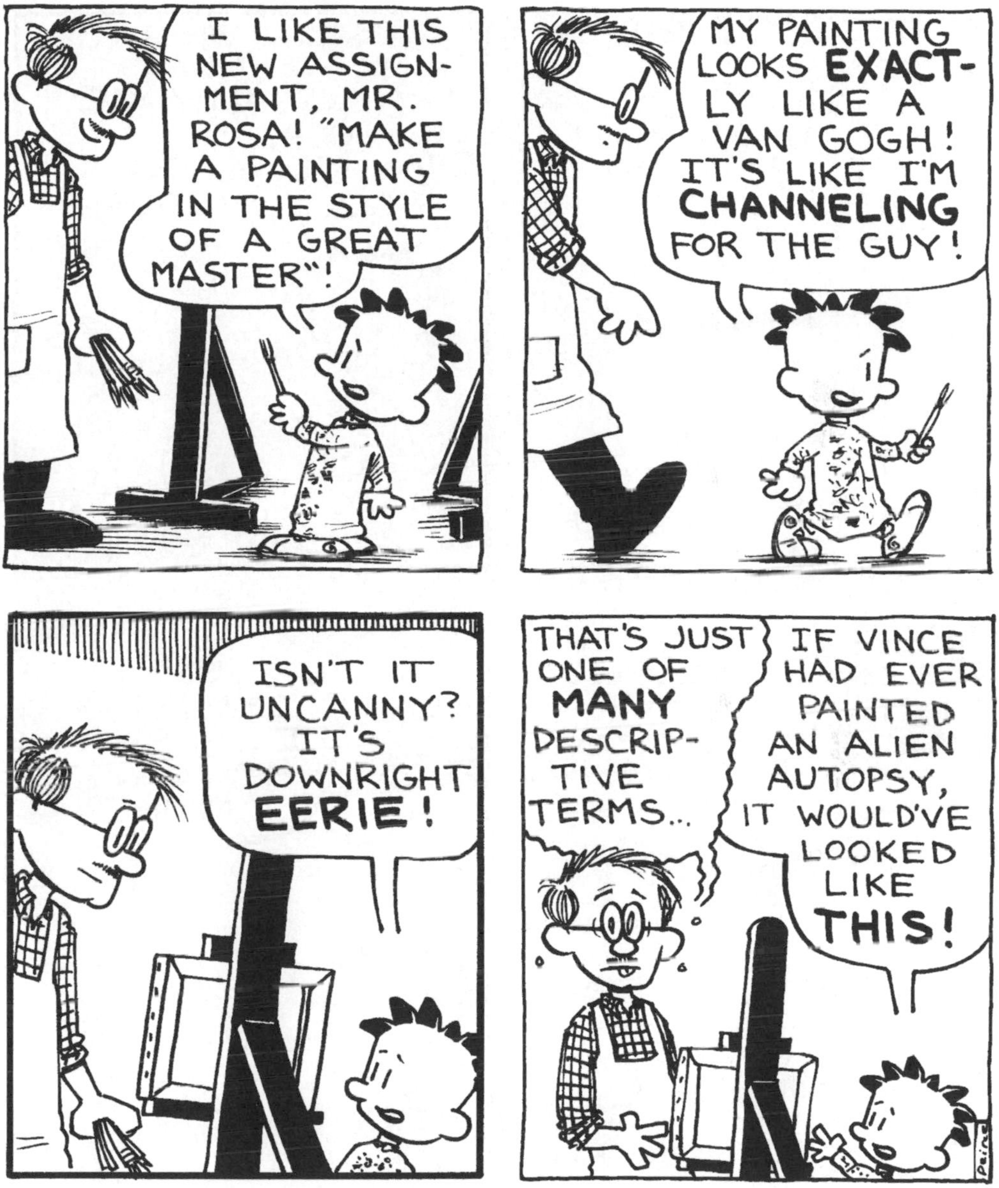
I LIKE THIS NEW ASSIGNMENT, MR. ROSA! "MAKE A PAINTING IN THE STYLE OF A GREAT MASTER"!
MY PAINTING LOOKS **EXACTLY** LIKE A VAN GOGH! IT'S LIKE I'M **CHANNELING** FOR THE GUY!
ISN'T IT UNCANNY? IT'S DOWNRIGHT **EERIE**!
THAT'S JUST ONE OF **MANY** DESCRIPTIVE TERMS...
IF VINCE HAD EVER PAINTED AN ALIEN AUTOPSY, IT WOULD'VE LOOKED LIKE **THIS**!
Peirce

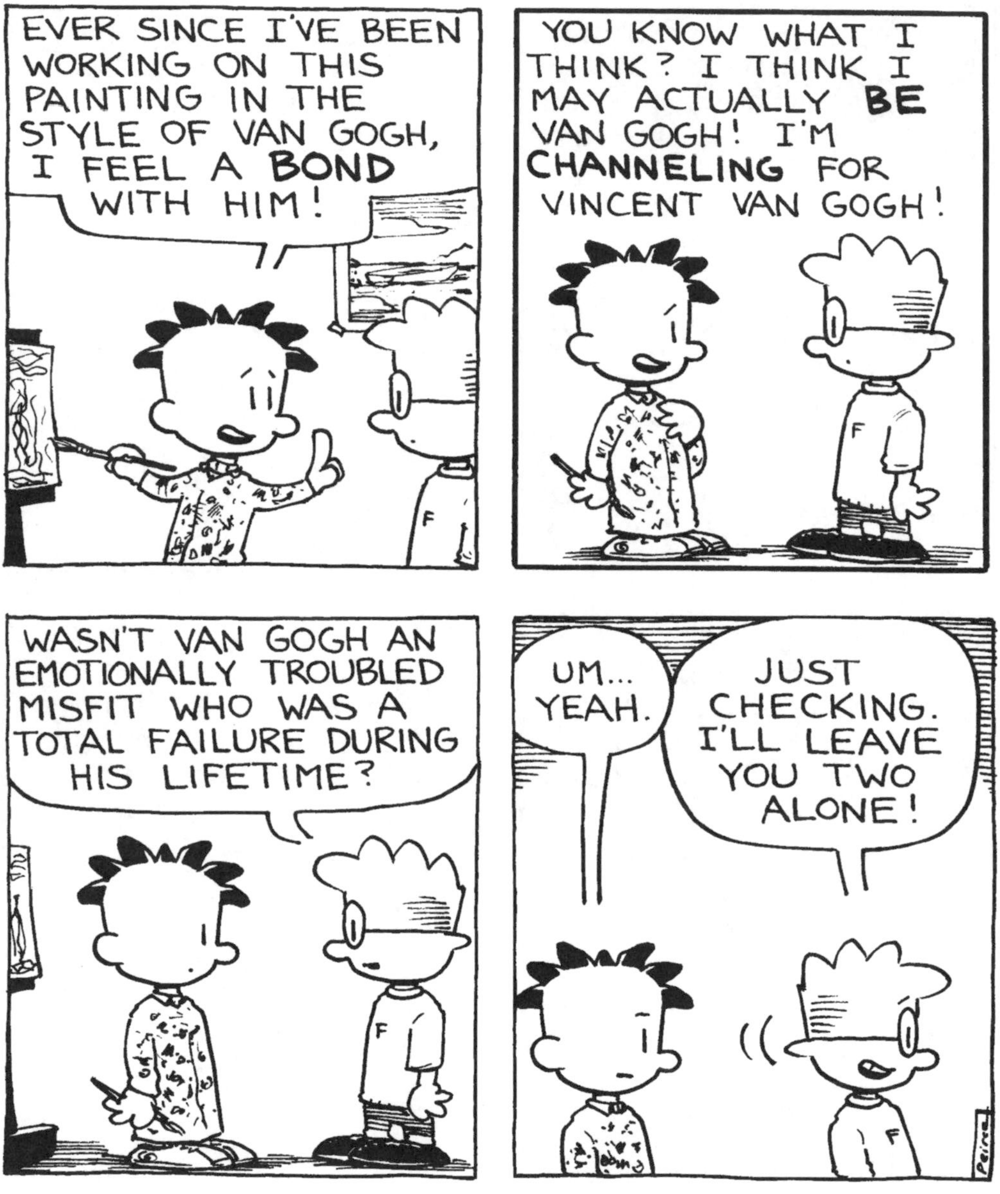
EVER SINCE I'VE BEEN WORKING ON THIS PAINTING IN THE STYLE OF VAN GOGH, I FEEL A **BOND** WITH HIM!
YOU KNOW WHAT I THINK? I THINK I MAY ACTUALLY **BE** VAN GOGH! I'M **CHANNELING** FOR VINCENT VAN GOGH!
WASN'T VAN GOGH AN EMOTIONALLY TROUBLED MISFIT WHO WAS A TOTAL FAILURE DURING HIS LIFETIME?
UM... YEAH.
JUST CHECKING. I'LL LEAVE YOU TWO ALONE!
Peirce

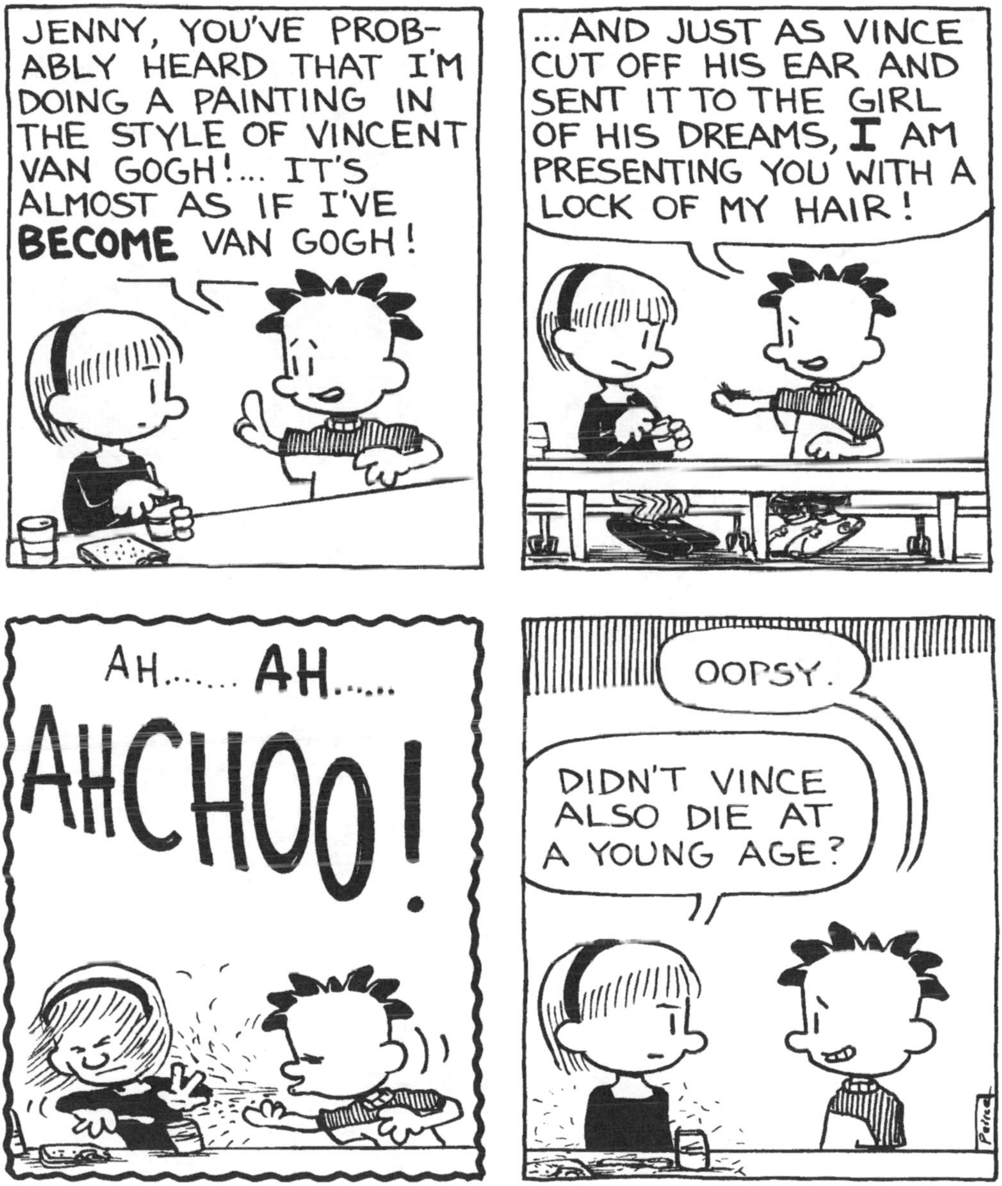
JENNY, YOU'VE PROBABLY HEARD THAT I'M DOING A PAINTING IN THE STYLE OF VINCENT VAN GOGH!... IT'S ALMOST AS IF I'VE **BECOME** VAN GOGH!
...AND JUST AS VINCE CUT OFF HIS EAR AND SENT IT TO THE GIRL OF HIS DREAMS, **I** AM PRESENTING YOU WITH A LOCK OF MY HAIR!
AH...... AH.....
AHCHOO!
OOPSY.
DIDN'T VINCE ALSO DIE AT A YOUNG AGE?
Peirce

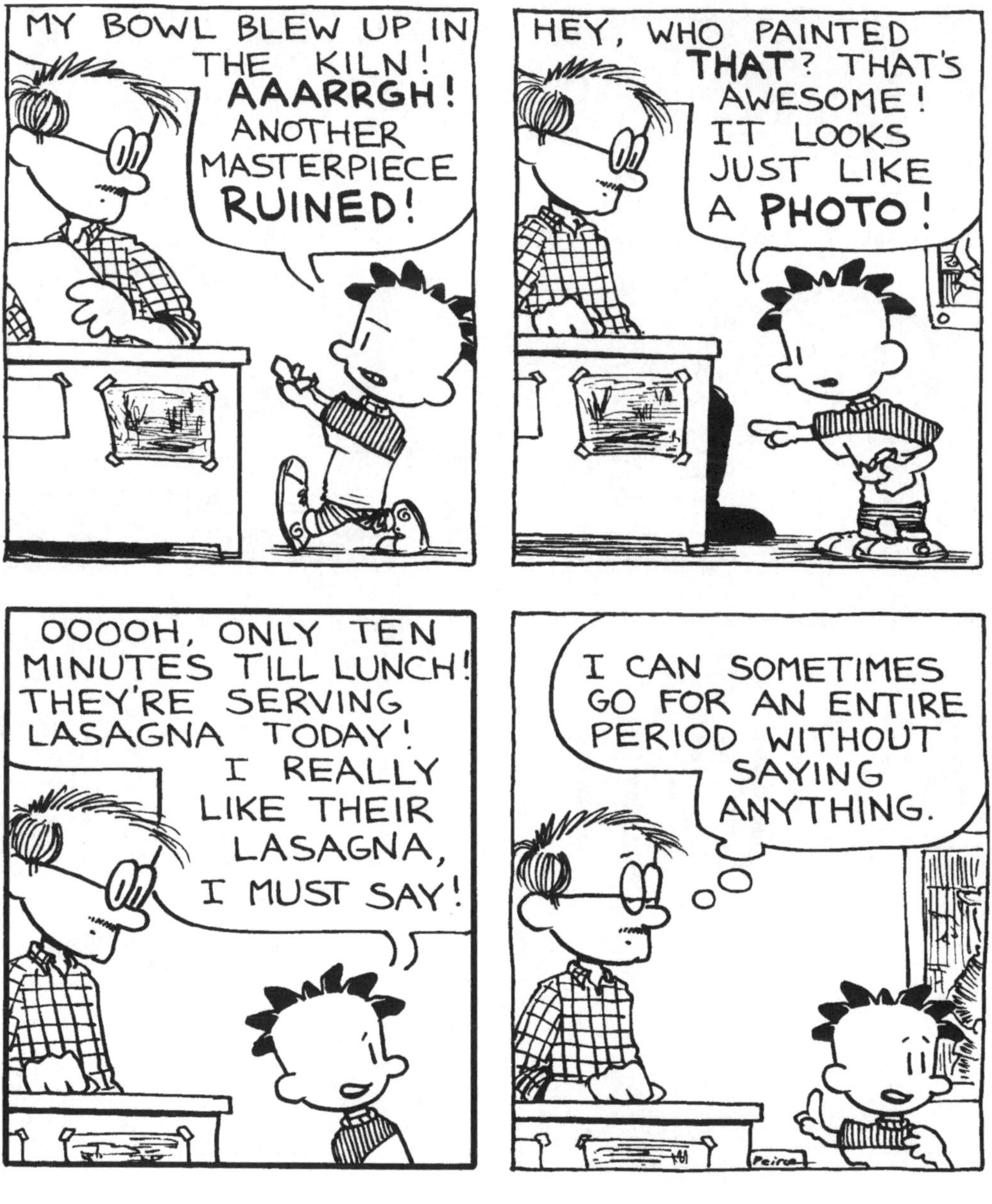
MY BOWL BLEW UP IN THE KILN! **AAARRGH!** ANOTHER MASTERPIECE **RUINED!**
HEY, WHO PAINTED **THAT**? THAT'S AWESOME! IT LOOKS JUST LIKE A **PHOTO**!
OOOOH, ONLY TEN MINUTES TILL LUNCH! THEY'RE SERVING LASAGNA TODAY! I REALLY LIKE THEIR LASAGNA, I MUST SAY!
I CAN SOMETIMES GO FOR AN ENTIRE PERIOD WITHOUT SAYING ANYTHING.
Peirce

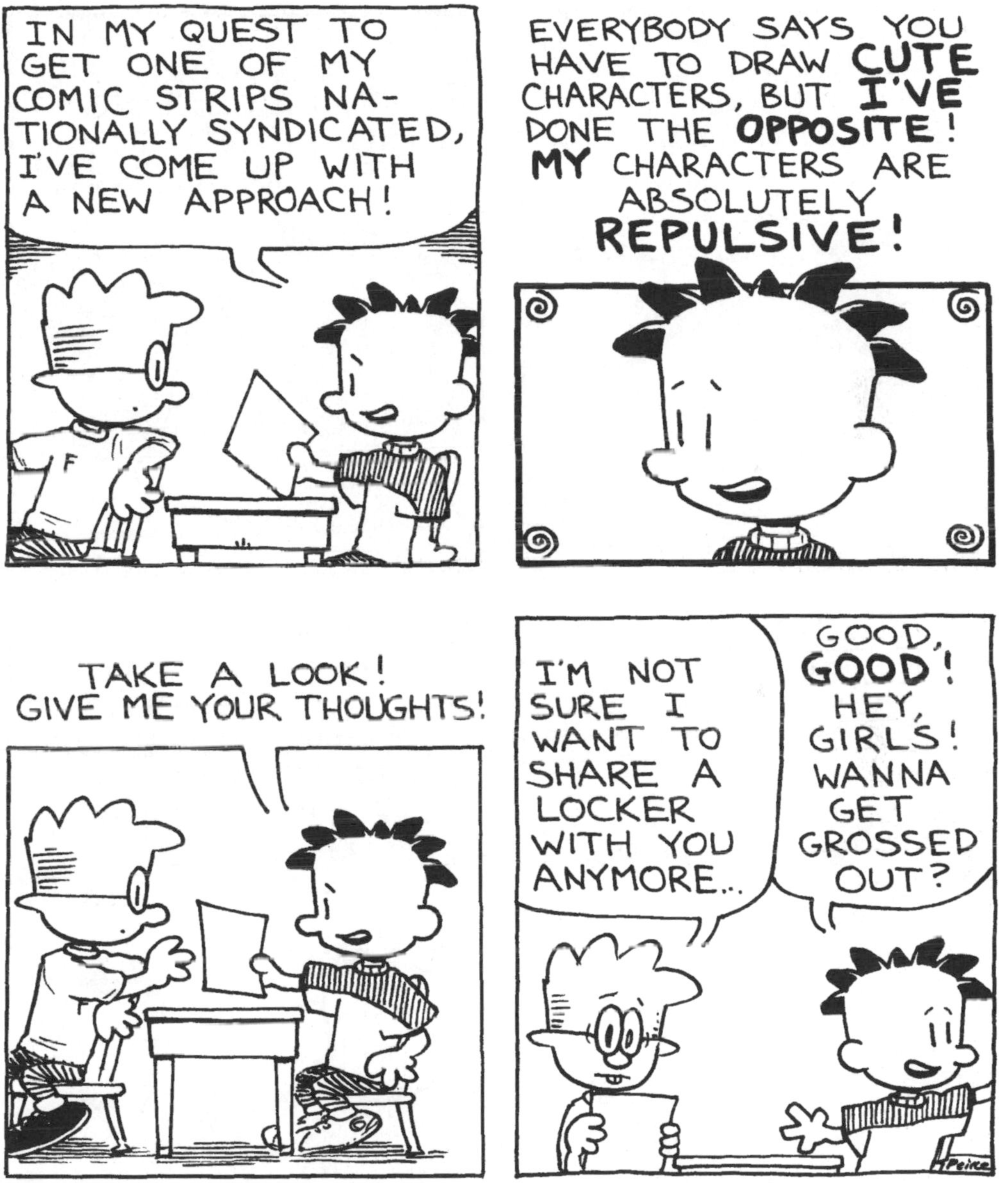
IN MY QUEST TO GET ONE OF MY COMIC STRIPS NATIONALLY SYNDICATED, I'VE COME UP WITH A NEW APPROACH!
EVERYBODY SAYS YOU HAVE TO DRAW CUTE CHARACTERS, BUT I'VE DONE THE OPPOSITE! MY CHARACTERS ARE ABSOLUTELY REPULSIVE!
TAKE A LOOK! GIVE ME YOUR THOUGHTS!
I'M NOT SURE I WANT TO SHARE A LOCKER WITH YOU ANYMORE...
GOOD, GOOD! HEY, GIRLS! WANNA GET GROSSED OUT?
Peirce

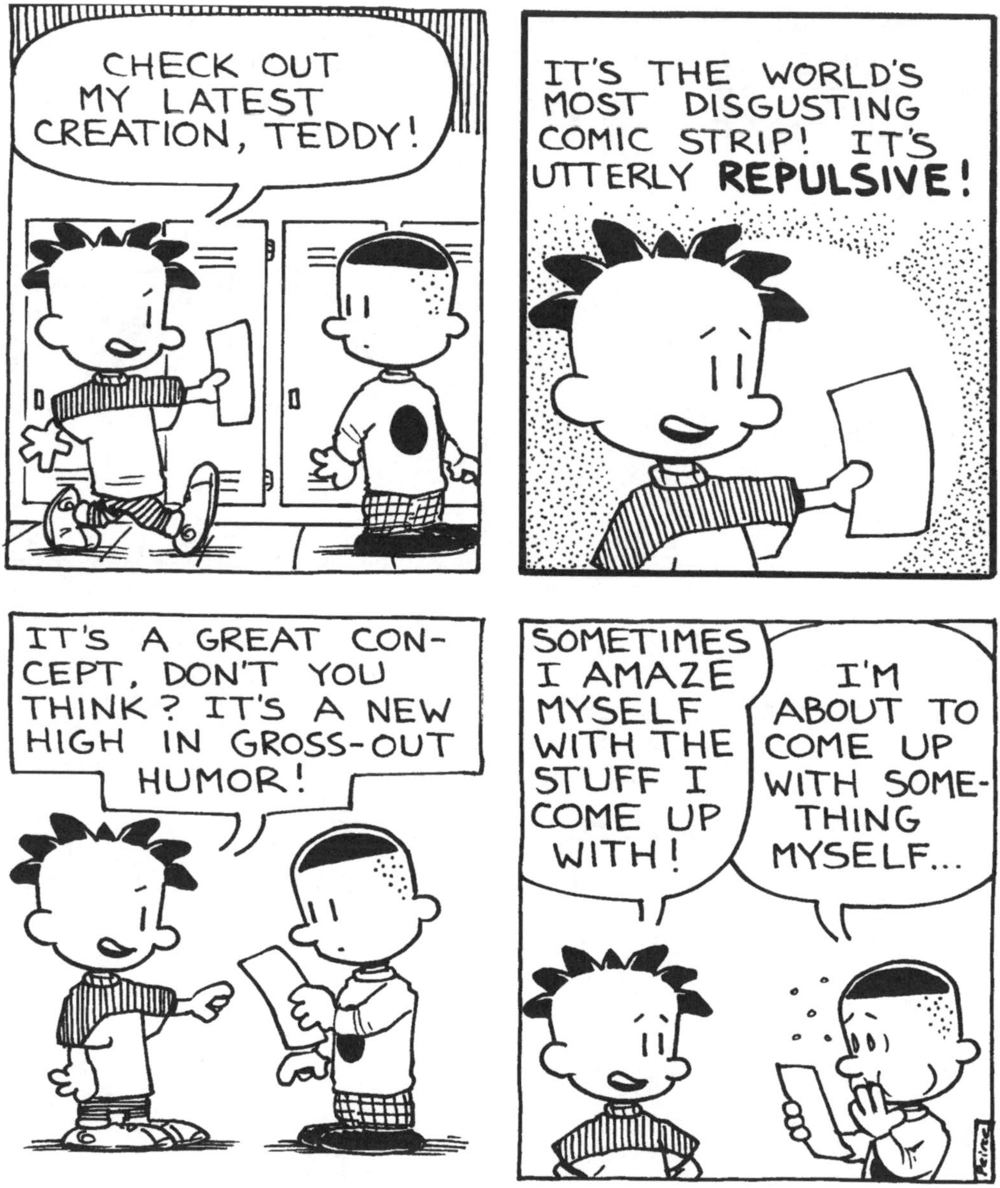
CHECK OUT MY LATEST CREATION, TEDDY!
IT'S THE WORLD'S MOST DISGUSTING COMIC STRIP! IT'S UTTERLY **REPULSIVE**!
IT'S A GREAT CONCEPT, DON'T YOU THINK? IT'S A NEW HIGH IN GROSS-OUT HUMOR!
SOMETIMES I AMAZE MYSELF WITH THE STUFF I COME UP WITH!
I'M ABOUT TO COME UP WITH SOMETHING MYSELF...

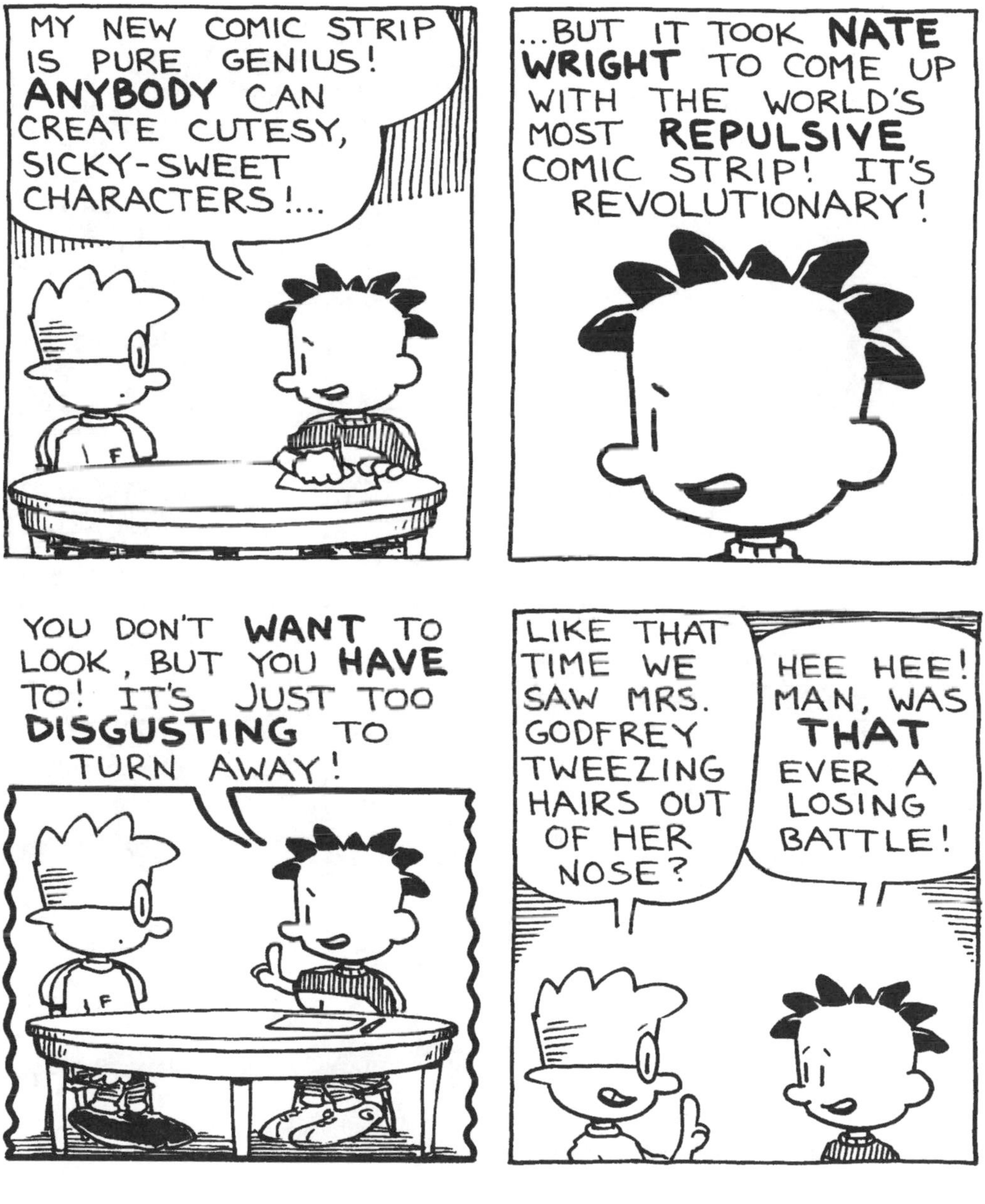
MY NEW COMIC STRIP IS PURE GENIUS! **ANYBODY** CAN CREATE CUTESY, SICKY-SWEET CHARACTERS!...
...BUT IT TOOK **NATE WRIGHT** TO COME UP WITH THE WORLD'S MOST **REPULSIVE** COMIC STRIP! IT'S REVOLUTIONARY!
YOU DON'T **WANT** TO LOOK, BUT YOU **HAVE** TO! IT'S JUST TOO **DISGUSTING** TO TURN AWAY!
LIKE THAT TIME WE SAW MRS. GODFREY TWEEZING HAIRS OUT OF HER NOSE?
HEE HEE! MAN, WAS **THAT** EVER A LOSING BATTLE!

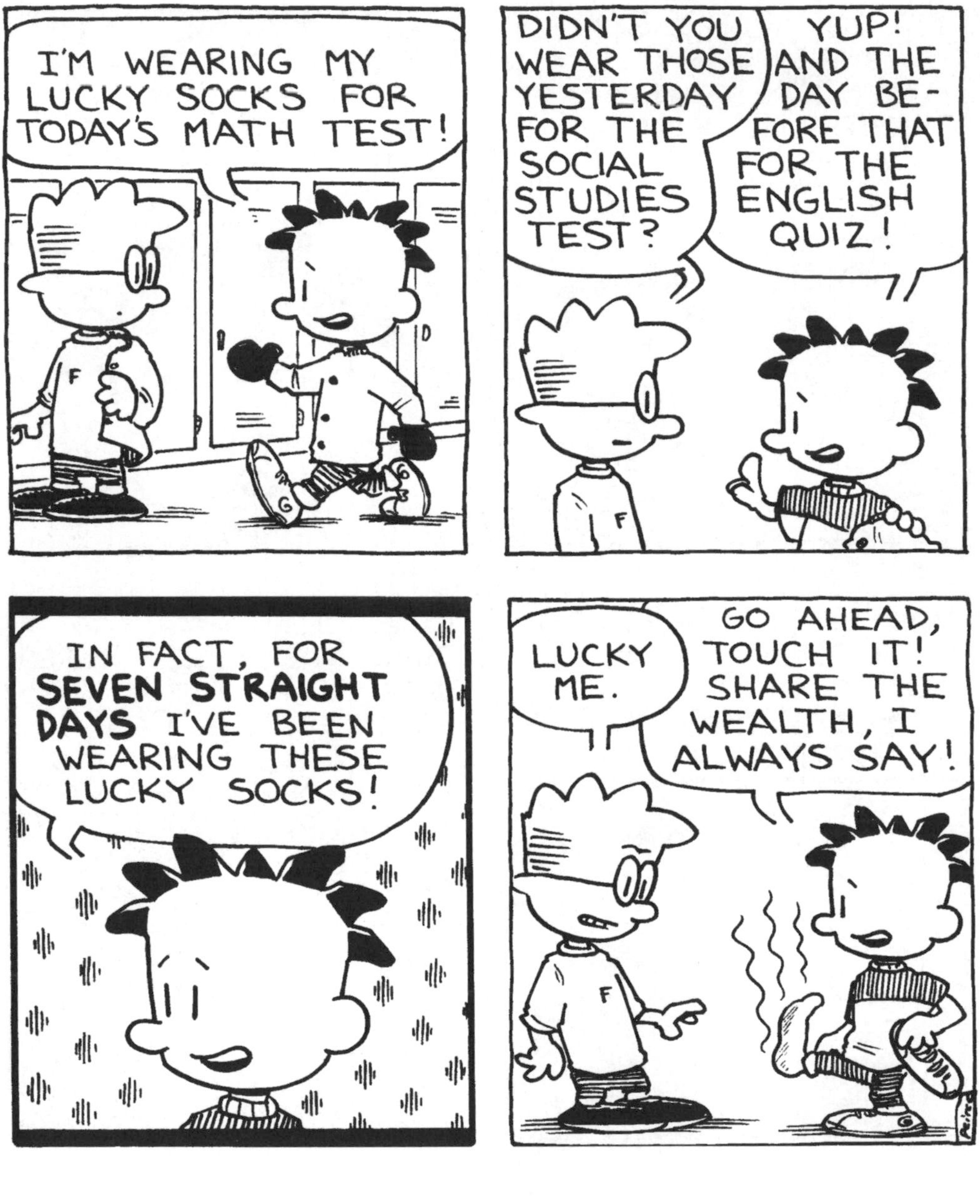
I'M WEARING MY LUCKY SOCKS FOR TODAY'S MATH TEST!
DIDN'T YOU WEAR THOSE YESTERDAY FOR THE SOCIAL STUDIES TEST?
YUP! AND THE DAY BE- FORE THAT FOR THE ENGLISH QUIZ!
IN FACT, FOR **SEVEN STRAIGHT DAYS** I'VE BEEN WEARING THESE LUCKY SOCKS!
LUCKY ME.
GO AHEAD, TOUCH IT! SHARE THE WEALTH, I ALWAYS SAY!

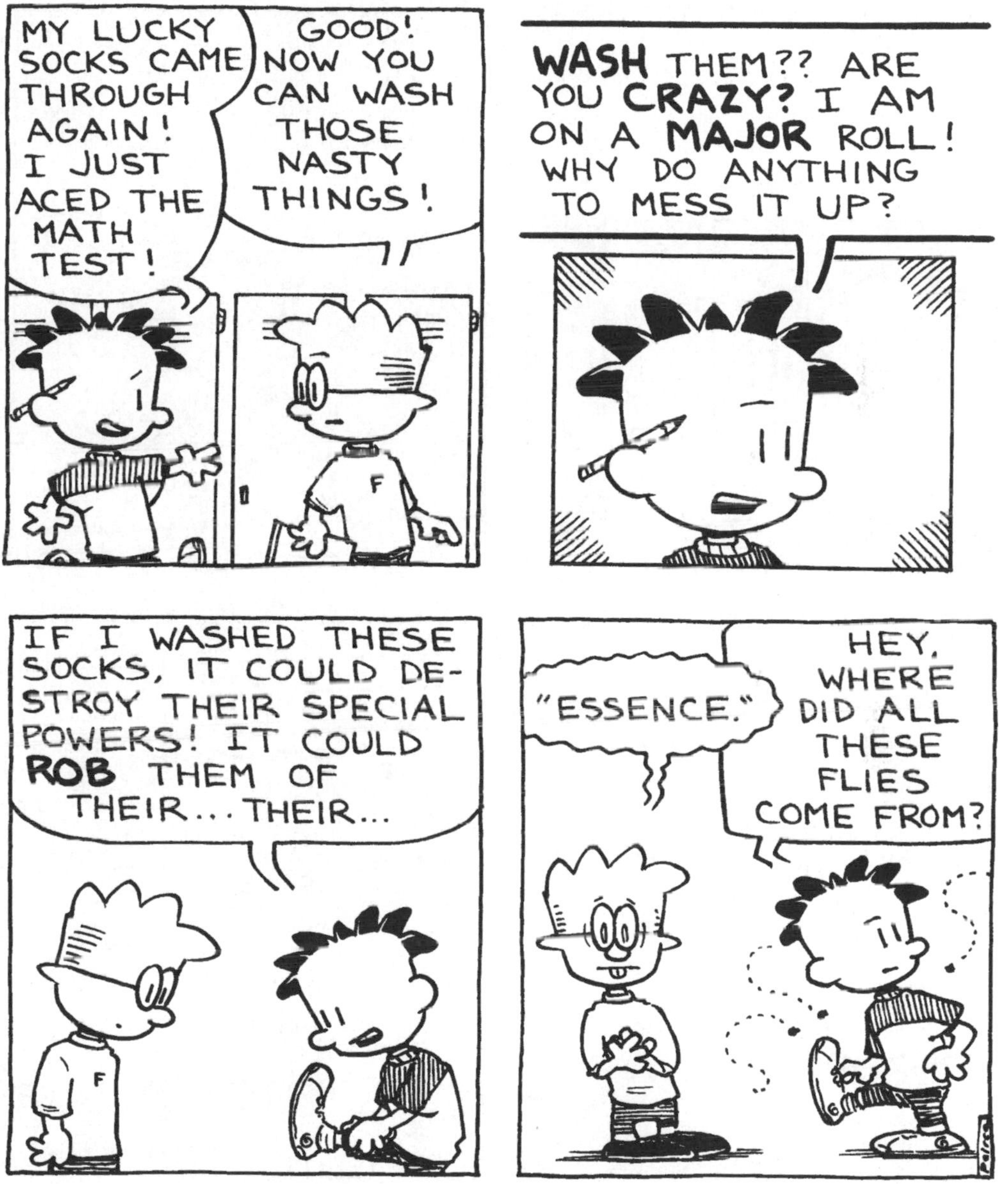
MY LUCKY SOCKS CAME THROUGH AGAIN! I JUST ACED THE MATH TEST!
GOOD! NOW YOU CAN WASH THOSE NASTY THINGS!
WASH THEM?? ARE YOU CRAZY? I AM ON A MAJOR ROLL! WHY DO ANYTHING TO MESS IT UP?
IF I WASHED THESE SOCKS, IT COULD DESTROY THEIR SPECIAL POWERS! IT COULD ROB THEM OF THEIR... THEIR...
"ESSENCE."
HEY, WHERE DID ALL THESE FLIES COME FROM?

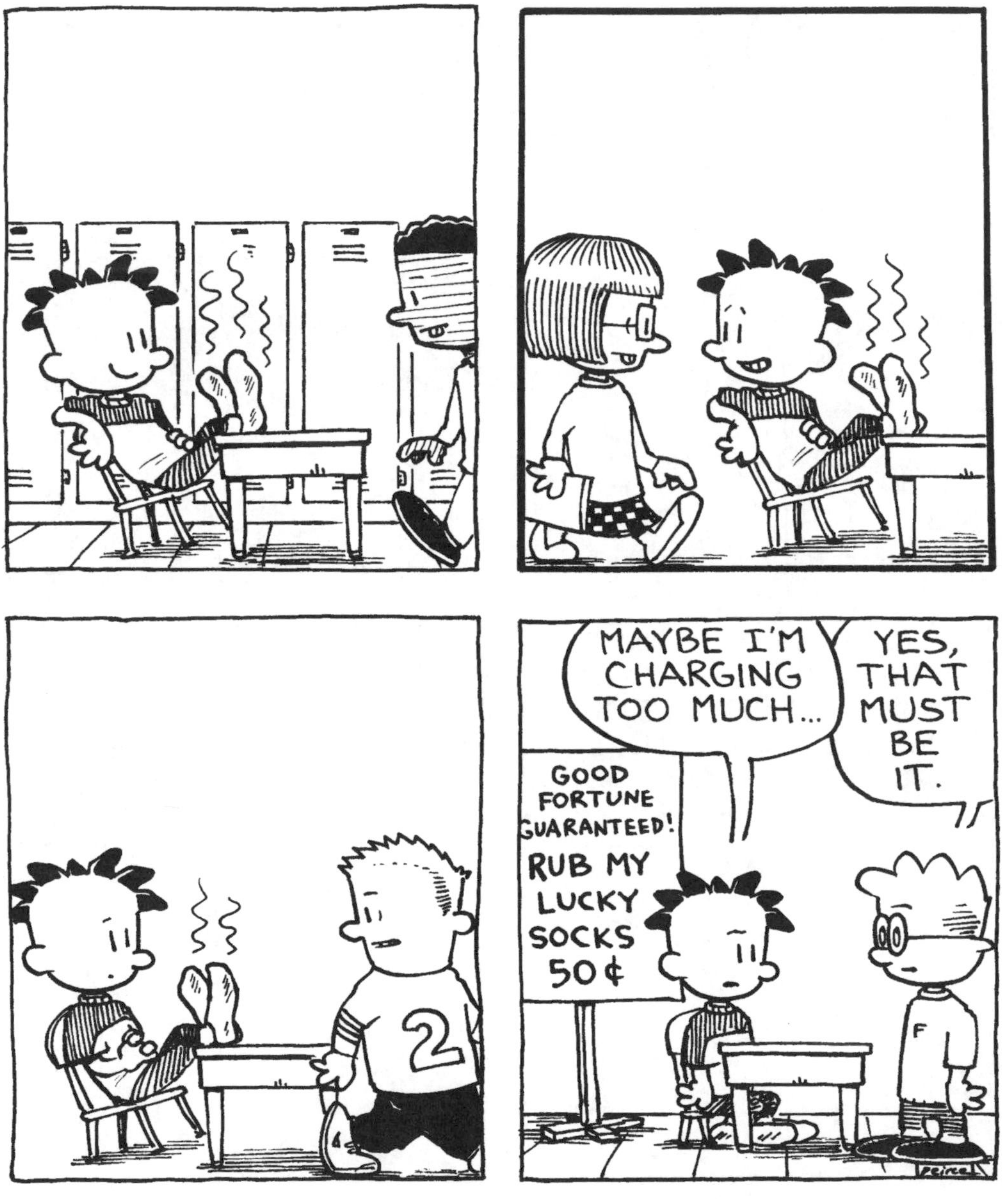
MAYBE I'M CHARGING TOO MUCH...
YES, THAT MUST BE IT.
GOOD FORTUNE GUARANTEED! RUB MY LUCKY SOCKS 50¢
peirce

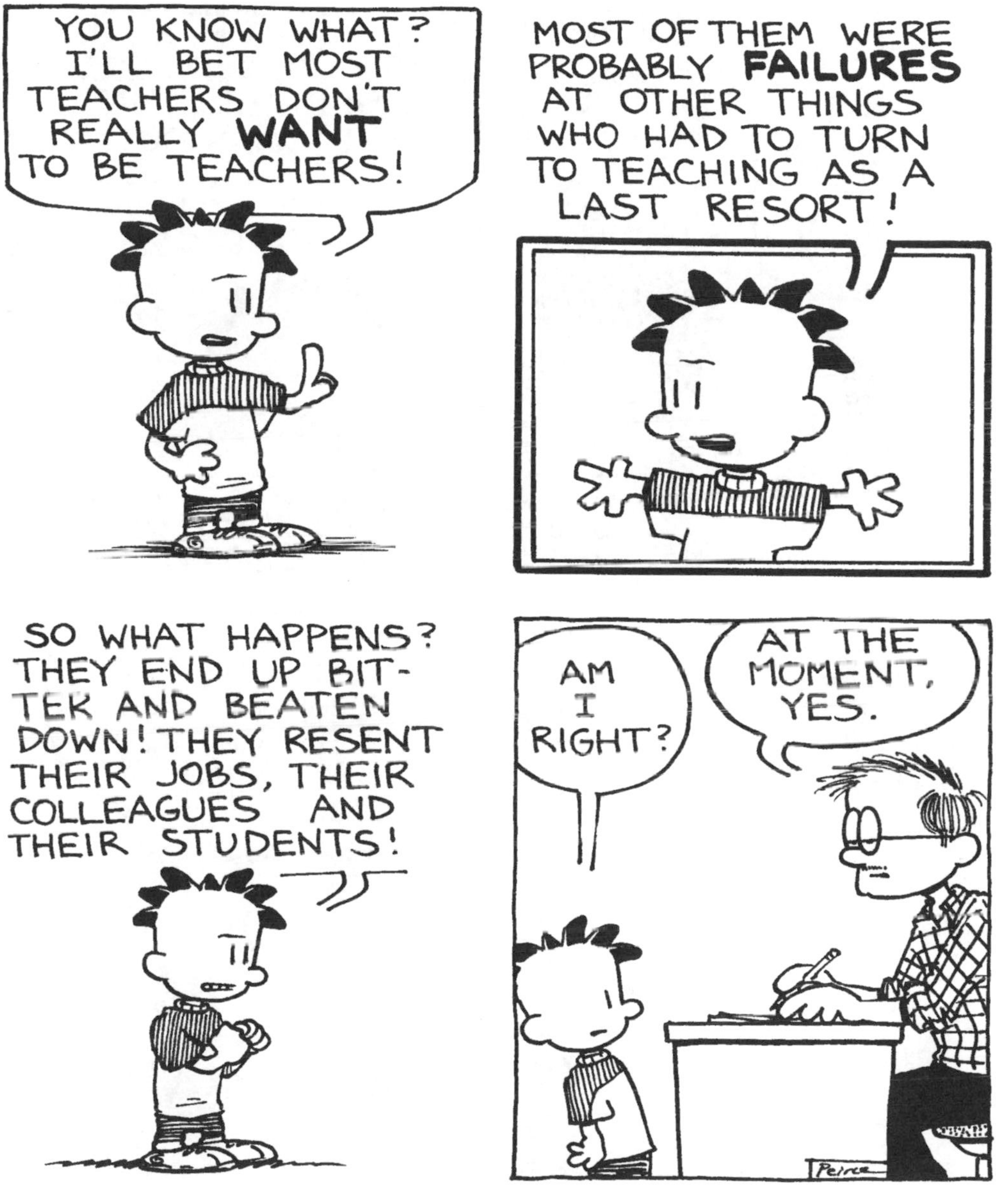
YOU KNOW WHAT? I'LL BET MOST TEACHERS DON'T REALLY **WANT** TO BE TEACHERS!
MOST OF THEM WERE PROBABLY **FAILURES** AT OTHER THINGS WHO HAD TO TURN TO TEACHING AS A LAST RESORT!
SO WHAT HAPPENS? THEY END UP BIT-TER AND BEATEN DOWN! THEY RESENT THEIR JOBS, THEIR COLLEAGUES AND THEIR STUDENTS!
AM I RIGHT?
AT THE MOMENT, YES.
Peirce

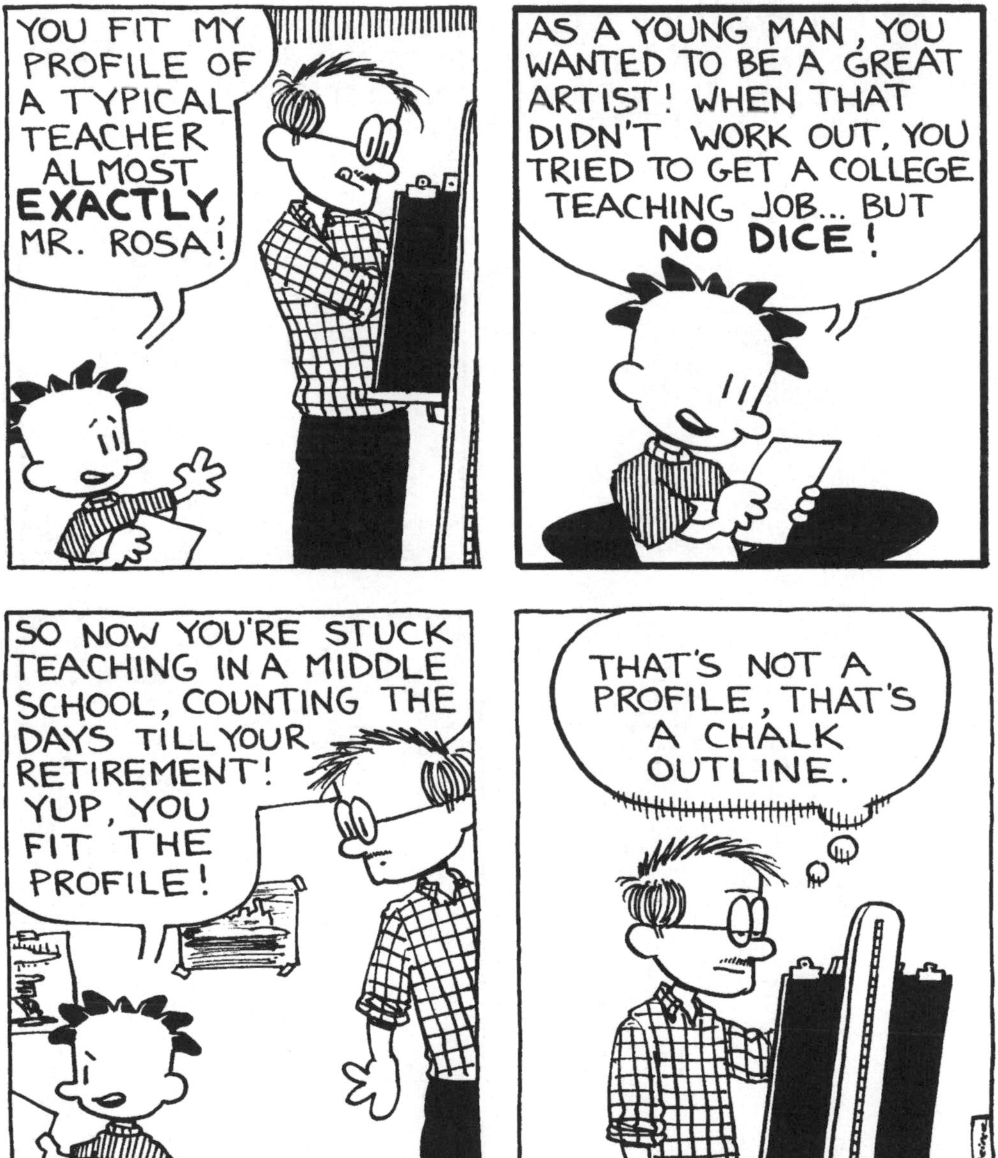

YOU FIT MY PROFILE OF A TYPICAL TEACHER ALMOST **EXACTLY**, MR. ROSA!
AS A YOUNG MAN, YOU WANTED TO BE A GREAT ARTIST! WHEN THAT DIDN'T WORK OUT, YOU TRIED TO GET A COLLEGE TEACHING JOB... BUT **NO DICE**!
SO NOW YOU'RE STUCK TEACHING IN A MIDDLE SCHOOL, COUNTING THE DAYS TILL YOUR RETIREMENT! YUP, YOU FIT THE PROFILE!
THAT'S NOT A PROFILE, THAT'S A CHALK OUTLINE.

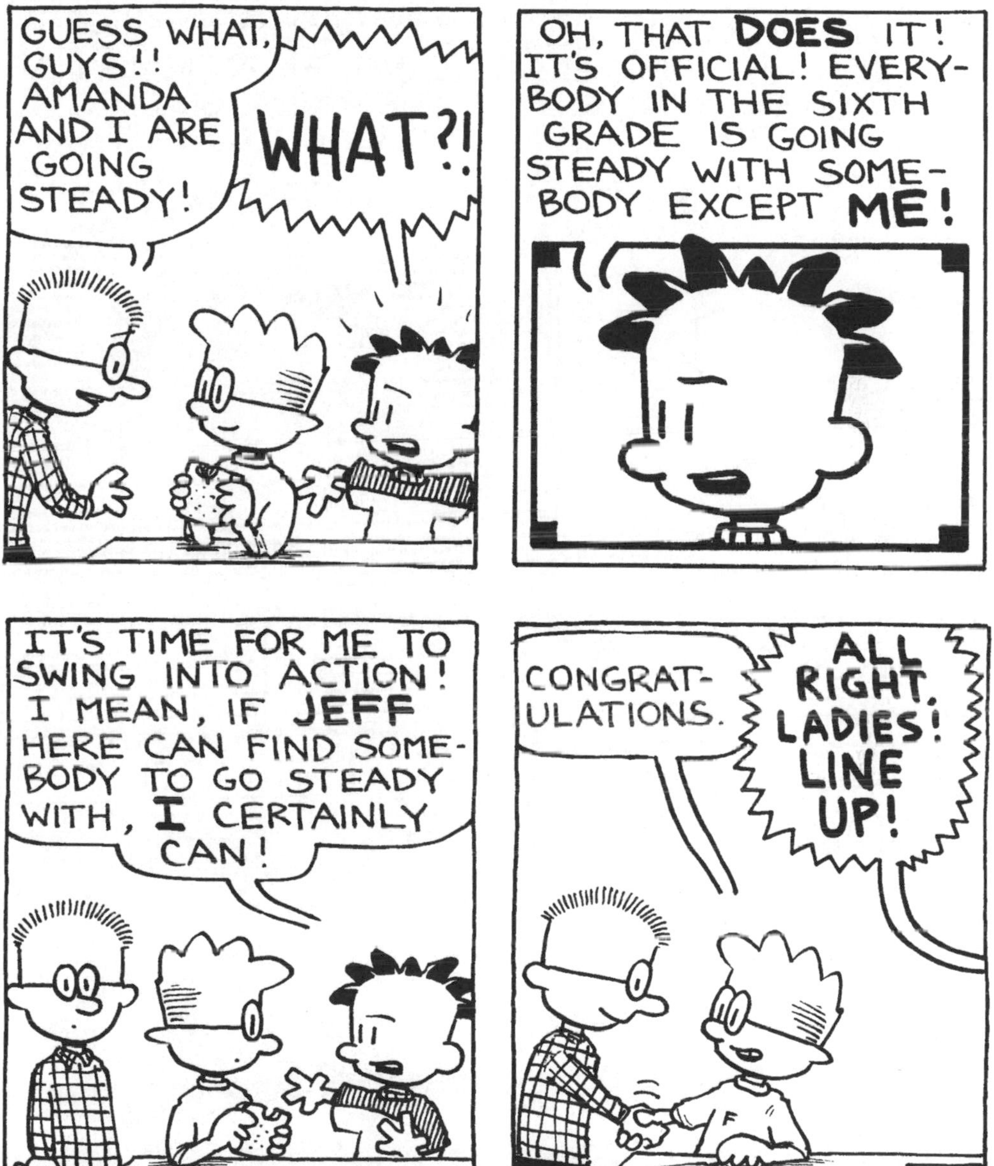
GUESS WHAT, GUYS!! AMANDA AND I ARE GOING STEADY!
WHAT?!
OH, THAT DOES IT! IT'S OFFICIAL! EVERYBODY IN THE SIXTH GRADE IS GOING STEADY WITH SOMEBODY EXCEPT ME!
IT'S TIME FOR ME TO SWING INTO ACTION! I MEAN, IF JEFF HERE CAN FIND SOMEBODY TO GO STEADY WITH, I CERTAINLY CAN!
CONGRATULATIONS.
ALL RIGHT, LADIES! LINE UP!
F
Peirce

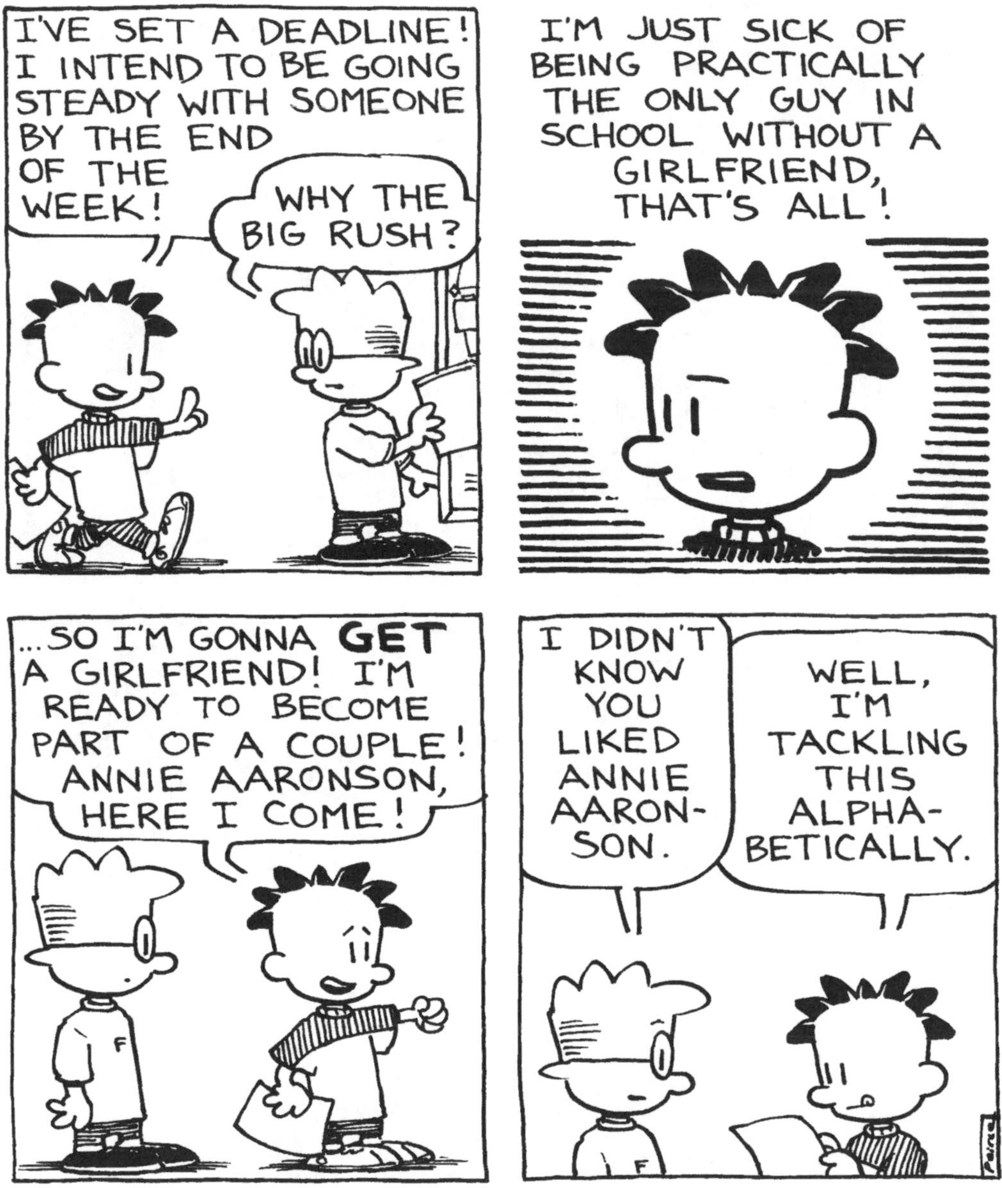
I'VE SET A DEADLINE! I INTEND TO BE GOING STEADY WITH SOMEONE BY THE END OF THE WEEK!
WHY THE BIG RUSH?
I'M JUST SICK OF BEING PRACTICALLY THE ONLY GUY IN SCHOOL WITHOUT A GIRLFRIEND, THAT'S ALL!
...SO I'M GONNA **GET** A GIRLFRIEND! I'M READY TO BECOME PART OF A COUPLE! ANNIE AARONSON, HERE I COME!
I DIDN'T KNOW YOU LIKED ANNIE AARON-SON.
WELL, I'M TACKLING THIS ALPHA-BETICALLY.
PEIRCE

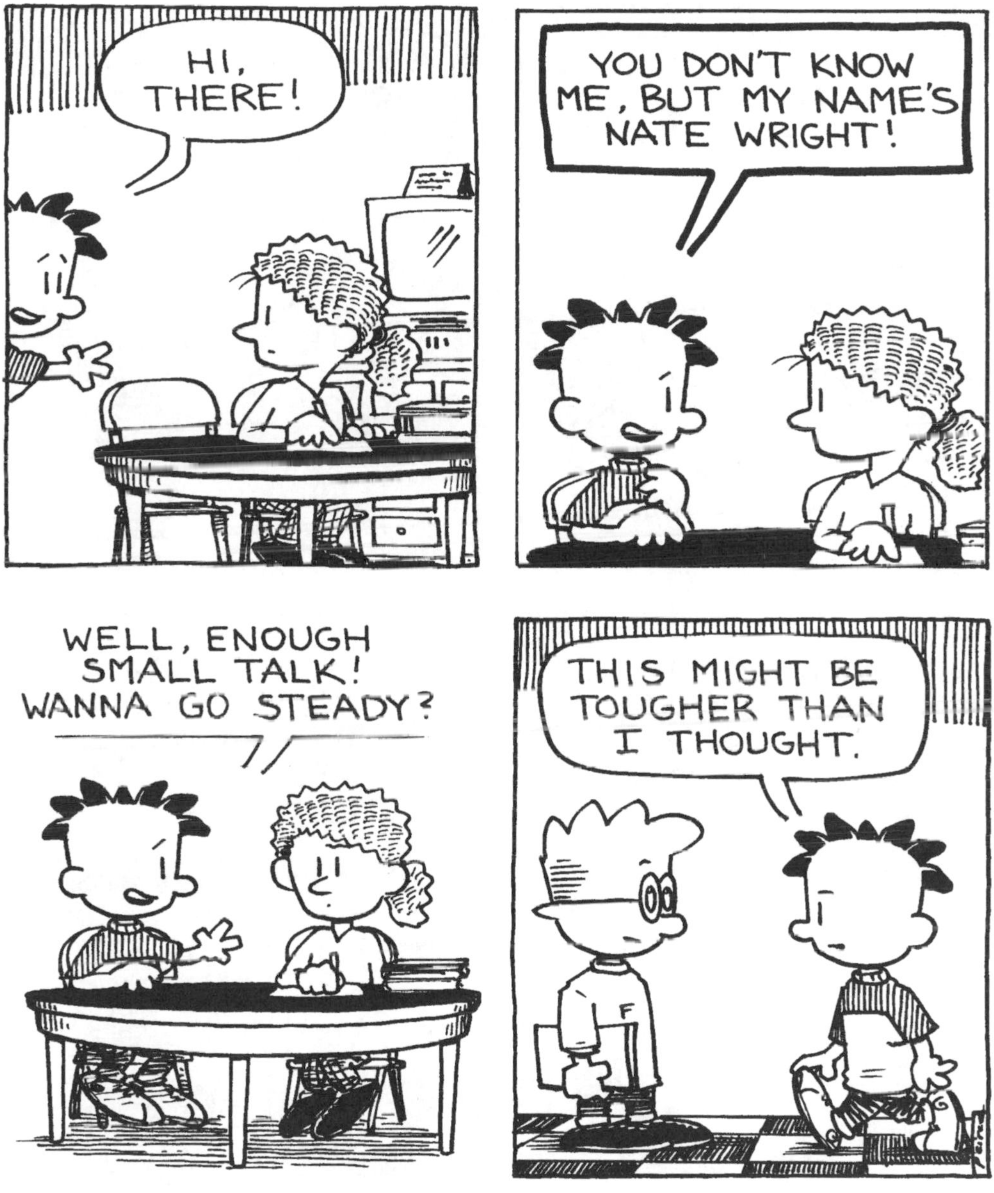
HI, THERE!
YOU DON'T KNOW ME, BUT MY NAME'S NATE WRIGHT!
WELL, ENOUGH SMALL TALK! WANNA GO STEADY?
THIS MIGHT BE TOUGHER THAN I THOUGHT.

HI! AREN'T YOU CYNTHIA PETERSON?
UH-HUH.
I'M NATE WRIGHT! HOW ABOUT YOU AND I GO STEADY?
WHY ON EARTH WOULD I WANT TO GO STEADY WITH SOMEBODY I DON'T EVEN KNOW?
SHE NEEDS SOME TIME TO THINK ABOUT IT.

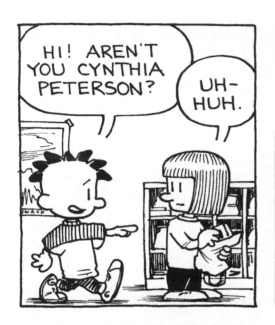

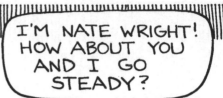

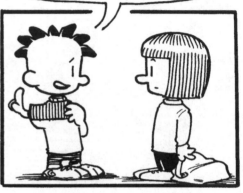

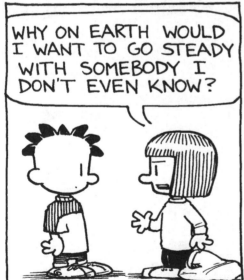

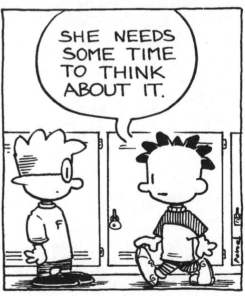

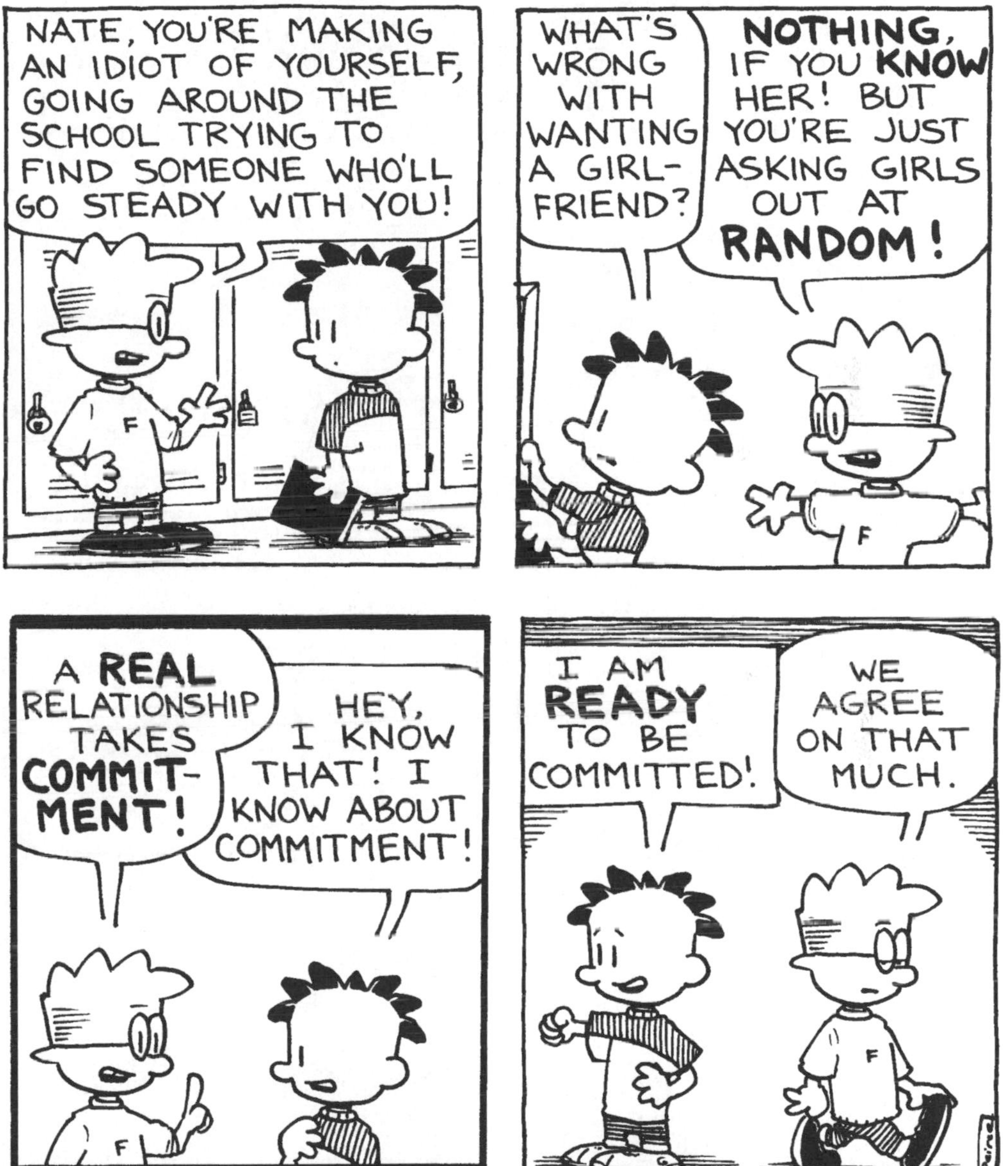
NATE, YOU'RE MAKING AN IDIOT OF YOURSELF, GOING AROUND THE SCHOOL TRYING TO FIND SOMEONE WHO'LL GO STEADY WITH YOU!
WHAT'S WRONG WITH WANTING A GIRL-FRIEND?
NOTHING, IF YOU KNOW HER! BUT YOU'RE JUST ASKING GIRLS OUT AT RANDOM!
A REAL RELATIONSHIP TAKES COMMIT-MENT!
HEY, I KNOW THAT! I KNOW ABOUT COMMITMENT!
I AM READY TO BE COMMITTED!
WE AGREE ON THAT MUCH.

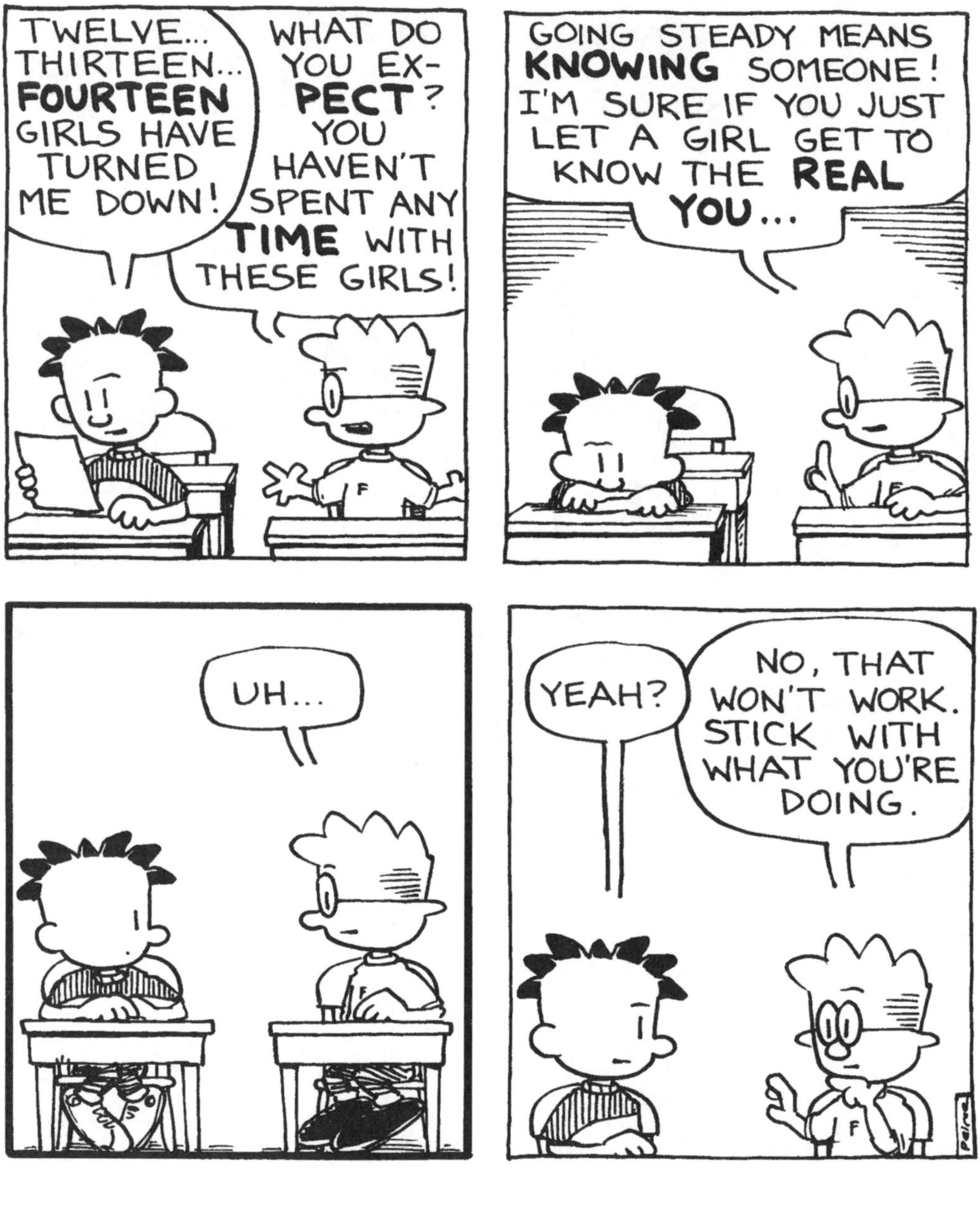
TWELVE... THIRTEEN... **FOURTEEN** GIRLS HAVE TURNED ME DOWN!
WHAT DO YOU EX-**PECT**? YOU HAVEN'T SPENT ANY **TIME** WITH THESE GIRLS!
GOING STEADY MEANS **KNOWING** SOMEONE! I'M SURE IF YOU JUST LET A GIRL GET TO KNOW THE **REAL YOU**...
UH...
YEAH?
NO, THAT WON'T WORK. STICK WITH WHAT YOU'RE DOING.
Peirce

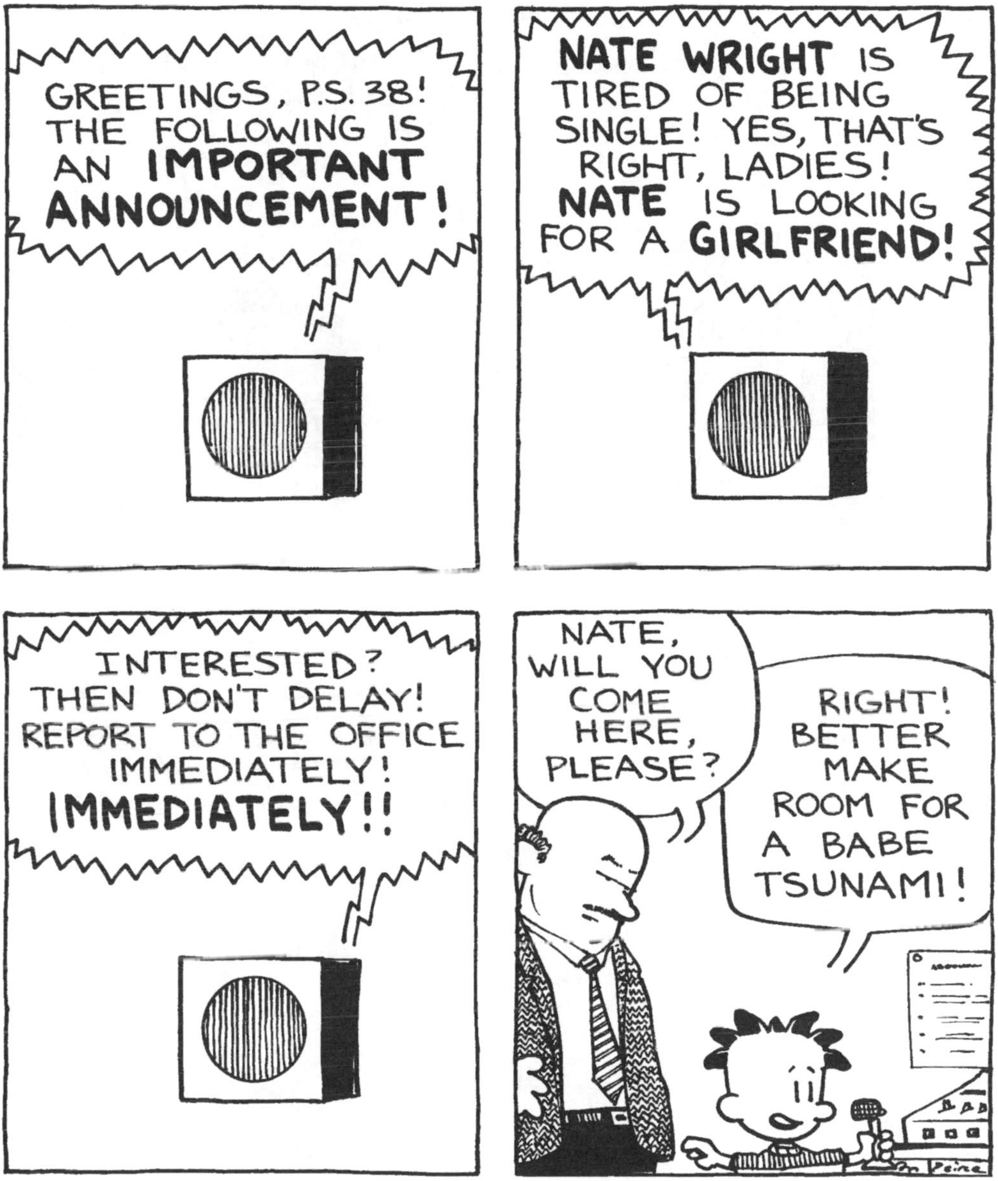
GREETINGS, P.S. 38! THE FOLLOWING IS AN IMPORTANT ANNOUNCEMENT!
NATE WRIGHT IS TIRED OF BEING SINGLE! YES, THAT'S RIGHT, LADIES! NATE IS LOOKING FOR A GIRLFRIEND!
INTERESTED? THEN DON'T DELAY! REPORT TO THE OFFICE IMMEDIATELY! IMMEDIATELY!!
NATE, WILL YOU COME HERE, PLEASE?
RIGHT! BETTER MAKE ROOM FOR A BABE TSUNAMI!

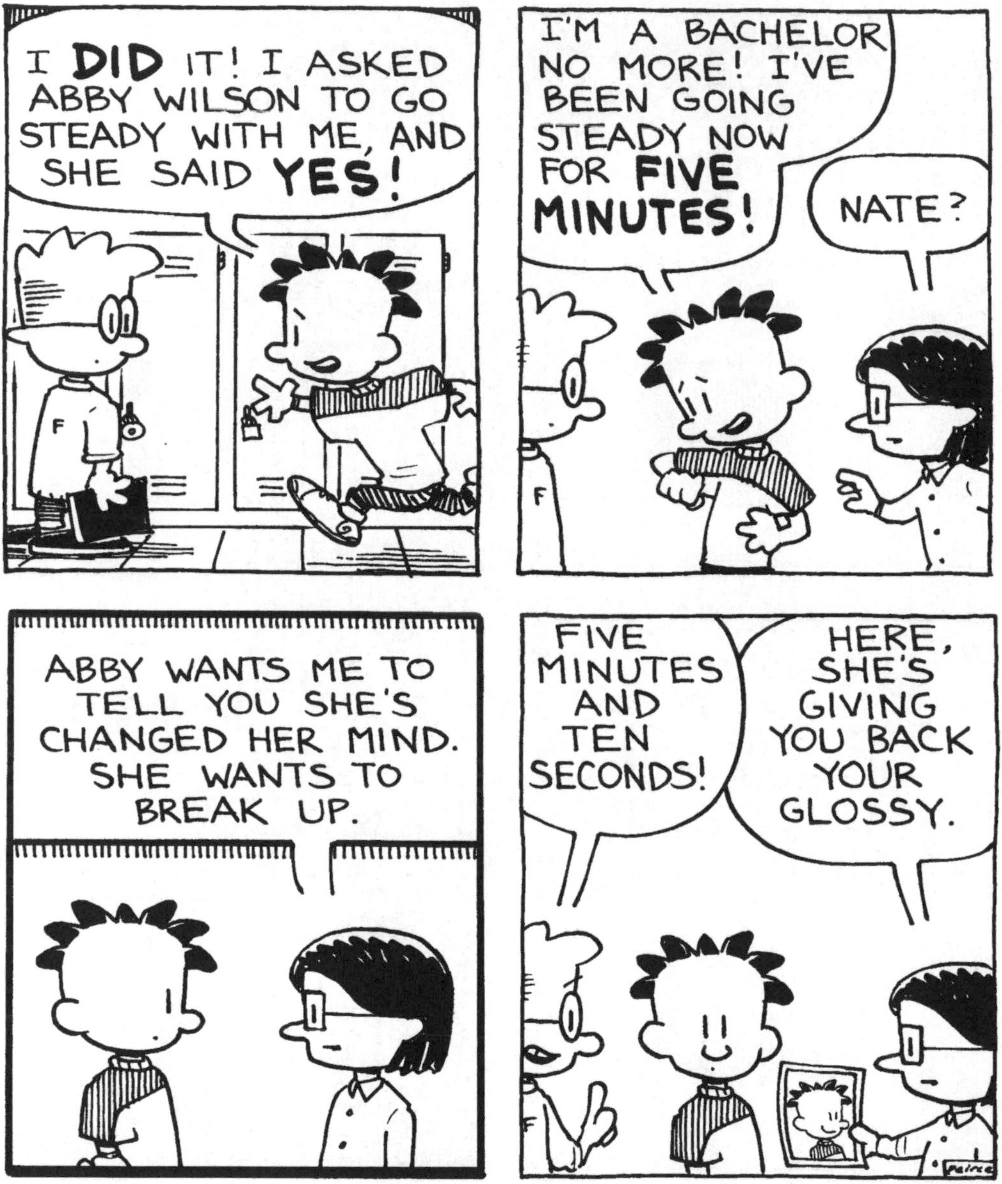
I DID IT! I ASKED ABBY WILSON TO GO STEADY WITH ME, AND SHE SAID YES!
I'M A BACHELOR NO MORE! I'VE BEEN GOING STEADY NOW FOR FIVE MINUTES!
NATE?
ABBY WANTS ME TO TELL YOU SHE'S CHANGED HER MIND. SHE WANTS TO BREAK UP.
FIVE MINUTES AND TEN SECONDS!
HERE, SHE'S GIVING YOU BACK YOUR GLOSSY.

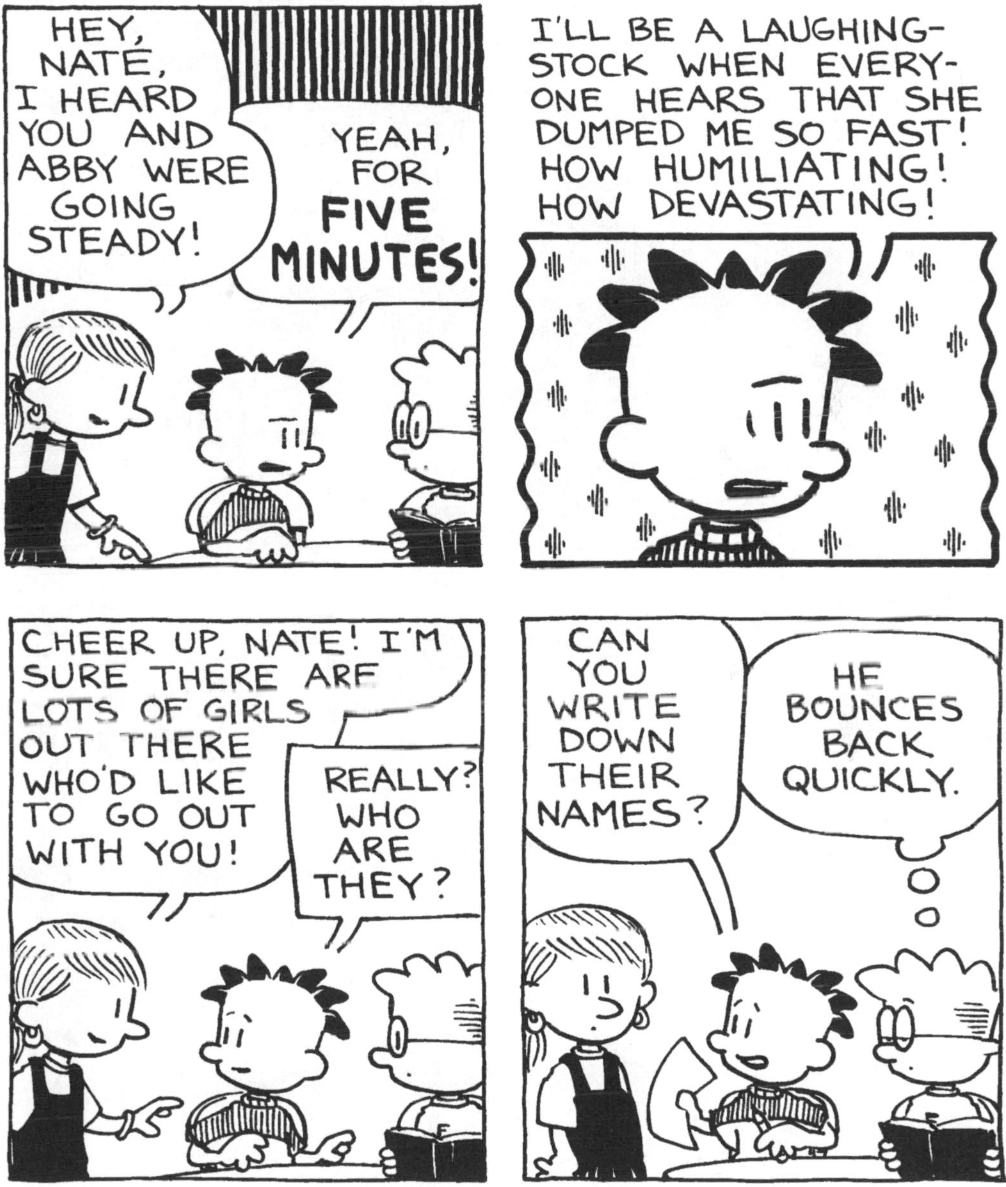
HEY, NATE, I HEARD YOU AND ABBY WERE GOING STEADY!
YEAH, FOR **FIVE MINUTES!**
I'LL BE A LAUGHING-STOCK WHEN EVERY-ONE HEARS THAT SHE DUMPED ME SO FAST! HOW HUMILIATING! HOW DEVASTATING!
CHEER UP, NATE! I'M SURE THERE ARE LOTS OF GIRLS OUT THERE WHO'D LIKE TO GO OUT WITH YOU!
REALLY? WHO ARE THEY?
CAN YOU WRITE DOWN THEIR NAMES?
HE BOUNCES BACK QUICKLY.

I'M READING AN ARTICLE ABOUT "TEACHER COMPETENCY TESTING."

APPARENTLY, THERE'S A LOT OF CONCERN THAT SOME TEACHERS JUST AREN'T QUALIFIED TO TEACH!

IT WON'T BE LONG UNTIL ALL TEACHERS ARE TESTED ROUTINELY! THEY'LL HAVE TO MEET CERTAIN ACADEMIC STANDARDS TO KEEP THEIR JOBS!

PAYBACK TIME!

The Continuing ADVENTURES of...
MOE MENTUM,
Hollywood Stunt Man!
On the set of "The X-Files"...
Moe! Welcome!
Hi, J.B.
Moe, we're filming our end-of-the-season episode, and we really want to make it memorable! That's why I want YOU to do the stunts!
You're the best in the business, Moe! With you on board, we'll make an unforgettable cliffhanger!
A cliff-hanger! WOW!
You'll be playing the part of Cliff.

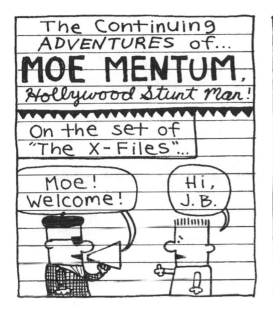

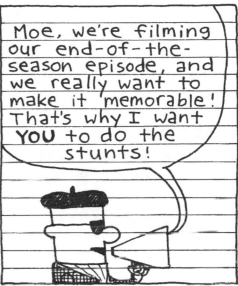

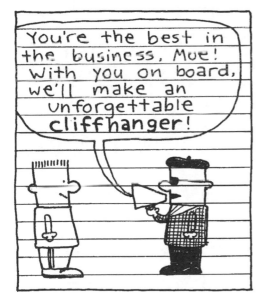

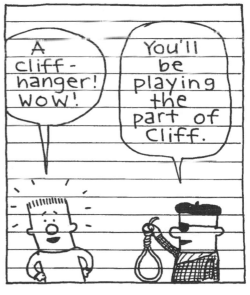

★ MO' MOE!! ★
HE'S...
MOE MENTUM,
Hollywood STUNT MAN!
On the set of "The X-Files"...
In this next scene, Moe, you play a corpse!
A CORPSE?? Wait a minute, J.B! You mean I'm just going to lie around? I thought you said I had an important role to play!
You're not just ANY corpse, Moe! You're ESSENTIAL to the plot! You're going to be autopsied by Special Agent DANA SCULLY!
Ooooh! Things are looking up!
I'll be pulling this foot-long slug out of your
PLACES, PEOPLE!

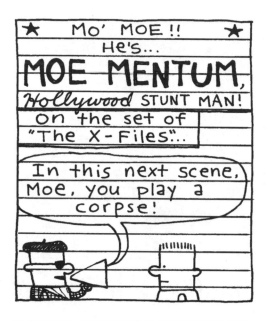

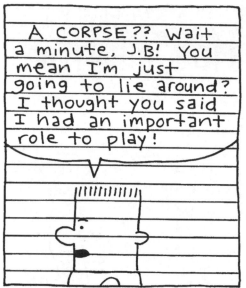

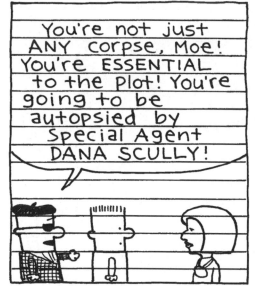

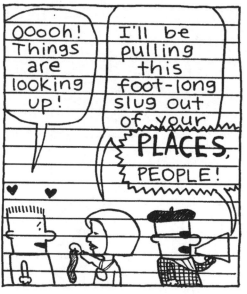

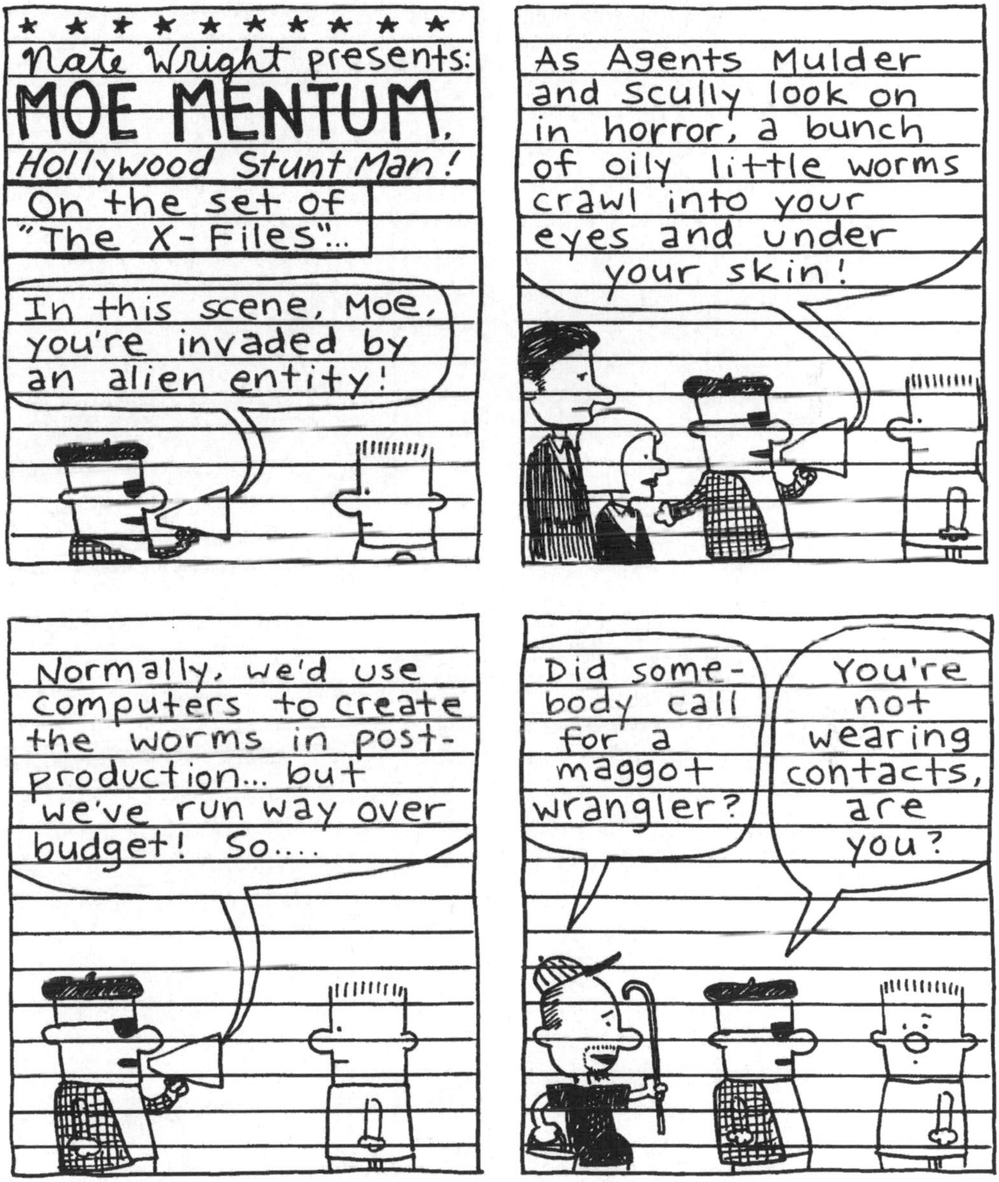
★ ★ ★ ★ ★ ★ ★ ★ ★ ★
Nate Wright presents:
MOE MENTUM,
Hollywood Stunt Man!
On the set of "The X-Files"...
In this scene, Moe, you're invaded by an alien entity!
As Agents Mulder and Scully look on in horror, a bunch of oily little worms crawl into your eyes and under your skin!
Normally, we'd use computers to create the worms in post-production... but we've run way over budget! So....
Did somebody call for a maggot wrangler?
You're not wearing contacts, are you?

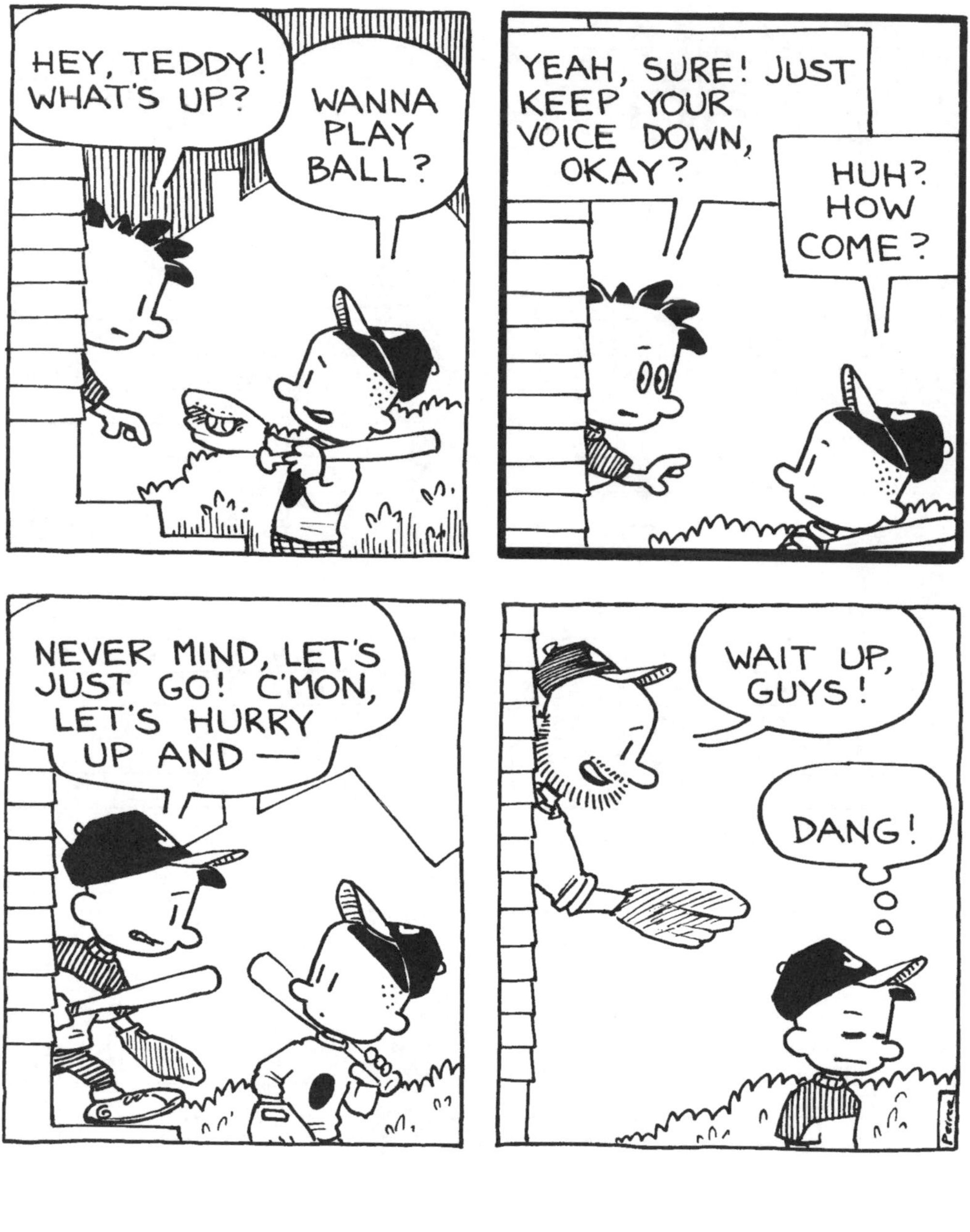
HEY, TEDDY! WHAT'S UP?
WANNA PLAY BALL?
YEAH, SURE! JUST KEEP YOUR VOICE DOWN, OKAY?
HUH? HOW COME?
NEVER MIND, LET'S JUST GO! C'MON, LET'S HURRY UP AND —
WAIT UP, GUYS!
DANG!

AH, SHAGGING FLIES! WHAT A GREAT WAY TO KICK OFF THE SEASON!
ISN'T IT EXHILARATING, NATE? SPRING IS IN THE AIR! YES, SPRING IS IN THE AIR!!
SO'S THE BALL.
WHAT?
Peirce

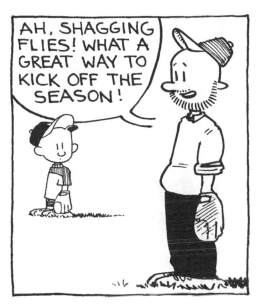

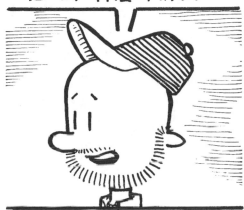

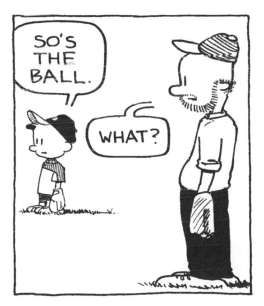

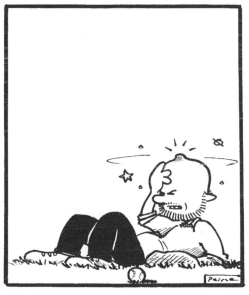

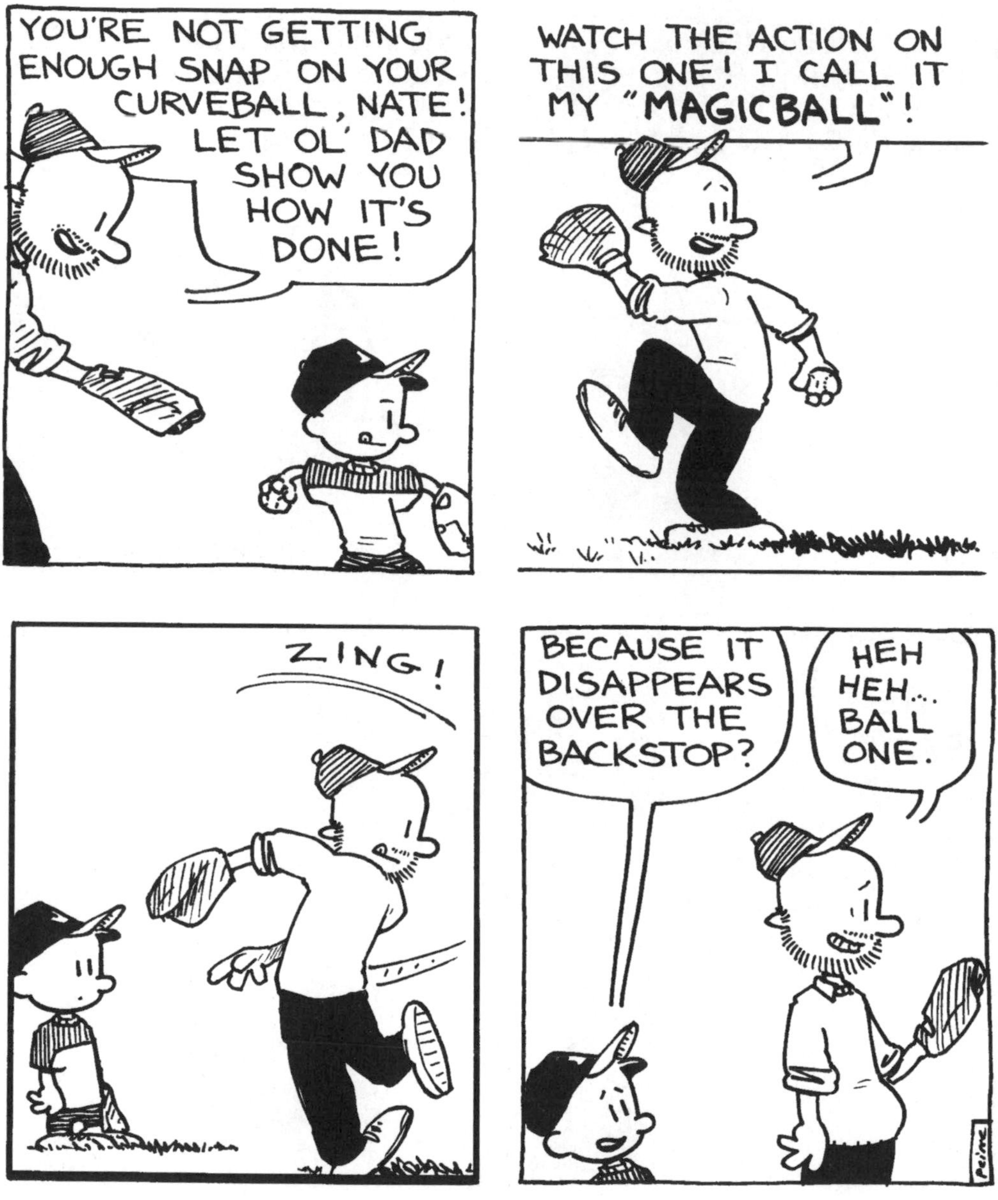
YOU'RE NOT GETTING ENOUGH SNAP ON YOUR CURVEBALL, NATE! LET OL' DAD SHOW YOU HOW IT'S DONE!
WATCH THE ACTION ON THIS ONE! I CALL IT MY "MAGICBALL"!
ZING!
BECAUSE IT DISAPPEARS OVER THE BACKSTOP?
HEH HEH... BALL ONE.
PEIRCE

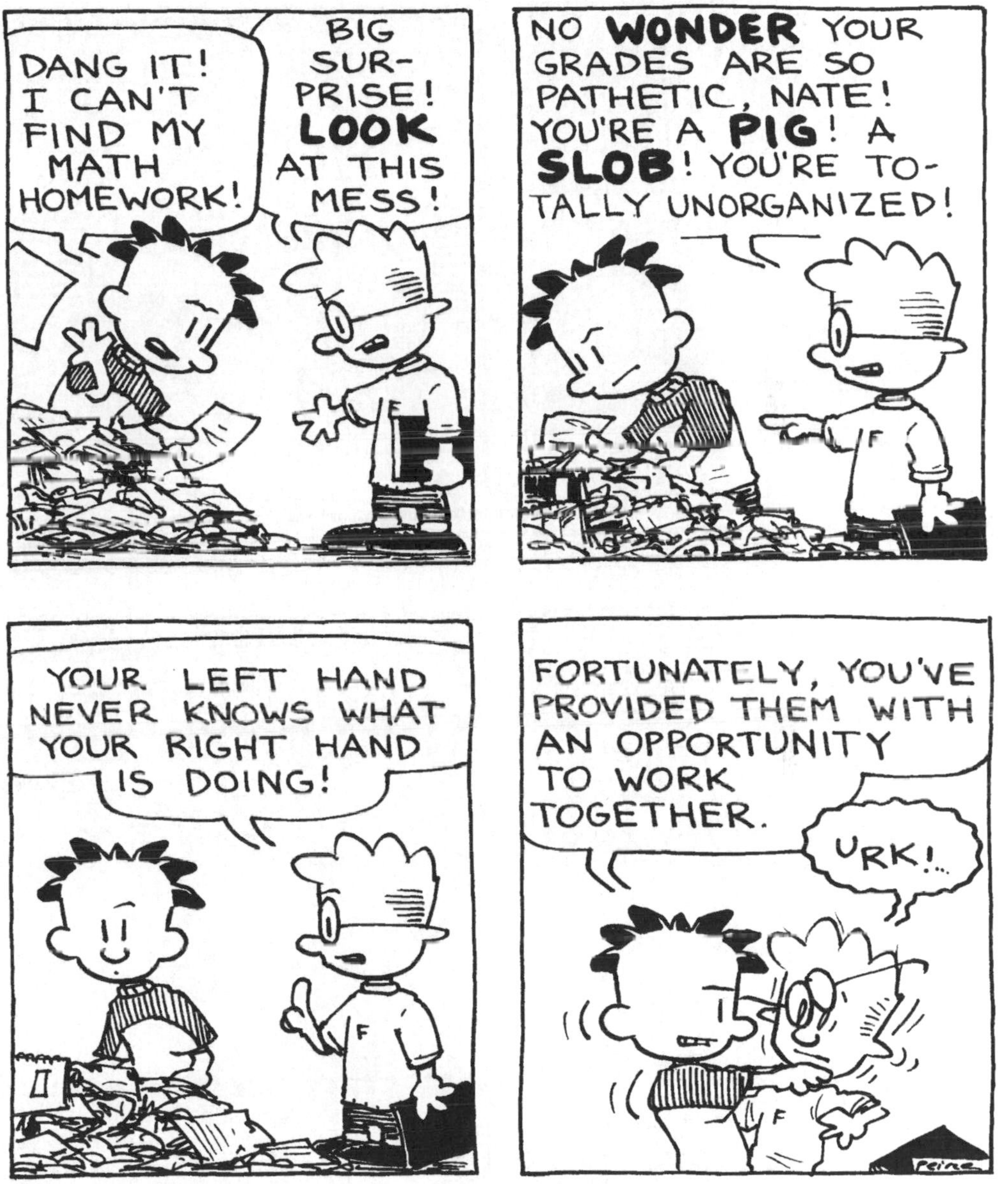
DANG IT! I CAN'T FIND MY MATH HOMEWORK!
BIG SUR-PRISE! **LOOK** AT THIS MESS!
NO **WONDER** YOUR GRADES ARE SO PATHETIC, NATE! YOU'RE A **PIG**! A **SLOB**! YOU'RE TO-TALLY UNORGANIZED!
YOUR LEFT HAND NEVER KNOWS WHAT YOUR RIGHT HAND IS DOING!
FORTUNATELY, YOU'VE PROVIDED THEM WITH AN OPPORTUNITY TO WORK TOGETHER.
URK!...

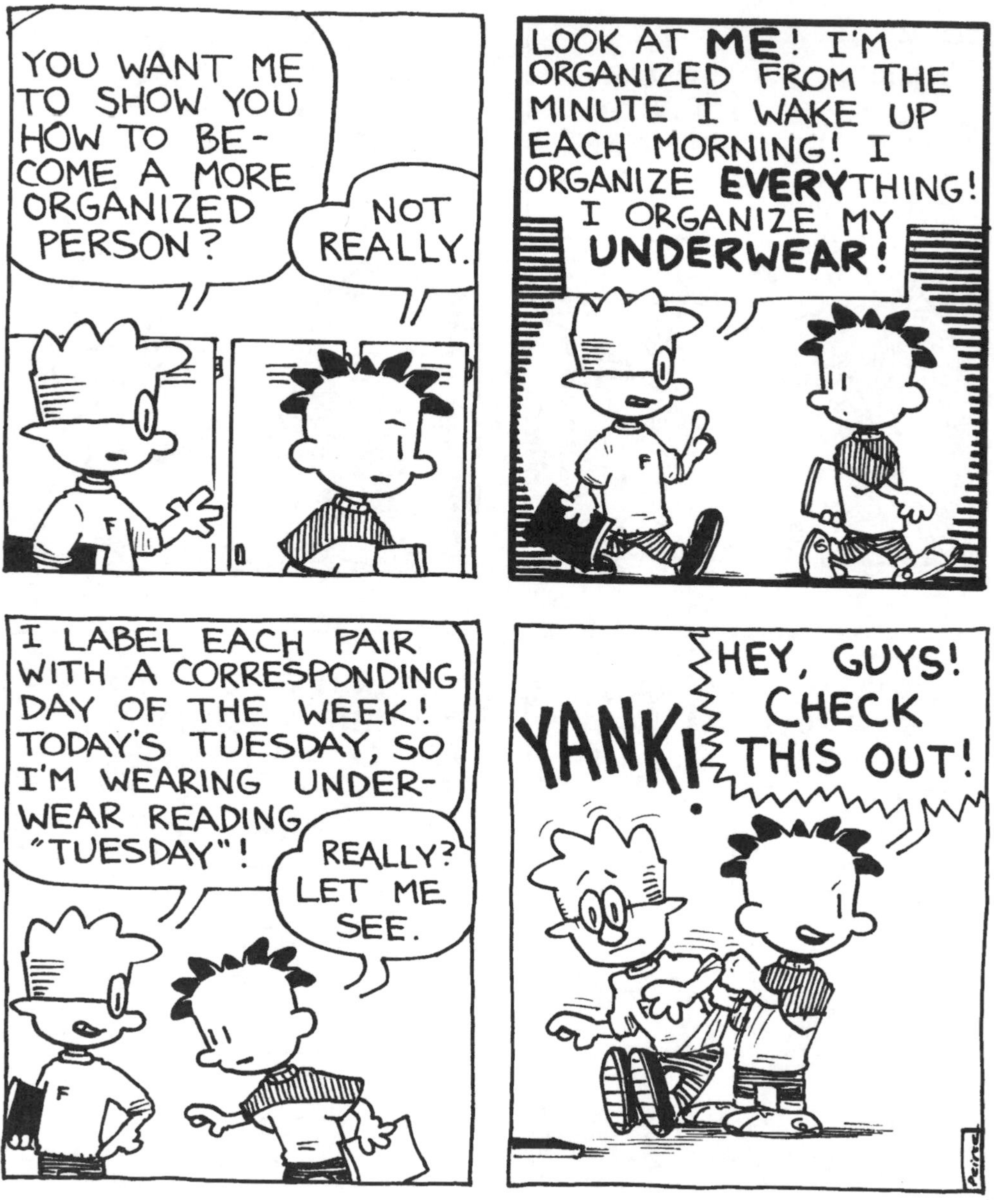
YOU WANT ME TO SHOW YOU HOW TO BE-COME A MORE ORGANIZED PERSON?
NOT REALLY.
LOOK AT **ME**! I'M ORGANIZED FROM THE MINUTE I WAKE UP EACH MORNING! I ORGANIZE **EVERY**THING! I ORGANIZE MY **UNDERWEAR**!
I LABEL EACH PAIR WITH A CORRESPONDING DAY OF THE WEEK! TODAY'S TUESDAY, SO I'M WEARING UNDER-WEAR READING "TUESDAY"!
REALLY? LET ME SEE.
YANK!
HEY, GUYS! CHECK THIS OUT!

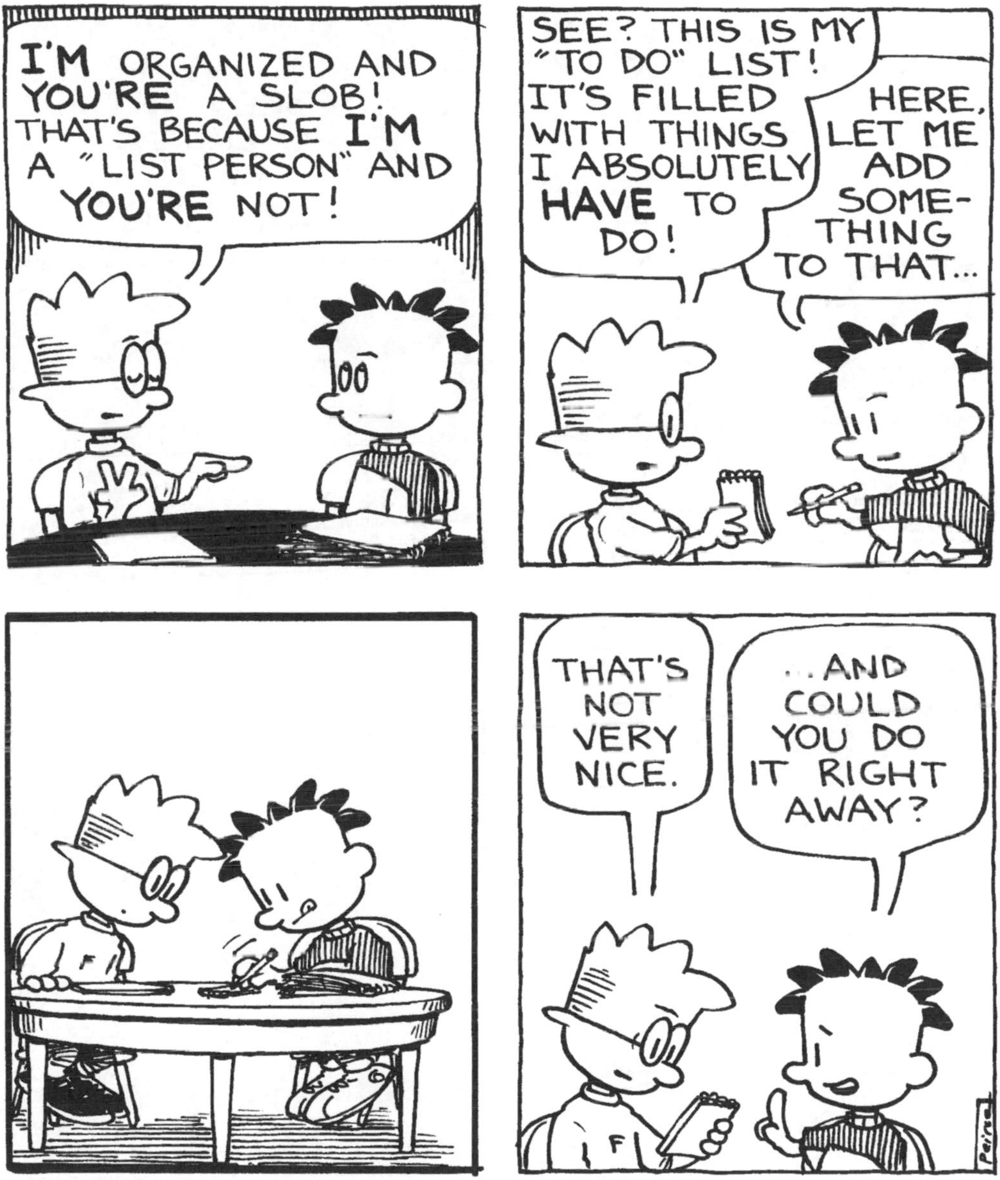
I'M ORGANIZED AND YOU'RE A SLOB! THAT'S BECAUSE I'M A "LIST PERSON" AND YOU'RE NOT!
SEE? THIS IS MY "TO DO" LIST! IT'S FILLED WITH THINGS I ABSOLUTELY HAVE TO DO!
HERE, LET ME ADD SOME-THING TO THAT...
THAT'S NOT VERY NICE.
...AND COULD YOU DO IT RIGHT AWAY?
Peirce

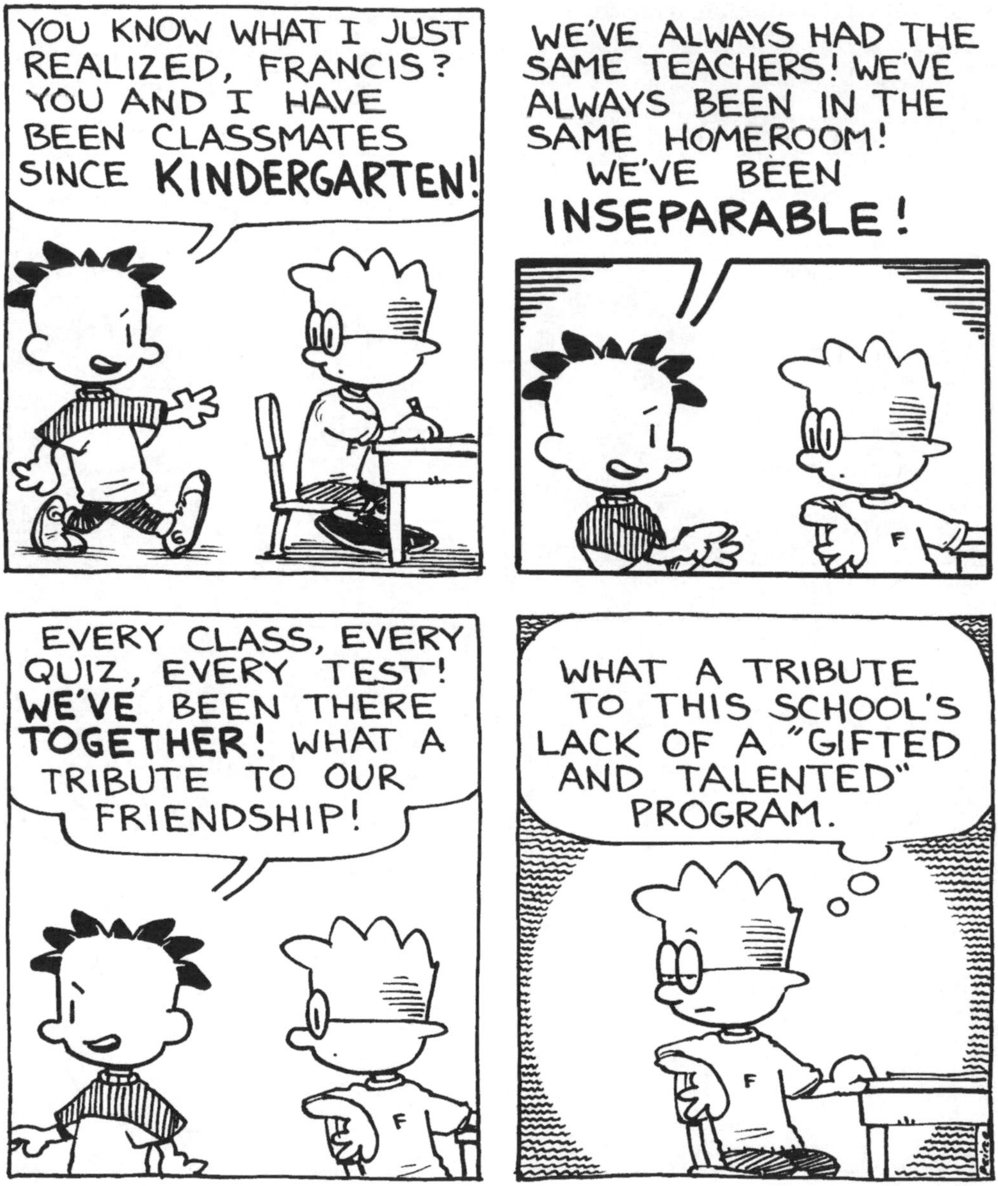
YOU KNOW WHAT I JUST REALIZED, FRANCIS? YOU AND I HAVE BEEN CLASSMATES SINCE KINDERGARTEN!
WE'VE ALWAYS HAD THE SAME TEACHERS! WE'VE ALWAYS BEEN IN THE SAME HOMEROOM! WE'VE BEEN INSEPARABLE!
EVERY CLASS, EVERY QUIZ, EVERY TEST! WE'VE BEEN THERE TOGETHER! WHAT A TRIBUTE TO OUR FRIENDSHIP!
WHAT A TRIBUTE TO THIS SCHOOL'S LACK OF A "GIFTED AND TALENTED" PROGRAM.

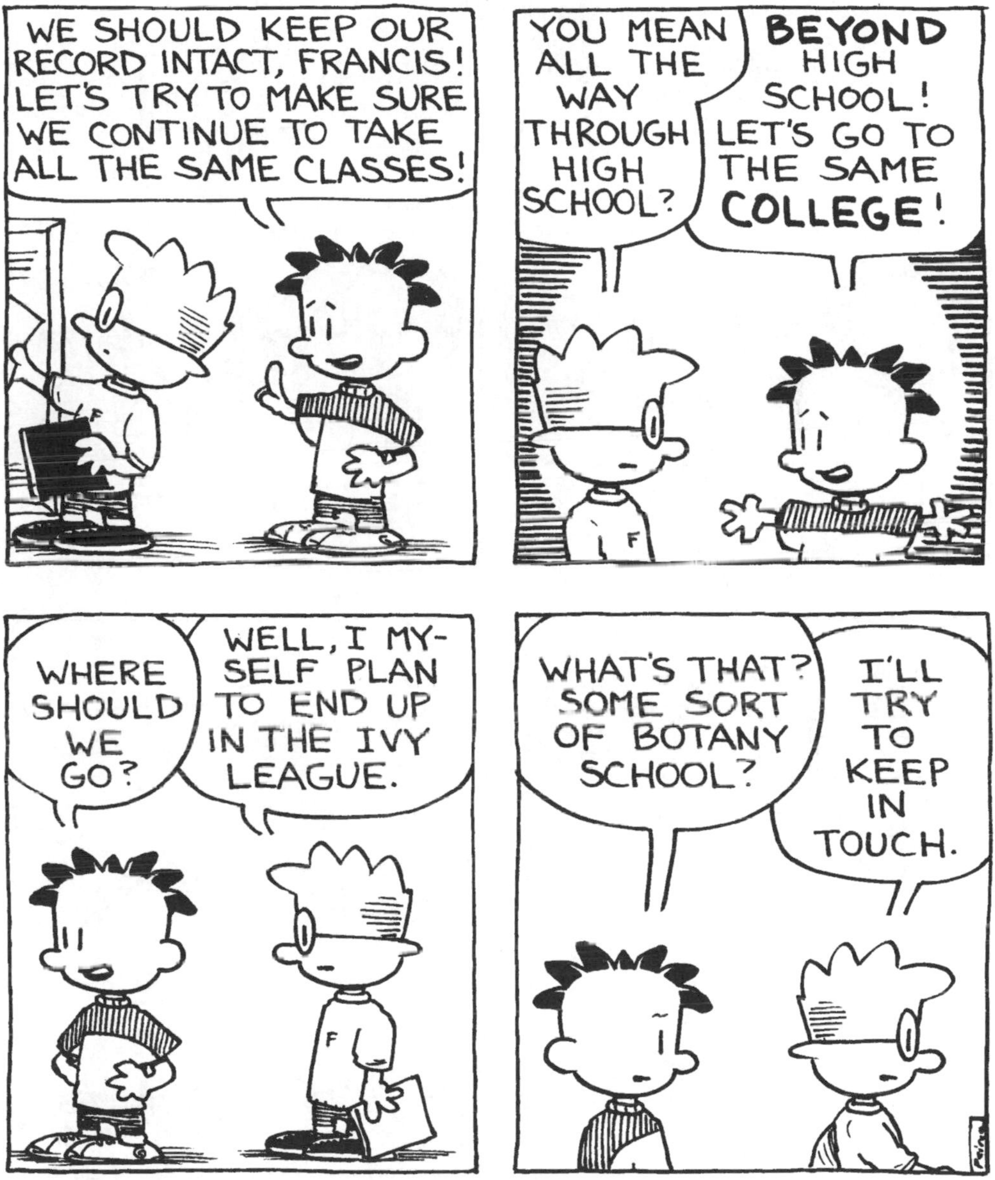
WE SHOULD KEEP OUR RECORD INTACT, FRANCIS! LET'S TRY TO MAKE SURE WE CONTINUE TO TAKE ALL THE SAME CLASSES!
YOU MEAN ALL THE WAY THROUGH HIGH SCHOOL?
BEYOND HIGH SCHOOL! LET'S GO TO THE SAME COLLEGE!
WHERE SHOULD WE GO?
WELL, I MYSELF PLAN TO END UP IN THE IVY LEAGUE.
WHAT'S THAT? SOME SORT OF BOTANY SCHOOL?
I'LL TRY TO KEEP IN TOUCH.

ELLEN... CAN I BOUNCE SOMETHING OFF YOU?
SURE.
BOING!

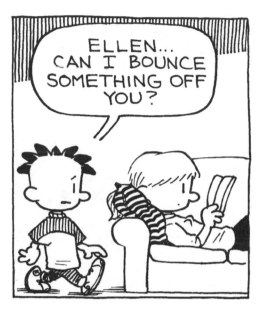

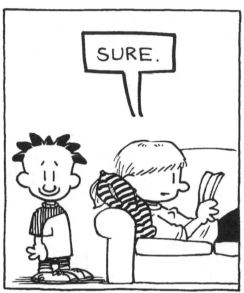

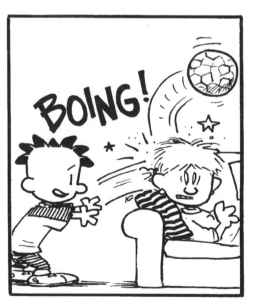

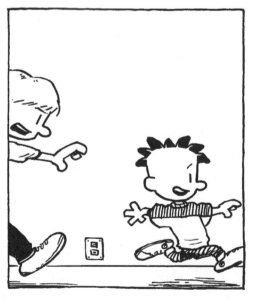

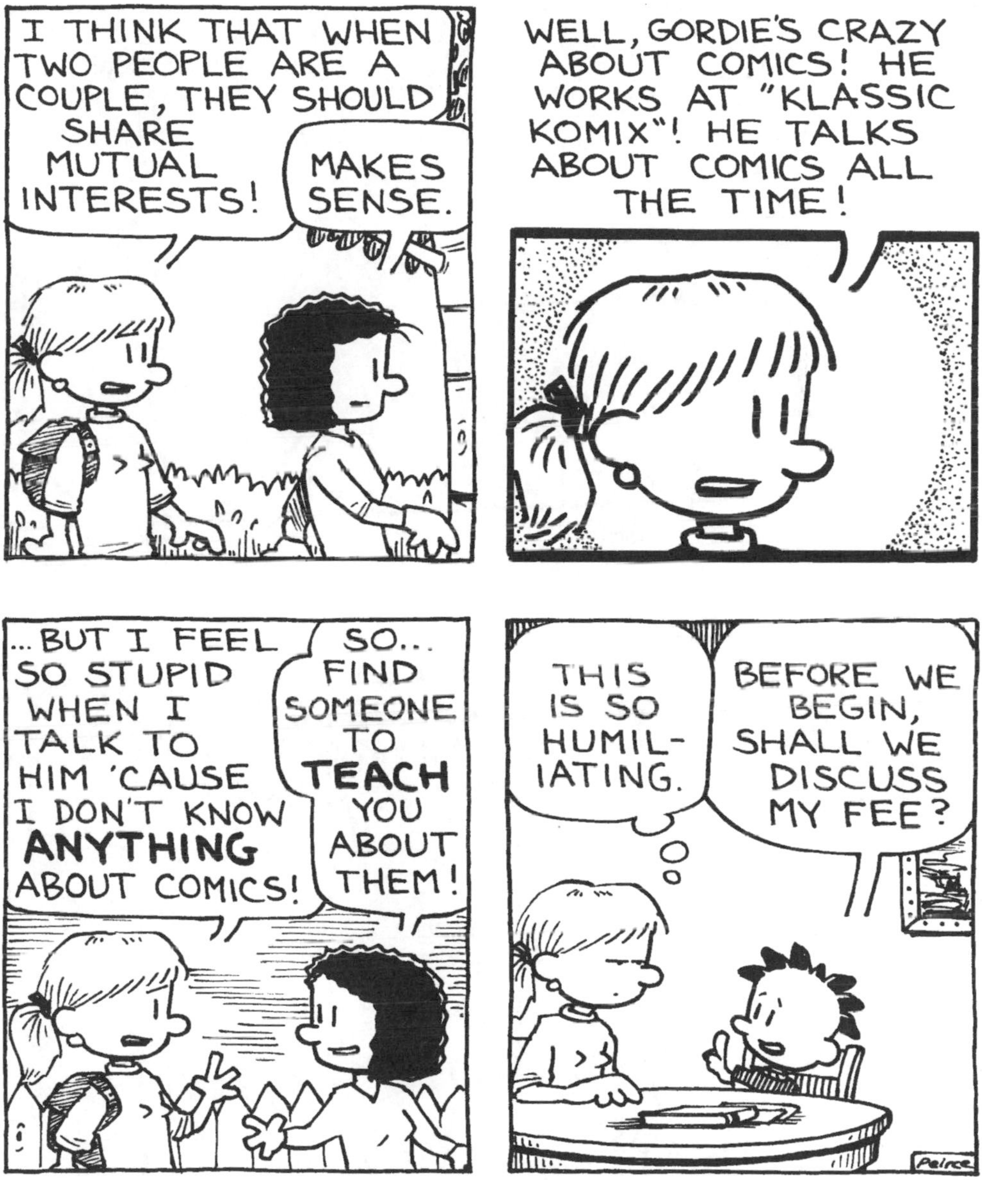
I THINK THAT WHEN TWO PEOPLE ARE A COUPLE, THEY SHOULD SHARE MUTUAL INTERESTS!
MAKES SENSE.
WELL, GORDIE'S CRAZY ABOUT COMICS! HE WORKS AT "KLASSIC KOMIX"! HE TALKS ABOUT COMICS ALL THE TIME!
...BUT I FEEL SO STUPID WHEN I TALK TO HIM 'CAUSE I DON'T KNOW **ANYTHING** ABOUT COMICS!
SO... FIND SOMEONE TO **TEACH** YOU ABOUT THEM!
THIS IS SO HUMILIATING.
BEFORE WE BEGIN, SHALL WE DISCUSS MY FEE?
Peirce

OKAY, YOU WANT TO LEARN ALL ABOUT COMIC STRIPS SO YOU AND GORDIE WILL HAVE MORE IN COMMON...

THE **FIRST** STEP IS TO TEST YOUR KNOWLEDGE OF COMICS! SO, ELLEN...... NAME THAT 'TOON!

UMMMM... NANCY?

NO, WAIT! **SLUGGO!** **SLUGGO!**

IT'S WORSE THAN I FEARED.

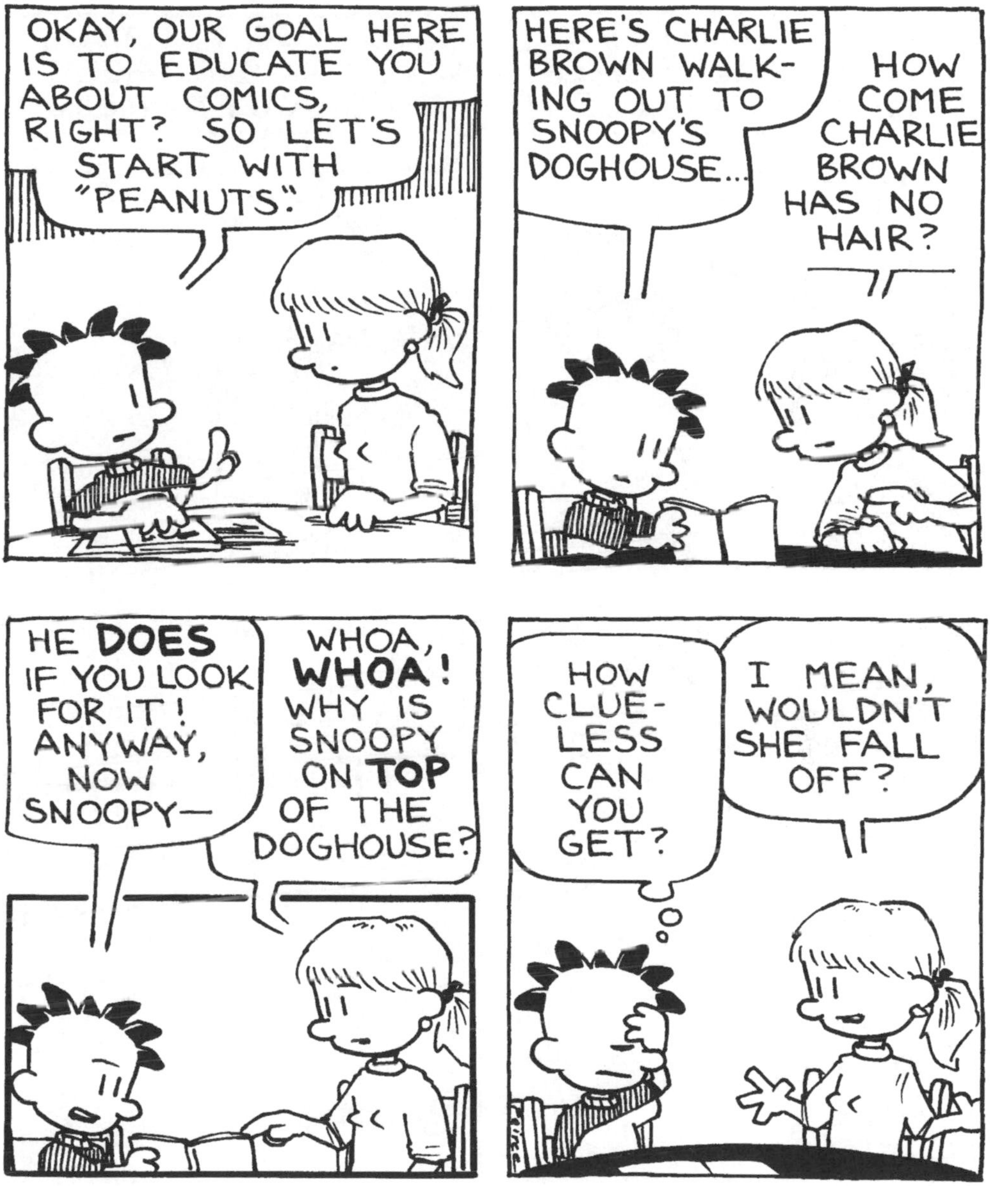
OKAY, OUR GOAL HERE IS TO EDUCATE YOU ABOUT COMICS, RIGHT? SO LET'S START WITH "PEANUTS."
HERE'S CHARLIE BROWN WALKING OUT TO SNOOPY'S DOGHOUSE...
HOW COME CHARLIE BROWN HAS NO HAIR?
HE **DOES** IF YOU LOOK FOR IT! ANYWAY, NOW SNOOPY—
WHOA, **WHOA**! WHY IS SNOOPY ON **TOP** OF THE DOGHOUSE?
HOW CLUELESS CAN YOU GET?
I MEAN, WOULDN'T SHE FALL OFF?

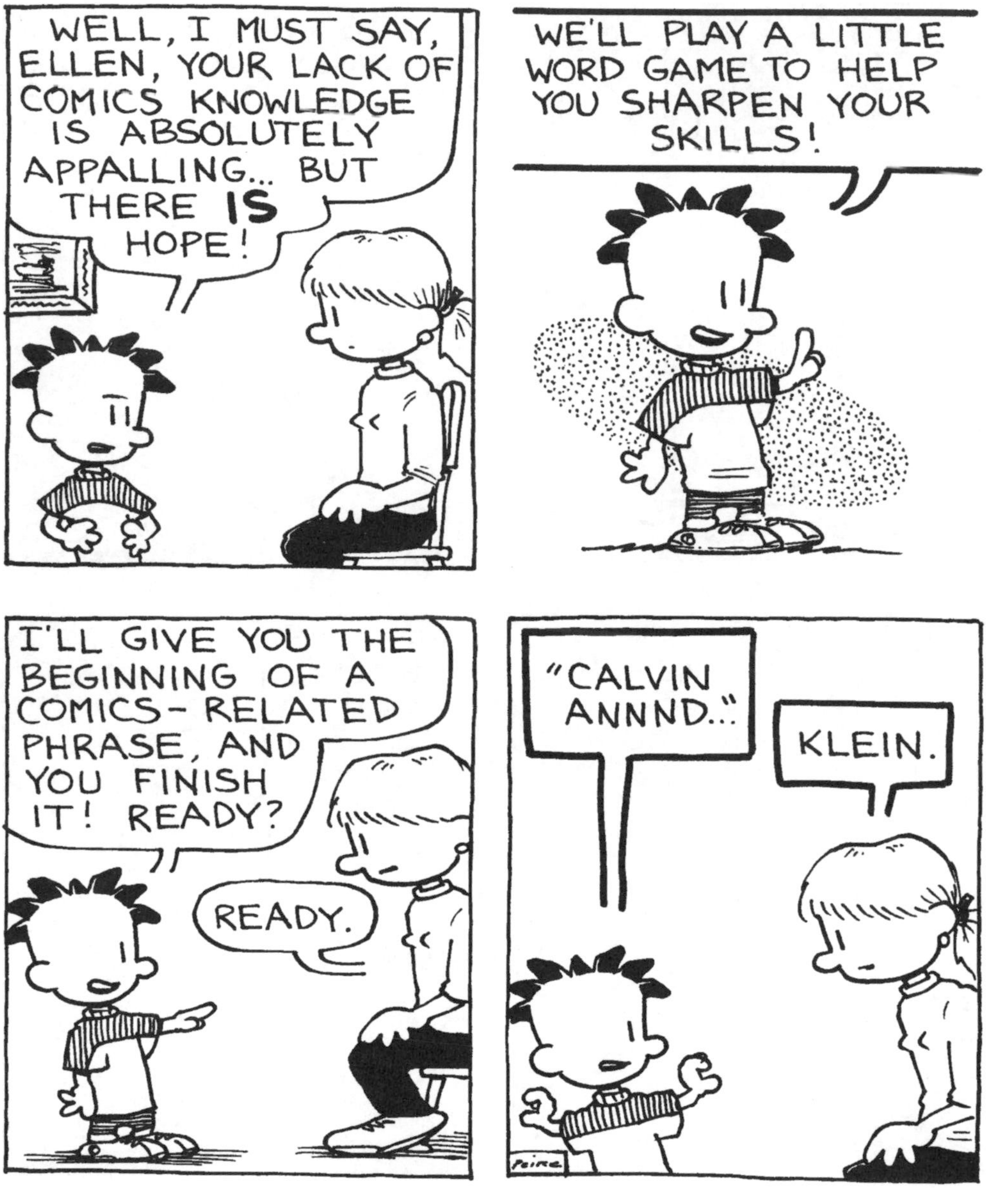
WELL, I MUST SAY, ELLEN, YOUR LACK OF COMICS KNOWLEDGE IS ABSOLUTELY APPALLING... BUT THERE **IS** HOPE!
WE'LL PLAY A LITTLE WORD GAME TO HELP YOU SHARPEN YOUR SKILLS!
I'LL GIVE YOU THE BEGINNING OF A COMICS-RELATED PHRASE, AND YOU FINISH IT! READY?
READY.
"CALVIN ANNND..."
KLEIN.
PEIRCE

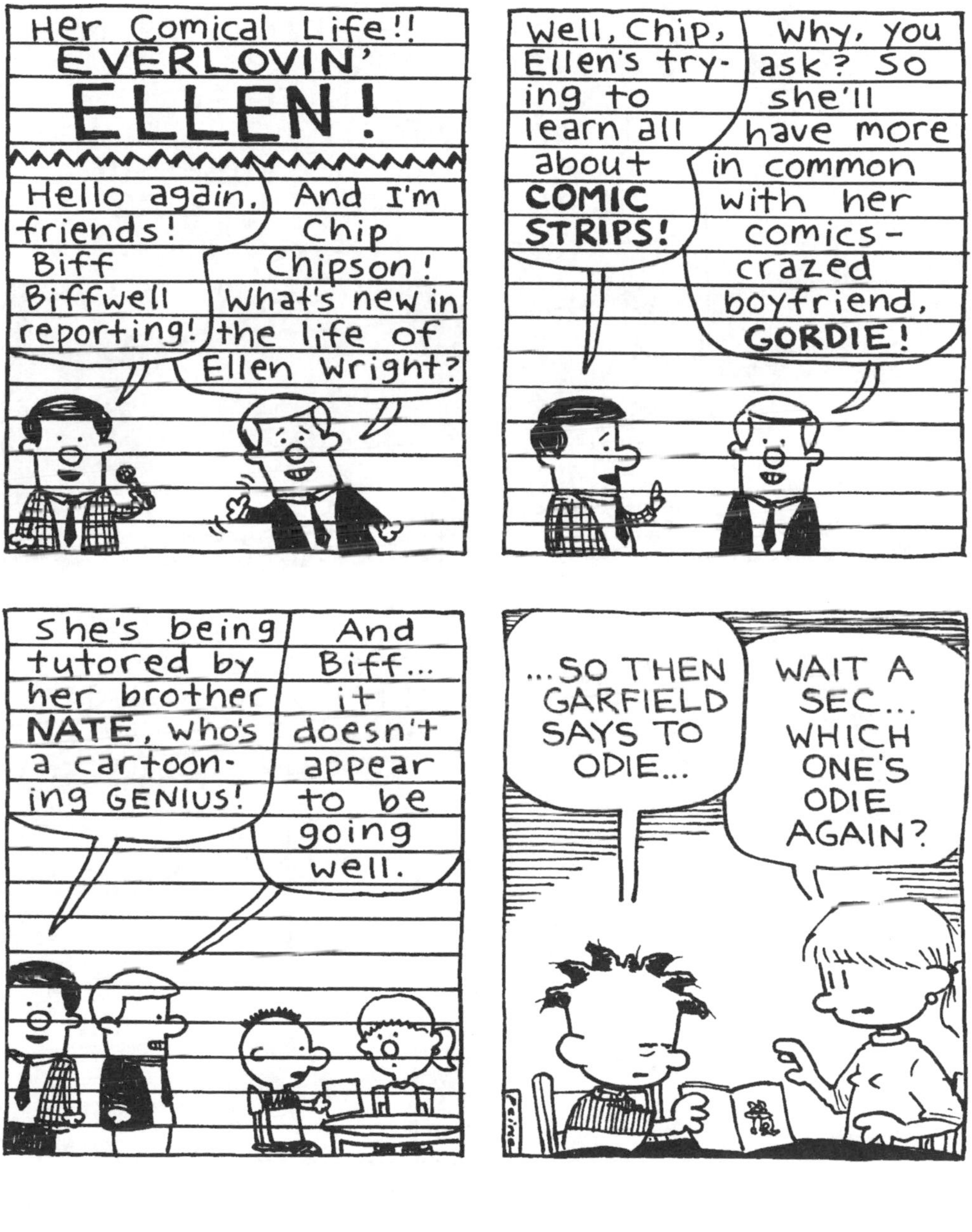
Her Comical Life!!
EVERLOVIN' ELLEN!
Hello again, friends! Biff Biffwell reporting!
And I'm Chip Chipson! What's new in the life of Ellen Wright?
Well, Chip, Ellen's trying to learn all about COMIC STRIPS!
Why, you ask? So she'll have more in common with her comics-crazed boyfriend, GORDIE!
She's being tutored by her brother NATE, who's a cartooning GENIUS!
And Biff... it doesn't appear to be going well.
...SO THEN GARFIELD SAYS TO ODIE...
WAIT A SEC... WHICH ONE'S ODIE AGAIN?

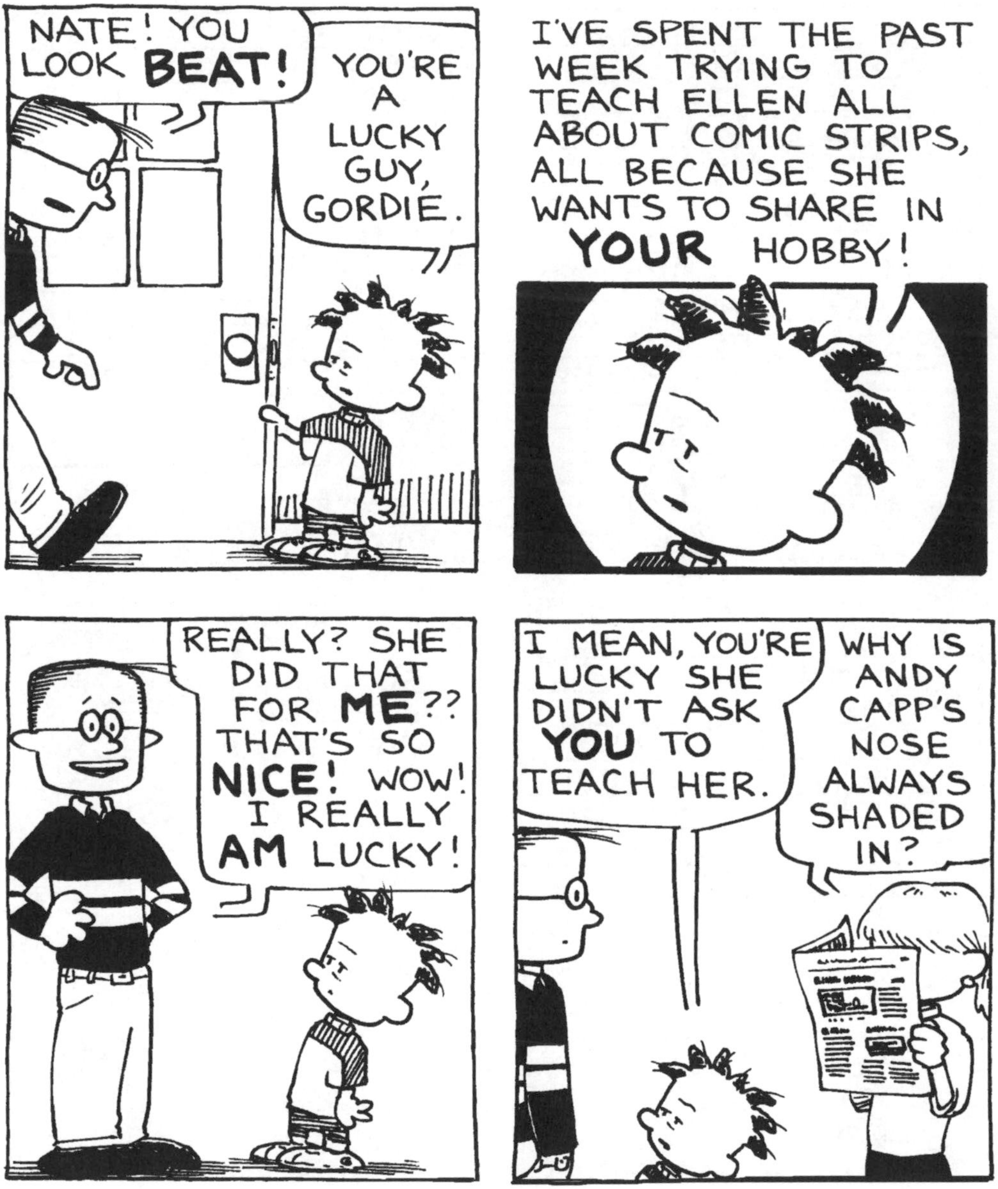
NATE! YOU LOOK **BEAT**!
YOU'RE A LUCKY GUY, GORDIE.
I'VE SPENT THE PAST WEEK TRYING TO TEACH ELLEN ALL ABOUT COMIC STRIPS, ALL BECAUSE SHE WANTS TO SHARE IN **YOUR** HOBBY!
REALLY? SHE DID THAT FOR **ME**?? THAT'S SO **NICE**! WOW! I REALLY **AM** LUCKY!
I MEAN, YOU'RE LUCKY SHE DIDN'T ASK **YOU** TO TEACH HER.
WHY IS ANDY CAPP'S NOSE ALWAYS SHADED IN?

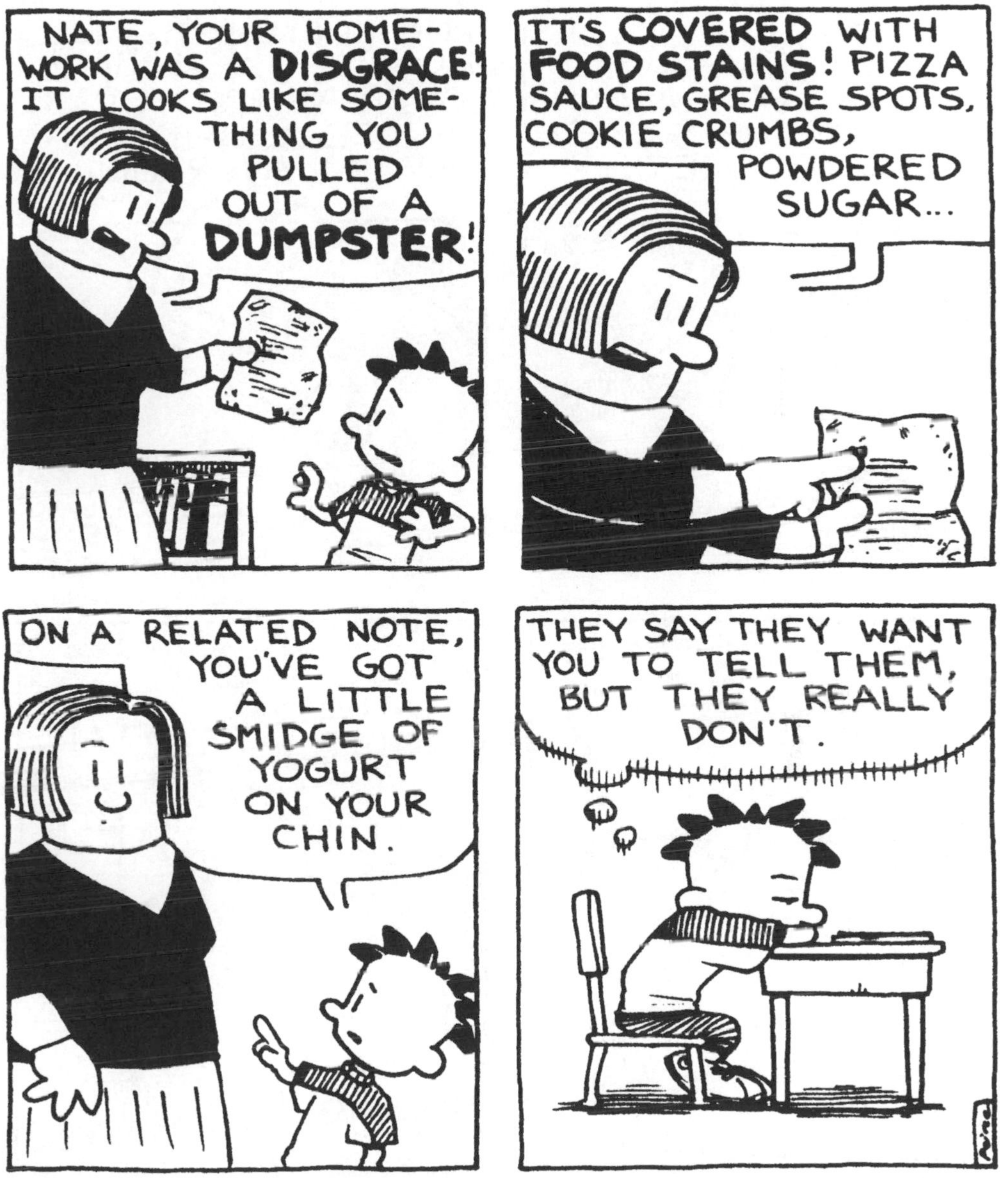
NATE, YOUR HOME-WORK WAS A **DISGRACE**! IT LOOKS LIKE SOME-THING YOU PULLED OUT OF A **DUMPSTER**!
IT'S **COVERED** WITH **FOOD STAINS**! PIZZA SAUCE, GREASE SPOTS, COOKIE CRUMBS, POWDERED SUGAR...
ON A RELATED NOTE, YOU'VE GOT A LITTLE SMIDGE OF YOGURT ON YOUR CHIN.
THEY SAY THEY WANT YOU TO TELL THEM, BUT THEY REALLY DON'T.

HEY, FRANCIS! WANNA TEAM UP AND WORK ON THE SCIENCE PROJECT TOGETHER?
HMM... WELL, LET'S SEE... I CAN GET A TWELVE ON THAT PROJECT AND STILL MAINTAIN MY "A" AVERAGE...
I CAN'T RISK IT.
HEY!
F
Peirce

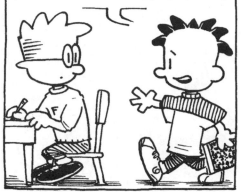

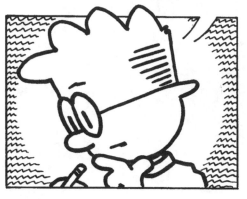

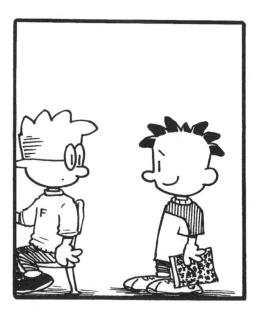

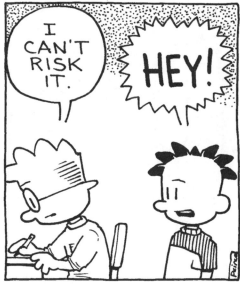

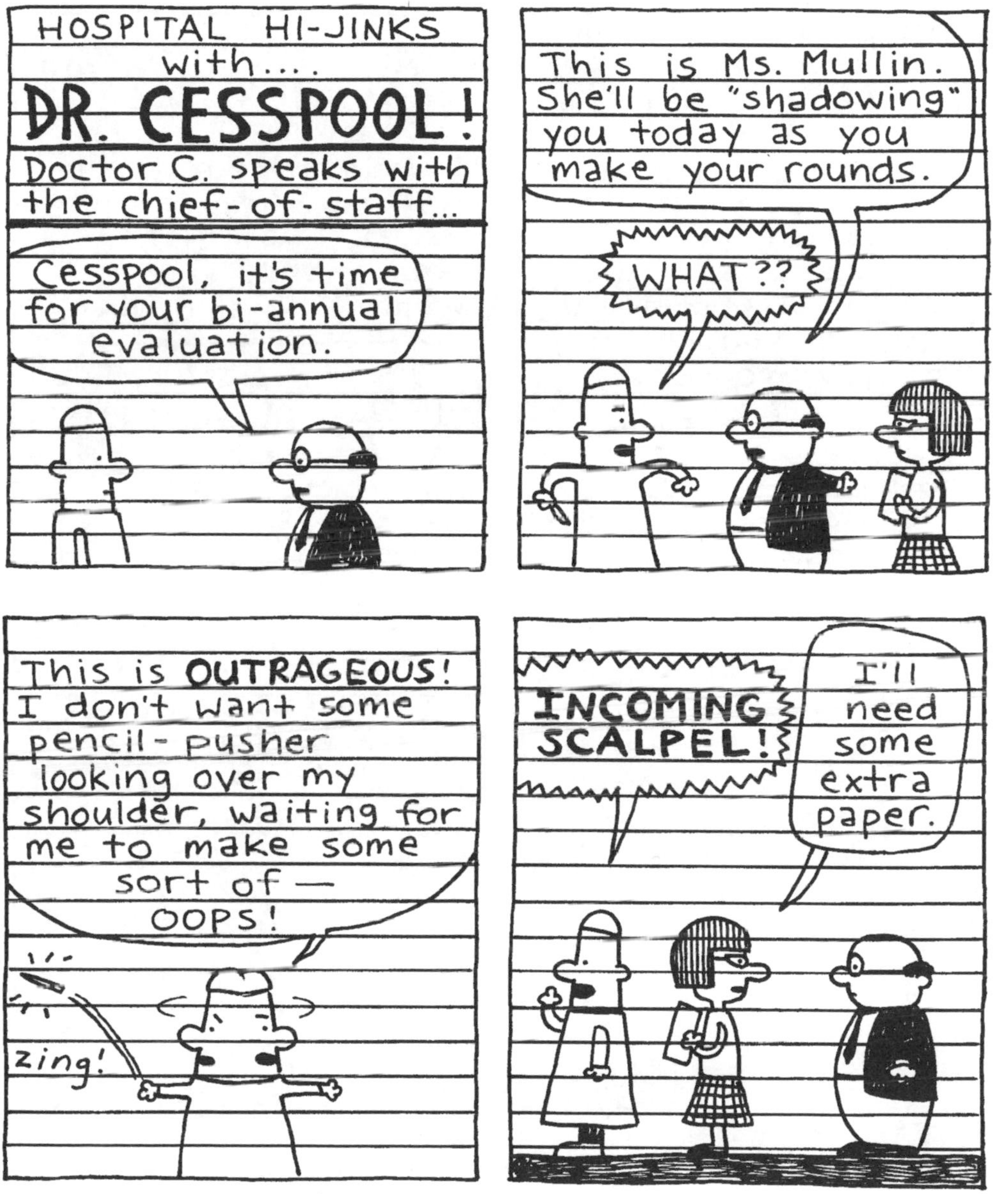
HOSPITAL HI-JINKS with.... DR. CESSPOOL!
Doctor C. speaks with the chief-of-staff...
Cesspool, it's time for your bi-annual evaluation.
This is Ms. Mullin. She'll be "shadowing" you today as you make your rounds.
WHAT??
This is OUTRAGEOUS! I don't want some pencil-pusher looking over my shoulder, waiting for me to make some sort of — OOPS!
zing!
INCOMING SCALPEL!
I'll need some extra paper.

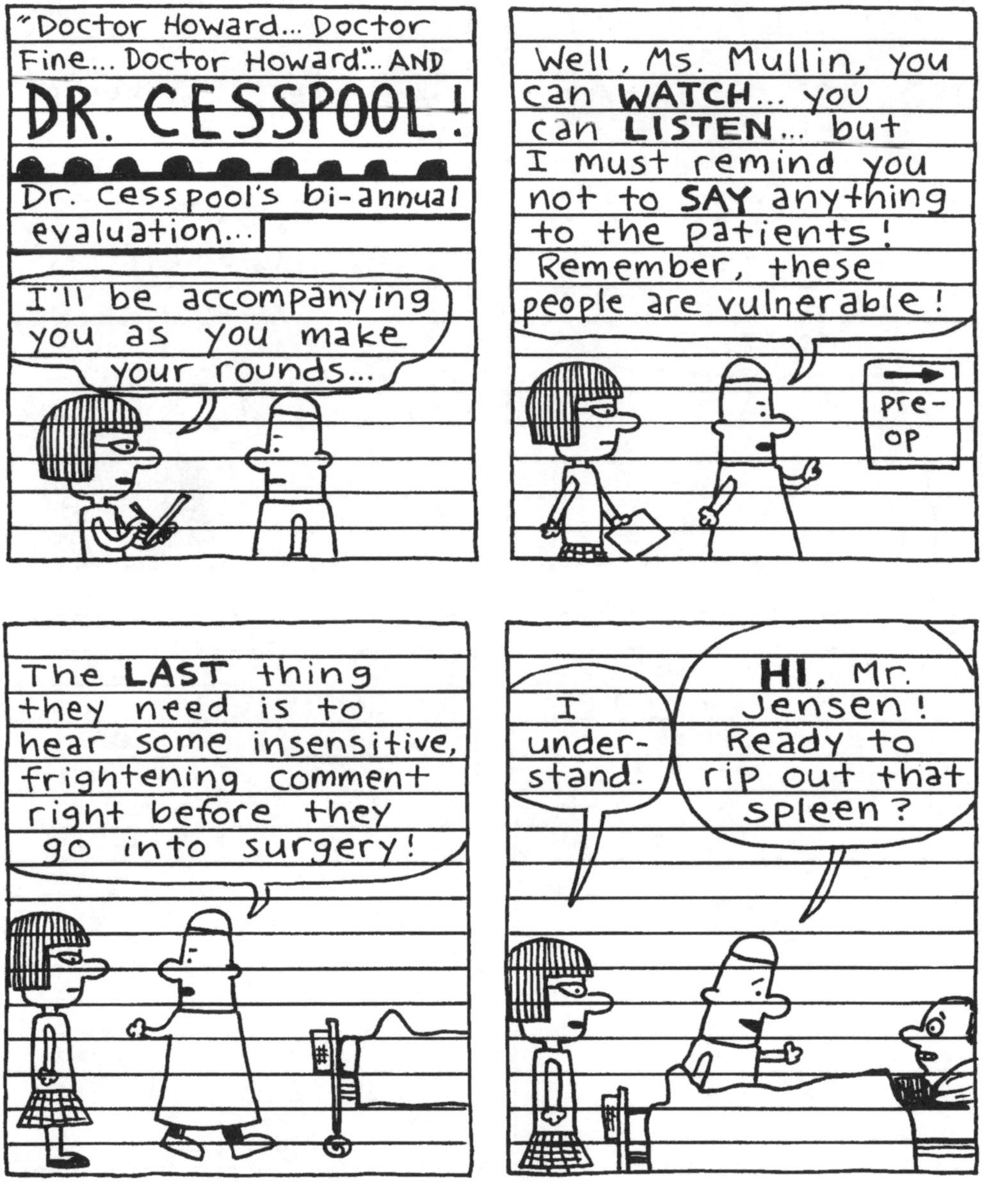
"Doctor Howard... Doctor Fine... Doctor Howard"... AND
DR. CESSPOOL!
Dr. cesspool's bi-annual evaluation...
I'll be accompanying you as you make your rounds...
Well, Ms. Mullin, you can WATCH... you can LISTEN... but I must remind you not to SAY anything to the patients! Remember, these people are vulnerable!
pre-op
The LAST thing they need is to hear some insensitive, frightening comment right before they go into surgery!
I under-stand.
HI, Mr. Jensen! Ready to rip out that spleen?

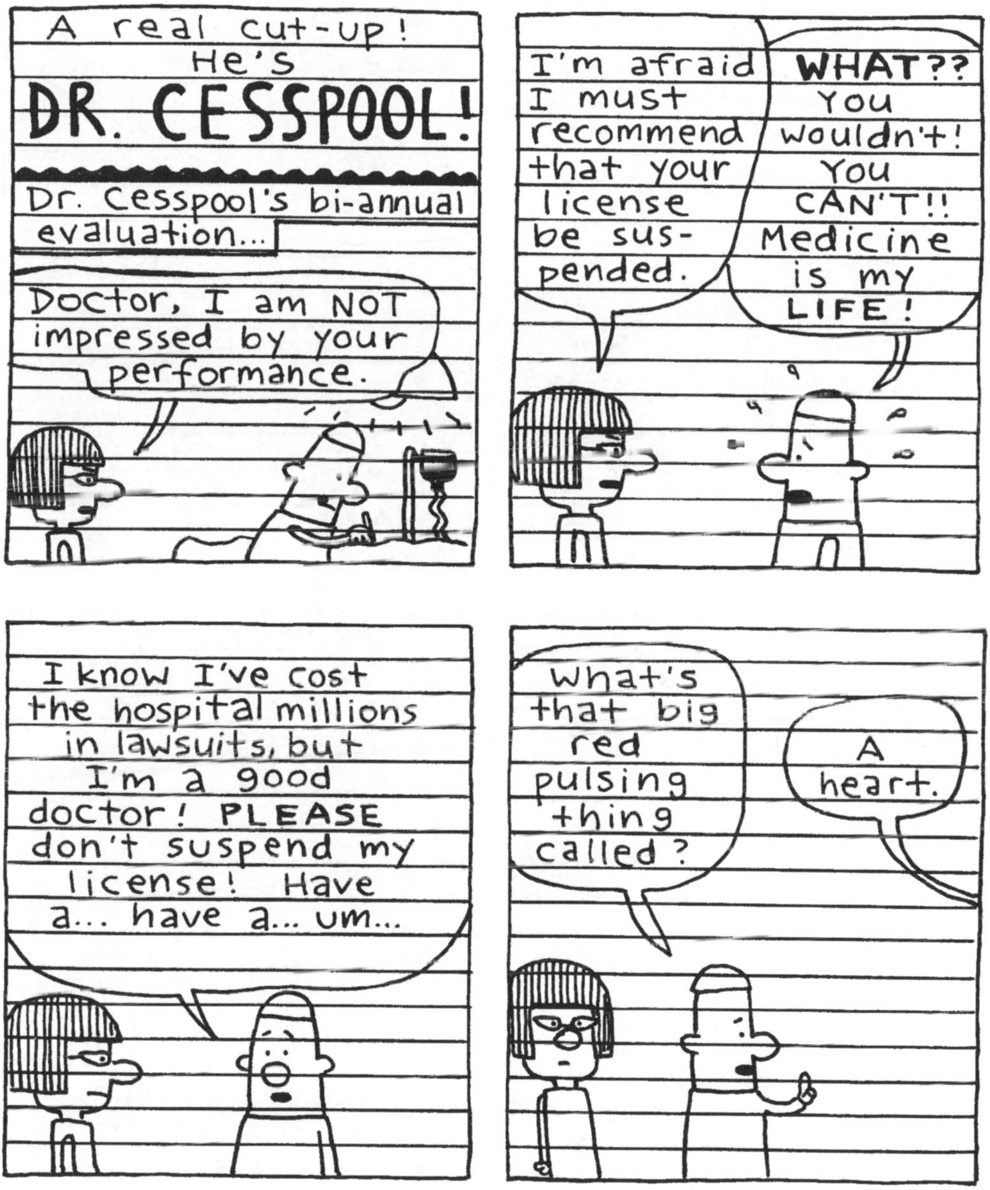
A real cut-up! He's
DR. CESSPOOL!
Dr. Cesspool's bi-annual evaluation...
Doctor, I am NOT impressed by your performance.
I'm afraid I must recommend that your license be suspended.
WHAT?? You wouldn't! You CAN'T!! Medicine is my LIFE!
I know I've cost the hospital millions in lawsuits, but I'm a good doctor! PLEASE don't suspend my license! Have a... have a... um...
What's that big red pulsing thing called?
A heart.

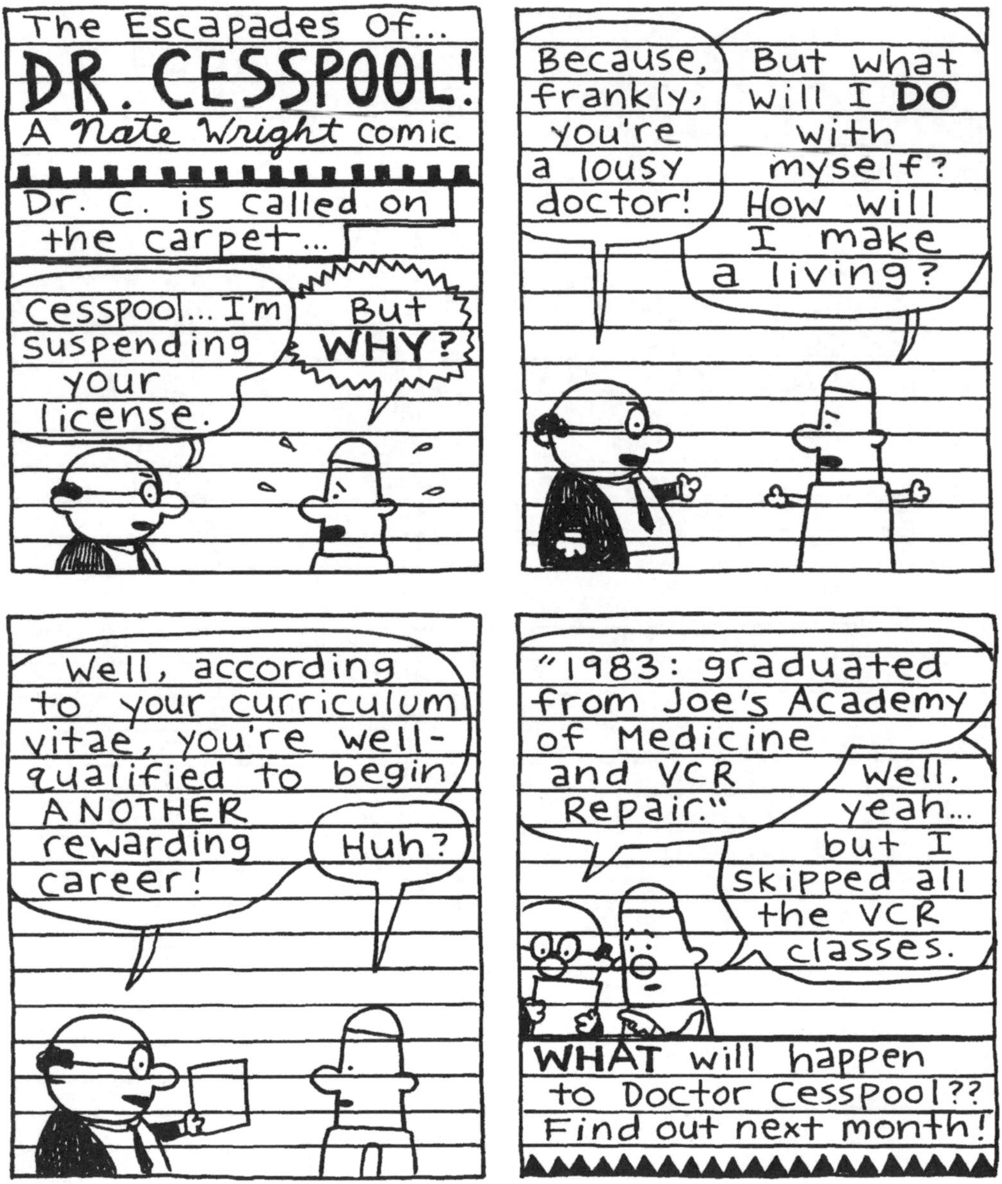
The Escapades Of...
DR. CESSPOOL!
A Nate Wright comic
Dr. C. is called on the carpet...
Cesspool... I'm suspending your license.
But WHY?
Because, frankly, you're a lousy doctor!
But what will I DO with myself? How will I make a living?
Well, according to your curriculum vitae, you're well-qualified to begin ANOTHER rewarding career!
Huh?
"1983: graduated from Joe's Academy of Medicine and VCR Repair."
Well, yeah... but I skipped all the VCR classes.
WHAT will happen to Doctor Cesspool?? Find out next month!

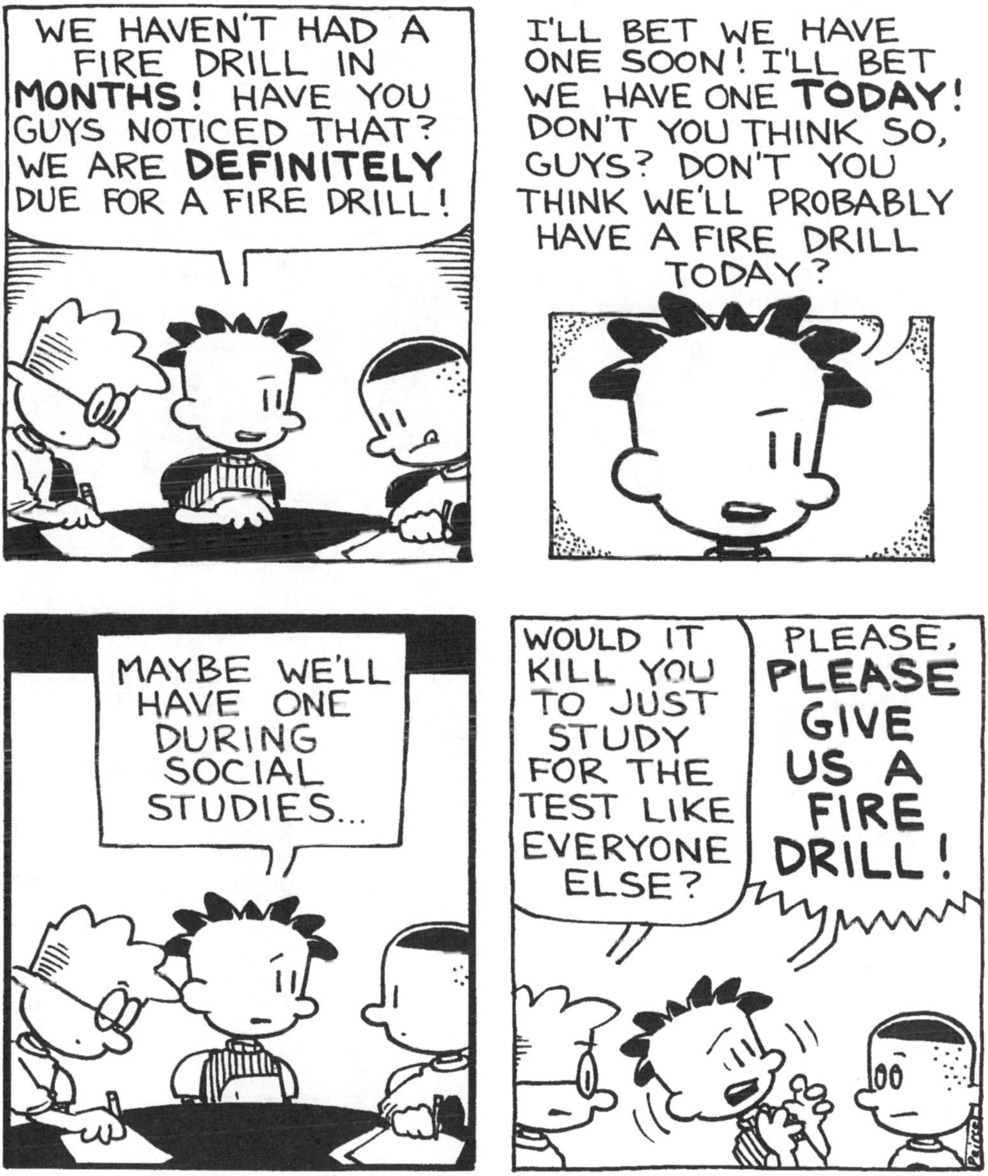
WE HAVEN'T HAD A FIRE DRILL IN MONTHS! HAVE YOU GUYS NOTICED THAT? WE ARE DEFINITELY DUE FOR A FIRE DRILL!
I'LL BET WE HAVE ONE SOON! I'LL BET WE HAVE ONE TODAY! DON'T YOU THINK SO, GUYS? DON'T YOU THINK WE'LL PROBABLY HAVE A FIRE DRILL TODAY?
MAYBE WE'LL HAVE ONE DURING SOCIAL STUDIES...
WOULD IT KILL YOU TO JUST STUDY FOR THE TEST LIKE EVERYONE ELSE?
PLEASE, PLEASE GIVE US A FIRE DRILL!
Peirce

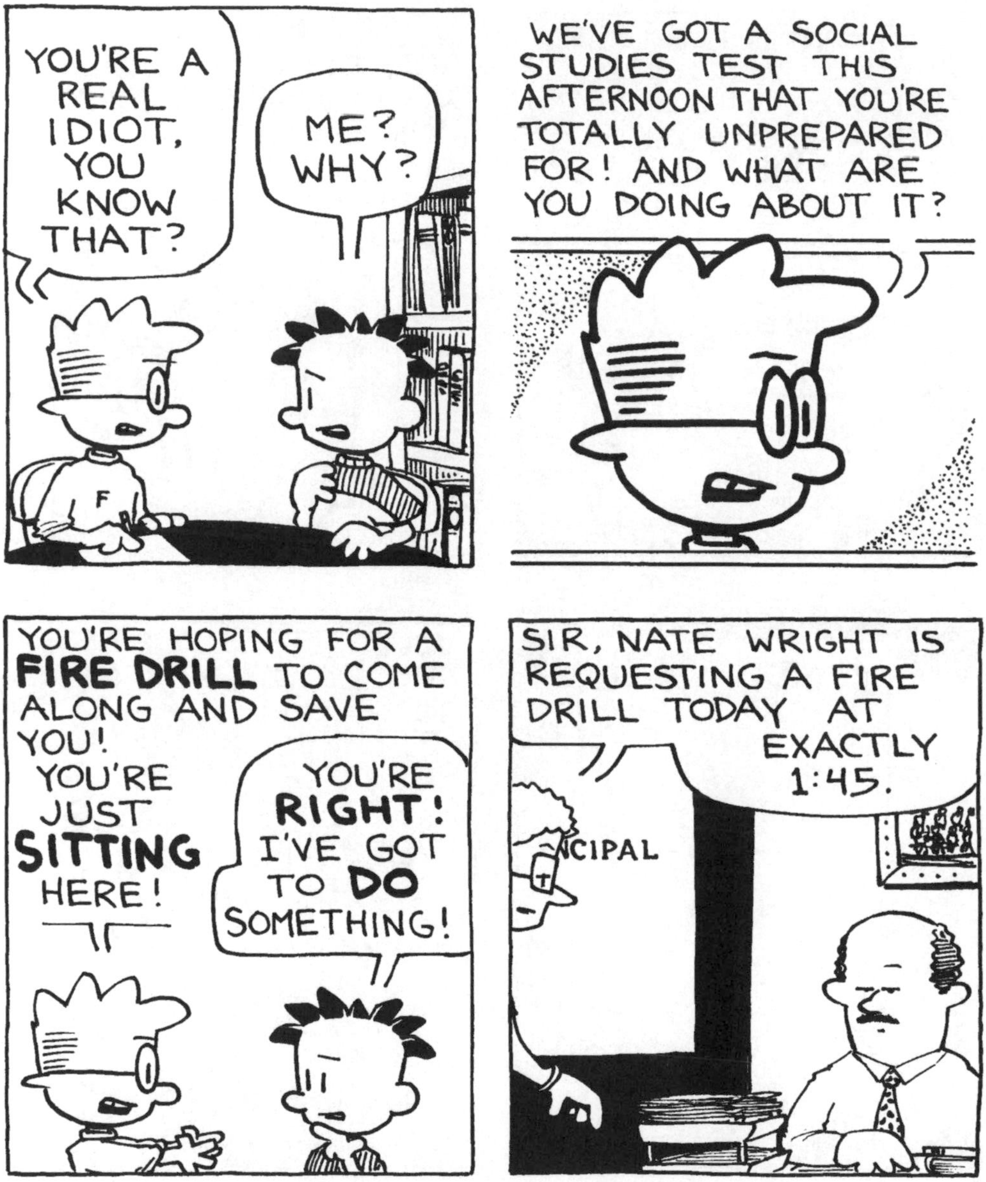
YOU'RE A REAL IDIOT, YOU KNOW THAT?
ME? WHY?
WE'VE GOT A SOCIAL STUDIES TEST THIS AFTERNOON THAT YOU'RE TOTALLY UNPREPARED FOR! AND WHAT ARE YOU DOING ABOUT IT?
YOU'RE HOPING FOR A FIRE DRILL TO COME ALONG AND SAVE YOU! YOU'RE JUST SITTING HERE!
YOU'RE RIGHT! I'VE GOT TO DO SOMETHING!
SIR, NATE WRIGHT IS REQUESTING A FIRE DRILL TODAY AT EXACTLY 1:45.
CIPAL

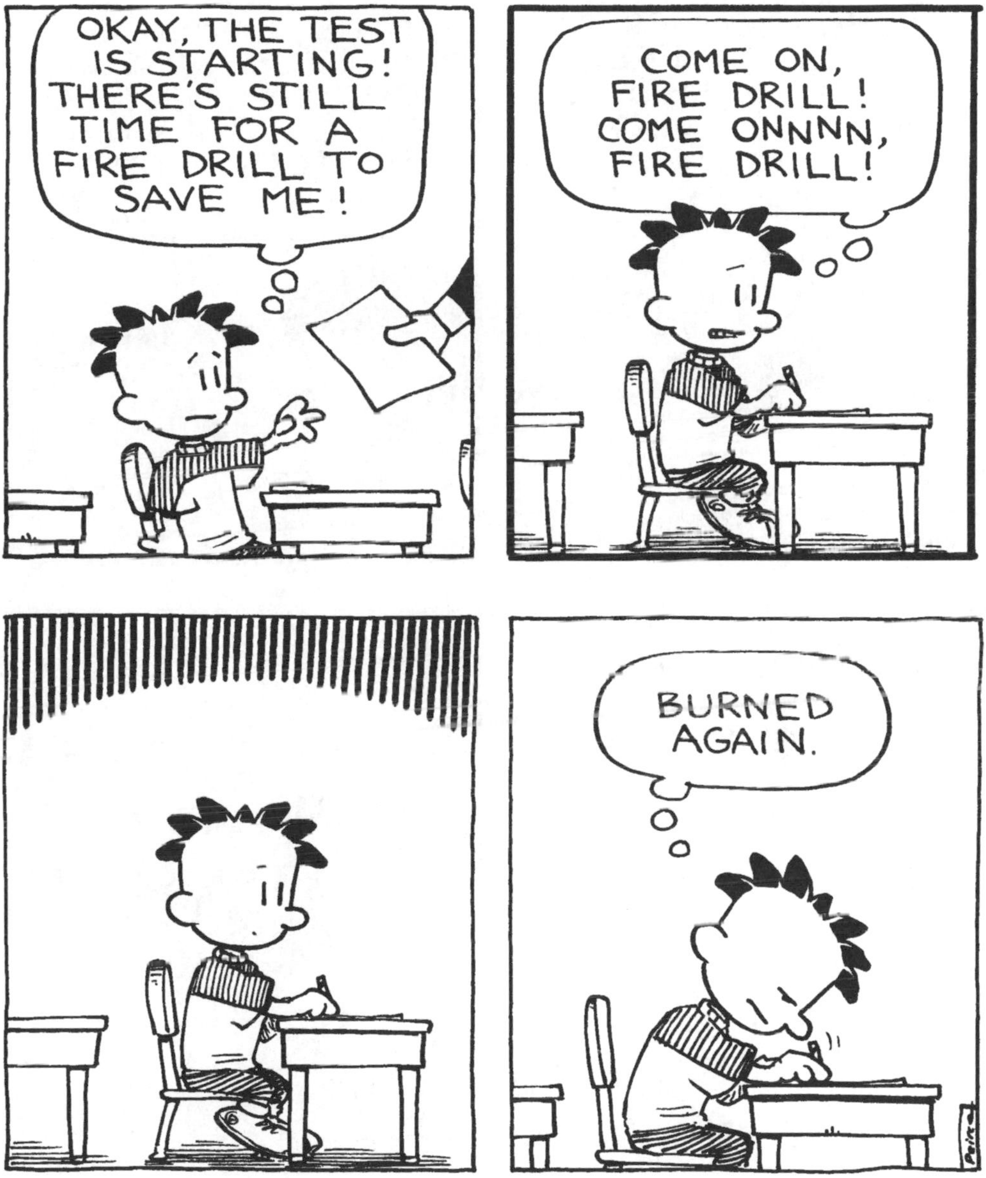
OKAY, THE TEST IS STARTING! THERE'S STILL TIME FOR A FIRE DRILL TO SAVE ME!
COME ON, FIRE DRILL! COME ONNNN, FIRE DRILL!
BURNED AGAIN.

LOOK AT THIS! WHAT A MESS! BOYS ARE SUCH SLOBS!
OH, GREAT! HERE'S SHEILA WITH ANOTHER ONE OF HER "ANTI-BOY" SPEECHES!
LISTEN, SHEILA, IF YOU HATE BOYS SO MUCH, THEN WHY DO YOU GO OUT WITH FRANCIS, HUH? ANSWER ME THAT!
BECAUSE FRANCIS ISN'T LIKE A BOY! HE'S SENSITIVE! HE'S SWEET! HE'S MORE LIKE A GIRL THAN A BOY!
WA HA HA HA
GREAT.
OOPS.

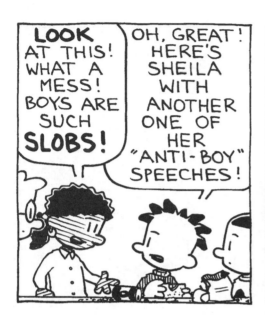

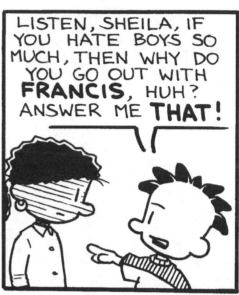

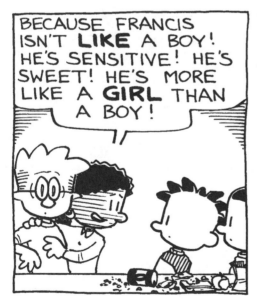

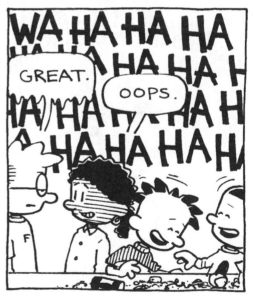

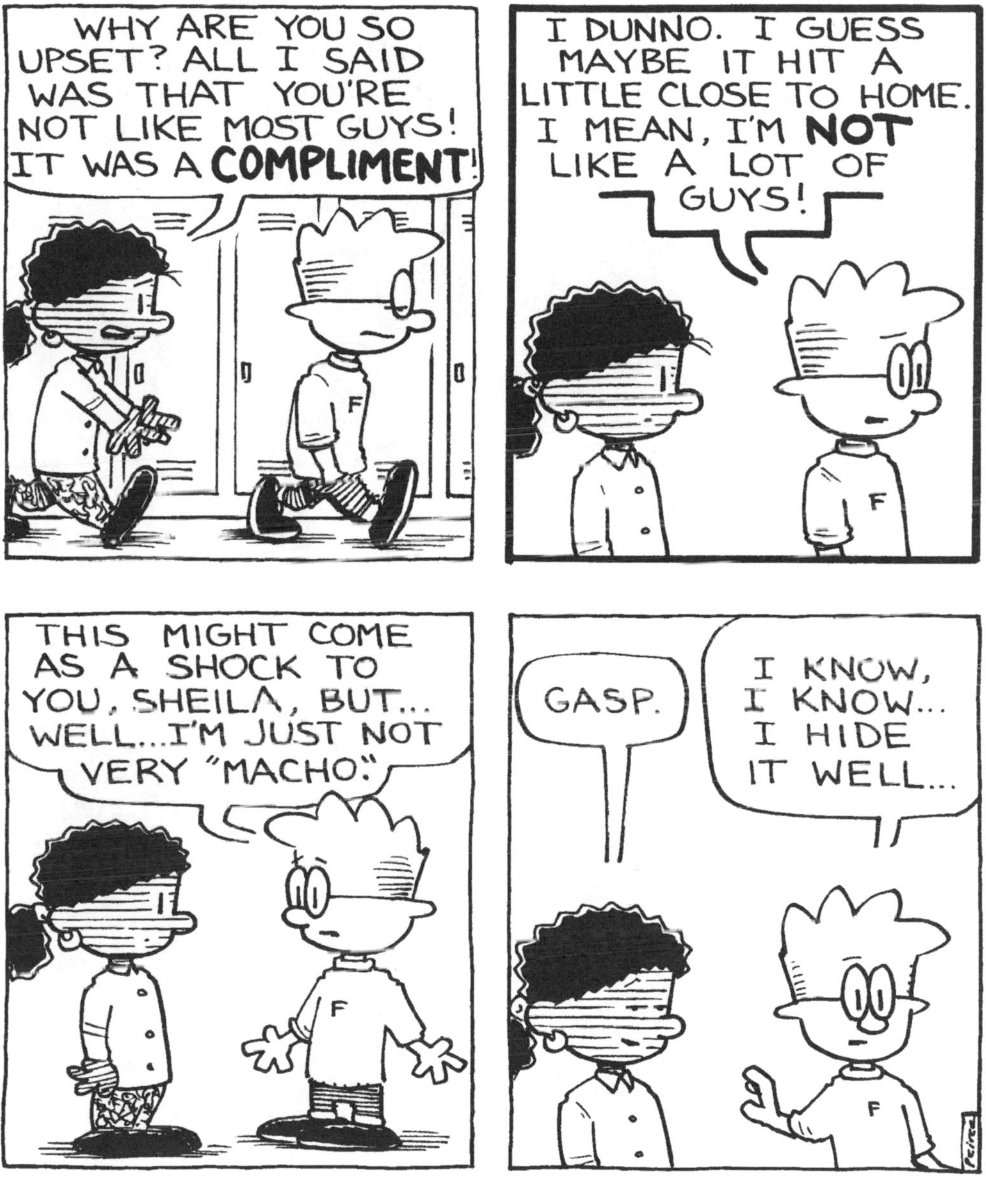
WHY ARE YOU SO UPSET? ALL I SAID WAS THAT YOU'RE NOT LIKE MOST GUYS! IT WAS A **COMPLIMENT**!
I DUNNO. I GUESS MAYBE IT HIT A LITTLE CLOSE TO HOME. I MEAN, I'M **NOT** LIKE A LOT OF GUYS!
THIS MIGHT COME AS A SHOCK TO YOU, SHEILA, BUT... WELL...I'M JUST NOT VERY "MACHO."
GASP.
I KNOW, I KNOW... I HIDE IT WELL...

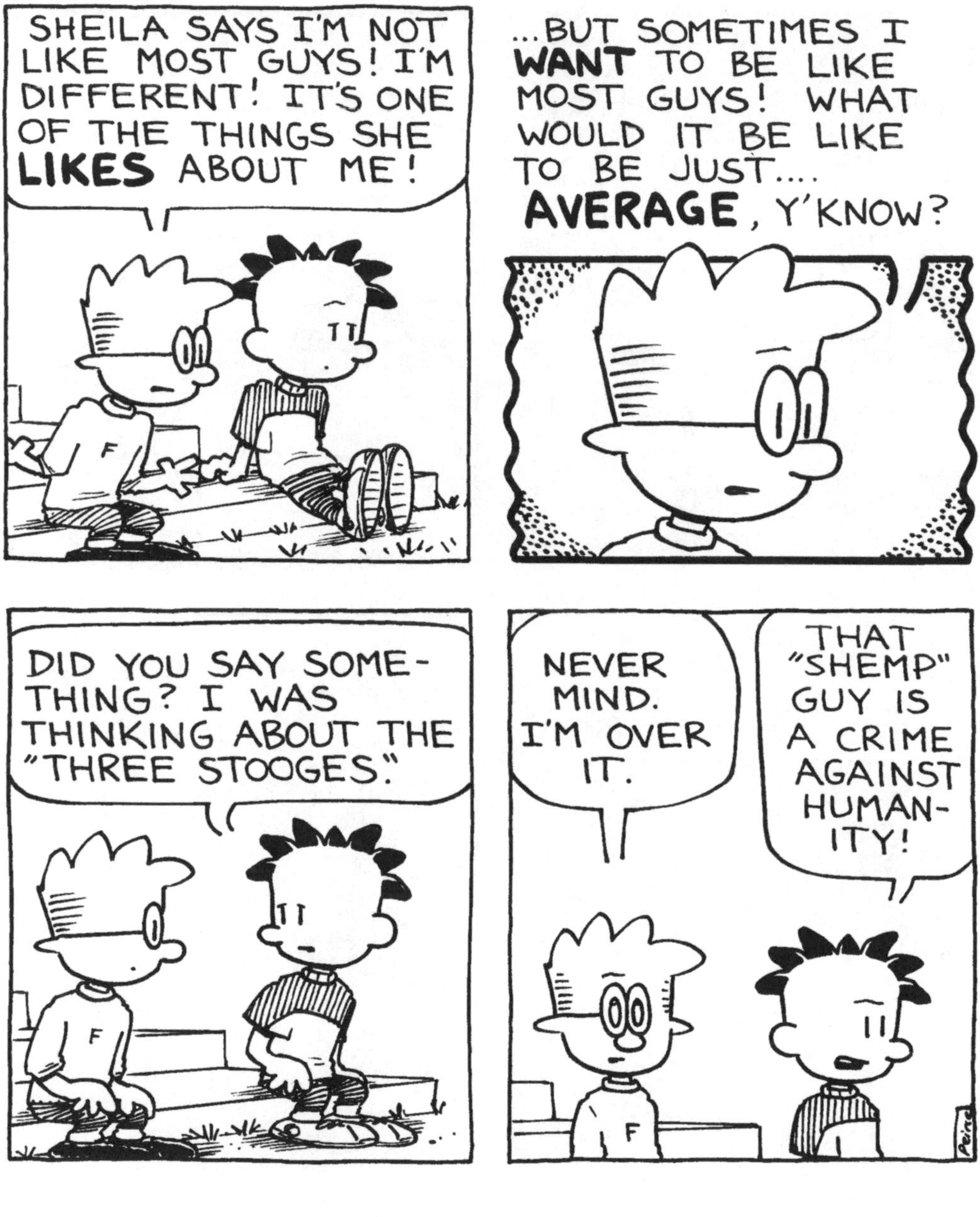
SHEILA SAYS I'M NOT LIKE MOST GUYS! I'M DIFFERENT! IT'S ONE OF THE THINGS SHE **LIKES** ABOUT ME!
...BUT SOMETIMES I **WANT** TO BE LIKE MOST GUYS! WHAT WOULD IT BE LIKE TO BE JUST.... **AVERAGE**, Y'KNOW?
DID YOU SAY SOME-THING? I WAS THINKING ABOUT THE "THREE STOOGES."
NEVER MIND. I'M OVER IT.
THAT "SHEMP" GUY IS A CRIME AGAINST HUMAN-ITY!
Peirce

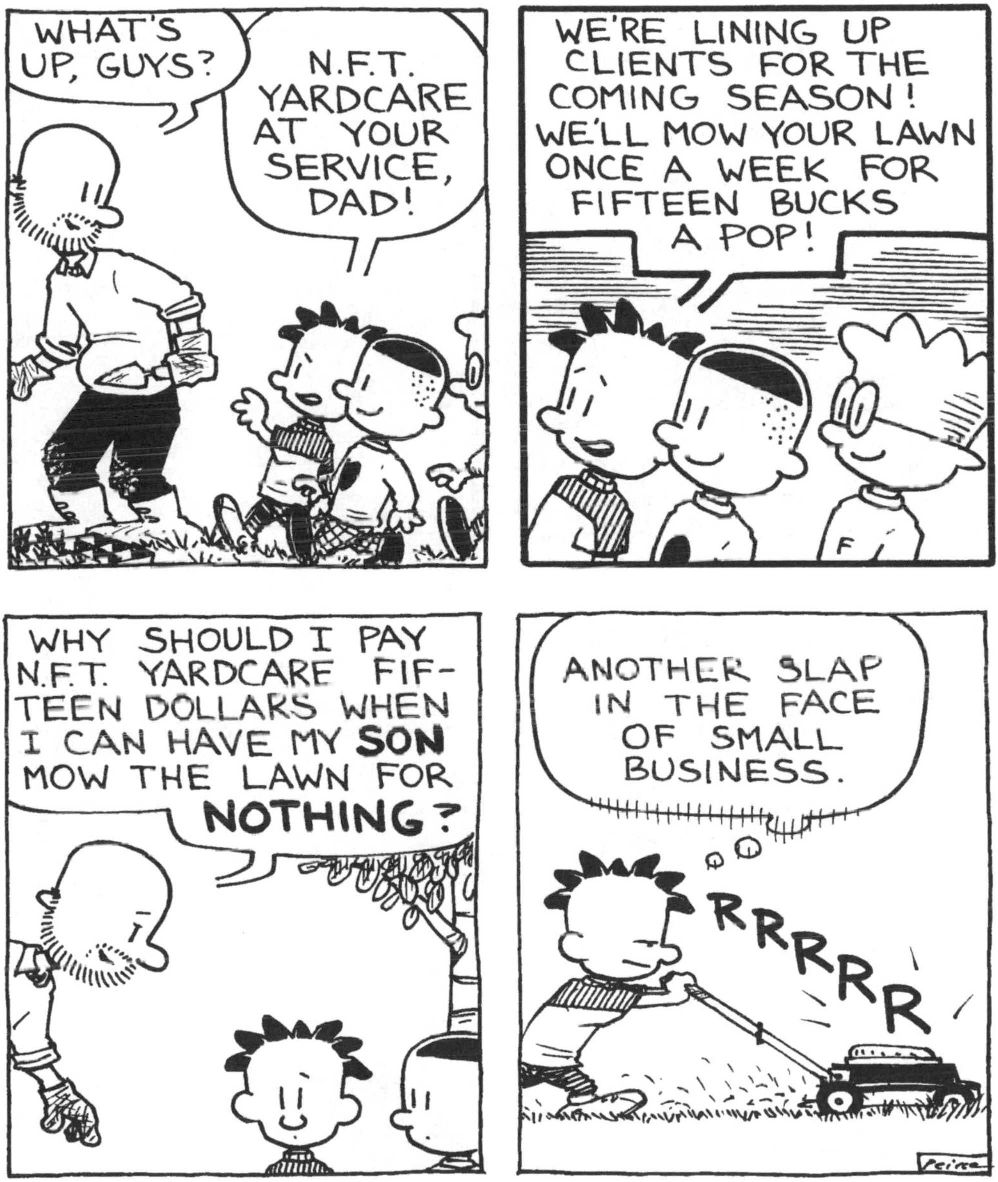
WHAT'S UP, GUYS?
N.F.T. YARDCARE AT YOUR SERVICE, DAD!
WE'RE LINING UP CLIENTS FOR THE COMING SEASON! WE'LL MOW YOUR LAWN ONCE A WEEK FOR FIFTEEN BUCKS A POP!
F
WHY SHOULD I PAY N.F.T. YARDCARE FIFTEEN DOLLARS WHEN I CAN HAVE MY SON MOW THE LAWN FOR NOTHING?
ANOTHER SLAP IN THE FACE OF SMALL BUSINESS.
RRRRRR
Peirce

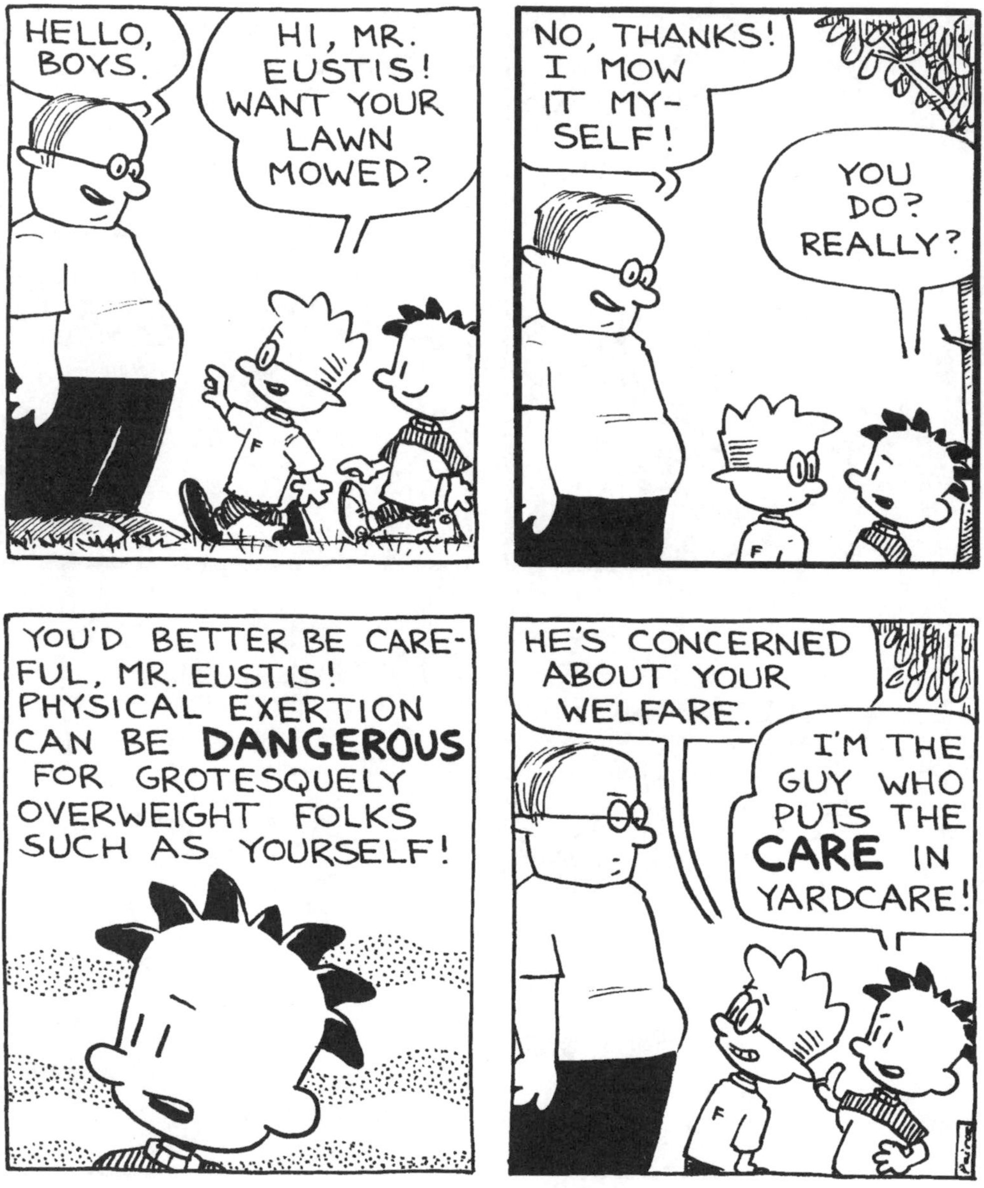
HELLO, BOYS.
HI, MR. EUSTIS! WANT YOUR LAWN MOWED?
NO, THANKS! I MOW IT MYSELF!
YOU DO? REALLY?
YOU'D BETTER BE CAREFUL, MR. EUSTIS! PHYSICAL EXERTION CAN BE **DANGEROUS** FOR GROTESQUELY OVERWEIGHT FOLKS SUCH AS YOURSELF!
HE'S CONCERNED ABOUT YOUR WELFARE.
I'M THE GUY WHO PUTS THE **CARE** IN YARDCARE!

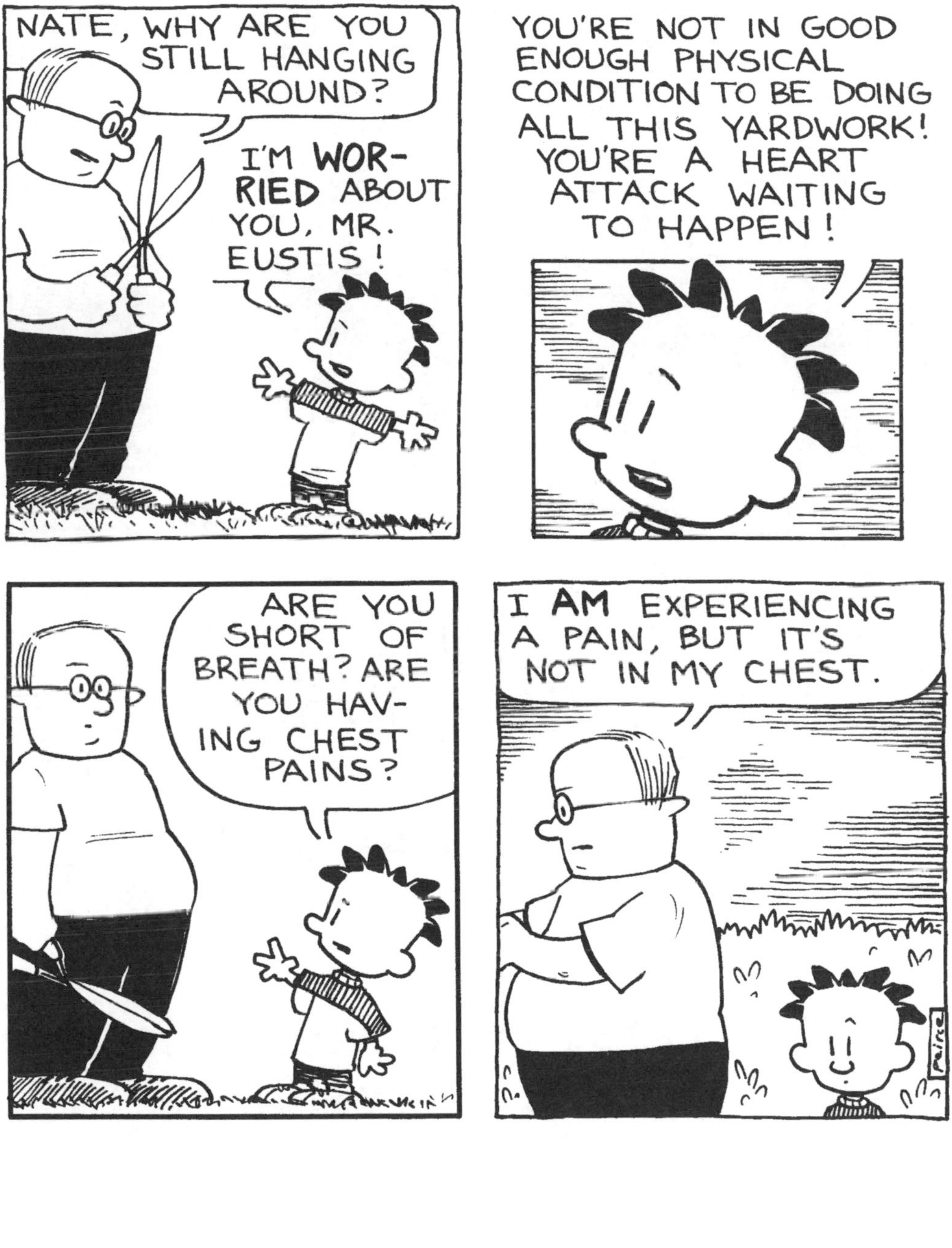
NATE, WHY ARE YOU STILL HANGING AROUND?
I'M **WOR-RIED** ABOUT YOU, MR. EUSTIS!
YOU'RE NOT IN GOOD ENOUGH PHYSICAL CONDITION TO BE DOING ALL THIS YARDWORK! YOU'RE A HEART ATTACK WAITING TO HAPPEN!
ARE YOU SHORT OF BREATH? ARE YOU HAV-ING CHEST PAINS?
I **AM** EXPERIENCING A PAIN, BUT IT'S NOT IN MY CHEST.
Peirce

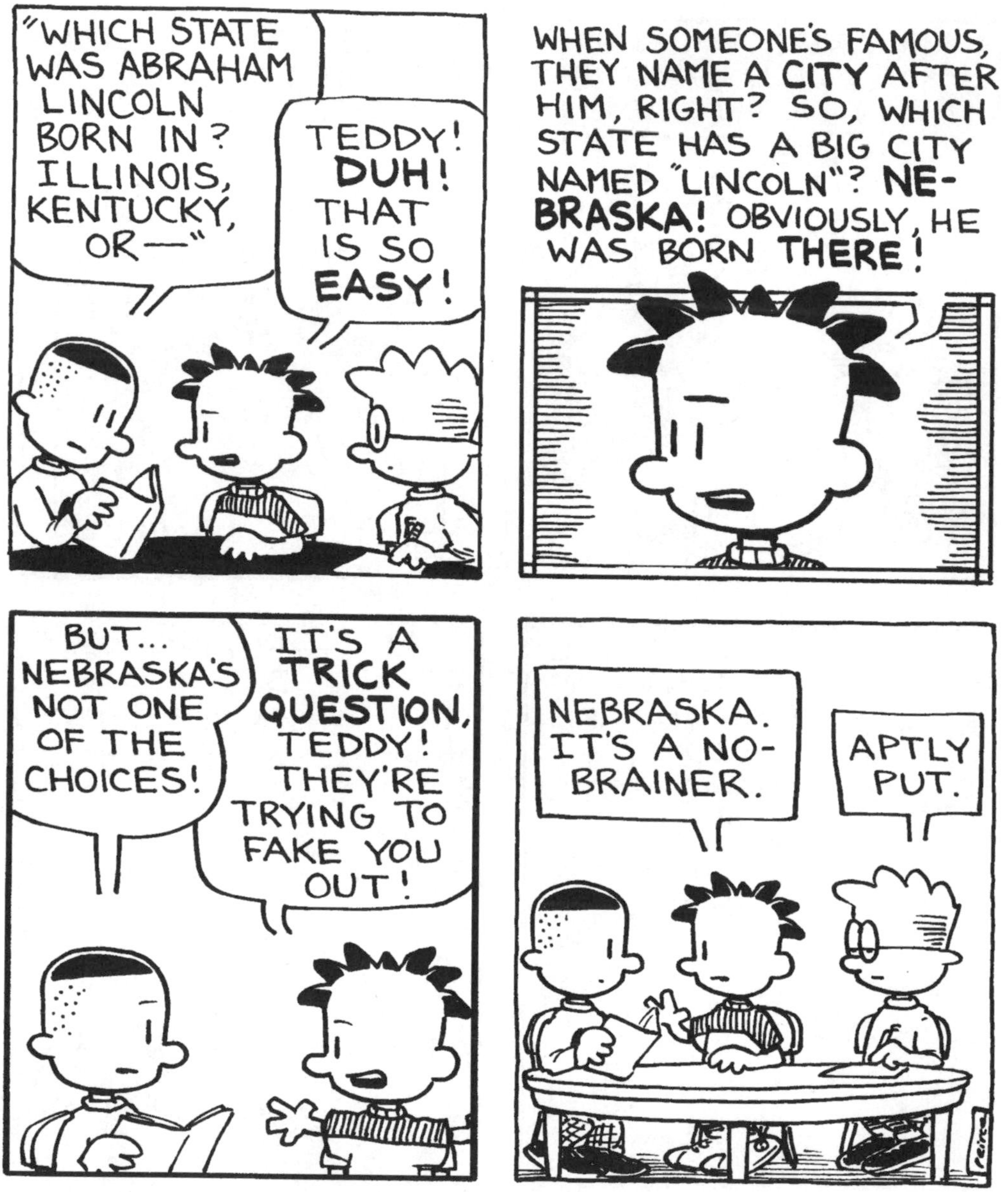
"WHICH STATE WAS ABRAHAM LINCOLN BORN IN? ILLINOIS, KENTUCKY, OR—"
TEDDY! DUH! THAT IS SO EASY!
WHEN SOMEONE'S FAMOUS, THEY NAME A CITY AFTER HIM, RIGHT? SO, WHICH STATE HAS A BIG CITY NAMED "LINCOLN"? NEBRASKA! OBVIOUSLY, HE WAS BORN THERE!
BUT... NEBRASKA'S NOT ONE OF THE CHOICES!
IT'S A TRICK QUESTION, TEDDY! THEY'RE TRYING TO FAKE YOU OUT!
NEBRASKA. IT'S A NO-BRAINER.
APTLY PUT.

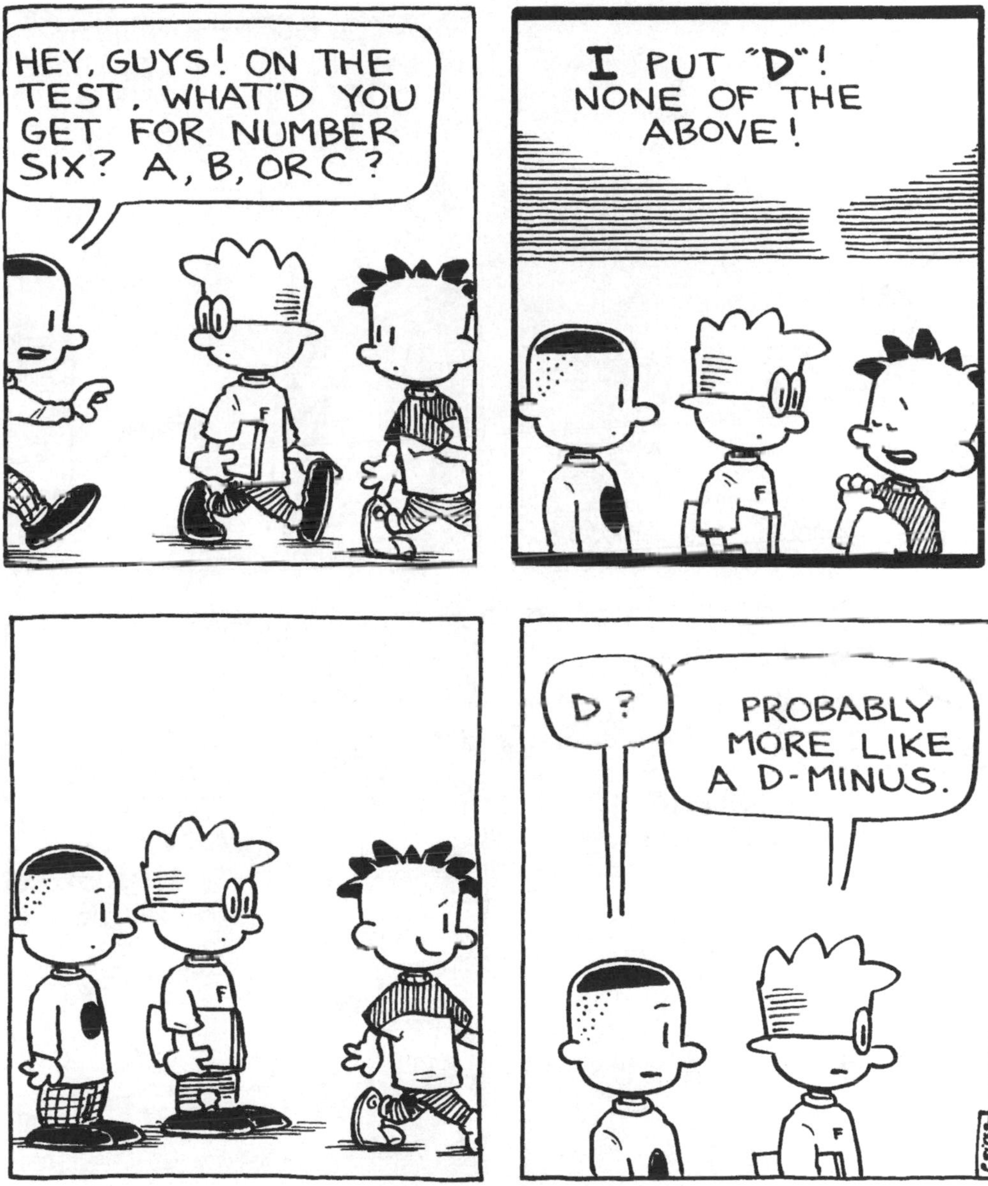
HEY, GUYS! ON THE TEST, WHAT'D YOU GET FOR NUMBER SIX? A, B, OR C?
I PUT "D"! NONE OF THE ABOVE!
D?
PROBABLY MORE LIKE A D-MINUS.
PEIRCE

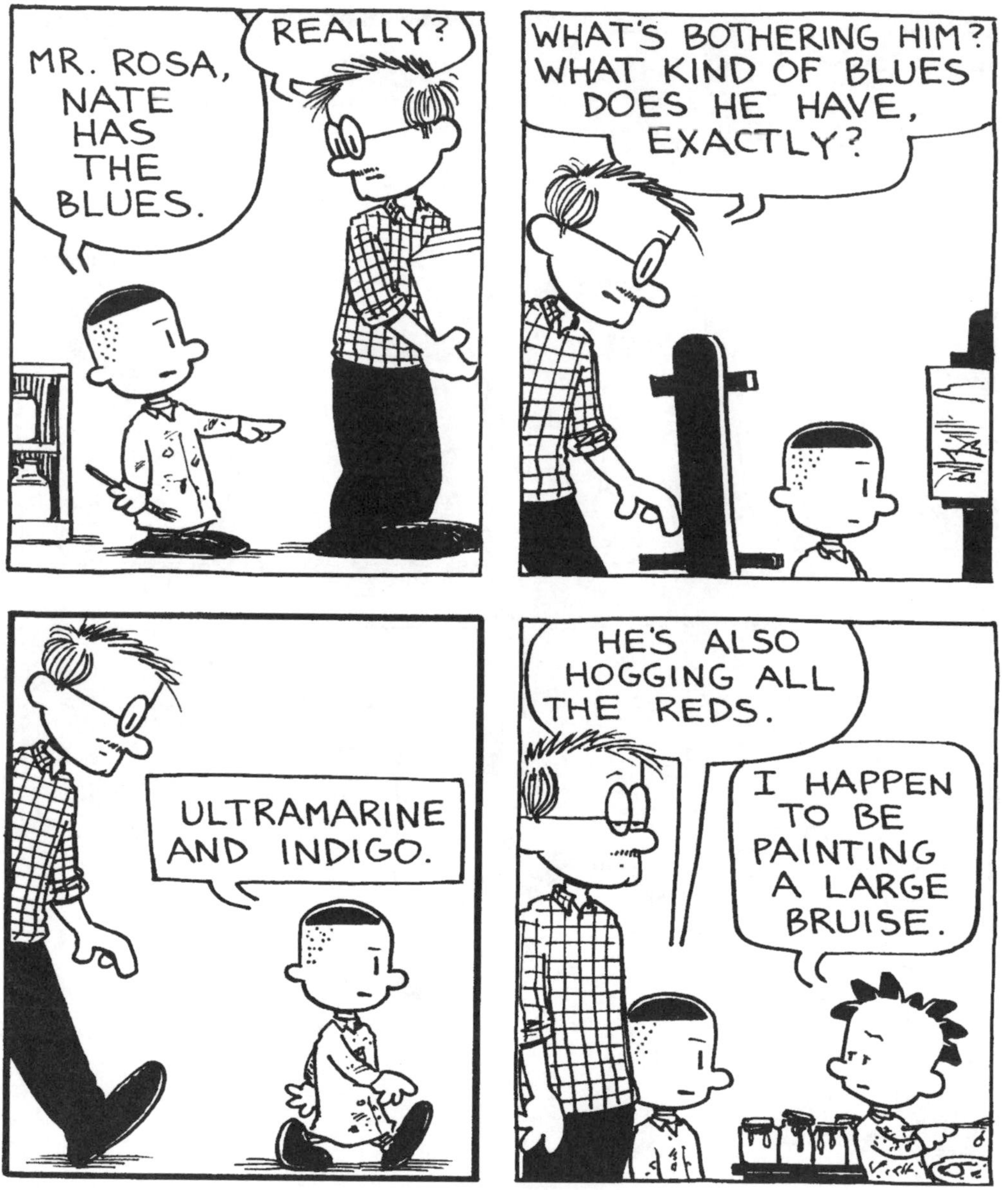
MR. ROSA, NATE HAS THE BLUES.
REALLY?
WHAT'S BOTHERING HIM? WHAT KIND OF BLUES DOES HE HAVE, EXACTLY?
ULTRAMARINE AND INDIGO.
HE'S ALSO HOGGING ALL THE REDS.
I HAPPEN TO BE PAINTING A LARGE BRUISE.

ABOUT THE AUTHOR

Lincoln Peirce has been drawing the *Big Nate*
comic strip for more than 20 years. Born in Ames,
Iowa, Peirce grew up in Durham, New Hampshire.
As a kid, he began creating his own strips in the
sixth grade. Peirce taught high school in New York City
and has created several animated pilots for
Cartoon Network and Nickelodeon. He lives in
Portland, Maine, with his family.

Big Nate is distributed internationally by Universal Uclick.

Andrews McMeel Publishing
a division of Andrews McMeel Universal
1130 Walnut Street, Kansas City, Missouri 64106

www.andrewsmcmeel.com

15 16 17 18 19 RR2 10 9 8 7 6 5 4 3 2

ISBN: 978-1-4494-7281-8

Big Nate can be viewed on the Internet at
www.gocomics.com/big_nate

ATTENTION: SCHOOLS AND BUSINESSES
Andrews McMeel books are available at quantity discounts with bulk purchase for educational, business, or sales promotional use. For information, please e-mail the Andrews McMeel Publishing Special Sales Department:
specialsales@amuniversal.com.

Check out these and other books at **ampkids.com**

big NATE
FROM THE TOP
by LINCOLN PEIRCE

big NATE
OUT LOUD
by LINCOLN PEIRCE

big NATE
AND FRIENDS
by LINCOLN PEIRCE

big NATE
MAKES THE GRADE
by LINCOLN PEIRCE

big NATE
GAME ON!
by LINCOLN PEIRCE

big NATE
I CAN'T TAKE IT!
by LINCOLN PEIRCE

big NATE
GREAT MINDS THINK ALIKE
by LINCOLN PEIRCE

big NATE
THE CROWD GOES WILD!
by LINCOLN PEIRCE

big NATE
SAY GOOD-BYE TO DORK CITY
by LINCOLN PEIRCE

big NATE
WELCOME TO MY WORLD
by LINCOLN PEIRCE

NATE el Grande
¡HOLA!
por LINCOLN
BIG NATE IN SPANISH!

Also available:
Teaching and activity guides for each title.
AMP! Comics for Kids books make reading FUN!

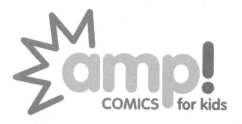

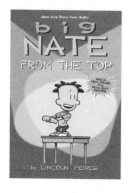

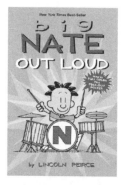

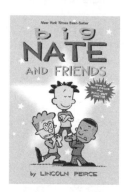

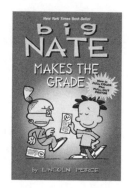

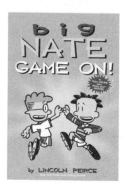

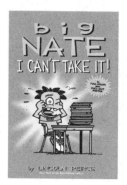

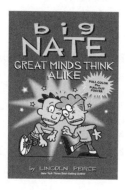

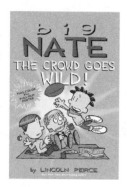

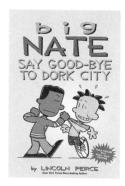

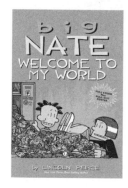

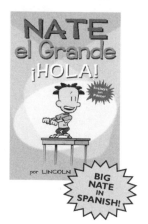